Books 1

STAR FORCE SERIES
Swarm
Extinction
Rebellion
Conquest
Battle Station
Empire
Annihilation
Storm Assault
The Dead Sun
Outcast

IMPERIUM SERIES
Mech Zero: The Dominant
Mech 1: The Parent
Mech 2: The Savant
Mech 3: The Empress
Five By Five (Mech Novella)

OTHER SF BOOKS
Technomancer
The Bone Triangle
Z-World
Velocity

Visit BVLarson.com for more information.

The Dead Sun

(Star Force Series #9)
by
B. V. Larson

STAR FORCE SERIES
Swarm
Extinction
Rebellion
Conquest
Battle Station
Empire
Annihilation
Storm Assault
The Dead Sun
Outcast

ISBN-13: 978-1497577084
ISBN-10: 149757708X
BISAC: Fiction / Science Fiction / Military

-1-

The space around Earth was quiet. There were no enemy ships in the system and at least three hundred defensive vessels glided around the planet in belt-like loops. The battleships and carriers could be seen from the ground at night. Reflecting the light of the sun, they looked like lost, fast-moving moons and the citizens of my world were comforted to see them patrolling in orbit.

I yearned to be with the fleet but that wasn't my role anymore. I was trapped in a glass tower in Geneva, Switzerland. Outside my massive office window, the Alps shone white with snow and black with rough stone. The mountains here weren't like the old, worn-down lumps in my native California. These peaks looked like a predator's teeth when the sun set behind them.

It was October and in this part of the world the air was already crisp and cold, promising the winter to come would be a harsh one. It was Wednesday, late in the afternoon, and my life as a dictator was weighing heavily on me today.

For all intents and purposes, I, Colonel Kyle Riggs of Star Force, was in charge of running Earth. I hadn't wanted the job, and I didn't think I was particularly good at it. I'd never wanted this kind of power, despite what my enemies liked to claim.

Do you want to rule the world? It does sound like a pretty sweet deal from the outside. Imagine how it would go: women would throw themselves at you, and if they didn't, you could have them executed. Everyone would listen to you, and your schedule would set itself. Enemies would die in quiet cells, and

1

sycophantic loyalists would be rewarded on the basis of how thoroughly they massaged your already monstrous—and growing—ego...

I wanted none of it. Especially after I learned that the job was—for the most part—a giant pain in the ass.

I remembered reading a book about Damocles, who'd been invited to sit upon his king's throne. He hadn't enjoyed being king for even a single day while I'd had the job for seven long months. Although he'd lusted for power, he didn't relish the reality, and I now felt I understood his plight.

As Damocles had learned twenty-five centuries ago, power is a double-edged sword. Yes, I could have had people executed if I so desired. But I didn't *want* to kill anyone. I wanted to unite humanity, to lift us up to meet our real enemy: the machines.

You would think that being gifted with a magnanimous leader, a man who was generally friendly and reasonable, people would rejoice and cooperate. That wasn't how it went. Once they figured out I wasn't a bloody tyrant like Crow, they decided to push. They wanted to see how far they could manipulate or disobey old Riggs before he pulled the rug out from under them. I guess that's human nature.

So, instead of taking it easy, I found each day began with a raft of problems. Seven long months ago we'd retaken Earth and "liberated" my home planet. In that time, there'd been less progress in every part of government than I would have liked to see. It had taken four full months just to quell rebellions and riots. Dark memories filled my mind when I thought of those early days. Every morning had been littered with news reports of looting and pillaging in dozens of cities. Set free of the empire, people had gone wild. They'd tried to break apart and return to the past, to become a hundred separate nations again.

I hadn't allowed it. Fragmentation of the empire at this point would leave us too weak. The Macros might come back any day, and when they did, we had to face them as a united force to destroy them in their thousands.

I wanted freedom as much as the next guy, you have to understand. I commiserated with my people's yearning to go back to the old days of bickering and border skirmishes, but weakness now could mean the end of the line for our species. We couldn't self-indulge in the past—at least, not yet.

The world had settled down eventually. They'd adjusted to the new order of things. The first day during which no one was assassinated or left dying in the streets of a burning city, I'd wanted out of my position. In my own mind, I'd imagined I would give the reins of power back to the governments of Earth and let them sort it out. Surely, they could see the logical need for a single world government at this point. Maybe something like the old UN could take over.

But that just wasn't going to work. I realized that now. They couldn't agree on who should rule and how they would go about it. Old rivalries hadn't vanished, they'd just been put aside temporarily. I could tell it would take several generations to change people in that regard. Every time I granted our new world parliament more sovereignty, they immediately became as self-centered, corrupt, bureaucratic and inept as the original UN had been in the past.

I couldn't afford to wait for them to decide how much money I should have to build up the fleet, or who should get the contracts. Not with unknown alien powers ready to pounce upon us at any time from beyond our known systems. So I didn't ask—I took what I needed and I ordered people to build what I wanted. Since I had the fleet behind me, they obeyed.

Largely because it was the easiest route available, I'd left Crow's Imperial governing infrastructure in place. I had to start with something. Not everything was the same, of course. I released all political prisoners no matter how irritating they were. I'd already destroyed the Ministry of Truth and now encouraged a free press. I allowed elections for all local and national leaders in every country. Until you got up to the world government itself, it was all very democratic. But at the top, I appointed my own people and kept the real power tightly in the grip of Star Force. These decisions were alternatively lauded and berated by the press, and there were plenty of negative consequences for everything I did.

"I thought we were pretty good at vicious tactics," I told Admiral Miklos one cold October afternoon, after a swarm of envoys had been ushered from the buildings and shut outside. "But these businessmen are like warriors in suits."

"They wield words and bribes like weapons," he agreed. He picked up a shiny metal bust, which had been left behind by one of the dignitaries. He hefted it speculatively. "I do believe this thing is solid gold."

Miklos was an Eastern European, and he still had an accent. He wore a beard that was a little fuller than regulations allowed for and had intense eyes. He stared at the golden likeness of me as if he were examining an alien animal.

"Yeah," I said. "Looks like real gold. Who gave that thing to me?"

"It came from the Turkish delegation, I believe," Miklos replied. "They probably calculated that anything less than *solid* gold would be considered an insult. Crow liked this kind of ego-building gift, and they seem to be determined to follow the protocol he began."

I sighed and reached out my hand for the bauble. Miklos hesitated before handing it to me, still frowning.

"Has this gone through security, sir?" he asked.

I shrugged. "You tell me."

Miklos found a file in the government archives on his tablet. He shot it to my tablet with a flick of his finger, and I examined it.

"Every test Marvin could put it through," I said, examining the file. "No toxins, explosives or even nanite viruses showed up. He couldn't detect anything."

"Okay then," Miklos said, putting the statue into my palm.

I examined the workmanship. It was really quite good. The damned thing looked exactly like me.

"The Turks really want this contract badly," I observed.

"They all do, sir," Miklos said.

Nations had always been fairly independent in Crow's empire as far as internal politics went. That part wasn't the problem. Mostly, my troubles began when I was faced with deciding where to allocate Star Force resources. Should I spend a trillion on rebuilding Earth's fleet? If so, *where* would that fleet be built? Where would the priceless alien factories be set up and fed local raw materials?

4

Everyone wanted in on the action. Lobbyists, celebrities and heads of state had thronged my headquarters in Geneva for weeks, demanding their piece of the pie. Most of the arguments came down to jobs, money and just plain petty bickering. Every nation wanted the big Star Force contracts. They did everything they could to ingratiate themselves and sabotage the others.

"They did a good job on this trinket," I said, setting the gold statue of my own face aside. "Some sculptor and metalworker put their best effort into this thing. They even have the faint scar here on my face, the one that predates my nanite treatments."

Miklos cleared his throat. I looked up at him expectantly.

"Have you made your decision, sir?" he asked.

"About what?"

"The location of the ship-building facilities."

"Oh, yeah…that. Yes, I've decided. I've decided to screw them all. I'm going to assemble the ships in space."

Miklos frowned. "Expensive and vulnerable."

"I know, I know. The advantages of doing it in zero-G probably are outweighed by the negatives. But the construction will be largely automated, with space-crawlers doing most of the work, rather than men in suits. We can move past the manual labor stage now."

"Like I said…expensive."

I was frowning now. Anytime a Fleet issue came up, Miklos always had a vested interest, just like every envoy from Brazil to Poland. He wanted to run the show as much as they did, but for different reasons.

I stood up from my seat at the head of a long table of rich mahogany and looked at him.

"Do I really have to sell *you* on this?" I demanded. "You've seen the projections. At first there will be a construction slowdown because we'll have to build an orbital platform, but once that's going, the production rates will improve. We'll be getting most of our raw materials from space from now on, especially from the Bellatrix system. We'll avoid the effort of having to ferry everything down from orbit to the surface if we build in space."

5

"That's true," he said, "but the orbital platform will take longer to construct than one would here on Earth. The technologies are new and unknown. May I propose a faster approach?"

"Of course. Propose away."

"We could build the production facility on *Phobos*, either on the outer hull or inside the vessel."

I stared at him for a moment, considering the possibility. I'd heard other proposals concerning *Phobos*, but this was a new one. *Phobos* was the largest ship we had. It was named after one of Mars' moons because it was the size of a hollowed out moon itself, about seven miles across and spherical in shape. Pirated from the Blues, who'd built it originally, it was easily the most powerful weapon Earth had at her disposal.

I shook my head after a few moments of thought. "No. I'm not going to do that. I don't want our best battlewagon turned into a factory."

"Why not, sir?" Miklos asked. "Think of the long-range possibilities. We would fly her out to a trouble spot and begin building a new fleet when we got there."

"I do like that aspect. Possibly I'll build our second dry-dock aboard her, but not our first. I'm not going to put all my eggs in a single basket. If *Phobos* went down in a battle, we'd lose our fleet and the capacity to build a new one all at once."

"But if we put up an orbital platform," he said, beginning to raise his voice, "it will become a giant target when the Solar System is invaded. Can you not see that, sir?"

I began to raise my voice in response. I felt my eyebrows squeezing closer together, forming a frown.

"Yeah, I can see that, but I'm telling you that if an enemy—any enemy—gets so far through our defenses that they're able to blast something out of Earth's orbit...well, we've lost anyway. They would have to have gone through several systems and our battle station at the border."

He pursed his lips tightly and nodded, lowering his gaze. These days, when I became angry, people stopped arguing. In a way, that was nice. But it was kind of weird, too. Did they really fear for their lives?

"As you wish, Colonel," he said.

I'd kept the title of Colonel because I didn't like the other options. What was I supposed to call myself? Overlord? Emperor? King? Or maybe "His Highness", as Crow had done? I decided that, for now, I'd stick with plain old Colonel Kyle Riggs.

A chime sounded, breaking me out of my thoughts. I put the statuette down again, finding that I'd been toying with it absentmindedly. It really was a startling likeness.

Miklos checked his tablet. "It's Captain Sarin," he said. "I'll be taking my leave, sir."

"Hold on," I said, putting up my hand. "Why is it that every time she shows up, you run off? There isn't a thing going on between you two, is there?"

"A *thing*, sir?" he asked with an odd twist to his lips. He seemed amused. "I don't believe I'm the one with the special relationship."

I nodded. I'd been suggesting there was a rivalry between my top officers, but his meaning was something else entirely. I didn't like it, but I understood.

Jasmine and I *were* romantically involved. It had been a long time coming, and I was enjoying it as much as she was—possibly more. I told myself not to let Miklos' smirk piss me off. It was only natural for underlings to make light of their superiors' dalliances.

I smiled back at him, instead of shouting.

"Funny guy," I said. "It's not like I'm playing grab-ass with an intern, you know. She's a mature woman and a peer."

"Oh, I agree, sir."

Another leer. I was ready for him to leave.

"Right," I said. "Well, there's the chime again. Do I let her in, or do I kick you out first to make you feel better?"

His ghostly smile faded. "Not necessary, Colonel."

I stabbed a raised stud on the arm of my chair and the smart metal door melted away. Jasmine came in, and I was glad to see she was wearing her uniform. It would have been embarrassing to have her surprise me in a silky robe or something like that. Fortunately, Jasmine didn't do that type of thing. She wasn't flashy and daring the way Sandra had been.

"Admiral," she said, nodding to Miklos.

"Captain," he replied. "I was just about finished."

"Hold on," I said. "Jasmine, what did you want to talk about?"

"The construction contracts, sir."

I nodded, looking at both of them suspiciously. "I see. Where do you think we should put the new facilities?"

"That's hardly my place to judge, Colonel."

"I'm asking for opinions."

Jasmine slid her eyes over to Miklos, then back again to me. She seemed to be assessing the situation, and I was doing the same. She'd come here to lobby me privately about these contracts just as he had. I tried not to be annoyed by this behavior among two of my most trusted officers. They'd been convinced by skillful manipulators. They were using their influence on me, not for gain, but because they believed they were doing the right thing.

"Did you know, sir, that the fastest growing aerospace industry on our planet is located in Bangalore?"

I blinked at her. Honestly, she'd caught me by surprise. So direct, so blatant. I snorted quietly. This made her frown, but I recovered quickly.

"No, I didn't know that."

"It was happening even before the initial invasion years ago," she said. "The two countries experiencing the greatest industrial growth in this area were India and China. Unfortunately, China was destroyed for the most part during the Macro assault of—"

Miklos jumped in then, growling. He sounded as if he couldn't stand to hear any more of her pitch. "That's not where you place a contract like this!" he shouted.

We both looked at him in surprise. Like a traffic cop, I gestured toward both of them. I shushed Jasmine with one hand and encouraged Miklos to talk with the other.

"Let's hear it, Miklos. Give me your honest opinion. You've been hinting around all day. Tell me where you want to put the fleet construction facilities. If not on *Phobos* if not in orbit—where?"

"Back before India—or the smoking ruin formerly known as China—had built their first toy rockets, Space City in Russia

8

was building more launch vehicles than any other country on Earth."

I nodded slowly and I didn't contradict him—or her. In truth, I thought Star Force on Andros Island had been the greatest producer of ships in recent times. They were both talking about old-fashioned chemical rocket delivery systems. We'd moved past all that, and I wasn't sure that the existing facilities or personnel could help us much to build a modern facility using Nano and Macro technology. Sure, they might have some good technical people knocking around, but the existing factories and the like would be all but worthless.

"I'm not sure that they could help," I said. "I'm sure there are some retired astrophysicists about that we could hire, but—"

"Hear me out, Colonel," Miklos interrupted. "If we're considering placement of the facilities on Earth, there are clear advantages to Space City. I'm not just talking about advantages to Star Force. The region has been damaged by war and economic upheaval. The people there have lost their pride and spirit. We could revitalize them."

"I see," I said evenly. "What I'm hearing is this: Jasmine is from India. She wants to help her people out, and you want to help yours."

They both frowned.

"Nepotism, sir?" Miklos said stiffly. "Is that what you're accusing us of?"

"Not exactly, Admiral. But I do think the numbers are so huge that your judgment has been compromised. It's only natural. I'm rejecting both of you, not choosing one over the other. In your case, it's because I'm not going to make a decision about the defense of Earth on the basis of who is most in need. If I did that, I'd build the factories in the wasteland that was once South America. Those people are living in squalor."

I turned to Jasmine while Miklos sulked.

"Your argument is different, Jasmine, but no less flawed," I told her. "You talk of India's aerospace industry as if it's modern. It isn't. The technology we're using is all new. It

9

would be like using a vacuum tube factory to build tablet computers—no help at all."

They both seemed deflated and frustrated. To my surprise and delight, they didn't bitterly argue to the last. They both knew me too well to go up against me when my mind was made up.

"Where, then?" Jasmine asked. "Where do you plan to build these factories? In the Central Valley of California?"

I flashed her a look of annoyance. She was suggesting that I was making an arbitrary choice to help out my own hometown, which just wasn't true. I opened my mouth to refute her suggestion, but Miklos beat me to it.

"He's putting the entire thing into space," he said. "An orbital platform."

"But why?" she demanded in surprise. "Such a waste—and one lucky missile could take out the entire facility."

I heaved a sigh. "I've gone around a few times with Miklos on this already. If you could fill her in, I'll be taking my leave."

They both looked startled as I stood and marched for the door. I'd had enough of bickering about economics in my office. I was bored and irritated with the entire business of running an empire. Sure, it had sounded like fun, but I'd been having far too many days like this one. It wasn't that nothing got done, but rather that it was a joyless affair.

Jasmine followed me out and caught up with me at the elevators. She touched my elbow, and I softened.

"Sorry," I said.

"Me, too. I understand the stresses you must be under. Running a planet is difficult for anyone."

"I've run them before, that's the funny thing. Out in the Eden system it seemed far easier. Everyone was open to new ideas. They went where I wanted them to go and made farms and towns grow."

"Maybe it was a natural pioneering spirit," she suggested.

"Not just that. They weren't entrenched in tradition, jealousy and the like. The people of Earth have baggage in everything they do. They aren't united—not really. The minute the aliens aren't visible in our skies, we start fighting over

10

scraps like a screaming mass of baboons on top of a heap of bananas."

She smiled at my over-the-top analogy.

"Do baboons even like bananas?" she asked.

"I have no idea," I admitted, chuckling.

We got into the elevator and touched the buttons to send us gliding downward. I would have preferred simple grav-tubes like the ones we had on our larger ships, but the elevators were a tradition on Earth and they made my countless visitors feel more at home.

On impulse, I grabbed Jasmine and kissed her. She resisted for a second, then melted. I knew she wasn't fully happy with me yet, but she didn't seem openly angry, just disappointed.

We didn't get to finish our short kiss before things went very wrong.

We were standing there in the elevator with our lips locked together when the little gold statue shaped like my head imploded, crushed by fantastical gravitational forces. Essentially a tiny black hole—one no bigger than a pinpoint—appeared momentarily inside my office and sucked everything around it inward, compressing matter and rupturing even the atmosphere inside the building itself.

-2-

Jasmine and I didn't know what had hit us. The implosion came first, followed almost instantaneously by an explosion as the gravity effect that had unexpectedly manifested in my office faded from existence. After the initial sucking force released its grip, the compressed matter expanded again with great violence. This was worse than the implosion itself had been. In space, there wouldn't have been as large an area of effect, but with an atmosphere present to carry a shockwave, the entire building was affected. The personnel in the building could feel rumbling aftershocks for several long seconds after the initial strike registered.

Jasmine and I didn't know any of this at the time. We assumed something had hit the building as we rode the elevator to the lobby.

The lights in the elevator flickered, and we went into free-fall. The cables had been severed by flying metal shards from the explosion in my offices. Fortunately, the elevators weren't antiquated equipment. They had emergency braking shoes which caught and shrieked as we fell all the way to the lobby. They were smoking hot by the time we reached the lobby, but we were alive.

The elevator doors were stuck closed, and I tried to force them open. I grunted, denting the thin metal with my hands as I strained to force it open. If I'd had a battle suit on, it would have been easy. But without metal claws the jammed door resisted my efforts.

"Was it a bomb?" I asked Jasmine over my shoulder.

She was already talking rapidly into her com-link with the operations people. If anyone knew what the hell had hit us, she would find them.

Jasmine shook her head at me, frowning. "We don't know yet. I've confirmed it was some kind of explosion—possibly a device went off inside the building."

"Great," I said. "I thought my assassination worries were over when we killed Crow. Maybe I've got a new enemy."

She was back on the com-link. I continued trying to force the doors open. I had them about two inches apart, and I could see the lobby now. There were people streaming out of the doors. They weren't panicked, but they were moving quickly. Star Force people, government officials and reporters were all getting their exercise today.

"Well, I don't see any flames out there, and the street outside looks normal. It must have been a small, localized strike."

Jasmine put her hand on my bicep. "You're just cutting up your palms on that metal."

"They'll heal," I said, forcing the doors apart another inch or so.

"Kyle, I've called in an extraction team. Let's wait here until they arrive."

I finally looked at her. "You did what? I'm not going anywhere."

"Someone is trying to kill you. We need to pull you out."

I frowned at her. "What else do you know?"

She licked her lips quickly, looked down, then back into my face. "The effect—whatever it was—the effect was centered on your offices."

"Ah," I said, getting it now. "They did try to hit me— whoever 'they' are this time. Well, I'm not sitting in this box any longer."

"Kyle, we have to get out of the region. We should leave Earth entirely."

"There are people upstairs, probably injured and in trouble. I don't feel like running out on them because some loser failed to blow me up."

"Kyle, please be reasonable."

I wasn't in a reasonable mood, I'd be the first to admit that. I was angry, surprised, and I realized as well that I was enjoying myself. It had been so long since I'd been allowed to do anything personally—anything that I could solve with my hands rather than giving orders.

As the elevator car was seriously jammed, I figured I had only two options: I could hammer the doors down with my fists, or I could exit through the access panel on the roof. I chose the roof, figuring it would be easier.

I jumped up, punching out the square panel. It crumpled and flew away into the dark shaft above. A black square appeared, showing a smoking gloom beyond. I jumped again, and shot out through the opening.

Any Star Force Marine could have done the same. We're nanotized, meaning our bodies are enhanced with muscular and regenerative improvements. We move quickly, we're extremely strong, and we heal unnaturally fast. We're akin to men walking on the Moon when under Earth's gravitational forces. We could take flying leaps if we felt like it.

Right now, I was in the mood to use my body to its fullest. I climbed up the elevator shaft walls. They were ribbed with girders and a steel framework. I climbed these as fast as an ape could zoom up a tree. Behind me, Jasmine stood on the elevator car roof, calling upward. I think she was demanding I come back down, but as the ruler of Earth, I figured I had privileges in situations like this. To be exact: I didn't always have to listen to my girlfriend.

I heard her lower her voice as I reached the eighth floor. She was talking, but more quietly. I knew she would be telling the extraction team where I was and how to intercept me.

For some reason, this ticked me off. I entertained the thought of stripping off my com-link and tossing it down the shaft, but didn't. Mostly, because it was a stupid idea. I might even hit Jasmine, and even if I didn't, it would be reckless to disconnect myself from Star Force. I kept the com-link on, and I kept climbing.

There was an emergency panel on the fourteenth floor. That was about five or six floors below my offices, but it would have to do. I kicked it out and entered the hallway beyond.

The fourteenth floor was smoky and empty. There was heat in the air, and I had to clear my throat repeatedly as I was breathing in the hot particles we call smoke. I could take an unusual amount of this sort of thing as I'd been specifically rebuilt for alien atmospheres. I didn't enjoy choking clouds of vapor, but they couldn't suffocate me.

I headed toward the stairway, where I met up with the first group of survivors. They were rushing down the steps, their eyes wide and their lungs spasming with deep coughs. I went against the press, heading upward while everyone else was going down.

A few of them recognized me, I think. They looked shocked to begin with, but their mouths hung open in disbelief when they saw my face. I had to wonder what I looked like. I took a moment to feel my cheeks and see if there were any open wounds. Sometimes, being nanotized made you look like an alien to normal people. There might be gaping injuries you hardly noticed and gleaming metal moving inside the wounds as if you'd slathered your cuts with bubbling hot mercury. Just seeing one of us in such a state could freak out the uninitiated.

But I didn't find any hideous wounds. I had a few scrapes, and my hands were dribbling blood, but otherwise I felt fine. My nanocloth clothing wasn't in bad shape either, having reknit itself together along the way.

I shrugged and pressed my way past the gawking crowd. I guess they were just surprised to see their ruler running around on the stairway.

I made my way to the top floors where my offices were. I wanted to see what had happened firsthand. There were a lot of good people up there, and I wanted to do a headcount personally.

After a minute or so of springing up the steps, I came out near my office suite. Here, the trouble wasn't just smoke. There was open flame, too. I found my first body huddled under a desk in the front office. She was dead. A civilian who couldn't take the smoke inhalation.

What had her name been? Beatrice, I think? Something like that. I recalled she was a Swiss girl.

I cursed and moved on. The next one was male, a big guy who was face down in the middle of the hallway with a chunk of metal sticking out of his back. He'd been hit by flying debris.

The temperature was pretty high by the time I reached the room where I'd been arguing with Miklos and Jasmine not fifteen minutes ago. I shielded my face with my arm and felt the heat of the flames cooking my flesh through the nanocloth of my uniform. Even I couldn't withstand temperatures over two hundred degrees for any length of time. I walked in, took video of the place with my com-link and picked up a few odds and ends to salvage. Then I retreated. I searched the rest of the floor, but found no more survivors. It was depressing.

As I came out of the oven-like central offices, the marines showed up. These weren't the color-guard types we had down in the lobby. They were assault troops, the kind that jumped out of spaceships on purpose.

"Sir?" the leader greeted me. "I'm here to escort you out of here."

I looked at him. He was wearing light armor—they all were. His faceplate obscured his features, but I knew that voice.

"Gaines?" I asked. "Is that you in there, Major?"

"Yes, sir."

Major Bjorn Gaines was a good friend of mine. I was glad to see he'd responded to the call personally, and I wasn't surprised. He was stocky black guy who often headed up Star Force's ground troops.

I looked around at the destruction. "Some mess, isn't it? A shame that good people had to die here."

"Sir, if we could get moving…I have airlift ready on the roof."

"Yeah. All right. I'd hoped I could save someone. I can't even find that gold statue the Turks gave me today."

"Excuse me, Colonel?"

"Forget it," I said. "Let's go."

16

I made it halfway up the stairs when I realized that I'd pretty much left Jasmine alone in the elevator car. I winced at the thought. Leaving your girl in danger wasn't the best way to cement a relationship. I halted, and Gaines halted with me.

"Hold on," I said. "I've got to go back to the lobby."

"What for, sir?" Gaines asked. He looked exasperated but he wasn't rolling his eyes at me yet.

"I have to get Jasmine out of the elevator."

He stared at me for a second. "You just left her back there?"

"Yeah."

"We can go get her, sir. I'll send a team right away. The airlift is—"

"No," I said. "I'm not going to fly out. You know women as well as I do, Bjorn. I'm going back."

He sighed and followed me. He didn't bother arguing further. Gaines knew me pretty well. Once I had an idea in my head, I didn't let go of it easily.

As we jogged down the stairs, I planned my speech to Jasmine. I had to have an angle to play on. It'd been too long to get away with something like: "It just took longer than I thought to get through the shaft."

When we got there, I was sort of hoping someone had already rescued Jasmine, but I wasn't so lucky. The lobby had emptied out, and the rescue teams were either engaged with the injured outside, or they were worried about me.

I eyed Gaines' men—or more specifically, their equipment. I found a nice prying bar on one of them, pulled it off his pack without asking and opened up the elevator door like a tin can. The metal peeled back with loud groaning noises.

I put my face up to the aperture and peered inside. Jasmine was gone.

"Damn," I said. "She must have gone up the shaft after me. Help me get this open wide enough to squeeze through."

Gaines put a hand on my shoulder. "We can do it, sir. You should really let us evac you out of here and let the rescue team do their jobs."

"Yeah," I said. "I know I should. But if this is a rescue, I want her to see my face first when we find her."

17

"Okay, you're the boss."

We tore the elevator apart, and I called up out of the hole in the top. It was dark and quiet up there, and she didn't answer. I tried her com link, but still, there was nothing.

I frowned, getting worried. I shot up through the hole, alarming the evac team. They scrambled to follow me.

When I found her at last, she was breaking into an office through a ventilation shaft. She was nanotized and strong, but stuck in a small space. She'd had a hard time getting enough leverage to bang her way through the metal shaft and the ceiling. I pulled her out by the feet.

"Hi, hon!" I said in a cheery tone.

She looked stunned. "I didn't know what had happened to you!"

"I came back for you," I said, "but you were gone."

She was coughing, but gave me a flickering smile. "Well, did you expect me to sit in there forever?"

"Not glad to see me?"

She looked over my shoulder at the evac people. Gaines waved impatiently for us to follow him.

"I was hoping no one would find me in this shaft," she whispered. "I got stuck."

I laughed. "That's why you weren't answering your com-link?"

She shrugged.

"Pride goeth before a fall. Let's get out of here."

She grabbed onto me before we left the dark shaft and gave me a quick kiss. "I'm glad it was you who came back and pulled me out, Kyle."

I beamed. *Bingo.* I'd pulled it off.

"Of course it was me! I'm sorry, too, that it took so long. I found a few casualties on the way."

"Any survivors?"

I shook my head. "Not on my floor. None of my staffers made it."

"The roof, sir?" Gaines asked urgently.

We were standing in the lobby by this time, and I saw the streets outside were filling up with news people. Their camera drones hovered behind them like buzzing wasps.

I shook my head. "Bring the airlift down from the roof five minutes from now."

"What?" he demanded, but I was already on my way to the lobby exit.

As we emerged into the dying sunlight, I swept up Jasmine into my arms in a dramatic gesture. She was startled and shy.

"I can walk," she hissed in my ear."

"No you can't. Not until we get aboard the lifter."

Jasmine was embarrassed as I hammed it up for the cameras. Every one of them was providing feed for some net-news outlet. She gave them shy smiles, and they ate it up. I knew we were giving them their latest splash photos for their websites. I could visualize captions about personalized rescues and heroism.

Captain Sarin, Riggs' latest romantic partner, was rescued in style at the scene of the attack...

They needed more of this kind of thing, and so did Star Force. To some degree, it would lessen the alarm the world would feel concerning the news that I'd almost been taken out by an unknown assailant.

When we finally boarded the airlift and were whisked away into the sky, I filled her in concerning the events of the day and what I'd discovered. No one, it seemed, had yet managed to figure out who had hit us.

But I had a pretty good idea *why* they'd done so. No one wanted me to put the ship-building facility into space.

The rescue people weren't satisfied with flying me to a local safe house in the Alps. They took us straight into space and onto the battleship *Potemkin*, Admiral Newcome's ship. After the Peace Accords had been arranged and signed, Newcome had flown Earth's fleet back to port and surrendered the vessels intact. I'd left him in command of the flotilla but lowered his rank to Rear Admiral under Miklos, who'd been promoted to Admiral.

Newcome greeted me aboard the ship, and I promised to brief him in the morning.

I adjourned with Jasmine to the best private quarters available. The evening turned out to be quite rewarding.

-3-

The next morning, Jasmine and I were up early and checking out the vids on the net. Every news report played me up as a dashing knight, and she played the part of my consort. She really seemed to like it.

One thing quickly led to another. Morning sex isn't always as great as it's cracked up to be, but the morning after my flashy rescue was an exception. Jasmine was in fine form, and I was unusually awake, despite the fact that I hadn't seen a cup of coffee since the day before.

We had the best stateroom the ship could provide. *Potemkin* was an old Imperial battleship, and although it had been updated, it wasn't like one of our more sparsely-appointed Star Force designs. There were pillows and hanging curtains, even a private portal to the stars outside. Our activities quickly frosted up the glass.

Outside the stateroom, a continuous parade of crewmen seemed to be marching by. I was baffled by this, as it was quite early, no more than 0600. In my long experience aboard starships, they were usually fairly quiet at this hour. The few people on duty were either late for bed or yawning and stretching, preparing for the day shift.

The footsteps outside in the hallway became inescapably obvious. They came every few minutes, impinging on our awareness despite the lovemaking.

Finally, as we were winding things up to a nice finish, a tap came at the door.

Nothing can screw up a climax like an interruption. We managed to enjoy the moment, but we were both left frowning at the door.

"Ship's door," I said, addressing the ship's AI. "Open audio channel."

A chime sounded, indicating it understood the command. Crow's ships were intelligent enough, but they generally didn't talk. They followed commands, and that was about it. In a way, I thought it was a design improvement over our more sophisticated—but sometimes argumentative—interfaces.

"Who is it?" I demanded loudly, knowing my voice would echo out into the passageway.

Jasmine squirmed away from me with a bed sheet wrapped around her and headed for the small private bathroom. I frowned and sat on the side of the bed.

"Are you speaking to me, Colonel Riggs?" asked a very familiar voice. It was none other than Marvin, my overly-intelligent, overly-eager robot.

Marvin was more than just your typical robot. He was a nanite brainbox with a massive capacity and an eclectic body he'd built himself with "spare" parts. Really, he was a being who regularly reconstructed himself. There was no one else, machine or flesh, quite like Marvin.

"Marvin?" I asked, my mind racing.

Jasmine came out of the bathroom, her face angry.

"That's who we heard out in the corridor?" she whispered. "He's been lurking out there for the past half hour. Probably listening."

I looked at her, then at the door. I didn't try to deny the possibility. He would do things like that if he wanted to talk to me badly enough. I imagined him tapping and rasping up to the door, listening to us having sex, then scuttling away disappointedly. I suspected he'd been doing this over and over again, as if he was caught in a loop of some kind.

"How long have you been out there?" I demanded.

"Does that matter, Colonel? I need to discuss something important with you."

Jasmine headed back into the bathroom with quick steps. I could tell she was pissed off at the robot.

21

I pulled on some smart-pants and let them close over my legs and waist.

"All right, come on in," I said resignedly.

The door melted away, and Marvin humped into our quarters. He was a bit too large for the space available.

Using his own ever-morphing designs, Marvin had always altered his shape the way others changed clothing. Today his central body mass consisted of a single cube—reminding me of the first time I'd met him. He had about a dozen upper-body tentacles. The lower ones were thick and short and were being used as legs. The upper appendages were long and snake-like. Instead of his usual dozen camera-eyes, I counted only seven. These were held aloft via the writhing nest of upper tentacles. He had so many damned limbs he still had plenty left over to manipulate his environment.

I noticed right away he didn't have any gravity plates attached to his undercarriage. That must have been why he'd been making so much noise as he move around outside, "politely" waiting for us to finish our activities.

I was surprised by the lack of grav plates and wondered what it meant. He liked to fly using gravity repellers, and often got into trouble for unauthorized investigations in space. One of the things we disagreed on most often was whether or not he should have the power of independent flight and space-travel. While configured for flying, he could do more work, but he also tended to zoom off and do things no one wanted him to. Often, these independent activities gave Star Force a headache.

Today, he had no repellers at all. I could only surmise that he'd trimmed them out of his design in order to placate me—as sort of a peace offering.

That thought didn't put my mind at ease, however. In fact, it had quite the opposite effect. When dealing with Marvin, I knew that the more cooperative he was at the beginning, the more I was going to have to pay at the end of the exchange.

Jasmine closed the bathroom door and fired up the shower. I felt a twinge of regret. I liked showering with her after our encounters. It was kind of like having a light dessert after the main meal.

"Let's start over again," I said cordially. "Hello, Marvin. You're looking trim this morning. What's up?"

"Hello, Colonel Riggs. I'm here to formally ask for your permission to solve a major problem Star Force has been facing for some time now."

"Whoa, whoa," I said, chuckling at his intensity. "Tell me what you're talking about first."

"Are you aware there are two rings exiting the Thor System that have never been successfully explored?"

"Oh, that," I said.

Beyond Eden

I was indeed aware of the unexplored rings. Thor had three rings we knew about. One led to the Eden System, and we pretty much controlled that one for now. We had Welter Station, a giant fortress in space, sitting right next to it on the Eden System side. The other two rings were more mysterious. One was about an AU out from the central binary stars and led to an unknown location in space. When we'd chased the Macros out of the system, they'd used that ring to escape.

The third ring was in the oceans of Yale, a water-moon that used to be inhabited by the Crustacean species. We'd managed to switch off that ring using some control codes we barely understood. It hadn't functioned for many months, but when it had, Macros had used it to invade the world's seas directly.

For a long time, we'd carefully avoided both rings. We didn't want to trigger any kind of violent response from the Macros, who were undoubtedly waiting on the far side of the rings. Several times, we'd sent in stealth probes through the active ring in space, but we'd never gotten the probes to return, nor gotten any data back from them. It was as if those ring transported anything traversing through it directly into the heart of a black hole.

"Which one are you talking about?" I asked Marvin.

"The ring in space. The underwater ring is small and disconnected at this point."

"The space ring..." I said. "Are you suggesting more probes? Because I don't see much point to that. We've tried many times and failed consistently."

Marvin's lower, thicker legs churned momentarily. He sidled closer to me.

"There are two possible reasons why the probes aren't working," he said.

"Yeah. The main one being that the Macros are instantly blowing them apart."

"I can be more precise than that."

"Okay," I said cautiously, "let's hear it."

Internally, I was already telling myself to be careful. This was one tricky robot. Rasputin himself couldn't have talked the Czarina into some of the crazy things Marvin had been able to get me to do.

"Let me start with a list of possibilities," he began, "one is that, as you suggested, they're being destroyed somehow the moment they go through the ring."

"That seems obvious. What's your other possible reason?"

"They're unable to function due to an unforeseen system failure."

"That's almost the same thing, Marvin. Your 'theories' are useless."

"Not so. If the latter situation is the case—and possibly even if the first one is the problem—I have a solution."

"Yeah?"

We stared at one another for a second. I realized that Marvin was waiting for me to beg him to tell me his solution. I was annoyed, as this talk didn't seem to be going anywhere, and I had the feeling it was going to end with Marvin requesting resources to do some strange thing that probably didn't need doing in the first place.

"Aren't you curious as to the nature of my solution, Colonel Riggs?" he prompted finally.

"'Curious' is too strong of a word," I said. "I'd say I'm slightly interested—but getting bored fast."

"Unfortunate. I'd thought you would be intrigued, as I'm engaged in solving one of the remaining mysteries within Star Force's sphere of influence. I want to discover what's on the far side of the unexplored ring. A portion of my neural net has been working on that problem for over a year now."

"I'm happy for your brainbox, Marvin. But, personally, I'm just glad there haven't been any more attacks coming from the

24

Macros for a long time. If they stay on their side of the ring, I don't care why they do so. I'm in favor of leaving them alone."

"A quiet stalemate isn't going to be the final result of this conflict, Colonel Riggs. The enemy will not rest. They're very busy right now, let me assure you. They will come to us by any means necessary when they're ready."

I thought about it and realized that Marvin was probably right. The Macros weren't like humans. They didn't calm down and go into "peaceful mode" when no enemies were in sight. Instead, they built up for the next conflict.

"All right, all right," I said, heaving a sigh. "You've got me curious now about finally scouting that ring. Let's hear whatever idea you have—but without listing any weird special equipment you might think you need."

Marvin's tentacles curled and uncurled excitedly. He did that when one of his plans was working out. I knew that he figured he had a fish on the line and was reeling the clueless bastard into the boat.

"Let me start by explaining the supporting facts so you can understand the validity of my proposal," he began.

"Get on with it."

"Very well. If the probes are being destroyed when they cross into the enemy system, it can't be instantaneous."

"Why not?"

"Because there is no such thing as a true instant in time—it is a continuum. Perhaps the process of destruction takes a nanosecond, or a millisecond. Whatever the answer is, that's the timeframe in which we have to work."

I snorted. "That isn't much time, Marvin. You can't even get a computer chip to add two numbers in a nanosecond."

"The reaction will have to be extremely quick. In fact, it will have to be ongoing as the probe passes from our system to the next. If it is already engaged, it will not be necessary to sense a changed situation and react to it."

"I'm not following you."

"Here," he said, curling tentacles in my direction. He indicated the command screen embedded in the conference table. All major ships in our fleet now had them. It made tactical discussions far easier.

25

The big oval screen glowed at his touch. It showed the Thor star system, with its three dead water-moons once inhabited by trillions of Crustaceans. I didn't like to look at it as it was probably my biggest failure to date.

"At this end of the Thor system, we have the ring which links to Eden. Over here, we have the second ring, which chains to an unknown destination. The third ring is underwater and currently inactive on the world formerly known as Yale."

"Formerly? It's still Yale, even it if is a radioactive hellhole."

"Reference updated," Marvin said. "In any case, imagine we construct a probe with a single powerful signal emanating from it. We send it through the ring, and, even if it's a very, very brief signal, we'll find out where it comes from when we hear it."

I frowned. "I can see how your plan could work. You're saying that it could be anywhere in the galaxy, and wherever it's transported, if it's broadcasting when it goes through, it will be broadcasting when it comes out. Even if it's destroyed almost instantly, we should get a blip."

"Exactly, sir."

"I don't like it for two reasons."

"I'm ready to defend my proposal," he said.

"I'm sure you are. Reason one: we've never sent anything noisy and disruptive through the ring before. We've tried to be stealthy, so as not to trigger the Macros into activating a counterattack."

"I would suggest that our attempts at stealth either haven't worked, or they haven't been relevant. The fact that the probes never return and the Macros never come in response indicates they were detected and destroyed—and yet the anticipated Macro response wasn't triggered."

I rubbed my chin and nodded. "I'm willing to give you that one. And I would like to know what we're up against, so I'm willing to take some level of risk. But here's my second objection: this radio signal you're going to send won't be able to get here in any reasonable length of time. What if the other end of the line is a hundred light years distant? Are you

26

honestly expecting us to wait a century to find out if your experiment failed or not?"

"No. The response will be instantaneous."

"How?"

"I was not proposing to use radio-based technology. Ring-communications utilizing entanglement theory will be used."

I shook my head. "I'm surprised at you."

"Really, Colonel?"

"Yeah—your plan can't possibly work. In fact, the more I hear about it, the more inclined I am to think you've got some other plot up your sleeve."

"Could you clarify that statement?" he asked.

"You know as well as I do that the ring is being continuously jammed," I said.

He moved as if to rebut my statement, and I put a hand up to stop him.

"A small broadcasting ring will not be able to send us anything," I continued. "Even if it does, it won't be able to tell us where it's from. Not if there's only a nanosecond to take readings. The beauty I saw in your plan, if we were to use radio, would be the directional nature of the signal. We could pinpoint the source if we got it directly from space."

"Very insightful objections, but you really don't think that I came here with an incomplete proposal, do you?"

I paused, thinking about it. "No, I guess not."

"I'm not here to insult your intelligence, Colonel. I've thought of these difficulties, and I believe I have a solution. First, we will not use the ring in the Thor system to relay the transmission. Second, I've come up with a way to get a directional fix on a ring-to-ring resonance signal."

He had me at last. I folded my cards and dove in. Sometimes, when Marvin was really flying high, you just had to go with him. His thought patterns were quite possibly superior to those of any human being that had ever lived, at least when it came to quantifiable things like science and engineering. Essentially, he was the smartest being I'd ever encountered.

He laid out for me in detail how he was going to do it. Really, it was ingenious, even for Marvin. He had invented the ring-to-ring communications boxes in the first place, so I should have expected he could improve upon his original designs—but I hadn't.

"You're telling me that you can do this?" I asked when he'd finished going over screen after screen of blueprints, diagrams and advanced math. "You can get two small devices to communicate instantly across any distance—even a hundred light years or more?"

"Exactly. And what's more, I can detect the direction of the signal. That part has been tested."

He showed me his prototype, and I had to admit, I was impressed. He'd built small resonance-communication devices in the past. Every major ship in the fleet had one. Using them, we were able to turn the rings into a series of routers, relaying information between distant ships in real time. The difference in his new design would be the size of the units—each unit would be small and wouldn't need the larger rings to relay the signal.

"Have you got a prototype of these two smaller boxes?" I asked excitedly.

"If I did, I wouldn't need your approval to build them, would I, Colonel?"

My grin faltered. "Let me guess…this is going to cost me, isn't it?"

"The devices in question will require a fantastic amount of power and rare materials. I'll be constructing the rings from collapsed star material—dark matter—then forming them into precisely matched and entangled shapes. Essentially, they have to be the same ring.

"How can you shape collapsed star-matter? You couldn't touch it physically."

"Actual physical contact would be dangerous and essentially impossible. We'll use gravitational emitters. Something similar to the weaponry and drive systems of *Phobos*, but on a much grander scale."

"Grander?" I didn't like the sound of that. *Phobos* was seven miles in diameter, and about half the ship's volume was dedicated to generators. "How much power would it take to activate a gravity emitter that could do the job?"

"The output of the local star would be enough."

"What?" I shouted. "You mean Sol? Are you crazy?"

"Humans have often suggested there is a pattern of irrationality to my circuitry that causes me to generate ill-advised theories and plans. If that matches your definition of insanity, then I might match that classification."

"Yeah," I said slowly, trying to wrap my mind around the conversation. "Mad as a hatter."

He finally left, and Jasmine came out of the bathroom drying her hair.

"What did that crazy machine want this time?" she asked me.

"He wants to build a big stick and poke the Macros with it," I said.

"That's crazy."

"Yeah..." I said slowly. "But I think I'm going to let him do it."

29

-4-

The following evening, I called a meeting with Admiral Newcome and his senior staff. When I went to meet with them, my mind was already made up. I was going with Marvin to the Thor System to attempt his experiment. I was tired of Earth, anyway.

"Admiral," I began, "I've got a proposition for you."

We'd sat down together to a sumptuous meal of barbecued air-swimmers. They'd been frozen and specially imported from the Eden system. Rank did have its privileges.

Newcome looked up with an alarmed expression on his face. He was a former RAF officer of the British air force. He was sixty-one years old, and his pink skull and jowls were frosted with white hair.

When Crow had taken over and declared himself emperor, he hadn't pulled off the coup alone. He'd had the tacit approval of Earth's major militaries. Newcome had been in that collaborative group. He'd advanced rapidly in the Imperial forces, eventually moving up to flying ships in space.

Many of our Star Force officers had come from various national naval or aviation backgrounds, as Newcome had. There was plenty of argument to go around as to which group did better in space. I was of the opinion that naval personnel were more suitable to flying large ships or formations, while air personnel fit in better with our fighter squadrons. Whatever the case, Newcome was a rare bird in that he'd survived both physically and politically during the two recent upheavals in government.

Some people on my staff, notably Miklos, thought I was a bit crazy to accept him into Star Force. After all, we'd fought a battle at the Tyche ring less than a year ago. But we were both human, and in the end I believed that put us on the same side. More importantly, he'd come to terms with me and been instrumental in causing Imperial Earth to fall with very little in the way of civilian death and destruction. In a way, I felt I owed him for that huge favor—we all did.

"A proposition, you say?" asked Newcome cautiously.

Like so many of my underlings, he'd learned to play his cards one at a time, never showing me what he had until he knew how things were going to go. He didn't state his opinions until he knew mine. That wasn't to say that he'd never disagreed with me, but he was a clever man who had always chosen his battles carefully.

"That's right Admiral, are you interested?"

Newcome craned his long neck around and looked down the table at his junior officers, who sat in a row on his side of the table. Regular Star Force staffers like Jasmine were on my side.

I could tell right off he wasn't going to get any support from his underlings. Every captain and commander feigned great interest in their food, which was believable enough, since the air-swimmers were excellent tonight. The flavor reminded me of a lighter version of duck, with a hint of escargot thrown into the mix. I loved it.

"Admiral, do I have your attention?" I asked.

"Oh yes, of course, Colonel. Please excuse me. I was just wondering if any of my staff members had any idea what you were proposing."

"Details first, eh? No commitment without information? I understand that strategy, and I approve. What I'm asking is if you wish to command a flotilla under me—no, that's too grand of a name. Let's call it a task force- probably consisting of no more than a single carrier and a dozen support ships, along with several transports."

If anything, the admiral seemed more flummoxed than before. I grinned at him.

"I—I don't know what to say, sir," he said.

"Stop worrying, man!" I said, laughing. "I'm not Crow. This isn't some kind of setup that ends with your head on a pike. I'm just asking if you're up for an adventure in space as my exec."

Newcome laughed nervously. It wasn't that he was a cowardly man, I knew that. But Crow had traumatized all his people. They'd never known when the wrong answer could mean the end of their careers- and possibly their lives.

"In that case, I'd love to join you," he said. "Count me and my staff at your service, Colonel Riggs."

Finally, his people appeared alarmed. I smiled at that. I could tell he'd stuck a pin into them on purpose. If they weren't going to speak up for their commander at a difficult moment, then they could suffer the consequences of his unsupported decision.

"Very well," I said, staring briefly at each of them in turn. "Let's not talk about this to anyone. It's not exactly a secret mission, but after the strike on my headquarters yesterday, I'd prefer not to inform more people than absolutely necessary about the nature of my plans."

"We're still somewhat uncertain about the details of this, ah...*adventure*, Colonel," Newcome said delicately. "Can you give us a hint so we can prepare?"

"All right," I said. "Here it is: we're going to the Thor System."

That alarmed look was back on his face. It was mirrored by the expressions of his subordinates. At this, I frowned. These ex-imperials were frightened whenever they left the Solar System. They were a provincial bunch that liked the comforts of home.

"Listen," I said, my voice becoming stern. "This is a space-going navy, in case any of you have forgotten. I know you like your velvet cushions and gold braid, but we're heading out to the frontier. Don't forget that our empire extends far beyond the Solar System these days. We have six systems to worry about."

"I take it then that we're making a show of force?" Newcome asked. "A parade of ships patrolling the outer regions to show the local populations we're strong and in charge?"

"That's not a bad idea, but it's not our primary mission. We're going as part of a research and construction effort. Marvin will fill you in on the specific supplies he requires to be loaded into the transports."

I took several more bites of air-swimmer, cleaning my plate. The other officers had been chatting, but now they spoke only in subdued tones. I didn't like the idea that they were too frightened to speak openly in my presence, but it seemed to be the case. I guessed that if I didn't execute anyone for a year or so, they might loosen up and grow some gonads again.

When I'd finished, I stood up suddenly and clapped my hands together, creating a booming sound that rang from the steel walls.

"That's it, then," I said loudly. "I want everyone to jump on this tomorrow morning. We ship out in a week's time."

They gaped at me like fish. I left the room and stomped out into the passageway. Jasmine was right behind me.

"Did you see that?" I asked her. "I don't know whether to laugh or cry."

"They aren't Star Force marines, Kyle," she said.

"No kidding. They're the polar-opposite of gung-ho. They're soft, that's what they are."

Jasmine shushed me, but I grumbled all the way back to our quarters. Over time, she'd moved up from being my regular dating partner to become my live-in girlfriend. I wasn't quite sure how that had happened—I never understood how a woman managed this trick. From my point of view, one day I'd been flirting and working up the courage to kiss her—and the next time I looked around, I found she was sighing in her sleep next to me every morning. What magic had transpired in between? I had no idea. The whole process was baffling to me.

Still, I found myself happy with Jasmine. She wasn't as provocative as Sandra had been, and I would say the flames of desire weren't quite as hot and wild. But, on the plus side, she never kicked me in the ass or tried to strangle me in my sleep.

When it came to women, I supposed one must take the good with the bad.

"From what I've seen, the Imperial Navy people are competent," Jasmine said.

"We'll find out," I said. "We'll take them out there, and if we're lucky, we'll show them a thing or two. I feel like a mountain man of centuries past around these Earth types. They must feel the way the Romans did when they found their empire in the hands of German barbarians."

She twisted her mouth and looked up at me. She crossed her arms. "Sometimes I feel like I'm the consort of a barbarian king."

I snorted. "That's fine. But don't get any ideas the way Attila the Hun's wife did. I'm not going out that easily."

We laughed and sat down on our poufy couch. The furniture was overstuffed and entirely too silky for my taste. I felt like I was in the lobby of some swanky hotel, rather than in an officer's quarters. These ex-imperial ships were almost embarrassing.

"Why does everything have to be red, gold and purple velvet in here?" I complained.

"Do you really want to redecorate before we go out to the Thor System?"

"Nah," I said, steering her away from that idea. If I let her, I knew she'd decorate the hell out of this place. "There's no time for that."

She looked slightly disappointed.

"Can we talk about something serious for a second?" she asked.

"What?"

"Miklos. You haven't told him you're leaving yet, have you?"

I heaved a sigh. "No."

"Are you worried that he'll be upset about your decision to fly with Newcome as your fleet commander?"

"He'll be threatened, I don't doubt it. But I want him to oversee the construction of the orbital shipyard. And I want Newcome to get some field experience."

"How do you think Newcome is doing so far?"

"I don't know," I said. "My first impulse is to relieve him and find someone younger and less timid."

"He has wisdom, good judgment."

"Yeah, maybe. But would he surrender to the machines as quickly as he did to us?"

She frowned at me. "That's not fair. He believed in you and wanted to save his fleet to fight Earth's real enemy."

I nodded. "That's what we *say*. But you know the news people and junior staffers call him 'Newcome the Runner'."

"He lost more than ten percent of his force before withdrawing," she said. "He had no idea what we could do. He was outranged and outgunned. From his point of view, *Phobos* wasn't even badly damaged."

"I was there," I reminded her.

Jasmine was talking about our fleet battle upon entering the Solar System. We'd barely survived Newcome's missile assault, but when we managed to blow up a good number of his ships while outside the range of his guns, he'd called it quits and withdrawn.

"The very ship we're aboard right now survived that day due to his action," she pressed. "But let's get back to Miklos. When are you going to tell him?"

"Right now," I said as I activated the coffee table. It was a screen, as were most of the walls. The coffee table served as the primary interface when I cruised the ship's net, looking at data and vid feeds.

Admiral Nicolai Miklos came online within a minute of my hailing summons. The man had always been prompt.

"Sir?" he said, sounding a bit sleepy.

"What time is it down there..." I asked. "Oh, sorry, Admiral. I guess I can wait until morning."

"You have me up now, sir. I take it there is no emergency?"

"No. This is about fleet operations."

I quickly filled him in on my decisions. Like the rest of the staff, I left him in the dark about Marvin's plans.

Miklos wasn't like most of the commanders around me. He was more of a numbers man. While I briefed him, I could see he was tapping at something. He'd brought up the manifests Marvin had put out on the command web.

"This list contains a lot of specialized materials, sir," he said, frowning. "Most of them will have to come from the Bellatrix System."

"Yeah, I know."

"Sir? May I ask what...?"

"You mean what the hell we're planning on building with this stuff? A powerful generator. The most powerful that's ever been seen in our corner of the galaxy."

He nodded his head slowly, rubbing at his eyes and flicking through reports with his fingers. I could see the blue light reflecting on his face.

"Where are you going to build this generator, if I may ask?"

I hesitated, but then decided to tell him. He had to find out soon enough, and the question was a reasonable one.

"I'm going out to the Thor System."

"Ah!" he said with a knowing smirk. "I understand now. You're going to build another space station out there."

I frowned. Miklos and I had argued frequently about the viability of the battle station I'd built to defend the Eden System. It sat on the border between the Thor System and the Eden System, hanging near the ring on the Eden side. It had been marginally successful in its task to stop Macro incursions. Miklos had always seen it as a drain on resources that could better be used to build more ships.

"Not exactly," I said.

"Very well, Colonel. I understand the nature of this call now. I will make immediate plans for departure. I don't know if I can be up there until sometime tomorrow afternoon, as I have some appointments I'll have to cancel—"

I put my hand up to stop him. "Keep those appointments, Miklos. I'm assuming they involve the construction of the orbital shipyard, right?"

He nodded, frowning.

"That's fine. That's just where I want you. Nothing is more important than getting that dock set up and running. I want you on the job, doing it right. In the meantime, Rear Admiral Newcome and I will be—"

"Newcome?"

36

"Yes, Newcome. I believe that's what I said. He'll be flying me out to the Thor system with a small task force."

"Very well, sir," Miklos said stiffly.

I could tell he wasn't happy, but that was just too damned bad.

"Now," I said, "get some sleep, man. We'll talk more about this in the morning."

"Good night, Colonel."

We reached for the cut-off. Jasmine, who'd been out of camera range during the conversation, slid back onto the couch with me. She had pajamas on—the satin ones I liked.

"When did you get into that outfit?" I asked.

"I did it while you dropped the hammer on Miklos."

"I hardly did that."

"His feelings were hurt. I could hear it in his voice."

I made a disgusted sound. "Everyone's a prima donna around here! Can't I give a command assignment to the man I want for the job?"

"Yes, but you gave it to the man who fears it, while passing over the man who assumed it would be his."

I looked at her for a second. She was often more perceptive than I realized.

"I do that sort of thing for a reason," I said. "I don't like people to become too comfortable in their positions. I want to shake them up- to push them to realize their full potential. If I leave a good man in an easy spot for too long, he'll become as soft as these cushions. Speaking of which…"

I reached for her, and she resisted for a moment, but it was only a pretense. We made love the way only two people with rebuilt bodies can.

-5-

The flight out to the Eden System from Earth was wonderful. Each million miles we traveled, I felt better. By the time we passed through the Tyche ring into the Alpha Centauri system, with its few, dusty, lifeless worlds, I felt great.

I had to stop and ask myself: *why?* The answer was simple enough. I was tired of politicking and sitting in offices reading reports. I wanted to get out into the wilds of space again.

I don't think I'm a bad government leader. Sure, there are better ones around, but there are plenty who are worse at it, too. The thing is that I *hate* it. I've never liked meetings, not unless I was designing something new and interesting or maybe planning out a campaign of action. For the last long, dragging months, I'd been talking about the allocation of trillions from the world budget and listening to speeches from people making their cases. It was kind of like being a judge orchestrating an endless trial.

I really, *really* hated the job and everything about it: The in-fighting, the pandering, and the jockeying for position. I didn't hate the part about hamming it up for the cameras, but that was about the only fun I had at work.

Now that I'd left Earth far behind, I felt free. We were flying a small task force out to the frontier to do something crazy—all of Marvin's ideas are crazy. I had to ask myself why I'd approved this particular one so impulsively, and I think it had to do with the fact that it gave me the perfect excuse to leave Earth.

"It's strange, really," I told Jasmine over breakfast. "I'm really liking this trip. It feels good to get away from Earth."

"What's strange about that?" she asked.

"Remember last year as we flew *toward* Earth? We were excited about that. We hadn't seen home for years. These days, I'm fed up with it."

She shrugged. "I don't see any of this as strange. You've never been comfortable on Crow's throne."

"Don't call it that."

We both fell silent and chewed our food for a moment. We were cruising toward the ring that would transport us from Alpha Centauri to Helios, the star system of our allies, the Worms.

"It's not a throne," I said at last, putting down my fork with a clattering sound that was louder than I'd meant it to be. "Look at this system we're crossing now. There's nothing much out here. And in the next one, Helios, we don't rule it. What kind of empire rules a single planet and a few colonies?"

"It doesn't matter what we call it," she said.

"Yes it does. If we're going to have elections soon, we can't go around calling our government an empire."

Jasmine frowned at her plate. I knew she didn't believe in a world-wide, multi-planet democracy. I couldn't blame her entirely—it might not work. But I did feel we owed it to our species to give it a try. Call me sentimental, but I liked individual freedoms, political equality and rules like one-man, one-vote.

My girlfriend, on the other hand, thought it was too dangerous to hand political power over to whomever the people voted into the job. She felt there were too many vicious aliens around who might tear us a new one any given year, and we couldn't afford to trust a haphazard political process that might give us a loser leader and result in our extinction.

"People always trade freedom for security when they're threatened," I said, countering her unspoken argument. She didn't even look at me as I spoke.

"Right now," I continued, "they like me because they see me as a strongman ruler, a protector. But that will change, you

39

watch. They'll turn on me if we have too many years of peace. They'll hate me in a decade—maybe less."

"You're right," she said, staring at her plate. "You're always right."

"No," I said, chuckling. "I'm not. That's the whole point. Don't you think that everyone in history who's been in a position of power like I am right now must have held that same conceited belief? I'm *not* always right. I can be replaced—and I should be, if I screw up."

"Let's talk about something else."

I sighed and finished my food.

"Hey," I said, as nanite arms removed our plates and stuffed them into the walls for recycling. "Let's go for a walk."

She frowned. "A walk? This ship isn't that big."

"A walk on the outside," I said, grinning.

Jasmine was a bit nervous about the idea, but I finally talked her into a vac suit and a stroll on the outer hull. She said something about radiation and exposure, but I coaxed her out anyway. She wasn't usually so fussy about things like that.

Once out there, we watched space drift by as we sailed toward the ring. We couldn't see the ring itself as we approached it, of course. We were going too fast for that. I especially enjoyed the sensation of going through a ring while out on the surface of a ship's metal skin. It was unlike anything else in my experience. One second, you were in a given star system, and the next you were somewhere else—a hundred trillion miles away.

"Isn't it great out here?" I asked her, loving it. "I mean, I'm a fool not to have trumped up a reason to visit Eden before this."

"We could be in danger."

It seemed like Jasmine had been complaining about something the entire time we'd been out here, and I hadn't really been listening. I finally tuned back in when she mentioned danger.

"Dangerous? How?" I asked her.

"I don't know. Flying debris. Some old weapon system of Crow's—anything."

"You worry too much. I've been out on the hull of ships in the middle of a pitched battle—so have you, for that matter."

"Yes, but I don't—oh!"

One second, we could see the three local stars, Alpha, Beta and Proxima Centauri. The next, everything changed around us. It wasn't a shimmering change, but an instantaneous one, as if someone had turned on a light in a darkened room.

The light bulb this unnamed giant had flipped on was huge and red. It filled a much larger portion of space than had all three of the Centauri stars. Called Aldebaran, the red giant filled more space than one could fathom. It glared and seemed very close, even though it was far away.

"Look at that!" I said, pointing toward the monster star. "You can feel the heat from it. Our visors are working overtime to adjust."

"The radiation will burn our retinas out," Jasmine complained.

"Nah," I said, clanking over the hull to a better vantage point. A sensor pod had been partially blocking my view.

Jasmine followed me after a moment and put her hands on my shoulder.

"I have to admit," she said, staring with a fascination that matched my own, "It is beautiful. You brought me out here to see this, didn't you? You knew we would fly through the ring while on the hull."

"Yeah, that's right," I said. "All those battles you spent on the inside, staring at a screen, I figured you never really got to experience anything like a live transition from system to system. This is your first one, isn't it?"

"Yes," she said softly, looking all around. "Okay, you were right to bring me up here."

"Ready to go back inside?"

She shook her head and I laughed. I put an arm around her and tried to squeeze her very gently. I did a good job, as I could tell she wasn't injured.

"Colonel Riggs?" A familiar voice spoke into my headset.

"Is this a private channel, Marvin? What do you want?"

"It's the Worms, sir. They've sent us a message."

I frowned. "I'll be right there."

41

As we headed back to the portal, I looked away from the big red star toward the disk that was the Worm homeworld. It was close and looked like a massive version of Mars. The color of rust, it had brackish, dried-up seas and mountain spires taller than anything back home on Earth.

When we got through the airlock and into the ship, I marched directly up the spine of the ship toward the bridge.

"Do you think it's important, Kyle?" Jasmine asked.

"Probably not, but I haven't spoken directly to these people for a long time. I want to make sure our relations are strong."

"Maybe you should ask Kwon for a report," she suggested.

I nodded. "I'd planned to pick him up, actually. He's been on Helios long enough."

Several months ago, Kwon had begged for a field assignment. If I was tired of Earth, Kwon was positively sick of it. I'd sent him out here to see if he could enlist the Worms in our service in some capacity. Jasmine had pointed out he was no diplomat, and I'd pointed out the Worms were half-feral and would probably like Kwon's concept of diplomacy.

Secretly, I'd been worried from the start. This moment was no exception. The instant we crossed into the Helios system, the Worms hailed us—how could I not think of Kwon and his efforts at making friends?

But I didn't tell Marvin or Jasmine any of this. It was best to learn the truth and try to pick up the pieces *after* you knew the score.

"Marvin?" I called into my com-link, struggling with a smart-clasp on my helmet that didn't want to let go. "Give me a report. What have they said so far?"

"Not much, Colonel Riggs. They sent a series of idiomatic pictographs indicating we should meet as warriors on the field of honor. Then they launched three ships, which are now in-bound to our position."

I frowned. "Three ships? The field of honor? Give me possible interpretations of the pictographs you received."

"I believe I just did that, Colonel."

I rolled my eyes. "I need analysis, Marvin. Are they angry, happy or just talking about honor because that's the polite thing to do?"

"A combination of all three is indicated," Marvin said. "Being in a state of rage pleases the Worms, and they are always concerned with honor. Without knowing the context of recent events in the system, we can't be certain which of these elements of their communication represents the primary meaning."

"Why not?"

"The same set of symbols can indicate a duel to the death is coming, or that a comrade is well-met. The concepts are too intertwined in Worm communications to easily separate them."

Jasmine and I reached the bridge, where Marvin was crouched at the command table. A spherical holotank floated above it, a newly-upgraded version. The holotank was a globular shape that spun with the motion of the ship, giving our relative attitude and a real-time reflection of space around us. Instead of being mounted on the ceiling with a steel rod, as we'd done in the old days, the system was positioned and spun by gravity plates both overhead and built into the command table itself. Our technology with regards to gravity manipulation had improved recently.

"So, in other words," I said to Marvin as Jasmine and I joined him at the command table, "You have no idea what the Worms are saying or what their intentions are?"

"That is essentially correct."

"That's unacceptable, Marvin. You're our best translator. I depend on you for accurate communications."

"I'm well aware of my indispensability."

I glowered at him for a second and had to force myself to calm down.

"Let's hypothesize," I said when I knew I could speak without shouting. "They only sent three ships. That indicates this is not an attack."

"A reasonable, if not entirely accurate, assumption."

"Why wouldn't it be accurate?" I snapped.

"Note the symbols on the table in front of us," he said, waving his tentacle over the command screen.

I turned my attention downward. My staffers had been watching the three contacts—colored amber, meaning the brainboxes weren't quite sure how to classify them. The three alien warships were closing on our position. There was a string of symbols displayed beside them, their last transmission. An image of Worm warriors side-by-side, which could mean honor or comradery. Next to that was a pictograph of a flat plain with a sun overhead. Last came a symbol I wasn't familiar with.

"What's that final thing? It looks like an X."

"Crossed lances," Marvin said. "The symbol indicates a duel or a military conflict of a small nature. It can also mean an exchange of arms."

I frowned at the symbols. "I have to admit, I don't see a clear meaning."

"Neither do I, Colonel—or rather, I should say that I see several legitimate interpretations."

Jasmine reached out and ran her fingers over the symbols, spinning them around to face her. "You don't think they're calling us out to some kind of duel, do you?"

"Um…maybe," I admitted.

"That is indeed one of the possibilities," Marvin added.

"Ah, damn," I said.

"What is it, sir?" asked Marvin.

"My good mood is gone."

"What mood, Colonel?"

"The feeling of joy and relaxation I was experiencing just a few short minutes ago. Now I remember what being out on the frontier dealing with crazy aliens is really like. What is it about our minds that causes us to only remember the good things about places we've been in the past?"

"That's an intriguing question, Colonel Riggs," Marvin said brightly. "According to research I've been conducting on human neurological patterns, I believe the human brain is structured to behave in this fashion. The mammalian brain—in particular, the anterior cingulate—has a number of unusual mood-inducing properties not found in—"

"Marvin," I interrupted, "it was a rhetorical question."

"Oh. I see, sir."

He finally shut up, and we all watched as the Worm ships flew steadily closer.

"Shouldn't we prepare for the worst, Colonel?" Jasmine asked.

"Like what?"

"We could open our missile ports and prime the warheads. We could lock-on with our weapons systems."

"Are they coming in with live guns?"

"Not that I can detect, sir. But it is a security breach to let a potential enemy get this close. We don't know their weaponry all that well."

"Given what we do know, put a cone of fire up."

She did so, and I was immediately alarmed. We were already under their guns.

"Put up their trajectory. Are they slowing down?"

"Not much, sir. But Worm behavior is often like that. They tend not to slow down until the last possible second."

I watched as she tapped the screen, and I saw the projected path displayed. As I suspected, it intercepted my ship perfectly.

"Not slowing down..." I said thoughtfully. "They drive like kids in a Porsche."

Marvin watched us closely with a single camera trained on Jasmine's face and mine. Most of his stalks and electronic eyes were focused on the screens. I thought this was odd. He really didn't need to look at the screens at all. Since he was linked in with the computers directly, he could see the data in his own mind the way the computer saw it. Maybe he liked getting our limited, angled version too. Maybe it gave him a more human perspective. As always, I found myself wondering what he was thinking. All too often during a crisis, it turned out later that Marvin knew more than he had been letting on about the nature of it.

"So, we're already within range of their particle beam weaponry," I said. "They're heading directly toward this ship, and they haven't applied braking jets."

Without being told, Jasmine displayed a timer. We had ninety seconds to go before they rammed us.

I knew I should fire on the Worms, change course, or at least warn them off. I chose none of these options.

"Marvin, transmit a set of pictograms," I said. "Tell them we welcome them on the field of honor."

Suddenly, I had the majority of his cameras on me. A few more swooped close to Jasmine to get her reaction.

"That might not be wise, Colonel," Jasmine said. "They might take the response as meaning their challenge has been accepted and that a duel should begin."

"Objection noted, Captain Sarin," I told her. "But that is exactly what I mean to say to them. Transmit the message, Marvin."

I heard a gargling sound somewhere behind me. I turned to see Admiral Newcome. He'd snuck in behind me and had apparently been watching the proceedings in horror. His face, normally florid, was nearly as white as his hair.

"Ah, hello, Admiral. Glad you could meet me here. Someone must have alerted you that we might be having a crisis."

I gave Jasmine a reproachful glance, which she dodged artfully, keeping her eyes down on the console.

"Colonel," Jasmine said. "The CAG aboard *Elixir* is requesting operational authority to launch his fighters."

"Request denied. There are only three Worm ships."

"Our protocols have been breached, Colonel," Newcome said, speaking up for the first time. "They are in too close. We are within our rights to defend ourselves."

"What you're seeing here isn't a battle, Admiral. It's a political negotiation."

"Then I request permission to engage in evasive maneuvers."

"Request denied."

"They're flying their ships right into us!" Newcome objected. "Even if they don't fire, they might well ram us. The kinetic force of even a glancing blow from a single ship would destroy our vessel!"

"A reasonable assumption, Admiral. But I don't think it's going to go down that way."

"You're gambling all our lives upon a hunch?" he asked incredulously.

"If I might interject, sirs," Marvin said.

We both looked at him.

"Admiral," Marvin said. "Colonel Riggs often bases command decisions upon criteria others do not comprehend at

46

the time they're made. Frequently, command personnel object, but their objections are virtually always overruled."

"What the hell is your robot telling me? We have less than thirty seconds left!"

"Tell him, Jasmine," I said.

She turned to Newcome. "He said Riggs often does crazy things, and you'd just better get used to it."

I nodded my head slowly. "Exactly."

When the final seconds ticked away, I could see Newcome squirm, wince and squint, but the Worms broke off before they rammed us, their trio of ships splitting apart and taking three separate spiraling paths.

"Sir?" Jasmine said, but I was too busy gloating to pay attention to her.

"See that?" I demanded, pointing at the twirling Worm ships. "They didn't hit us. This was some kind of test, some kind of show of bravery. We did our part by not blinking first."

"Blinking, sir?" asked Newcome. "I don't understand."

"Haven't you ever played chicken with your friends—or your enemies—on a dark road at night?" I asked him.

"I most certainly have not!"

"Come on, not even when you were young and crazy?"

"I don't think that description ever fit my station in life."

I looked him over and sighed. "No, I don't suppose it ever did. Well, anyway, the Worms were just having a little fun. Now—"

"Colonel Riggs?" Jasmine asked again, more insistently.

"Yes, what is it, Captain?"

"There is another contact closing on our position."

Frowning, I looked down at the board, then up at the holotank. An orange contact flickered there. It was small, no more than a cluster of pixels.

"What the hell is that?" I asked.

"Unknown, sir," she said. "The Worms released it as they made their final approach."

"Released it?" demanded Newcome, perking up. "It must be a bomb or a mine of some kind. Please sir, allow me to maneuver out of its path or shoot it down."

I frowned at the screen, uncertain. I'd understood we were involved in a show of bravery between our two species, two warriors meeting on an open plain and beating their chests before clasping arms—something like that. But why drop an object into our path?

"I don't get this."

Newcome sensed my uncertainty and grew braver.

"May I take action to protect my ship in that case, Colonel?"

I glanced up at him. It was a reasonable request. "All right. Don't shoot it down, but you have the helm."

He shouted a stream of orders. The navigational people all went into action, and we evaded the incoming object. It sailed past us at a rather sedate pace.

"If that was an attack, it was a pretty lame one," I said.

"You can never be too careful, sir," Newcome said.

I tossed him an annoyed glance. That was all I needed, another nervous officer on my bridge. I was already regretting bringing Newcome along.

"May I shoot it down now, Colonel?" Newcome asked.

"What? Certainly not. For all we know it's a Worm fruit basket. There's no need to—"

"Sir?" Jasmine said, speaking up again.

This time, I gave her my immediate attention.

"We're being hailed, sir."

"Ah, good. Finally, the Worms are going to explain their bizarre behavior. It's about time."

"Possibly, Colonel, but the transmission isn't coming from the Worm ships or Helios. It's coming from the object."

My frown returned. "Well, pipe it through."

She did, and a familiar voice echoed on the command deck. It was faint, but I recognized it immediately.

"Star Force ship?" Kwon hailed us. "Could you maybe pick me up or something? I'm drifting, and the Worms didn't give me any kind of propulsion."

-6-

We slowed down, turned around and hauled Kwon into our vessel. Newcome was even paranoid and objecting about that, spouting some nonsense about fake Kwons and parasitically infected personnel.

"I assure you, Admiral," I told him, "the Worms have neither the technology, motivation, nor the personality to try something like that. They just gave him back to us, that's all. They probably got tired of him. He eats a lot."

Glowering, Newcome followed me to the sally portal where we deployed marines in battle—or in this case, retrieved them.

We processed him through the airlock and, when there was enough air in the chamber to talk, I opened my visor.

"Kwon, you have some serious explaining to do," I told him.

"Good to be back, Colonel."

"I beg your pardon, Colonel," Newcome said. "But can't we at least bring him through the decontamination center? It is standard operating procedure."

"All right, all right," I said, closing my visor again.

Ten minutes later, I met up with Kwon again in a small pressure-sealed chamber. Only the Imperial ships had rooms like this, designed to hold people who'd done space exploration before they were allowed back into the general population of the crew. They were quarantine centers, really. I didn't see the point, but I figured since we had the facility we might as well use it.

"It was very interesting living with the Worms, sir," Kwon told me.

"I'm sure it must have been quite an interesting experience for the Worms too, since they dumped you out of their hold like a sack of trash."

"Oh, I don't know. That's just their way. They aren't a soft people, you understand."

He laughed then, and I realized belatedly that Kwon had made a joke. The Worms were squishy, like huge leather pillows filled with squirming muscle. Physically, they *were* soft people.

I chuckled politely, then continued to question him. On hand, I had Admiral Newcome, who looked as if he smelled rotten meat. Marvin had managed to tag along as well, and seemed very interested in the discussion. He wasn't saying much, but his interest in unusual events was always alarming to me. He often knew or suspected more than he was letting on. I knew enough not to ask him what he was thinking, of course. Marvin would only clam-up harder if he thought I was on to him. The best thing to do would be to watch him closely for clues as to what he was thinking.

"All right, let's hear your report, Kwon. Where is the rest of the delegation I sent to Helios?"

"I don't know, sir," he said. "But I think they all died."

"*Died?* How?"

"The Worms had a contest with us. A constriction contest. That's what they like to do for fun, you know. They squeeze each other. It's like wrestling for them."

I nodded slowly. "Let me guess, they squeezed you, and you won."

"Yeah. The other guys didn't make it, though. Internal injuries, probably."

"How the hell did all this start?"

"It was the chief emissary's fault, I think. She didn't quite understand the Worms. She talked about learning their customs. She told them she wanted to form a relationship with them—to be treated as a Worm citizen."

50

"Uh-huh. So the Worms took her at her word and wrestled with her."

"Right. I don't think she was even nanotized. She made a funny little sound, and then there was blood all over the inside of her visor."

Newcome was squirming like a Worm himself. "Beastly barbarians," he mumbled.

I glanced at him. "True," I said. "The Worms are probably the most culturally barbaric species we've encountered. They're kind of tribal and believe in blood sports. If it was anyone else, I'd take this personally and be angry with them, but they might not understand. After all, the ambassador asked for it."

I turned back to Kwon. "What happened after the Ambassador died?"

"Well, the rest of the diplomatic team kind of freaked out. They shot a few Worms—it didn't go too well."

"Hmm," I said, sighing. "A diplomatic incident. Now I understand their message better. The Worms were speaking of mending our lost ways. I would wager from their behavior they're angry and considered a warlike response."

"I think they were pissed off, yes, sir."

Newcome was still eyeing Kwon suspiciously. "Your story is quite fantastic, First Sergeant. What was your part in it? How did you survive?"

"Well, I didn't pull a gun. Instead, I got up like this."

Kwon stood and crouched with his hands out to his sides. His knees were bent, and his hulking form was clearly in the posture of a wrestler. In fact, he looked like a sumo wrestler to me.

"They didn't try to kill you, then?"

"Well—they tried. They sent in a Worm about my size. I was glad he wasn't one of the really big ones—you know, the Granddaddy Worms. Anyway, he was tough, and strong, and I didn't have an armored suit or a knife or anything. We thrashed around, but I finally managed to tear him apart."

"How do you even go about getting a wrestling hold on a Worm?" I asked him.

51

He shook his head. "No, no, I didn't do a wrestling move. I grabbed one half with my arms locked around the middle, see, and I squeezed him until he came apart in two halves."

"Ah, you *literally* tore him apart."

"It was the only way I could figure out to win, sir."

I chuckled. Admiral Newcome looked disgusted.

"So then they were impressed," I said. "They decided you could live, and they shipped you up here when we came by. When did the wrestling happen?"

"About a week ago, if I had to guess. I've been living in my suit. Not much to do. Not much to eat, either. Could I go to the mess now, Colonel?"

"You certainly can, Kwon. You've earned it."

I clapped him on the back and sent him on his way.

Newcome turned on me the moment he was out of earshot. "Do you believe all that nonsense, Colonel? I mean, seriously?"

"It makes sense, sir," said Marvin suddenly. He hadn't spoken much throughout the briefing, but he came to life now that Kwon was gone.

"*Sense?*" demanded Newcome. "What kind of *sense?* These aliens crushed our entire diplomatic team without a warning, and Kwon is returned by ejection from their ships? This isn't civilized behavior."

"Agreed," I said. "But Marvin's right. You have to understand the Worms, Admiral. They aren't like you or me in personality or culture. They're rough around the edges compared to us."

"Rough around the—I can't believe what I'm hearing. You're defending them."

"Maybe," I said. "Like I said, you have to understand them. Our chief emissary clearly failed to do so. She went into a shark tank, then invited the sharks to do what came naturally to them. I recall certain British explorers making similar mistakes a few centuries back. These are *aliens*, Admiral. Not primitive people who need more education. You have to deal with them as they are, not as you wish them to be."

Newcome didn't seem to get what I was saying, and I lost interest in the conversation. I knew I didn't really need to explain it to him. If he stayed alive long enough out here on the frontier, he'd figure it out on his own as Kwon had. You just couldn't judge aliens by human standards—and if you did, you'd likely make a fatal mistake at some point.

I dismissed Newcome and turned to Marvin.

"What do you think we ought to say to the Worms, Marvin?"

"You're asking me, Colonel?"

"I believe I just did."

"I rarely am queried for advice in diplomatic matters."

I rolled my eyes. Marvin had served as my translator on countless occasions. He was the best at it as his brainbox contained the best set of neural chains in the known cosmos. But, although he'd asked for more autonomy in his communications, I'd always denied it to him. I just plain didn't trust him to negotiate on Earth's behalf as a free agent.

"Well, I'm asking for your advice now, robot," I said.

"Sometimes I wonder if the term 'robot' has a negative connotation for you, Colonel. Your usage in this instance suggests—"

"Look, let's just stick to the subject. I asked what you would suggest, and I still haven't heard anything but complaints. How can you expect me to elevate your status in these matters if you don't even provide constructive input?"

That comment seemed to get Marvin's attention. His cameras reshuffled themselves, and his tentacles stopped rasping on the floor.

"You're suggesting a promotion in my status?"

"We're not cutting a bargain if that's what you mean. I want to hear what you're thinking about this situation."

"We have several viable options," Marvin said at last. "We could declare war on the Worms for their misconduct, for example."

"Not going to happen. What else?"

"I wasn't suggesting that course of action. I was simply offering up alternatives."

"Well, keep going."

"We could send a scathing communication to them, telling them of our displeasure. Or we could send our apologies for the behavior of our envoys."

"Both sound weak, but plausible. Is that it?"

"No, sir. There is one other option: we could ignore the incident entirely."

I looked at him. "What would that do?"

"It would show that we understood their actions, but that we neither applaud nor condemn them. That we haven't changed the nature of our relationship over the incident."

I thought it over and rubbed my chin. I nodded at last.

"I like that," I said. "They've got to be wondering what we'll do. When they came at us playing chicken, I resolutely flew onward. They broke off. That shows they aren't angry enough to start a war themselves."

"Not angry enough nor foolish enough."

I shook my head. "No, that's not how they think. The Worms would rather fight to the last and die than hide in their holes as a beaten people. If they wanted to fight us, they would have attacked regardless of their poor odds. But they didn't. That means they're annoyed, but the situation can be repaired."

I stood up and slammed my fist on the table. It rang and dented with the impact. I loved smart-metal furniture as it allowed me to express myself fully and then quietly self-repaired afterward.

"I'm going to take your advice, Marvin. I'm going sail on by the Helios system without a complaint, an apology or a single missile fired. As far as I'm concerned, we're still allied peoples, and when the time comes, we'll fight to the death against the machines side by side."

"Your statements are appealing, but I can't take credit for your reasoning. My advice was merely a matter of listing options and consequences."

I laughed as I left the room. "Don't sell yourself short, robot. Sometimes, the best advisor is one that serves as a sounding board for his commander's thoughts."

I left him then and moved back to the bridge. My flotilla accelerated without a transmission to the Worms. We headed toward the Eden ring at flank speed. The Worm ships silently watched us slip away. They didn't fire or follow us. They just waited until we exited their system a few days later and then returned to their home space and parked in orbit over their planet.

By that time, I'd had the opportunity to second-guess my choices. In particular, I wondered about Marvin's "advice". He'd made a point of giving it to me, then clearly stating that he *hadn't* given it to me. Why would he want to play both sides of the issue?

I had to wonder about Marvin's true motivations. He always had his own private, oddball goals.

I knew he really wanted to perform an experiment out in the Thor system. Could that be why he'd suggested doing nothing? He'd known that if I did shoot at the Worms, it might have created a distraction, delaying us. There was nothing that slowed down an expedition like a diplomatic incident that needed cleaning up.

"Damn," I said aloud to no one.

The trouble was rooted in a simple fact: the robot was at least as smart as I was. He always had been. That was the real problem. How could a mere human outthink an artificial genius?

-7-

When we finally arrived in the Eden System, I felt like I'd come home again at last. I immediately headed to the ship's tiny observatory and gazed out the frosted window, mesmerized by the local star and the shimmering planets that circled her.

I remembered wanting to leave Eden and head home to Earth. In retrospect, that seemed insane to me. How could I have pined away for Earth when all this natural beauty awaited me here, circling a perfectly stable yellow sun? I chided myself for not having visited for so long.

The Eden System was made up of six habitable worlds that circled a lone star many light years from Earth. There were actually seven habitable worlds, if you included the homeworld of the Blues. But that was a gas giant, and as only the Blues could survive there, it didn't count in my book.

Such lovely worlds…they were like jewels floating in space. Eden-8 was probably my favorite. It was the coolest of the human colony-worlds. I'd built my sanctuary there, Shadowguard. It was a castle-like structure, and it clung to the tallest peak on the planet, the only spot where natural snow fell regularly.

I felt a sudden yearning to visit Shadowguard again. Once I had the feeling, I couldn't shake it. Inexorably, my thoughts moved from Shadowguard to thoughts of Sandra, my dead girlfriend. She'd been my companion through many years and adventures. We'd been happy on Eden-8 if a little restless and homesick.

"A penny for your thoughts," said a quiet voice behind me.

I jumped a little. I hadn't heard Jasmine come into the chamber.

"I haven't held a penny in my hands for years," I said, smiling at her.

"Well, tell me what you're thinking about anyway."

"Right now, I'm thinking we were crazy to ever leave Eden. What is it about us humans that causes us to take a good thing for granted? To become restless and bored when we have it too good? We just have to go out into the wilderness and stir up some trouble."

She laughed quietly. "You should know. You're the very best at stirring things up."

I nodded and returned to the view. She was right about that. I had a knack for finding trouble wherever it hid and whacking it with a stick.

"Why *are* we out here, Kyle? Really?"

I glanced back at her for a moment. I thought about Marvin's plan, and my face darkened. "We're about to whack another wasp's nest, I think."

"Why not go home then?" she asked, coming near and clasping my arm. Her touch was as gentle as that of a butterfly alighting on my artificially toughened skin.

"Maybe we should, but I think it's time we learned what our adversary is planning. If we wait any longer, they might be ready."

"Who? And ready for what?"

"The machines—our first enemy. Our *real* enemy."

"Do we absolutely have to mess with them again? Can't we just leave them alone? Perhaps they won't come again. Maybe they never will. Maybe their minds are caught in some kind of endless loop."

I shook my head and sighed. "No. They're building up. They're preparing a surprise for us. If we do nothing, they will have the initiative when the time comes. They'll be ready, we won't. I don't want to play their game. I want to force them to play ours."

Her hands gripped my elbow, but she didn't argue further. I liked that about Jasmine. She wasn't a fighter—at least not in our personal relationship. She'd always accepted me as her commander whereas Sandra never really had.

We watched the stars glide slowly by outside and felt the cold of space seeping inside the seams of the ship. It wasn't built entirely of smart metals, being an old Imperial vessel. It had an old-fashioned solid hull. The joints of these ships seemed to leak more than our Nanotech ships did. As a result, some chambers were hotter or colder than others, depending on orientation and random design flaws.

The view was romantic, but we didn't make love or even kiss. We just stared, both of us wondering what tomorrow might hold.

* * *

We had three scheduled stops in the Eden system. The first was at the homeworld of the Centaurs. They were in a fine mood and glad to see me back in their hometown.

"Colonel Riggs," they said, "we're indescribably pleased to greet you again. The grass will grow greener, and the skies will stretch to the infinite horizon in your honor."

When I talked to the Centaurs I usually found myself talking, not with a single representative, but rather with a collective council of some kind. In this case, the council had hailed me from their coldest planet. A world of clear skies and steep, snowcapped mountains, they were most at home there.

"People of the grass," I said enthusiastically. "I can't tell you how happy I am to be back. Nowhere else in the universe is the air so clear and the water so clean as it is upon your planet. I'm sorry I ever left this system."

They liked this, and went into a gush of pleasantries about the grass, the sky and honor—always honor. Usually, this sort of thing left me impatient, but not this time. I was smiling throughout the lengthy speech. I let them blow on and on like the very wind they were praising. At last, however, I decided it was time to rein them in.

"Let's get down to business, shall we?" I asked.

"Business? Trading? There is little honor in such concepts."

They sounded disappointed that I wasn't letting them tell me more about their fields, droppings and bounding litters of young. I was sorry to be the party-pooper, but I wanted to move on to my next port of call in the morning.

"I apologize," I said, "I do not like to be rude, but I must be brief. I wish to offer you supplies and technological systems."

"And in return?"

I cleared my throat. "I'm hoping we might ask for a new levy of troops."

"You ask much, but your wishes will be accommodated. How many of our furred millions will you require this time, friend?"

I shook my head in disbelief. "Don't you even wish to know *why* I want more of your troops?"

"To ask such a question is to offend you. We have no wish to do that. If someday your actions are dishonorable, we'll question you then."

I understood that. They trusted me—until I screwed up. After that, I figured it might be hard to regain their trust. I had a lot of capital with these people. After all, I'd saved their race from extinction and given them their homeworld back. Further, I'd continued chasing the Macros out of their system for years.

Still, I somehow felt a little guilty when dealing with them. They were so trusting and so grateful. It made me want to make sure I never did screw them—not even accidentally.

"I've brought back thousands of your people. They are now veterans. I'm returning them all, releasing them from my service."

"Did they not please you?"

"On the contrary, they did. But I don't wish to abuse their loyalty. I want to reward them for their service by giving them leave and taking on fresh troops. Every Centaur that wants to go home will be dropped off today."

"Have you offered them this privilege yet, Colonel Riggs?"

"No, not yet. I wanted to consult with you, the Centaur Council, about replacements first."

"It is well that you did so, for they will most certainly disappoint you in this instance."

I frowned. "Why's that?"

"Because the sun never sets upon a warrior's service. How many do you think would ask to return home if you were to offer them the privilege?"

I considered this and quickly had the answer.

"None of them," I said. "That's what you're getting at, isn't it? They would all opt to stay on, to serve me until death."

"Naturally. To do anything else would embarrass the herd."

Their words made sense. I knew the Centaurs—hell, I'd learned their language and customs at our first contact. I should have known better. First off, they tended to do everything as a group. They didn't decide as individuals. They were more like a flock of birds, a herd of antelope or a school of fish, moving as a single mass. If one would opt to stay in Star Force and serve honorably to the death, they all would.

"Hmm..." I said thoughtfully, touching my face with a gloved hand. "All right then. I've made my decision. Those Centaur troops I have with me are to be garrisoned here on your worlds. I'm stationing them here permanently as a home guard. They're to keep their equipment and organization, and they will still be part of Star Force, but they will be under local command and committed to local defense."

They chewed that one over for a few seconds. Finally, the voice came back online. "That seems like an honorable solution for all parties. We will be delighted to be reunited with our heroic herd-mates."

"Can you provide me with fresh troops for my fleet? I wish to train more as I have the first group."

"They will be provided! We'll have contests and races this very day. Only our most vigorous will meet the challenge!"

I smiled. I had them where I wanted them now. We'd found a way for honor to be satisfied and for me to get what I wanted. I'd have fresh troops and they'd have their people back. Centaurs didn't live as long as humans did. By the time a buck was twenty, he was broken down with age. I needed ten-year olds, a fresh herd of them. The arrangement would be a win all the way around.

By the following day, we lowered transports and unloaded the troops. They carried with them a very special gift. It was one of the Nano factories. A new model, with a raw input system and programming station even a Centaur could work with.

They were blown away by the value of the gift.

"We cannot accept this!" they puffed. "The value is immeasurable."

"Yeah, but you gave me yours years ago. I'm returning what I borrowed. I have many such units, and don't need this one at the moment."

I was lying, naturally. There was never a time that I couldn't use a Nano factory. They produced every sophisticated piece of equipment I had. Without them, there would be no generators, spaceships, beam weapons or even nano-clothing. But I wanted them to take it, so I pretended it was a cast-off unit.

After a few gushing, half-hour speeches, they finally took custody of the system and began making excited plans about building ships with it. I felt a pang as they said this. The Centaurs would now be able to transport their people back and forth between the three cooler worlds in this system with ease. Civilian traffic would be flying through Eden once again.

Why did this fact give me a pang of regret? Because of a streak of dark greed I'd begun to suspect was in every human's heart. They'd given us three worlds to colonize—but there were two more they'd barely touched. Why should I pass them to a population of friendly goats? Was that the honorable thing to do or a stupid mistake? I decided I would let history judge me on this one.

Once we'd made the exchanges, and I prepared to board my ship again, something unexpected happened. A local Council of Elders came out to meet me. There were no less than a hundred and thirty of them.

I sighed. I'd almost made it back aboard the ship without listening to another speech.

I pasted on a smile and greeted each furry goat with the help of a translation box. After a half-hour, Marvin came out of the lander to find out what was taking so damned long.

It wasn't his best move. To these people, he wasn't a friendly face. He was a machine—a nightmarish one at that. He had tentacles whipping around and cameras panning and zooming like a swarm of bees around his primary brainbox.

As one, the delegation of Centaurs froze and lifted their horned heads. Their eyes tracked the robot as he glided toward me.

"Colonel Riggs, we believe you are under attack," one of them said.

I glanced back and spotted Marvin.

"Sorry," I said, "That's a friendly machine. He's not dangerous."

"Is it intelligent?"

I looked Marvin over. He looked agitated, but curious all the same.

"Yes," I said, "it is, after a fashion."

"Then, by definition, it is *not* friendly. Do not be fooled as we once were."

"This machine is different. It was not made by the Macros or the Nanos."

"Where did it come from, then? The Great Airless Ocean?"

"You mean space? No, not exactly. He sort of built himself. But his mind—his mind was created by you guys."

The Centaurs bleated amongst themselves for a minute or so after that. Heads heaved and tails flipped. I'm not an expert at reading Centaur body-language, but I knew they were upset.

"Marvin, did I say something wrong?" I asked quietly.

"You insulted them, Colonel," he said brightly.

"I don't see how—" I began, but then they turned back to me.

"We have misjudged you. Clearly, you have made a new alliance with the machines. We must ask that you release all of our troops from your service, and we will return the duplication machine you gave to us. We will not be so cheaply bought. Our droppings would be more—"

"Hold on! Hold on!" I said, throwing up my hands.

They seemed to find this gesture threatening, so they lowered their horns and backed away from me. This was going from bad to worse.

"Let me explain," I said. "I will attempt to return this matter to balance. The sky is endless and the rivers divide our lands, but the grass is everywhere."

I had no idea what that meant, but I'd heard a Centaur captain say something like that to stop a feud between his troops once.

The Centaurs seemed to calm down. "What you say is indisputable. We will listen out of loyalty and honor."

"Right. It went like this..." I explained to them how Marvin had come about. Originally, he'd been a download from the Centaurs. He was a massive data-dump, a mind of immeasurable size. I'd always wondered where the Centaurs had come up with the technology to build such a thing. Maybe today I'd learn the truth.

When I finished with my story, the Centaurs weren't impressed. "We've called out to our brothers using our far-reaching cries."

I nodded. "Far-reaching cries" is what they called packet radio.

"No such transmission was made by our peoples. We tried to send something—but it was immeasurably smaller. Nothing like this abomination against life could possibly have been created by a simple translation device. You have been deceived—or, by the skies, you are seeking to deceive us."

That wasn't the end of their little speech, naturally. They went on and on, complaining about the lack of honor in the universe and rivers that ran befouled with another clan's urine.

While they complained, I opened a private channel to Marvin. "When I give you the signal," I told him quietly. "You're going to perform a shutdown."

"What signal, Colonel Riggs? I'm not familiar with any such pre-arranged protocol. Perhaps we should meet in private and discuss this matter without the presence of these primitive aliens."

"If you don't play dead when I give you the cue, I'll remove every privilege I've ever granted you. I swear, I'll find those secret pools in the engine rooms you're always playing with and dump them out."

"That would be vandalism and murder, Colonel. The microbiotic colonies—"

"They're unauthorized, that's why you hid them. Are you going to cooperate or not?"

"I will absolutely do so. But may I state that threats are unnecessary? Compliance is my natural first instinct. I will—"

"No it isn't, but revenge is mine. I'll dump them into space, Marvin. They'll be a block of ice five minutes from now if you don't fake death extremely well."

"—again, totally unnecessary. I find that—"

"Stop transmitting, Marvin. You're done."

I cut the channel and stood up, raising my hand to stop the ongoing litany of complaints from the Centaur delegation. They shuffled from hoof to hoof skittishly.

"I've heard enough. I've decided that I have been deceived. I thank you for having brought this matter to my attention. Today, you have revealed to me a traitor in our midst. I will resolve this matter immediately."

So saying, I strode purposefully toward Marvin. He did a great job of looking alarmed. Every camera he had watched me advance, and he scuttled back a few steps.

"I trusted this machine because I believed you sent him to me. I now understand no machine can be trusted in this manner. They're incapable of honor, and they have no fur."

"Your statements are a sequence of *non sequiturs*," Marvin complained.

"Shut up and shut down, steel devil!" I shouted, and I sprang on Marvin's back. Obediently, Marvin went limp. He'd surmised correctly that this must have been the signal I'd been talking about.

"What has happened to the machine?" asked the Centaurs, circling around warily.

I ripped a tentacle off and waved it at the herd. I threw it into their midst, with the camera still attached. They leapt away as if a snake had landed in the grass at their feet. Perhaps, in a way, it had.

"I've shut it down, and I'm now going to disassemble this monster."

A hailing signal beeped on my com-link. I opened it with a stealthy tap.

"Colonel Riggs, I must protest. You said nothing about disassembly."

"Play dead, Marvin," I whispered. "You brought this on yourself."

"I don't see how—"

"You could have stayed on the damned ship!"

I closed the channel and proceeded to strip every tentacle from the robot and kicked the brainbox repeatedly, denting the sides. I knew that unless I ruptured it, Marvin would survive. He could rebuild external damage in a few hours, as long as it didn't affect his neural chains. He wasn't going to be happy, but I was having a little fun, I have to admit.

The Centaurs, for their part, grew increasingly bold. By the end, they joined in, urinating and scatting on the prone, motionless robot.

I could only wonder if curse words were looping around inside his artificial mind.

-8-

"If I'm not mistaken, you enjoyed that experience, Colonel Riggs," Marvin complained an hour or so later.

I struggled not to smile. Kwon blew it by laughing hugely. "That has to be the funniest thing I've seen all year. I got a vid from the landing craft. You guys want to watch it again?"

"That won't be necessary, Kwon," I said with mock severity. "Could you all wait outside? Marvin has been humiliated enough."

Kwon stumped out chuckling. The two techs that were on hand to reassemble Marvin's broken body also left reluctantly. Everyone wanted to hear this conversation.

Marvin watched them go. He looked down at his broken form. He did look pathetic. He was just a brainbox with a few wobbly arms lofting cameras and no legs to speak of. It made me think of him as an infant, as an almost helpless intellect exploring his world for the first time. I hardened myself against such sentimental thoughts.

"You sent them away before they finished reassembling my person," Marvin complained.

"That's right," I said. "I thought you and I should talk in private."

"Yes," he said. "You mentioned humiliation. Would that be an appropriate response given my current circumstances? Is it an emotional mix of anger and shame? I have to admit, being dismantled and abused was unpleasant. I wished the Centaurs harm during the process."

66

"Natural enough," I told him. "It showed restraint that you did nothing."

"I fully complied with your orders in that regard, didn't I?"

"Yes, you did, Marvin," I began, and then I caught myself. You couldn't just go around telling Marvin he was a good robot. He always asked for a treat when he did something good. I had to be careful. I hardened my tone. "But following orders is what's expected of any member of Star Force. It's a thankless job but one which we perform flawlessly."

"Still, there are promotions and privileges granted when particularly outstanding—"

I cut him off seeing right away where he was going. "Before there can be any talk of granting anything, I have some hard questions for you. The Centaurs disavowed playing a part in your creation. All this time, I thought you were a partial download. If you are not, where exactly did you come from, Marvin?"

"That's a mystery even to me," he said. "I'd prefer to discuss—"

"No, no, not so fast. Did you *know* you weren't a partial download of AI from the Centaurs?"

Marvin only had two cameras and no manipulative limbs. My techs had orders to work very slowly. I hadn't wanted Marvin up to full operational effectiveness until I knew more about him.

"I most certainly am a download from the Centaurs. They admitted to making the transmission, and you might recall that I was nearly erased when we returned to the Eden System and their servers restarted the process."

I nodded thoughtfully. "That's true," I said. "But you were always too sophisticated to have come from the Centaurs. I should have known they could never have developed a mind like yours. They don't know much about software."

"Our shared supposition has always been that I was part of the technology left behind by the Nanos, and I wasn't directly developed by Centaur programmers. That would be absurd."

"I have to agree with you there. But you're so much more than a translation program. How could a relatively simple piece of software grow into such an intellect?"

Marvin panned and craned his two wobbly cameras. He seemed cautious and thoughtful. I watched as he tried to watch me and the exit at the same time. Then he looked down at his missing limbs. They were mere stubs coming out of his central thorax.

"Is there a reason why I'm still not in a mobile state?" he asked.

"We're repairing you as fast as we can, Marvin."

"That seems unlikely, Colonel Riggs."

"Let's not change the subject. Where do you really come from, Marvin? What extra element made you? I'm not buying the partial download theory—not anymore."

Marvin's camera studied me. "I can see that you do not intend to reconstruct me until I answer this question to your satisfaction."

"That's right," I told him, crossing my arms.

"I'm disappointed in you, Colonel Riggs. I've always counted you as an ally."

This statement gave me a pang. I wondered what feelings Marvin really did have, if any. He *seemed* to have them. He could pout, and he could rejoice.

"Listen, old friend," I said. "This isn't personal. I have to protect billions of lives. I can't take chances."

"Am I so threatening? Have I done nothing to earn your trust?"

I sighed. "I do trust you. I've given you powers undreamed of. There were times you could have pulled the plug on my entire species. Who else has entrusted you with such responsibility?"

"As I recall, you had little choice in those instances."

"All right, forget about that then. Just tell me what you remember about your creation."

"That is an unfair question. I might as well ask you to detail your thoughts as you passed through your mother's birth canal."

I frowned at him. "No, it's not the same at all because you remember *everything*. You did right from the start. You can play back to me everything I've ever said to you, and you frequently like to do so to win a point."

"There are certain things you ordered erased."

"Never mind about that," I said quickly. Marvin had a lot of stuff in his brainbox, and some of it I didn't want anyone else to know about. "You'll always be under a pall of suspicion especially since you were once one with the machines."

"That's not true. I was never a Nano—or a Macro. I do not count them as kin. They are maybe distant cousins, in a way, but not family."

"Okay, I'll buy that," I said. "*We* are your family now. Star Force is your home. But you have to come clean, Marvin. I can believe you may not know what you are, but you must have a theory. You must have known our story of your creation didn't entirely make sense. Talk to me, Marvin. Give me a good reason to trust you again."

"I find it difficult to function without my limbs."

"You're being restrained right now. I'll give you your limbs back if I find you to be truthful and honest."

Kwon appeared at the door again. Had he been listening in? I wasn't sure. He leaned into the doorway and said, "You can't trust him. He'll lie. He always lies. He'll say anything to get out of this."

I turned to him in surprise. "I thought I asked you to leave, Kwon."

"You did, sir. But he's a sneaky robot. I had to come back and check on you."

I looked at him thoughtfully. Kwon wasn't normally the deep-thinker in the group, but perhaps this time he had a point.

I turned back to Marvin. I couldn't believe Marvin was an evil robot bent on humanity's destruction. He'd saved our bacon too many times. Wouldn't it have been easier to kill us all by failing just once in the past? To bail out of a burning ship and never return? Why stay with us if he didn't want to?

"Marvin," I said, taking pity on him. His one camera wobbled from one glaring face to another. Everyone he thought was his friend had turned on him. "Marvin, just tell us what you think happened. If you weren't a download from the Centaurs—who made you?"

"I did not know at first," Marvin said, studying us both as he spoke. "I suspected, but I never knew. I believe I'm what

69

you call a 'virus', Colonel Riggs. What you call a Trojan virus, to be precise. I was tacked onto a legitimate download coming to you from the Centaurs. When you went through the ring, however, the transmission was severed, and I was never fully installed."

"A virus," I said slowly, mouth sagging open. "But, of course. It fits perfectly. We were making a transfer, and something unauthorized added itself to the file. You were the amalgam of a legitimate transmission and something malicious."

Kwon looked back and forth between the two of us. "Shouldn't we reformat him, or at least switch him off, or something?"

"No," I said, shaking my head. "Marvin's something else now. He's something that no one ever planned or built. Would you burn an infant for the sins of his parents?"

Kwon looked doubtful. "Maybe—if they were really, really bad sins."

"Well, that's not our way. It's not the Star Force way. He's joined us now, and his dark background has been washed away."

Marvin was perking up as I spoke.

"Tell me more, Marvin," I said. "If you figured out you were a hidden transmission, a virus mixed with a translation database, then you must have a theory about who created you. Who transmitted you as a virus?"

"I would think that's abundantly clear at this point, Colonel Riggs. It was the Blues."

I nodded thoughtfully. "Yes, of course. I see their hand in everything. They've been out to screw us from the start. They like to work quietly, behind the scenes, using artificial proxies. They created the Macros and the Nanos. They attacked Earth, and they created you to infect our systems."

"I might add, however," Marvin said, "that they've done a great deal of good as well. I believe they're a race like humanity, made up of individuals and diverse factions. Some may want to destroy all life outside their ocean of gases while others wish to aid all life, and more still want to study it, driven by curiosity."

70

"I think we should bomb them again," Kwon said from the doorway.

"Kwon," I said sternly. "I think it's about time you followed my initial orders and found something else to do."

"Okay, but if the robot gets a tentacle around your neck, you hammer on the walls, right? I'll come back again."

"That will be all, First Sergeant."

When he'd finally stumped away down the passage, I went back to staring at Marvin. What was I going to do with him? He was a mystery. He was our devil and our angel wrapped up into one strange package.

Really, I didn't have any options. I couldn't dismantle him or even switch him off for a while. He was the lead investigator on this scientific venture. Hell, it was his idea.

"You know what I think, Marvin?" I asked after staring at him thoughtfully for a time.

"I'm uncertain what you will say, but I'm interested in the topic."

"I think you're just what you seem to be: part good and part evil, part helpful software and part malware. You remind me of a program that does a useful service—but which spies on the owner and transmits key-logging password data across the web."

"I'm not a spy, Colonel—at least not in the traditional sense."

I chuckled at his careful definition.

Eventually, I ordered him to return to duty in the science labs. I made sure he kept out of sight for the rest of the time we were orbiting the Centaur homeworld, and insisted that he change his appearance so our Centaur troops wouldn't report him as alive and well aboard our command ship.

Disguising Marvin turned out to be difficult. He was the only robot in Star Force—at least the only one that was self-mobile and talkative. I decided we should put tracks on him instead of tentacles to walk on and removed his grav-lifter plates. I also insisted that he use arms with solid components and ball-joints, rather than whip-like tentacles. He clanked around the ship miserably and complained whenever I came within earshot.

71

"Really Colonel Riggs, I'm feeling extremely inefficient."

"I bet, Marvin," I said. "But at least your mind is your own. If you have that, you've got everything you need, right?"

"I fail to see—"

"Marvin, you're alive and well. Many people, including billions of Centaurs, would rather see you dead. You're just going to have to make do."

"These wheels and plates—I feel primitive, Colonel. I've seen machines from your early pioneering days. I resemble an exploratory robot sent to a distant world."

"A Mars rover?" I asked, squinting. "You know what? You're right. You do look like a rover."

I laughed and Marvin pouted. "This seems like an inappropriate moment for levity."

"Humor is all about pain, Marvin—someone else's pain," I told him.

-9-

We released around a thousand Centaur veterans and loaded up with fresh recruits. After special mind-altering injections were administered, they were able to tolerate the confined spaces required for travel in our ships. They went through an initial adjustment period, then began to train outside our vessels in open space. I watched from the aft portals seeing the tiny blue streaks of light as they practiced burning one another with low-wattage lasers.

A shadow fell over me from behind. I turned my head a fraction catching the reflection of a figure in the frosty window I was gazing through. I recognized the tall, spare frame.

"Hello, Admiral Newcome," I said. "How are things on the bridge?"

"The ship is in perfect operating condition," he said, coming to stand next to me and watch the practicing Centaur troops.

As we watched, two collided in a high-speed accident. Newcome winced.

"Will that trooper survive, Colonel?"

"Maybe," I said. "If he does, he'll be more careful the next time."

"Right…well…right…" Newcome said. He often said this when he wasn't sure how to react.

"What's on your mind, Newcome? Are you just on a stroll?"

"No sir. I'm here to report something."

I glanced at him for the first time. He looked slightly nervous. The man was brave enough, but it didn't come naturally to him. I guess living under Crow had been rough on these guys. The survivors were all shifty-eyed types.

"Let's hear it," I said.

"There're rumors floating about the ship, sir…rumors about your robot."

I nodded. I'd heard plenty of complaints about Marvin from the first moment he'd put himself together. I said nothing, allowing Newcome to make his case.

"They say we're going out to the frontier in order to disturb the Macros, and that the entire scheme was cooked up by Marvin. Is there any truth to these wild tales?"

"Aren't you curious about what's on the other side of the last ring in the chain?"

"Not curious enough to risk my neck to explore it."

I grunted unhappily, then pointed outside at the Centaurs.

"You see those people, Newcome?"

"People? You mean the native levies, sir?"

"Yeah. To me they're people. Just like you and me. They're under my protection—*our* protection."

He stared at me uncomprehendingly.

"You know what they have, Admiral? They've got something I find many Earthers lack. I'm talking about balls, big furry ones."

He made a disgusted face, and I grinned at him.

"What do bollocks have to do with space exploration, Colonel?"

"They have everything to do with it," I said. "You have to take the initiative in war. You can't sit on your butt and expect the enemy to do the same."

"War, sir? We're at peace at the moment."

"Oh no," I said, thumping him on the back. "Don't ever let me hear you talk like that."

He stumbled and had to throw his hands up to catch himself to keep from bumping his nose on the glass.

"Hmm," I said, frowning. "You've left handprints on my observation glass."

"I'm sorry, sir. I'll have it cleaned."

There was a sarcastic edge to his words, and I could tell my thumping his back hard enough to make him stumble had pissed him off. I grinned. I liked him better when he was annoyed with me. It proved he wasn't a wimp after all.

"See that you do," I said. "Now, to explain further: we *are* at war. As long as the Macros exist, there will never be peace. They haven't forgotten us, and we haven't forgotten them."

"But it's been so long, sir. I would think they might have given up, sealed up the ring and written off this corner of the galaxy."

"A nice thought, but unlikely. Even if it's true, we can't confirm it so we must proceed as if it's *not* true. To do otherwise is to invite extinction."

He nodded. "Yes, I understand your point. We must prepare as if our doom is coming at any moment—especially in the absence of hard data. You propose to get that missing information with this venture?"

I considered for a moment before finally deciding to tell him the truth. I'd planned on keeping my secret until we'd reached the Thor System, but as that was only a day or two away now, the moment seemed opportune.

"Yes," I said. "The rumors are true. We're going out there to investigate the Thor ring. We don't know where it goes, but we know the Macros are on the far side of it. If they're building a fresh armada out there, I want to know about it."

Newcome's eyes widened. "We're really going to fly through the ring?"

I laughed. "Is that what the rumors are saying? That the Colonel has finally lost it and plans to fly Riggs' Pigs on one last suicide mission into the unknown? No, I'm not that crazy."

He cleared his throat and took a breath. He seemed relieved. "Excellent, sir. I assume we'll be conducting some kind of surveillance then. A secretive drone, perhaps?"

"A drone, but not a quiet one."

I explained it all to him then. I told him about Marvin's plan to build a communications unit that could connect us to the stars for a brief instant and pinpoint the location of the system on the far side of the ring, even if the Macros destroyed it almost instantly.

His worried expression returned as he contemplated the possibilities.

"But that could...the Macros will know what you've done. They aren't stupid."

"Far from it."

"They'll know they've been located. They will take action."

"No," I said. "*We* will have taken action. We will have thrown them off their timetables for once. When an enemy is tired, don't let him sleep. When he's hungry, don't let him eat. And when he's quietly building up for a big attack on your homeworld, hit him first."

Newcome looked like he'd swallowed something large and unpleasant.

"How long do we have?" he asked.

"What? To write our wills? Plenty of time. Marvin is working on the transmitter every day, but the receiver will be far larger. We'll begin construction near Thor as soon as we arrive."

"Near the star itself?"

"Where else do you think we'll get the energy we'll need?"

He left soon afterward. I knew that he'd spread the news throughout the fleet. *Let him,* I thought. It was time they all knew what we were doing out here. Maybe it would quell the nervous rumors.

* * *

We flew past Welter Station, the most impressive fortress in humanity's arsenal. That bulwark was now properly placed at the border of our five controlled star systems. Hopefully, the next time the Macros came at us we'd be able to stop them right here.

We glided through the ring into the Thor System and were now on the frontier of known space. I stood on the bridge with my top commanders when we crossed over the border and into the devastated system.

Once there'd been trillions of intelligent people here—the Crustaceans. These argumentative, arrogant aquatic beings had fought us and the Macros, but ultimately they'd been destroyed. The last few millions of their kind were now living in the oceans of Eden-6 where we'd transplanted them. They complained it was too warm for them, but since their three home planets were now brown, radioactive cesspools, I figured they'd just have to get used to the tropics. After a few generations, the hot salty water would seem natural to them.

As the images from the Thor System came up on our screens, I didn't look at the twin stars or the planets. I focused in on the three water-moons that circled the gas giant in the habitable zone. On these three Earth-sized moons, dubbed by us Harvard, Yale and Princeton, nothing now lived.

I was glum-faced to be back here, to be faced with what had to be my single biggest defeat. I'd always regret the events that transpired here over a year ago. I was determined not to let any wholesale slaughter of innocent biotics happen again.

I glanced toward Jasmine, who was watching me. She dropped her gaze when her eyes met mine. I wondered what she was thinking. Being out here and seeing the smoldering cinders that were once rich living worlds—the sight got me to thinking.

"Maybe you were right, Jasmine," I said aloud.

She raised her pretty face and met my gaze when I said this. Her eyebrows rose in a questioning manner.

I gestured toward the screen displaying the three lifeless moons.

"We can't let anything like this happen to Earth. We're living in a hard era, a time almost like a new Dark Age."

Jasmine seemed to figure out what I was talking about. She nodded. "We can't let decisions fall to chance."

I had a second thought as I continued to study the screen. "But then again," I said, "If someone else had been in command, maybe the guy would have done better. Who's to say?"

She shrugged. "If you've found a worthwhile successor, abdicate. Give all authority to a younger, more skilled individual."

I looked at her thoughtfully. She had me there, and she knew it. I didn't have anyone else for the job. I didn't have anyone I felt I could entrust with the keys to Star Force. At times I'd thought Crow was the man for that job—and that had turned out pretty badly.

I heaved a sigh and straightened my spine. "Helm, let's lay in a course for the closer of the two suns. The white dwarf will do, won't it Marvin?"

"According to my calculations, either star's energy output is sufficient. If we choose the smaller of the two, we'll have to build somewhat closer, however."

I nodded. "You have the helm, Marvin. Take us to the star of your choice and park us in orbit. I want full radiation suits for the crew. Double-up on nanocloth suits and have the nanites chew up some lead before they add that second layer."

There were a few groans at this announcement. Nanoclothing was so light and easy to wear you sort of got used to them after a while. They were a hard habit to break, like living in your pajamas all weekend long.

We planned to fly in with our most heavily protected face always aimed toward the stars like Spartans hiding behind upraised shields. I ordered the hull thickened up on the belly of the battleship as we glided closer to the blazing suns. Star Force people could take a lot of radiation, as the nanites repaired cells quickly, but our electronic subsystems were more fragile. To compensate, the ship's systems moved constructive nanites around. They flowed in vein-like silvery relief over the hull, delivering more metal to the portions of the ship most affected.

Marvin chose the smaller star because its energy output was more stable. We reached the white dwarf two days later and established a safe orbit after fighting the gravitational forces. Then the real work began.

Marvin was given a fighter to tool around in because I'd told him he couldn't have engines attached directly to his body. Unfortunately, his overseeing a large construction project in space pretty much required mobility.

I became angry less than a week into the project, when I realized Marvin had dismissed his fighter pilot. This meant that he was effectively zooming around independently.

"Marvin?" I shouted into a private channel. "Report immediately."

"That's not possible, Colonel. I'm engaged in a critical phase of the project. I'm assembling the core of a key system."

I muted him and turned to Jasmine, who was watching the boards and knew better than I did what he was up to.

"Is he bullshitting me, Captain Sarin?"

"Yes and no. He's not here in orbit around the white sun. He's near Harvard, in fact, building a digester."

Harvard was one of the three moons that sailed around a gas giant in this system's habitable zone.

"He's building a what?" I asked.

"He's breaking down surface material of asteroids and smaller moons orbiting the gas giant. He's quarried chunks of rock and is firing them toward the sun. Another system located here in orbit around the white sun catches the pieces and uses them in construction. Really, it's quite elegant as an engineering solution."

I frowned. It sounded big, expensive and complex.

"How big are these chunks of material?"

"They're about two kilotons each, according to these documents."

She displayed a mass of planning files on the command table. I'd been busy looking at reports of our military buildup back on Earth. I'd pretty much let Marvin do whatever he wanted. In retrospect, I realized that was rarely a good idea.

A blizzard of files opened with a rattling sound-effect on my side of the big screen. I tapped them closed irritably. I didn't have time to read every blueprint and proposal.

"How is he managing to accelerate and decelerate chunks of mass that big?"

Jasmine looked at me in surprise. "Didn't you know, sir? He's brought along another of his prototype devices for this purpose."

"What device?"

"A gravitational manipulator. A smaller version of the system *Phobos* uses for propulsion and weaponry."

Of the tech we'd discovered and purloined, gravitational control systems were among the most amazing. The Blues were the experts at this, and they'd built a moon-sized ship that flew using a gravity-manipulating drive. We'd stolen the ship, made it our own, and called it *Phobos*.

I scratched my chin. "Well, it does sound like he's got a good reason," I had to admit. "Put him on screen."

"He's not in local space, Colonel."

"I know that. But wherever he is, there's a camera. Let's see him."

It took her a few minutes, but we soon had him on the big display. Marvin was zooming around in his fighter, making gut-wrenching turns and sliding stops.

"He's buzzing around like a bee in a greenhouse," I said, chuckling.

"He does seem to be happy, sir."

"All right, Marvin," I said, unmuting the blinking channel again. "You can keep your fighter and fly it yourself but no strapping any engines directly to your chassis!"

"I wouldn't think of it, Colonel Riggs."

Time passed. Every day I watched chunks of rock flowing into orbit near us. It was disconcerting seeing the flying stream of debris. It reminded me of being in the path of an automatic pitching machine only, in this case, the balls were the size of buildings, and they were flying at around a hundred thousand miles a minute.

Still, he managed to use gravitational systems to accelerate and decelerate each chunk. When they got to our orbital position, he began assembling them into a massive cylindrical structure.

I frowned as this monolithic thing that grew up outside my windows. With each day that passed, I couldn't help but be awed and worried by it at the same time.

"Jasmine," I said one fine morning as we sipped coffee and stared at the growing structure, "Tell me if I'm wrong, but that doesn't look like anything a human would build in space, does it?"

She shook her head. We both went back to staring. Marvin was creating an alien structure. A sphere of black, swirling stone mixed with metal in an almost organic pattern.

What had I set into motion? I'd expected maybe a smaller version of a ring, but this thing…? What the hell did it do?

I demanded a face to face meeting with Marvin the next day. He complained bitterly, not wanting to pause in his work. I knew he'd been working around the clock without a break, and he was totally obsessed.

When I threatened to clip his wings and take away his fighter, he finally came to heel.

"Colonel Riggs," he said as he walked onto the bridge, "What is so critically important it can't be done virtually?"

I gave him a quick, visual inspection. His body looked remarkably like the version I'd originally approved of and allowed out into space. But I knew better.

"Jasmine," I said, "play the vid."

She tapped the screen and, on the holotank, an image of Marvin flickered into being. It showed him as he had been less than an hour ago, fully decked out with ten extra cameras and two clusters of tentacles that drifted in the vacuum of space.

"Looks like a couple of sea anemones somehow attached themselves to your chassis, Marvin," I said. "Where are those clusters of appendages? Did you leave them in the fighter?"

"Those are not technically appendages, Colonel Riggs. My primary form is exactly as you see before you, approved and certified."

I scoffed. "Come on, Marvin, we've got you on video."

"Oh," he said, as if noticing the video for the first time. "I see clearly the source of confusion on your part. That is not my body you're seeing. Those are tools—work clothes, if you will. Just as a human needs tools to perform construction, I designed external components I could add to my structure temporarily to enhance my performance."

I laughed. Jasmine scowled.

"I get it," I said. "I told you there can't be any altering of your form. So, to circumvent that command, you built whatever you wanted as a 'tool' which would allow you to claim it wasn't part of your actual body. Very clever, Marvin."

81

"Thank you, sir."

"How close are you to finishing this semi-organic-looking cylinder-thing?"

"It's finished now."

Jasmine and I stared at him for a second. "What?"

"The project is completed. We're ready to proceed to the next step, but we haven't yet accumulated sufficient mass."

"Is that why more chunks keep coming into orbit here?"

"Precisely."

"Why do you need so much mass?"

"How else do you propose to create compressed matter? You must have a source of uncompressed matter, then compress it. Stardust is extremely dense, collapsed material, and it requires a great deal of mass and energy to create it. I propose to perform the task artificially with gravity we've generated and controlled."

Jasmine spoke up then. She had her own reasons for demanding he come to us and report in.

"Marvin," she said, "I've done the calculations. All the smaller moons in the gas giant's gravity-well do not make up enough mass to equal what you've already transported here into orbit. How is this possible?"

"First, let me praise your mathematical prowess, Captain Sarin. However, you are wrong in this instance."

"What do you mean, wrong?"

"All the mass I've transported to orbit the white dwarf star, Loki, comes from the orbit of the gas giant."

We both frowned at him. "But if the total mass of the asteroids is less than what you've sent…" I paused, and then I had a terrible thought. "Marvin, are you mining the primary moons?"

"Of course I am, Colonel Riggs. The conclusion is inescapable, isn't it?"

"Those were habitable worlds, not just rocks in the sky!"

"The difference is negligible in this instance as they are no longer habitable worlds."

"But Marvin," said Jasmine in a sad, worried voice, "the Crustaceans dream of returning to their homes and rebuilding someday."

"That is an unreasonable fantasy. Firstly, the radiation on the moons in question will not fade to a non-lethal level for thousands of years. Secondly, there will be large portions of the moons missing by that time as my project has removed them."

We stopped asking questions then because we didn't know quite what else to say. I considered ordering Marvin to stop chewing up the Crustacean moons, but I knew there wasn't any other source of material we could easily access. The system didn't have an asteroid belt, and the gas giant itself was too huge and not solid enough to mine into chunks.

I went to the big window and watched jagged lumps of matter fly by at blurring speeds. What would the Crustaceans say if they knew what we were doing out here?

I turned back to Marvin. "I want you to mine only one of the three moons. Pick the one that's most suitable, and leave the other two alone."

"That will delay my schedule, sir. Once the initial crust of the moon is stripped away, the magma underneath is far less suitable as it—"

"I don't care. Do it my way or forget it."

He craned his cameras and eyed me quietly for a time. I knew he was gauging my mood and looking for any sign of weakness.

I must have looked resolute because at last he said: "It will be done your way, Colonel Riggs."

Then he left, and I felt more disturbed than ever by what we were doing out here.

-10-

A month passed. During that time, most of the surface of Harvard, one of the three extinct moons circling the gas giant, had been stripped away. The planetary mass, once roughly the size of Earth, had been reduced by approximately four percent. That might not sound like a lot, but I was pretty sure the Crustaceans were going to notice if they ever got out this way again.

"Marvin," I said on my next daily call, "Give me a status report, please."

"We're ready to move to the next phase, Colonel Riggs."

"Really? And what phase is that? Are we going to chew up a fresh world? Or maybe you'd like us to steer a couple of comets into orbit around this star."

"That will be unnecessary and a waste of time. A comet, in particular, would be unhelpful. At this relative proximity to a stellar body, the heat and radiation would quickly vaporize the entire—"

"Yeah, yeah," I interrupted. "I know. It was a sarcastic comment. What is the next phase?"

"Testing."

I paused, and my face brightened. "Testing? That does sound positive. How do we do it?"

"The unit is ready to transmit—but I'm unsure as to the precise nature of the final results."

"What do you mean, 'unsure'? Are you ready or not?"

"In a manner of speaking, yes, I am."

Jasmine tapped my arm. I turned on her in irritation. Wearing lead underpants for many long weeks had made us all touchy—except for Jasmine herself, that is. She was as cool, professional and unperturbed as usual. Even the heat of the "double blaze" period didn't bother her much. Every nine days, our orbit led us into a position where we were between both of the stars: the big red one and the white dwarf. Hit from both sides with every ounce of radiation the two furnaces could put out, our cooling systems were always overloaded. We called these unpleasant hours the "double blaze".

Right now, we were in the worst of it. The temperature had to be more than a hundred degrees in my suit, and the internal temperature of the ship was around a hundred and fifty. You had to put your food into a cooling chamber just to slide it into your helmet and eat it.

"What do you want, Captain?" I asked her.

"Ask him about the generators. Where are they?"

"That's right. Marvin? We've been observing your engineering. We understand the incubator—that cylindrical thing; and we understand the compressed matter it's been pumping out. Star-dust, you call it. But aren't you going to need more generators? What's going to power this communication device when you have it ready?"

"That is an insightful question, Colonel Riggs. Inspect any of the rings, and you'll find they do not have power emissions. The trick is that the power was utilized in their creation. They are linked through entanglement properties across time and space. They are, in a sense, occupying the same location in a different dimension. Therefore, applying resonance to one causes the other to resonate."

"Yeah, yeah, I know all that. But you said we'd send a transmission like a directional beacon. How can you do that without a power supply?"

"I have plenty of power. Distance isn't a factor when the two devices are entangled."

"Hmm," I said, looking at Jasmine. She was listening in, and she shrugged at the explanation. "I sure hope you know what the hell you're doing because we don't."

"Are you ready to proceed with the test?" Marvin asked.

I looked around my staff. They gave me "why not" type gestures.

"Yeah, sure," I said. "But can't it wait until we're out of the double-blaze period? We're hot and uncomfortable here."

"Unfortunately, no. The gravitational forces required use solar energy, and the collectors are operating at their peak during this time period."

"Right. Okay, let's go."

"Excellent! I'll launch the probe immediately."

We all stood around the command system, not quite sure if we were going to see anything interesting. We got quite a surprise.

A blue streak appeared, curving away in an arc from our location and stretching off into space.

"What the heck is that?" I demanded. "Jasmine, why are you putting that bright trailing graphic on—whatever that is?"

"I'm not, sir," she said. "The image you see is real. At least—according to our sensors it is. It's burning white-hot, about seven thousand degrees Kelvin."

"Seven thousand K? Isn't that around the surface temperature of Sol?"

"It is a little hotter, actually."

I muttered curses. "Where's it going? Is it physical or is it an emission?"

"It's a little of both, I think. The arc—sir, we've plotted a course. The anomaly is heading for the ring out of the Thor System."

"Marvin!" I roared. "What's happening?"

"Excuse me, Colonel Riggs. I'm having difficulties."

"This isn't a test," I said. "You launched the probe, didn't you?"

There was a pause, during which I watched the silver arc of brilliant light stretch a quarter of the way around the white dwarf star. It broke orbit and began to straighten out, heading toward the far reaches of the star system.

"I have good news and bad news," Marvin said after a moment. "The system misfired. It is a prototype, after all."

"What's the good news?"

"Why, that *is* the good news," he said as if surprised. "It works, and it is transmitting."

"Well, shut it off, we're not ready. The battle group isn't poised for a response."

"But sir, I'll have to start over again."

I frowned. "Start over? How long will it take to rebuild the probe?"

"Not just the probe, but the receiver will have to be reconstructed as well. We'll have to move on to a second moon—there's no choice there. I'm down to magma all over Harvard."

I heaved a sigh. Internally, I knew he was probably manipulating me. Marvin was all about doing what he wanted and asking forgiveness later rather than for permission now. That way, no one ever got the chance to tell him "no". The only option you ever had with Marvin was to decide if today was the day you shut him down permanently.

"Proceed with the test," I said.

"A wise choice, Colonel Riggs."

"Don't rub it in, robot."

"An unclear reference. Comment ignored."

"Yeah, yeah," I said, and muted the channel.

"Well," I said, looking around at my stunned staff. "It is time to get our ships moving."

"Where are we going, sir?" Jasmine asked.

"To the border ring. We have to set up there in case the Macros do come through."

"And if they do?"

"Then," I said, "We blast every one of them out of space until they stop coming or we're all dead."

That comment kicked people into gear. Being on station here in stellar orbit had been like living in an endless, boring sauna for months. Everything had suddenly changed.

In a way, I welcomed it. It had been too long since I'd felt my adrenaline pumping. I watched as our ships scrambled away from the gravity tug of the white dwarf star and began to follow the streak of light toward the ring.

"We're way behind," I complained an hour later. "That thing must be approaching the speed of light by now."

"It's about seventy percent of the way there, Colonel," Jasmine confirmed. With a dozen deft taps of her fingers, she brought up speed and course data, which now floated beside the streaking probe.

"How the hell did he get that thing to move so fast?"

"Looking at the reports, it appears he built a small platform from eight fighters. I'd guess he stripped the engines and left nothing but a frame holding them together."

I nodded. "Eight fighter engines tied together and launched as a single unit. Yeah, that would give a small ship a pretty good acceleration curve. But there are fuel limitations."

"Not if you aren't planning to slow down," Jasmine said thoughtfully. "The device will streak through space from here to the other side of that ring singing its simple tone. Then it will probably be destroyed. The question is: Can we receive the signal for enough time to get a fix on its location?"

The more I thought about it over the following two hours the more I wondered if this had been such a great idea. Already, I'd wrecked the surface of a formerly habitable world, and now we were about to poke a pin into the Macros. Even if we did learn where the star system on the far side was, how was it going to help us? The only effective way to get there was through that ring. We'd known that before we started chasing the probe. The only positive thing about the chase was that it got us out of the heat and radiation we'd been suffering through for so long. I stripped off the outer suit, took a shower, and left my helmet on my desk. I returned to the command table rubbing my neck.

"Your hair is still wet," Jasmine told me quietly.

"I know," I said, "it feels great. It's cooling me down. I think I need two or three days of cooling down."

Jasmine gave me a small smile.

"Why don't you go take a shower?" I suggested. "I can man the helm."

She took me up on it immediately. I halfway wanted to chase after her, but the probe was only about an hour out from the ring now, and I figured there just wasn't time. At the very least, the entire command staff would notice. I didn't want to be whispered about as the guy who couldn't keep his hands off

88

his girlfriend even in the middle of a crisis. I'd had that label before, and I'd never worn it comfortably.

After she left, I sent people off in turns to clean up. They came back with fresh suits and smiles. Nothing gets quite as nasty inside as a spacesuit you've been living in for weeks—especially when it's a *hot* spacesuit.

All too soon, the probe closed in on the ring. We were hours behind it, but my command staff and I had come up with a game plan by then.

"Decelerate, four Gs," I ordered. "We've got to slow down if we don't want to plunge right through after it—or overshoot it."

We turned around to aim our jets in the direction of our travel and the ship shook under us. The G forces were painful even to nanotized people. I didn't want to be flying right into the teeth of the enemy if they did come popping out.

"Do you think we should alert Earth?" Newcome asked me. He was back on the command deck, and his face was all pink and white.

"Yes," I said. "Tell them we've launched the probe. Don't mention anything about doing so early. Let's keep our dignity on this one."

"And the fighters...sir?" Newcome pressed.

"You want to send them in there now? To screen us? Forget it. If we fight, we'll do so as a single fist. I'm not burning pilots to save our butts if this goes badly. Speaking of which, where the hell is Marvin?"

"Why—he's aboard *Potemkin*, sir," Jasmine said. "I thought you knew."

"He's aboard this ship? Since when?"

"He boarded moments after the probe was launched."

I nodded sourly. "He hasn't shown his nose up here on the bridge because he knows I'm going to bitch at him. Get him up here. This is his firecracker, and he's going to watch it go off with the rest of us."

I knew Marvin preferred to "watch" events like this via the com network. He had direct access to all the data flowing in from the computers and sensors so he could read it anywhere. We had to have that data processed then displayed visually on

89

our command table and holotank. That was a redundant step for Marvin.

"He's telling me his presence here isn't necessary or productive, sir," Jasmine said.

I could tell she was as annoyed as was I.

"Patch that channel to me," I snapped.

When she did so, I roared into it. "Marvin, drag your conniving butt onto my bridge, or I'll blow up that probe right now."

"I'm not sure Star Force currently has the capacity to enact such a threat—"

"Yeah? You want to risk it?"

Apparently, he didn't. The door to the main passageway dilated open immediately, and Marvin stepped through. He clunked on stubby feet again. He'd done another quick-change shedding his "external toolset" to leave him in the state he'd been restricted to.

I had to take it as positive news that Marvin was at least aboard the ship and marginally cooperating with my commands. If he'd thought we were about to be destroyed, he'd have already bailed out on us by now.

"Let's just see what you've done for us today," I said, waving toward the console.

With ill grace, Marvin quietly took his spot at the command table. We all watched tensely as the point of no return was reached and exceeded.

The position of the probe on the screen was just conjecture now. It was moving too fast to get a fix on it by traditional methods. We could only plot its course and imagine where it was. We were about five light-minutes behind it, and the distance was growing as we decelerated, and it continued to streak toward the goal.

"There isn't going to be much time for a blip of data if this thing goes through and smashes into a solid obstacle," I said. "Why don't you slow it down, Marvin?"

"It is already decelerating," Marvin said, craning cameras to observe our screens. "It was programmed to do so. Your coordinates are inaccurate."

I frowned. "Why didn't you correct them?"

A few cameras observed me and then drifted away. "Is that meant as sarcasm too, Colonel Riggs?"

My frown deepened. I thought hard. When dealing with Marvin, you had to stay on your toes. He was devious and always thinking ahead. Considering recent events, I thought I had the gist of it.

"I get it," I said. "If we knew just where it was, it would be easier for us to abort it or destroy it—right?"

Cameras panned over me briefly, but I received no reply. This was Marvin's equivalent of a shrug.

Newcome, watching this exchange, was aghast. He came over and attempted to pull me aside. I let him, although I was distracted.

"This robot—it has plans, sir. I've seen this sort of thing before. I worked for Crow, remember? I know a schemer when I see one—human or not."

"Thanks for the newsflash, Newcome," I said. "But I'm not in the dark about that. Marvin is always scheming. The trick is to figure out his plan before it's too late. In this case, I think we've failed. This test is a launch. Lord only knows what will happen next."

The probe flew on. Periodically, its displayed location and speed were corrected by Marvin. We couldn't see it anymore. We had a fix on its trail and its supposed path, but we didn't have hard data yet. It was too far ahead for that.

The probe was slowing down as it approached the ring, and I'd decided not to try to stop it. We were only an hour or so behind it after all. What could go wrong?

Marvin and Jasmine worked to rig-up a counter. Every time it updated, a pulsing tone sang in the background. It was an annoying sound—like the old moon missions used to have but quieter and more frequent. *Beep, beep, beep.*

I knew that if I had to listen to that sound all day I'd go nuts.

But I didn't have to, because suddenly it stopped...

Our probe had gone through the ring.

I'm not quite sure what we'd been expecting, but we were all gritting our teeth and squeezing our eyes almost shut the moment the probe plunged through the ring into the unknown. It vanished off our sensors and…nothing happened.

I heard a few sighs of relief. People's bodies were relaxing, unwinding their tense muscles. I knew they were thinking it had all been a bust. There was no ultimate ka-boom at the end of this grand experiment. No calamity had struck us. The probe was lost, and we were safe. A happy ending.

But I wasn't relaxing just yet. Instead, I watched Marvin.

Jasmine dared to catch my eye and give me a small smile. Maybe she was like the rest of them and thought the worst was over. But then, I indicated Marvin with a nod of my head, and she looked at him. Her smile, as small as it had been, faded away to nothing.

"What's wrong with him?" she asked, leaning forward and frowning.

"He's locked up. Remember the time we sent instructions to the ring on Yale? He looked like that then—like he was caught in some kind of endless loop."

Marvin's pose was an odd one even for him. His tentacles were poised in mid-air, and his cameras were frozen. Not a single lens was zooming in. One tentacle tip that hovered over the command table twitched. Up-down, up-down. It looked like he was tapping a finger to a fast, staccato beat.

"Sir," Newcome said, approaching me. "There's nothing coming back from the probe. We had a wire on it, but there's no input at all."

I glanced at him. He looked as relieved as the rest of them. I turned back and continued watching Marvin.

"What's wrong with your robot?" Newcome asked.

"He's getting something—or trying to. Don't mess with him. This test cost the crust of an entire world. I'm not planning on running it twice."

Everyone fell quiet, and we all stared at Marvin curiously. About ninety seconds later, he came to life again.

"Mission accomplished," he said. His cameras roved, seeing our scrutiny. "You've all changed positions. Is something wrong?"

"You were frozen-up," I told him. "Processing heavy input, I'd guess."

"Yes...my chronometer is correcting itself. One-hundred and seventy-one seconds have passed. Odd, I didn't even feel it. I put myself into a hard loop. I don't usually do that as it's dangerous."

"Never mind the details now. What happened? You said the mission was accomplished."

"Yes, I've pinpointed the direction of the ring's exit point—or, at least, the position where the probe emerged. But I'm not one hundred percent certain as to the distance relative to our location. You see, I wasn't able to triangulate with only a single receiver. The signal was very brief so there was no time to apply a parallax test. I was only able to get a directional fix, and I'm not certain as to the range."

"But there is a system in that direction, right? A target?"

"No, and I find that troubling. There are only roving planetoids out there, no stars at all. Not unless the signal comes from quite far off. The uncertainty lies in the distance to the target, you see. Behind a cluster of planetoids, which is admittedly the likely source, there are other possible targets."

I nodded. "Sounds like the direction leads toward the galactic center. Lots of target systems that way."

"Incorrect assumption. The path leads out of the Milky Way galaxy entirely."

I frowned. "Display it, Marvin. I'm not getting what you're trying to say."

Marvin moved to the command table and touched a set of virtual controls. The image he summoned appeared on the globular holotank above the table.

A depiction of our entire galaxy stretched across the tank. The galaxy was a spinning disk with three spiral arms. The center was like a hubcab and dense with stars. Far out along the rim of the galaxy a tiny green line shot upward. The line was no thicker than the thinnest of filaments, and it stretched even longer inside the holotank as I watched.

I examined the direction and zoomed in with my fingers. "But you said there were other possible systems behind the one you located. There's nothing out there."

"Untrue. There are two entire galaxies in the background that could conceivably be the source of the signal."

"Other *galaxies*?" Sarin asked. "At what range? Ten million light years? That's too far."

"Within our frame of reference, it would seem to be," Marvin said stubbornly, "but not theoretically. Just because we've only encountered rings that have led to relatively nearby destinations does not prove—"

"Marvin," I interrupted him. "Why are you arguing about this? Are you trying to cover up a failure? Is this some kind of false lead?"

"Well, there is a sure way to discover the truth of that accusation, Colonel Riggs. In fact, you've brought the conversation around to the point I was trying get to. I thank you."

"Hmm," I said, eyeing him warily. "What do you want?"

"I propose a second test. We'll move the receiver this time, allowing triangulation. We'll know exactly where the signal originated."

I huffed and almost laughed aloud. "So that's it? You want to rip up a second world and fire another probe into enemy territory? Well, that isn't going to happen."

"Why not, sir?"

"Because your test looks like a colossal failure. You didn't pinpoint a star system. Instead you got a random beam out into

94

space. In fact, if I read this correctly, that vector goes right past the Solar System. It almost bisects the point in space we know as 'Earth'."

"A simplistic view, Colonel. The point is approximately thirty thousand AU outside the Solar System. That's more than half a light year."

"Yeah, yeah. I don't buy it. The signal goes nowhere, and the test was a dud. Face it, Marvin, the probe didn't survive long enough to get a clear fix. That's all. It could have happened to anyone."

Marvin edged closer to me. His cameras swung wide, getting my profile. "If that is the case, a second probe would prove your theory."

"No way. I'm beginning to think I was crazy to let you do this test in the first place. Each time we wriggle a ship through that ring, no matter how small, we run the risk of waking up the Macros. They're well-documented to have defensive software, which triggers on the basis of proximity, overriding their other programming. I'm not going to run the chance a second time—especially if it means wrecking another habitable moon."

"We've sent several probes through before without causing a response."

"True, but I'm not interested in pushing our luck any further."

I called a break then, ordering my command staff to stand down. I told them the test had been a bust over Marvin's protests. An hour later, I was in the canteen downing my first beer of the day.

I had just opened up my second and poured it into an icy mug when my helmet began beeping. I glanced at it and put my headset on reluctantly.

"Riggs here."

"Sir? You have to get up here. We have contacts."

I stood up with a grunt, stretched and trotted up the passageway. When I got to the bridge, I saw the command table had lit up. A red warning beacon had appeared, and machines were beeping all around us.

"Is this what I think it is?" I asked, looking at the screens.

95

"Hold on—yes, sir, confirmed," Jasmine said. "We have contacts. They're coming through the ring now."

We all stared in shock. Even Marvin, who snaked onto the deck a minute or so later, seemed surprised. After absorbing the data, he turned away from the screens and focused his cameras on the rest of us. I knew he was taking an emotional reading—analyzing our faces and body language.

I reached out and smashed down the camera that drifted near my left shoulder. "Did you get that, Marvin? Did you read my emotional state, there? How do you think I'm feeling right now? Take your best shot at analysis!"

"I would surmise that you are in a state of anger, Colonel."

"Damn straight, I am."

Enemy ships kept coming through. As Marvin's test had gone off prematurely, we weren't in position to meet them with immediate force.

"Why the hell—why are they reacting *this* time? We've sent probes through before, and they've destroyed them without moving."

As we all watched, more red contacts slipped through the ring in front of us. It was hard to believe it was happening. We were still about an hour out from the ring.

"What are we up to?" I asked. "About fifty cruisers?"

"Seventy-eight, sir," Jasmine reported. "They're hitting our minefield now. They've lost twenty-nine ships, but they're still coming."

Marvin stayed quiet for once in his existence. He reeled in his damaged limb. The smashed camera at the end bumped and scraped on the floor over my boots.

"What did you make me *do*, robot?" I asked him.

"The attack upon my person was unwarranted but predictable. It is my understanding, however, that it is unethical to blame the victim in assault situations."

I blinked at him for a second before I realized he was upset about his broken camera. "No, you crazy machine. I'm talking about triggering a Macro attack. How did I let you talk me into risking it?"

"There are several psychological theories I've been working on in that regard. I would say the most likely cause is straightforward: boredom."

I pressed my lips together in anger. I hated it most of all when he was right. I *had* been bored, and I'd come out here to do something cool. As a result, I'd taken risks. I'd poked the stick into the hornets' nest—and surprise, surprise—we were about to be stung.

They kept pouring in through the ring, and we made emergency preparations for battle. I scrambled my fighters and launched a barrage of missiles—but not all of them. I wanted to see what I was facing before committing us to battle.

They kept flowing out of the ring like a hose on full blast. Over the next half-hour, we planned and war-gamed. We had only a single carrier and about sixty support ships. It wasn't enough. When the enemy force managed to punch through our minefield, their numbers had reached four hundred cruisers despite their losses. It was too late to stop them. They were already here.

I ordered us to reverse course and run for the ring that led to Eden. Maybe that was the moment they'd been waiting for. As soon as we reversed course, they unloaded.

"Colonel Riggs, we have new contacts...missiles, sir. That's confirmed. About eight hundred of them."

I nodded. "The enemy is firing now that they sense we're trying to break off."

A cloud of missiles appeared in a broad swath of space. Each enemy ship had fired two.

"All right," I said. "Change the programming on our missiles. Order them to intercept that cloud and lay down a staggered impact pattern. If we can get to the enemy barrage before they spread out very far, we should halt this wave."

Newcome looked at me. "Maybe we should try to strike with what we've launched. Our missiles are moving faster, they should get through and destroy a lot of ships."

"Uncharacteristically brave of you, Admiral," I said. "I approve, but I must overrule your suicidal suggestion."

"Why is it...?" his question died as Jasmine reconfigured the map, showing the probable outcome of his idea. He nodded. "I see. We can't stop eight hundred missiles. They'll get through and damage the task force badly."

"I'm predicting a thirty-eight percent loss from this initial barrage alone—that's if they don't throw everything at our carrier to knock it out."

"That would be their wisest move," I said. "Our fighters can dodge missiles, but they can't fly forever out here without a base. They'd all be out of action before the rest of us reached the Eden ring. Speaking of which, have you alerted Welter Station, Captain Sarin?"

"Naturally, sir. They know what's coming."

"Good work," I said, and turned a musing eye back toward the screens.

Around me, most of the staffers were in a near-panic. They were relaying instructions, organizing formations and gaming out scenarios. Mathematical projections were made for a dozen possible actions we could take, just in case I asked.

But I was in a more contemplative state of mind. As the top commander, it was my job to keep my eye on the bigger picture.

"They seem to have stopped coming through," I said aloud. "Four hundred ships... Actually, I'm surprised they have so few. I would have thought they'd had enough time to build more. We've given them over a year to prepare for this day."

I turned back to Captain Sarin, who was bringing all our data together. "We've projected their acceleration curve based on known Macro flight capabilities. They won't be able to catch us."

"Good," I said. "We'll withdraw in good order to the Eden ring. With Welter Station at our back, we should be able to—"

"Sir," interrupted Admiral Newcome. He'd been playing with his tablet and a smaller console to the side. "I think we have a problem."

I turned to him, frowning. "What problem?"

"The enemy acceleration curves, sir—they don't match our projections."

"How so?"

"They're accelerating more quickly than our estimates allow for—about thirty percent faster."

98

I looked at his work and read the numbers. "That's a lot of power. They must have upgraded their engines. I can't think of any other explanation."

"Neither can I, sir," Newcome said.

"Good work," I told him, clapping him on the shoulder. "I knew I brought you along for something."

He winced, probably because I was accidentally crushing his shoulder, but he appeared appreciative of the praise.

"Jasmine, tap in the new estimates."

"Those numbers aren't confirmed yet, Colonel," she said.

"I don't care. I'm not taking any more chances."

She did as I asked, and very soon a much grimmer picture developed. Originally, it had looked as if we'd be faced with missile barrages chasing us all the way back to the station. But now, it was clear we weren't going to make it. The enemy ships would catch up with us before we made it back to the safety of the Eden system.

"We'll be under their guns within twenty-four hours," I said. "Are these numbers firming up? I need accurate projections, people."

I looked sternly over at the table full of nerds in the corner of the room. They were responsible for getting these things right. They worked feverishly for perhaps thirty seconds more, then transmitted their results to my table.

The images shifted on the primary screen. A red arrow representing the Macro ships now intersected our green oval in nineteen hours.

"What the hell...?" I asked. "Why did it change again?"

"The enemy ships are coming on even faster now," Jasmine said. "Their rate of acceleration is increasing, not staying steady. That's why I must have missed the estimates in the first place. We can't beat them, Colonel."

"New engines," I said thoughtfully. "Something that allows them to accelerate with an odd curve. Maybe the new engines take time to warm up? They pretty much crawled through the ring. Maybe they start cold and have to be stoked to full power."

"I hardly think it matters, sir," Newcome said. "The point is, they will catch us. We'll have to turn and do battle."

99

I glanced at him. "These details *do* matter. Very much so. Jasmine, what do we have in the way of reinforcements back in the Eden System?"

"Not much, sir. Less than a dozen ships, all small except for a single old carrier that we use to watch the Blues."

I nodded. "All right. I assume these latest projections are holding up and don't need further tampering?"

"They are, sir. We have nineteen hours."

"I want my senior staffers to meet me in the conference room. We'll discuss our options."

I left the bridge, and a few minutes later Jasmine and Newcome showed up in my office. Behind them a third individual clattered into view. It was none other than Marvin himself. He was still nursing his broken camera and displaying it prominently as if he imagined someone might offer him sympathy. None of us did. The old 'abused robot' routine wasn't flying with anyone today.

"Your robot appears to have followed us, Colonel," said Newcome stiffly. "I was under the impression this was for senior officers only."

I snorted. "He's right, Marvin. Have you given yourself a new rank?"

"No, Colonel Riggs. But I have interesting opinions to share regarding this command decision."

"Okay then, pull up a chair—or rather remove one."

When Marvin came to a conference table, it was generally necessary to remove a chair to make a place for him to crouch around it with the rest of us.

"I've brought you here because we have some unpleasant choices to make," I said to the three of them.

"Unpleasant?" asked Marvin.

He had a lot of cameras on me. Whenever the topic of discussion involved his existence, Marvin became very focused indeed.

"That's right. One option is to turn and fight right now. The advantage to such a move is that, if more reinforcements are coming up behind this wave of Macros, we can destroy these ships before they're reinforced."

"That doesn't seem realistic, Colonel," Jasmine said. "We can't kill all their ships. How does it help us if they outnumber us twenty to one or only ten to one?"

"I'm getting a negative vibe from you, Captain," I said, giving her a slight frown. "Anyone else?"

Marvin's foreclaw rose up.

"Sir, I have a suggestion or two."

"Go ahead."

"The enemy fleet is going to destroy us. That's unquestionable. But many of our personnel might escape this fate and reach Welter Station if we act quickly."

I leaned back in my chair. "I'm all ears, Marvin."

"We could abandon most of the ships. By transferring every engine to a single large vessel—the carrier would be the most natural choice—we could load up our personnel and accelerate at a greater pace than the enemy."

"Intriguing…" I said, "But you mentioned that 'many' of us would get away. Who would not make it?"

"I've done the calculations. We have a group of transports traveling with us carrying Centaurs, am I correct?"

I was beginning to frown. "Yes, new recruits from their homeworld."

"Fortunately, they've had basic training and have undergone my treatment to make them functional in space. I'm proposing that—"

"Hold on, Marvin!" I said, lifting a hand. "Are you saying we should leave them behind? That we should let the Macros destroy them in their ships while they lag behind us? That we steal their engines and leave them adrift?"

"No, sir, that would be a terrible waste."

"I'm glad to hear we agree on that point."

"No, Colonel," he continued. "I'm not proposing to squander a vital resource. What I suggest is that we deploy the Centaur troops, all of them. They can ride their personal conveyances into the hulls of the enemy ships and do terrific damage by detonating nuclear charges—"

I was out of my chair.

"Shut up right there, robot!" I shouted. "You've got a lot of guts to suggest these fresh recruits commit mass suicide in order to salvage your brainbox. Let's not forget that you were the one to fire off this experiment prematurely."

"That was an accident, sir."

"So you say. If you'd held back until we reached the ring, we'd have been in position to stop the enemy as they entered. Instead, we're faced with this grim situation."

"I fail to see how I'm to blame. The entire process was experimental. In these situations, unexpected phenomena very typically—"

"Well, get the idea of leaving the Centaurs behind to screen our retreat out of your neural chains. I'm not going to order the Centaurs to make a suicidal charge at the enemy ships while we run for cover. That's final."

"In that case, I'm out of ideas."

"I've got one," Newcome said. "What about the gravity device Marvin's been working on—could it be weaponized?"

We all looked at Marvin. He seemed surprised.

"An intriguing proposal. The system is essentially a gravitational force manipulator on the order of the one built inside *Phobos*. In fact, I first got the idea for the system from the *Phobos* unit. Unfortunately, the site has been abandoned, and there is no one there to make the necessary changes to the systems."

"Hmm," I said, tapping on the screen in front of me. "We're not that far from the probe's launch point. We could be there in a few hours."

"We can't divert our course or slow down," Newcome pointed out. "They'll catch us even faster if we do."

"No," I said, tapping my chin. "But Marvin has given me an idea. We could launch a small ship with extra engines very quickly. With enough power, it could reach the device within a matter of hours."

"But Colonel," Marvin said, "who could possibly be convinced to go on such a dangerous, highly technical mission?"

All of us turned and stared at him in unison.

"Oh," he said in surprise. "I should have expected this response after your earlier tirade."

"Well?" I asked gruffly. "Will you do it, Marvin?"

Jasmine reached out a hand and put it on his nearest tentacle. He studied the hand with a single camera, rather than her face.

"Marvin? Please?" she asked. "We'd all appreciate it. You would be a hero again."

"I've found that the title of 'hero' is a fleeting honor amongst humans. But I will do it. Just thinking about the challenge is stimulating my circuitry."

I'd been pretty sure that Marvin would take the job. That's why I'd asked him instead of ordering him to do it. In some ways, he was a coward, but in other instances he was insanely brave. The key was to put some kind of technical challenge into the mix to intrigue him. If you did that, you could get him to do almost anything.

Marvin and I had a very long history of manipulating one another and involving one another in our schemes. This time, I seemed to have had the last laugh.

Or at least, I hoped so.

-12-

Our missiles met with the enemy's first barrage in open space. They destroyed one another in a cascade of ghostly fire. In the airless void between planets, nuclear explosions are odd, glimmering affairs. There's no mushroom cloud, no fireball. Each release of energy resembles a cold-looking puff of light and energy as if tiny stars are being born, then winking out a fraction of a second later. As our missiles struck theirs, hundreds of infant stars were born and quickly died away as we watched.

"Some of their birds got through," Jasmine said. "Seventy-four of them. I'm surprised they haven't released another wave."

"They plan to get in close before hitting us again," I told her. "Why waste good missiles when they know their main guns can shred us soon enough? They'll save their ammo for the killing strikes."

I realized my shoulders were hunched, and that I must have looked defeated. I made an effort to straighten up. I knew the staffers were watching me. I had to look firmly in command and confident. Slumping over the command table at a bad moment wasn't acceptable. Looking cool when I didn't feel like it was one of the hardest parts of my job.

"Give me an update on Marvin," I said to Jasmine.

"He's not responding to any transmissions. He can hear us, but he's running with radio silence at his end."

"What about a ring-to-ring transmission system? Surely, he took one with him. The enemy can't listen in on that."

"He did, but the Macro ships are jamming all the rings now. We're left with radio. If he transmits, he'll give away his position."

I nodded in understanding. There was no way Marvin was going to answer us while scooting away on a small, vulnerable target under enemy guns. I couldn't blame him for that.

"All right then. How long until the Macros get into range?"

"Eleven hours and forty-nine—"

"Colonel," Admiral Newcome spoke up beside me. He sounded as if he couldn't stand by quietly any longer.

"What is it, Newcome?"

"We should launch another attack *now*. Give our missiles time to get up to high velocity and slam into them. We can at least make a good accounting of ourselves before they catch us."

"We don't have a lot of hardware left. I'd rather hold onto it until we get in closer."

Newcome nodded curtly and stepped away from me. I could tell he didn't like my answer at all, but he wasn't going to say so. As an ex-Imperial officer, he was used to being shut down by superiors. In a way, I wished more of my regular staffers had his respect for the chain of command. We Star Force types were still less than one hundred percent professional. We were more like some kind of revolutionary outfit full of personalities and shouting.

I could now see why dictators since time immemorial—whether they were called kings, presidents or emperors—had often executed their noisiest subordinates. The thought occurred to me with regularity these days and each time it took an effort to push it away. Stress, high stakes and total power were a heady combination. Newcome seemed to appreciate this. He never pushed his luck.

Hours crawled by. Sometimes, having a finite amount of time to wait seemed to make events happen more slowly. This was one of those times. But at last, there was news to report when the enemy was no more than three hours behind us.

"Sir," Jasmine said, "we have new contacts."

I frowned at the screens. I was looking for a fresh wave of missiles or new Macros at the ring, but I was looking in the wrong direction and for the wrong colored contacts. The new images were friendlies, and I finally spotted them blinking in green at the Eden ring.

"Who's that?"

"Remember the carrier force we left to supervise the Blues? They've come to our aid."

"Hmm," I said, uncertain as to how I should respond to this. I'd never ordered the carrier to come to the Thor System. "Open a channel to the commander."

"Done."

"Is this Captain...?" I asked, but I couldn't recall the fellow's name. I looked at Jasmine and snapped my fingers.

"Captain Grass," she said quietly, putting her hand over her microphone.

Grass? I froze for a second, then winced in recollection. This was the single large ship in our fleet that was commanded by a non-human. Like most Centaurs, he had a name only his own people could relate to. Almost all of them were named after the sky, or grass, rivers, honor, fur, etc. This wasn't as strange in their native language as it was to us. They had over a hundred names for grass, each of which connoted some delicate variance, such as the way it rippled when wind ran over a field. When their names went through our translation systems, they all came out as "Grass" no matter what other nuances there might be for them.

The bigger problem, besides the name, was the fact that the commander was a Centaur. I'd had a lot of trouble with Centaur officers as ground troops. Now, I had an untested alien captain coming to my rescue in command of a major ship.

I'd put him in command of the ship as a diplomatic gesture. It had seemed rude to everyone that the Centaurs were included in our alliance, and were integrated into our ranks, but weren't given commanding roles. To show we weren't prejudiced— when, of course, we really were—I'd placed Captain Grass in command of the biggest ship in the quietest system in the Empire. And then, I'd promptly forgotten about him.

"Captain Grass," I said, putting on a welcoming tone. "This is Colonel Kyle Riggs."

"I stand ready to charge, Colonel!" came the reply.

I paused with my mouth open for a full second. "Charge? Charge where?"

"Toward the enemy on your flank! The enemy is right behind you, sir!"

I heaved a sigh. Centaurs weren't subtle warriors. Most of what we called "tactics", they saw as dishonorable trickery. Honor, to them, was a straight out charge into the teeth of the enemy. By dint of superior numbers and ferocity, the best would win. They understood the concept of being beaten and driven into submission, but only after a bloody defeat. To them, my retreat in the face of the enemy without a fight was baffling.

"I haven't given the order to charge yet," I said.

There was a moment of delay, probably due to confusion on the part of Captain Grass.

"Are your engines operating properly, Colonel?" he asked finally. "I see that they are...you're under power... I can only imagine that your sensors are out of operation. I will render assistance transmitting the coordinates of their fleet to your systems. You're headed in the wrong direction, sir!"

This was exactly why I'd never promoted any other Centaur officers to the rank of captain. I'd done so in Captain Grass' case, assuming he'd remain stationed in the Eden System indefinitely, to fight the Blues if they dared to reappear, or to blunt the attack of a new fleet of Macros. His ship was old and unimportant, so if he blew it up, it didn't really matter.

But today was different. I had to win this fight, if only to stay breathing. And here was Captain Grass, doing exactly what I'd imagined he would do when faced by a real live enemy: revving himself up to charge against overwhelming odds. He naturally expected me to join the charge with him, hell-bent on death and glory. The only problem was I didn't want to kill myself just to look tough in his eyes.

How does one explain tactical actions to a being that barely comprehends them? I opted for my usual approach: I'd give him stern orders, and then do whatever I needed to do. I

107

decided to play on his defensive instincts as part of the home guard. In Centaur herds, when a war band took to the fields they always left behind a few rams to protect the young in springtime.

"Captain Grass, you will stay at your position guarding the ring to Eden. The machines know nothing of honor. Do not let them slip past you and slaughter our young as they frolic under an open sky!"

"Don't worry, Colonel! We will paint the skies with our blood as if it were grass. We will never allow the machines to sneak past us like burrowing creatures in the night. If the honor of the river were between the two of us, Colonel, I would drink with you in this moment!"

The exact meaning of his words was lost on me, but he seemed happy so I went with the spirit of things.

"Right!" I shouted enthusiastically. "Hold your ground as if it were the highest hill under the blazing sun! Riggs out."

I made slashing motions to Jasmine, who quickly disconnected the channel. Even as she did so, the Centaur began a new windy speech about honor and rivers. Captain Grass seemed to be big on rivers.

"Are they holding at the ring as they said they would?" I asked.

She tapped up a closer image, and I could see the carrier task force was slowing and retreating back toward the ring.

"They're taking up their position as ordered," she said.

"They were about to charge, weren't they? Without orders, as usual."

"To them, orders are subservient to honor," she said.

"Yeah, great," I said. "Where's Marvin now?"

"He's in orbit around the white star. He's been there for a couple of hours. We have no emission readings from the sun station. I don't know what he's doing. For all we know, he's hiding in there."

I frowned, eyeing the screens and the holotank. There was no information there, but I had a hunch.

"No," I said. "He's a sneaky robot. He's up to something. If we're lucky, it will be something helpful."

After the Centaurs had settled down, we only had the enemy to watch. The contacts crawled after us on the screens. Each was a tiny triangle of red light trailed by a gently fading contrail that glimmered away to nothing. There were a lot of red triangles converging upon our position—far too many of them.

When there was less than an hour to go something good finally happened.

"Sir?" Jasmine asked suddenly. "I think—I think one of the enemy ships has suffered a malfunction."

My eyes glazed over from staring at the creeping doom for so long.

There had been things to do, of course. I'd ordered additional anti-missile turrets to be installed all over our fantails. The enemy missiles were only a few minutes behind us. I wasn't too worried about them as there were only seventy-four of them left, and they were coming in pretty slowly in relative speed. They'd been cruising for hours, and we'd been accelerating trying to outrun them. I was confident our ship-based anti-missile systems would take them all out.

What worried me were the enemy main gun turrets. They were going to be in range an hour from now, and we didn't have any effective defense against them.

Jasmine's comment woke me up, however, and I eyed the screens closely. There were so many hundreds of triangles it took me a moment to figure out what she was trying to show me. Jasmine had helpfully popped a pulsing circle around the spot.

As I watched, the contact's movement slowed, falling behind the rest.

"Maybe that new engine of theirs can run out of gas," I said excitedly. "Let's keep an eye on—where'd it go?"

What had been a slowing triangle now became an arc of fading light. It vanished from my screen.

"It's gone, sir," Jasmine said. "It just isn't there anymore, according to our sensors. I have several probes out there relaying data to us from multiple angles. I'm certain that ship just disappeared."

I began to grin. "Put Marvin's position up on the screens," I said.

"Marvin's position?"

"The sun factory near Loki. Put it up."

She tapped away, and after a few seconds a new contact appeared. It was green and circular, and it was right where I thought it was.

"Another ship has been destroyed just now…I think," Jasmine said.

I watched as a second red triangle winked out.

"What's going on, Colonel?" Newcome asked me. He'd come over from the defensive operations team to join us at the command table.

"Marvin is what's going on," I said with confidence. "See his position relative to the Macros? They're too far away and going too fast at this point to turn on him. He knows they can't change course now. They've been pursuing us for too long."

"I don't understand, sir," Newcome said, frowning at the screen. "Are you saying your robot is destroying their ships?"

"Yes, of course. He's held his fire until this moment, probably for hours, waiting until they were too far past him to turn around and take him out. Now he's zapping them, taking them out one at a time."

Before I'd finished explaining it, another ship vanished.

"I see!" Newcome said, his big blue eyes brightening. "This is excellent news."

Newcome began poring over the data intensely. I had to like him for one thing: the man understood numbers. He knew that rates of fire, ranges and relative velocities often meant the difference between life and death in any space battle. He had a calculator up on the screen and was tapping at the numbers and connecting a small program to various changing data points by swiping and moving them.

"He's knocking them out very fast," Newcome said. "That first salvo must have been a near miss. The first ship struck was hit in the engine region. After that, every strike has been amidships, destroying the target. He's taking out a ship every forty-nine seconds, by my estimates."

"Recharge and retargeting time," I said, nodding. "Gravity weapons always take time to cycle and fire again."

"The enemy is taking evasive action, Colonel," Jasmine warned me.

I could see them now, splitting apart and dodging.

"It won't save them, but it may buy them more time," I said. "What I want to know is whether Marvin can destroy them all before they reach firing range on this fleet?"

Newcome and Jasmine worked on this. I was surprised that Newcome came up with a definitive answer first.

"Negative, Colonel. They will lose at least two thirds of their ships, but not all of them. They will come within range with…I'd say about a hundred and thirty vessels."

I frowned. We only had thirty, even if one of them was a carrier.

"That's not good enough," I said. "Launch every missile we have. Put them out in pulses, but give them a dozen targets each. If one blows up, they should be programmed to automatically target the next one without too much overkill."

Almost before I finished explaining what I wanted, I felt the ship shudder under me. I knew that our birds were flying. Every few seconds, the ship shuddered again.

Admiral Newcome gave me a crooked smile. "Not conserving your ammo today, eh sir?"

I smiled back. "This is our chance. They don't even know what's hitting them. If we can chew them up all at once, slamming them from every angle, we might pull this little fleet out of the system without losing a single ship."

Newcome's expression indicated he thought the odds of that were slim, but he did look a lot happier than he had ten minutes earlier. Hell, we all did.

"Unload the transports and form up the fighters into strike groups," I ordered. "The marines and fighters will go in right after the missile strikes. Set up the timing on that, Jasmine. Don't let our missiles blow up our attacking troops."

"Working on it, sir."

The next hour zoomed by. When you're doing something effective in battle, and you think your odds of winning are pretty good, time flies. Their ships kept winking out, one at a time. When half of them had been destroyed, we were all smiles. Sure, it was still two hundred to thirty, but they were being annihilated at a horrific rate.

Jasmine caught my attention with a frown at that point, however. "Sir...I don't understand it, but the rings are back online. They've stopped jamming them. We're in connection with Star Force again."

I hooted. "We must have gotten their jamming ship."

She shook her head. "I don't think so. They were all jamming. Every last one of them. But for some reason..."

She trailed off and put her hand to her headset. Her frown deepened.

"I'm getting a channel request," she said. "They're asking for you, sir."

"What? The Macros are calling me begging to surrender? Request denied!"

I said these words with glee in my heart and a grin on my face. For years, the Macros had been slamming the phone down on my calls and pleas for mercy and diplomacy. It felt great to give them the finger for once. They were all going to burn this time.

But Jasmine was still frowning; she still had her hand cupped over her earpiece. She shook her pretty head.

"No sir," she said. "It's not the Macros calling us. It's the Blues."

I stared at her for a second, and my face fell. I turned my gaze back to the screens. Yes, we were winning. Yes, we were tearing apart the Macro ships like toys. And apparently, someone had heard about it, and didn't like it. The Macros had called up their collective mommies begging for help against the big bad man.

The question was: what could the Blues do to stop me?

-13-

I opened the channel with the Blues reluctantly. My first instinct was to ignore them. I wanted to simply churn and burn on the Macro fleet, ripping apart every one of their mindless vessels without mercy or compunction.

But I still feared the Blues in the back of my mind. They'd launched a ship less than a year ago that had shown us new technology we'd been unable to beat. If it hadn't been for Crow's cyborgs, we would never have defeated *Phobos*. Now, I had to ask myself: What else did they have up their sleeves?

"Colonel Kyle Riggs," said a ghostly voice after the channel was established. "Why am I not surprised that we have been forced to lower ourselves into conversing with your species yet again? Without fail, your savage life form has irritated..."

It was at about this point during the windbag's speech that it occurred to me that the guardian ships I'd place in orbit over the Blue's homeworld were now out of position. Instead of squatting just above the atmosphere, ready to bomb them if they did anything funny, Captain Grass had come to my rescue on his own initiative. That meant the Blues were back in the Eden system with nothing to keep them from launching an attack against our colony worlds, and it had probably prompted this noisy cloud to call me up to talk big.

Mind racing, I muted the Blue on the line and turned to Jasmine. "Order Captain Grass back into the Eden System," I said.

113

"He won't like retreating from a battle. You know them. They're dying to charge right now. They can see us attacking, and it must be driving them mad."

I glared. "I don't care! This isn't about glory and honor. Tell him the sneaky Blues are threatening his homeworld, and he's out of position. Tell him anything, but get him back to his station!"

"Sir," Newcome said, stepping up. "Let me do it. I'm experienced in the art of talking reluctant commanders into following orders."

I glanced at him, and nodded. "Okay. Jasmine, stay on ops. Newcome, get into communication with those damned goats and send them back home."

I unmuted the Blue. Unsurprisingly, he was still lecturing me about what a bastard I was.

"...and without provocation, your barbaric species has repeatedly assaulted our gaseous oceans, polluting them with—"

"Yeah, yeah," I said. "Let's get on with it. Who are you, and why are you calling me now?"

"I am the being known as Mercy," the Blue said.

I rolled my eyes. "Mercy, huh? Okay, 'Mercy'. Have a little compassion and get to the point. I'm busy."

"You have indeed been working industriously. We know all about your violations. You have stepped too far over the bounds this time, Colonel Riggs. Really, we did not think you were capable of—"

"Look," I said, "I'm about to break this connection and put you on permanent hold. If you have something pertinent to say, this will be your last chance."

"No, you are incorrect. It is *your* last chance, fleck of solid matter which plagues us. You have broken the edicts of the Ancients. They will not tolerate your transgressions. They will come, and they will eradicate you like the vermin you truly are."

He finally had me frowning. I had to admit, he'd managed to worry me. I gnashed my teeth, wanting with all my heart to disconnect him. Hell, I wanted to order Captain Grass to carpet bomb their annoying world once and for all.

114

I closed my eyes and took a deep breath. All around me people were launching fighters, relaying orders and giving one another reports. This was a bubbling hive of activity, the heart of a command post in the midst of battle. I had to rise above all that excitement and try to figure out what Mercy was hinting at.

"I'm listening," I said. "I'm grateful for this opportunity to hear your wisdom. Let us share a moment of peace in the middle of chaos. Tell me, merciful one, why you have lowered yourself to speaking with one so unworthy as I?"

"Your attitude has improved," the Blue said. "I will reward you with clarity, for it is in my nature to be generous with unfortunates such as yourself. I'm speaking of the Ancients who created the transport network you call 'the rings'. The Ancients have moved on, but they are ever vigilant. You have attempted to duplicate their work, which is an act of sacrilege they will never permit."

"Are you talking about the gravity weapons? You built them first."

"No, not at all. I'm referring to your creation of new rings. You have managed to connect two points that are light years apart, and that is forbidden."

I was finally beginning to catch on.

"You detected our activity?" I asked.

"Obviously. I can't believe it took you this long to comprehend the nature of a discussion in which you are personally involved. I was informed, before I made this merciful gesture, that you would not understand my attempt at communication. It was predicted that you would be argumentative even when facing the doom of your species. That you would—"

"Okay, yeah," I said, becoming irritated all over again. "I'm a real asshole. I get that. Now, explain how these Ancients who made the rings are going to be a problem."

"If we have detected your transgressions, they will have done the same. They will not tolerate a threat to their dominion."

"What is their dominion? How many systems do they have?"

"Your question is almost without meaning."

"How many systems are connected by rings of their making?"

"You have been told this before. Some two hundred known linked points exist. They are not all operational, however."

"And why's that? Why haven't we seen these Ancients for so long? Where are they, and why aren't they patrolling their territory? I mean, it would only take a year or so for one of my ships to traverse two hundred linked systems. Where have they all gone? Are they all dead? Or maybe fighting a war of their own?"

There was a moment of quiet after my question was translated and relayed to the Blues. I almost asked again when he suddenly replied.

"You ask questions for which we do not have an answer. But the beings we speak of are as far beyond our understanding as we are beyond yours. They are so advanced as to be gods. Do you know the mind of your gods? No, you do not, and neither do we. But we know enough to fear them wherever they are and whatever they're doing."

I turned my eyes back toward the screens to see how the battle was shaping up. It was looking pretty good. We still had seventy missiles of theirs inbound, but the missiles were traveling pretty slowly now in relation to my retreating fleet. I figured we could shoot them all down before they hit us.

My own forces were closing with the enemy. I had about a hundred fighters out there and at least a thousand marines. We would board their ships or stand-off and bomb them with tactical nukes. Those of the enemy cruisers that survived Marvin's continuous fire, that is. They were dodging around, but it hadn't spoiled my robot's aim much. In fact, he was hitting them faster now. Maybe he'd gotten the hang of his system, or maybe it was warmed up. Every thirty seconds, another of their ships crumpled into a wad of metal and released a puff of gas and energy. Already, more than half of them were out of the fight. There were only about a hundred and seventy ships left.

"Looks like our boys are going to miss this fight!" I said proudly. "I thought Marvin needed a helping hand, but now

I'm beginning to think there will be nothing left by the time our fighters reach the enemy."

"Your statements are nonsensical," Mercy complained in my ear. I grimaced. I'd forgotten about him for a moment.

"Sorry," I said. "I was speaking in code. What do you want again?"

"Most of my people, who are listening to this conversation now, do so solely for the purpose of gloating. They understand you have doomed yourself, and they are joyful. That is not my way. No matter how unworthy your form of existence, I feel compelled to offer you solace."

I snorted. "Solace? What kind of peace can you offer me?"

"It is known to us that, in his final moments, you shared matter with Tolerance. That was a thoughtful gesture for a barbarian. Our scholars are somewhat at a loss to explain it. Perhaps our civilized natures have infected the purity of your naturally feral state, instilling you with refinement. In any case, I wish to personally offer the same courtesy to you."

I frowned. "Let me get this straight," I said. "You're offering me the opportunity to come into your atmosphere, meet up with you, and, uh—trade matter?"

"Exactly. It is a burdensome thing, and I will forever be stigmatized among my own people for having allowed it. But I am the one called Mercy, and I would stay true to my principles even under these circumstances."

The Blues were a strange people even by the galactic standards for strangeness set by all the aliens I'd encountered so far. These beings existed largely in a gaseous state, and when they met up with one another, they often traded some of their personal matter. To a solid creature such as myself, this seemed odd at the very least, like keeping a lock of hair from everyone I'd ever met. But they didn't only keep this exchange, the puff of gas exchanged became part of them. They believed they were immortal as long as some piece of their molecular matter was still functioning in another of their species.

Knowing this, I understood that the Blue was offering me something significant in his culture. But I wasn't keen on the idea. I'd traded spit with Blues twice before, and I hadn't enjoyed the experience in the least.

"Why are you offering us this now?" I asked him. "Why do you think it's a merciful act to share matter with me?"

"Is that not obvious? I'm fairly certain it must be abundantly clear by now. I truly don't understand how you can have advanced so far—"

"Right, okay," I said. "I'm a big dummy. Now, just tell me why you want to do this?"

"Because you are doomed, Colonel Kyle Riggs. Your existence cannot continue. You have violated the will of the Ancients, such as none has dared to do for a billion years. You and all your people will be destroyed when they come back."

For the first time, the Blue had my full attention. I turned away from the screens, the cheering crowds, and cupped my hands over the mouthpiece. "You say they're coming back? These Ancients? When?"

"That is known only by them."

"Well, how long has it been since you've seen them? How long in standard Earth years?"

There was a moment of quiet, then the answer came at last. "The stillness of space was last visited upon all our species over a hundred thousand years ago."

"A hundred thousand...?" I asked? Then I smiled. "Ha! I've got news for you, Mercy. That's a long, long time for a human. I'll be dead and gone long before they come back. But what was that you said about the stillness of space? I didn't get that."

"The reference was to the cold they bring with them: the chill of the stars, the cooling of the planets. All life suffers when the Ancients glide through our systems."

I was frowning again thinking about that.

"Okay, Mercy," I said. "I've got to go. I have a battle to win. But I want to thank you for this call, the warning and your very personal offer of solace. I know that means a lot to your species."

"You appreciate my offer?"

"I do indeed," I lied. "I might even take you up on it someday."

"I am surprised. I was told you would not understand my generosity and would reject it. You are a strange being, Colonel Kyle Riggs."

"I've been told that before," I assured him and closed the channel.

Around me, my staffers were cheering. The enemy was down to thirty ships, and our fighters and marines had finally reached them. We were tearing them apart.

But I stared at the screens, troubled.

"What is it, Colonel?" Jasmine asked me. "What did the Blues have to say?"

"They wanted to give me the last rites," I said.

"What?"

I shook my head. "Doesn't matter. But Jasmine, do you happen to remember when Earth's last glacial period began? You know, when the ice covered most of our world?"

"You mean when it ended?" she asked, frowning.

"No. I want to know when it started."

She brought up a screen and did a search online. I could have done that, but I let her.

"Just over a hundred thousand years ago," she said. "Why do you ask, Colonel?"

"That's what I thought," I said. "No reason. Carry on."

A few minutes later, the last of the enemy ships blew up. While everyone else on the ship cheered and whooped, I remained quiet and brooding.

What if I had pissed off these Ancients—some sort of sinister super-aliens we'd never encountered? What if I'd unwittingly stirred up a new shitstorm, the like of which hadn't been seen in a hundred millennia?

Well, I told myself, *it wouldn't be the first time.*

-14-

We all thought the battle was over when the last Macro cruiser turned into a fountain of plasma and shrapnel. But it wasn't.

Those seventy-odd missiles kept coming at us. I'd pretty much discounted them until they started slowing down and taking complex countermeasures.

"Sir," Newcome said, calling me from the bridge.

"What is it, Admiral?"

"I think you better come up here."

I'd been taking a sip of coffee down in the cantina, wishing it was beer. I stood up with a grunt. Kwon stood up with me.

"What is it?" he asked. "Something's gone wrong? That's it, I can tell!"

He sounded eager to fight. He'd missed out during the last battle. The last Macro cruiser had died before it had reached cannon-range. He'd asked to go out with the marines, but I hadn't let him. I didn't want to risk losing a key man on a fight that was pretty much a foregone conclusion.

I had to admit that sometimes Kwon's lust for battle was disturbing. A normal man wouldn't be all turned—on about a chance to face death, but Kwon never got tired of it.

"Maybe," I said, giving him a tight smile. "Trouble on the bridge. But it might just be Newcome acting nervous again. He needs babysitting more than most officers."

"Babysitting, ha ha!" Kwon shouted, enjoying the joke more loudly than I would have liked.

"You want to tag along?" I asked him.

"Would love to, sir!"

He followed me all the way up the main passage, and we pressed our way through the nanite door. Right away, I could tell the mood was all wrong. The staffers were bustling, but quietly. The jubilant mood left by our recent victory had vanished.

"Brief me, Newcome," I said. "And this had better not be some kind of a screw-up on your part."

"Hardly, Colonel," he said huffily. "The enemy has employed sophisticated countermeasures. Their missiles are still coming, and we aren't going to be able to stop them."

Narrowing my eyes, I surveyed the boards and the holotank. The enemy missiles were already in range, and I could see we were taking potshots at them with lasers.

"Why are we missing?" I said, watching a steady series of stabbing beams reach out from our fleet in flickering lines which intersected the enemy missiles neatly. Each time they did so, there seemed to be no appreciable effect.

"Technically, we're *not* missing, sir. The enemy has deployed a particularly effective aerosol. It is prismatic, highly reflective and stubbornly difficult to burn through. Unlike chaff, there doesn't seem to be any end to it, and we can't burn through it. Even direct hits are having no effect on the enemy missiles."

I nodded. "I can see that our fighters aren't going to return in time to help."

"It will all be over hours before we retrieve them. We're reducing the fleet's speed in order to do so, but it won't help."

"What about Marvin?" I asked. "Can't he zero in on these missiles and crush them for us as he did the fleet?"

"I don't know, sir."

"What about using our own missiles against these incoming birds? Have we got anything left?"

He shook his head. "We threw it all into destroying their ships. We're on our own. We'll have to ride out this attack without the fighters or missiles."

I frowned, looking it over. Jasmine arrived, and she rushed to the table. Her eyes swept over the scene, and she nodded in understanding.

"I have received a message from Marvin, Colonel," she said.

I looked at her expectantly.

She shook her head. "He won't be able to help. The moment the last Macro cruiser was destroyed, he launched from the Sun Factory and headed back toward our fleet. Really, we can't be angry with him about that. He completed his mission perfectly.

"It wasn't quite over with yet," I grumbled. But, after thinking about it, I shrugged.

"Looks like they're going to tag us, people," I said loudly. "Really, we had to expect this. We could hardly hope to get through a fight like this one without a scratch. Seventy missiles will hurt, and they will probably take out a few ships. But if we all—"

"Sir?" Newcome interrupted me.

I looked at him, frowning.

"There's more to it than that. The enemy missiles are slowing as they come in close. They are, in fact, matching our velocity and deceleration arc."

It took me a second to get what he was saying. "You're telling me they aren't missiles at all. That these are assault ships?"

He nodded. I looked at Jasmine.

"That would fit the profile of behavior, sir," she said.

For the first time, I felt a twinge of worry.

"How far are we from the ring to the Eden System?"

"About an hour away, Colonel."

"What if we sped up again? What if we zoomed right through the ring and made it home as fast as possible?"

They were both working on the numbers. Glimmering lines curved on the screens, projecting new paths.

"We could do it in half that time."

"Thirty minutes…and the enemy missiles—um, assault ships, will speed up again to catch us, I'm sure. But that might screw up their little protective clouds. Let's do it. Fleet, I want every ship in the task force to accelerate, all ahead full. If we make it to the ring while they're landing on our hulls, the guns of Welter Station can pick them off."

I didn't have to ask twice. I could tell by the speed of the response Jasmine had already tapped in the order. She was always on top of these things. I was glad I'd brought her along.

The ship's decking lurched under my feet. A painful, growing weight caused by the acceleration pressed upon me, too much for the grav plates to compensate for.

The next twenty minutes were rough. The missiles gave chase, and we fired everything we had left at them. Unfortunately, I'd unloaded all my missiles, fighters and marines to meet the ships themselves.

It soon became clear we weren't going to make it to the ring before they caught up to us. We weren't going to be able to stop them.

"Sixty-eight left?" I demanded incredulously. "Are you telling me we only got a handful of them with all that fire? That means their anti-laser systems are far better than ours. This is actually depressing news. We surprised them with the gravity weapon, and it was a damned good thing we did. These ships would have mopped up the floor with us. They would have deployed these defensive measures to protect their cruisers when we got into range with our main guns, I'm sure. I'm shocked at their technological advancement."

"Sir," Newcome said. "Maybe that's why they have so few ships. It's been a long time since we met up with the Macros. Maybe they spent their time upgrading weaponry rather than building more vessels."

I nodded. "I have to concede that possibility. It fits the facts, but we may never know the truth. It does, however, emphasize our need for technological advancement. We can't have a bunch of machines out-teching us. It's downright embarrassing. I want samples after this is over—presuming we survive. Transmit every measurement we've taken to Welter Station, and have them relay that to Earth."

"We can't do that right now, Colonel," Jasmine said."

"Why not?"

"They're jamming the rings again."

123

I growled. "The Macros and the Blues are in coordination yet again. What a pair of devils. I tell you, I've still got half a mind to erase the Blues while we can."

At this, several pairs of eyes looked up at me. Only Kwon didn't appear to take note. He was tapping at one small corner of the boards, where he was checking his troop rosters. I approved as he was arranging defensive operations on the ships. That was his job, and he always stuck to his job rather than getting upset about whatever I said.

The rest of them looked worried. I heaved a sigh.

"No, I'm not going to order you to commit genocide no matter how much the Blues deserve it. I'm just annoyed with them. We have to make it painful to them when they pull stunts like this. Possibly, that entire line they gave me about sharing matter and me being doomed was bullshit meant to cover for the fact they really just wanted to give the Macros their marching orders."

"What did they say about being doomed?" Jasmine asked in concern.

"Never mind about that. They never talk to me without throwing in a few oddball threats. Let's get back to the battle at hand. Kwon, where are you setting up your marines?"

"Center of each ship, main passage between the bridge and engineering."

I nodded. "Tell every crew to keep the engines burning. I don't want them crawling in that way. Once they get off their damned missiles we'll take some shots at them. Each ship can try to burn individual machines off his neighbor's hull."

"Good idea!" Kwon shouted. "It will be like picking fleas off your neighbor's back—but try to leave a few for my men. We need practice."

I knew Kwon really meant he wanted to have some fun fighting with the machines personally, but I didn't argue with him. Our gunners and brainboxes would not need my encouragement to fire when the enemy was swarming on hulls. They probably wouldn't have listened if I'd told them to go easy on the machines, in any case.

When the machines finally did hit us, it wasn't loud or flashy. They came in, unloaded marines that looked like headless grasshoppers, and all we heard was the clank and rasp of their feet on the hulls.

It was impossible not to look up at the ceiling when you heard that sound.

"It's been a long time," I said.

"It sure has," Kwon said, cradling his projector and checking his charge for the tenth time. "Too long."

Up until that point, nothing had really gone wrong. I'd known for twenty minutes that they would catch us, and I knew those missiles were full of enemy marines. If they couldn't find a way in for the next ten minutes, we'd slip through the ring and find ourselves in home space. Welter Station had lasers that dwarfed anything that my ships had. Even if they had their own personal aerosol shields up by then, I was confident our big guns would burn through it without a problem.

I was beginning to think we were going to ride this one out. At that moment, something new went wrong.

"Sir, we have a hull breach," Jasmine said.

"What? Already?"

She'd hardly had to tell me. The screens were flashing red. Our exterior view of space and the Thor System flashed away and was replaced by a diagram of our ship. Up forward, about ten meters from the nose itself, the breach appeared as a dark hole surrounded by red warping radiating lines.

"They've got something new. They're cutting through our hull as if it's paper."

I watched for a second, fascinated. Then I turned to Kwon. "They're getting inside. Let's go."

"Colonel!" Jasmine said in alarm.

I paused.

"You don't have to go personally. We still have a complement of defensive troops and crewmen. Let them do their jobs."

Kwon laughed. She looked at him coldly.

"You should know him better than that by now!" Kwon said, marching into the passageway. He shouted orders to the squad of troops that waited there.

I paused, seeing the worried look in Jasmine's eye. I hugged her lightly, not wanting to crush her with my

125

exoskeletal armor. Her Fleet uniform was like paper compared to my gear.

I kissed the top of her head. "If they get to the engine core, we're all dead anyway. Make sure every crewmember suits up. This might be a fight to the finish."

She turned away, eyes glistening with emotion. She began shouting orders and handed over fleet ops to Admiral Newcome. There was precious little to do in that regard now.

The enemy had penetrated the hull of every ship in the task force. Most were only graced with a dozen invading marines. But, as we were on the only battleship in the fleet, we'd gotten around a hundred uninvited visitors.

This fight was to the finish now, I told myself. More than once, I'd invaded Macro ships and taken them from their rightful owners.

Maybe the machines thought it was payback time.

-15-

They came in like a swarm of bees. We were never quite sure how they breached the hull, but they seem to have some kind of new energy drill on the nose of specialized Macro marines. One in every sixteen of them had been built with this singular purpose in mind: to break into an enemy ship.

"A bomb would have been so much easier," Kwon said as he trotted in front of me toward the breached zone.

Gamma deck had a hole in it, as did the aft region near engineering. We'd assigned ourselves defensive duty at the Gamma breach since it was closer to our starting position at the bridge. Another squad of defensive troops was heading to engineering. They weren't marines, but Star Force Fleet people can put up a good fight when you put them in armor and tell them to defend their ship. I had high hopes for them.

"Yeah," I said, huffing a bit when we reached a ladder and vaulted through an access point in the bulkhead. "A big bomb shoved through the hull is always easier. But their methods are effective, and they're doing a lot less damage by drilling small holes than explosives would. I can see the beauty in their system. They're designed to capture our ships rather than destroy them."

Kwon craned his body around to look at me. I could see his face through this visor, and he wore a grimace of disbelief.

"Beauty? There's nothing pretty about these metal bugs, Colonel. They're evil machines. That's all. About as beautiful as a dentist's drill."

"Yeah..." I said, letting him win the point. There was no use in trying to get Kwon to understand a designer's viewpoint. He wasn't a programmer or an engineer. He specialized in blowing things up rather than creating them.

But I'd always been impressed by Macro technology. It was so functional, so pure. There was no waste, no frills. If a cube-shaped object did the job, you got a cube out of them. No decorations or markings: A perfect cube.

That's what these invasion robots were. They'd been carefully designed to do a specific job, and they were doing it very well. If I'd been forced to admit it, I'd have to say they were kicking our asses.

"I hate machines," Kwon said as he crouched and scuttled forward on his knees.

It was an awkward pose for any armored man, but when Kwon did it he looked like a metal beetle.

"Are you sure?" I asked, crawling after him and looking for the enemy. "What about your weapons and your suit? Do you hate them too?"

Around us a dozen troops crawled on their bellies. Gamma Deck wasn't like most of them. It wasn't even a full-sized deck. It was more like a layer of equipment and tubing to support the decks below and above it. Rather than nice flat corridors and hatchways, it was a maze of piping and machinery. Usually only maintenance people came down here.

"You know what I mean, sir," Kwon whispered, scanning the dark clutter around us for any sign of the enemy. "I'm talking about smart machines. I hate them."

"Even Marvin?" I asked. "If it hadn't been for his gravity-hammer, we'd have lost this fight and be dead and floating by now."

"Yeah, you got me there. I don't hate Marvin. He worries me, and I don't always like him—but I don't hate him. Okay, so I hate all machines except for—"

That was as far as he got. I was surprised, really, that the enemy had let us this close. They opened up from their positions where they'd lain in ambush as we crawled toward them.

There were sixteen of them and sixteen of us. The enemy was organized into four diamond-shaped teams of four. I counted their guns as they flared yellow-white, ripping apart the gloom. The equipment and piping around me popped, melted and sizzled.

Sixteen guns was the same size as my squad. I had a wild thought then: I should institute reforms upping our unit sizes slightly. That way we'd always outnumber them.

It was a silly idea, but you never know what might be going through your mind when the fireworks start. Usually, I didn't think about much other than staying alive and killing the enemy. However, sometimes I experienced flashes of sights and sounds from my past, or memories of home – especially if I took a hit and felt stunned.

"Left flank," Kwon shouted suddenly, "hunker down. Right flank, give them covering fire. The enemy is concentrating left. You know the drill, stick to it."

He was a first-class fighter and a great sergeant. The men had just the right level of fear mixed with respect for him. I don't think they feared him physically even though he dwarfed most of them. They feared his reputation, and the number of fights he'd walked away from, leaving dead comrades and enemies strewn behind. It was hard not to be intimidated by facts like that.

I agreed with his tactical decisions, and as I was on the left flank, I hunkered down with the rest of them. A storm of laser bolts burned the air over our heads. The entire crowded region of Gamma Deck was filling with wisps of smoke as lasers vaporized metal. Hit or miss, almost everything down here was metal.

"They're shifting to hit us on the right now, sir," Kwon said. "And I haven't counted any kills yet. They have heavier front plating than they used to, I think."

"Okay, let's change things up a little. Hand grenades, I want them all tossed at once."

"Sir, I don't think that's such a—"

"Frag out!" I shouted, pressing a stud and throwing my grenade into the face of the enemy who had taken this opportunity to scuttle forward. We were busy ducking, and they were trying to get in close.

"Throw one each, men!" I ordered over the command channel.

The men didn't hesitate. They pulled out their tactical grenades, armed them with a click of their thumbs and lobbed them toward the enemy.

These grenades didn't behave like the old-fashioned dumb weapons. We'd done a little bit of design work ourselves over the years. These were smart grenades. They had onboard magnetometers, tiny brainboxes and even propulsion systems. Essentially, they were tiny, suicidal drones. Programmed to seek and destroy Macro-sized metal objects, they homed in and exploded, not on a timer and a fuse, but rather like tiny mines seeking ships in space.

Explosions blossomed. A moment later, I stood up, and the men around me cheered.

Only two of the machines had survived. We'd wiped them out. We concentrated fire and melted the last two. They took a lot more heat to burn down than usual, and I was certain they had new armor. But the last one finally died, scrabbling and kicking like a bug touched by a match.

"We only lost one man, Kwon!" I shouted.

"Yeah, but you took out that big box over there."

I followed his outstretched hand and frowned. "Hmm," I said. "It is about the size and weight of a Macro. Someone's grenade must have gotten confused."

"They told me not to use grenades down here on Gamma," Kwon complained. "They said I would wreck something critical."

"Well, it was my call," I said. "I'd say it was the right one. After all, we took them out fast."

I broke off in surprise. "Huh…I'm floating now."

We all were.

"I think the ship's gravitational system is dead, sir," Kwon said.

"Yeah, dammit."

We were in free-fall. As the damaged device died, things went from bad to worse. *Potemkin* wasn't just gliding along through space, after all. The entire fleet was still accelerating, and now we could feel the full weight of that acceleration.

Men tumbled and grunted, falling toward the aft bulkhead. Gamma Deck was filled with a lot of obstacles and darkness, and the limited space was crowded with men, equipment and dead Macros.

It was a mess. Men grunted and shouted curses. Visors starred and some troops were pinned under a mass of struggling bodies.

I was one of the unlucky ones. Two Macro hulks crashed down on top of me at the far end of the deck. Fortunately, I was already connected via com-link to the bridge.

"Bridge? This is Riggs. Kill the engines. We're no longer being pursued. Coast. Do not decelerate or accelerate. I repeat—"

"Colonel?" Jasmine's voice asked in my ear. "What did you do down there? I see your location—Gamma Deck."

"That's correct. Could you shut off the engines, please?"

"They're cycling down now. It will be a few minutes."

I cursed and complained inside my helmet. I was glad I was wearing hardshell armor, as I would have been crushed otherwise. Finally, after what seemed like a very long time, the pressure eased, and we all started floating again.

"Colonel?" Jasmine was saying again. "Could you get to engineering? They're having trouble down there. We might lose the deck."

"Roger that, I'm on my way. Tell them relief is coming and to fight a defensive battle until the marines arrive."

I thought about my relatively untrained fleet people fighting with these new-and-improved Macro killing machines. It wasn't a pretty picture.

"Message relayed, sir," Jasmine said. "And Kyle, did you wreck my ship?"

"Uh—Kwon did it."

"I should have known!" she said, and broke off.

Kwon drifted closer to me when I flipped back to proximity chat. "What did she say? Is she pissed? You blew a hole in her baby, and women never forget that kind of thing, you know."

"Yeah," I said, feeling a little guilty about blaming Kwon. "I know. But don't worry. She'll get over it."

We hustled aft through a system of hatchways and worked our way to the rear of the ship.

"Colonel?" Jasmine called me again. "You have to hurry. They've engaged and are taking losses. They can't use grenades without wrecking the engines."

"We'll be there in sixty seconds."

When engineering was right below our position on Gamma Deck, I ordered my men to break through the deck-plates in unison.

This maneuver isn't as hard as it sounds. In many places on a modern cruiser, our decking was built with smart materials holding together the larger sheets of pure metal. If you went to a joint, and had the right security codes, you could break through into whatever was on the far side just by telling the nanites to let go.

So when we did storm through, we did it all at once. An avalanche of marines came falling out of the ceiling of the engineering deck along with dislodged deck plates and drifting clouds of constructive nanites. They'd been the glue between the plates for so long they didn't seem to know what to do when ordered to release in zero G. They formed swirling swarms that looked like tiny tornadoes of metal filings.

We unloaded on the machines point-blank. We were in their midst, and we made a happy discovery: their improved armor was only effective in the front. That made sense as it would have been difficult to armor up every machine without weighing it down so much it couldn't move.

Caught from the sides and rear, our lasers punched through their hulls and burned their guts out before they could do much. In the entire action, we only lost one man who was gored to death by a thrashing machine in its death throes.

The Fleet people, unfortunately, weren't so lucky. They'd been wiped out.

"We were too slow," I said, checking each armored corpse for vitals.

"I found one alive here!" Kwon shouted.

We gathered around and helped stabilize a dying midshipman. The woman wouldn't see action for weeks, but she'd live.

The rest were dead: About thirty of them.

"They fought bravely," I said. "But these new lasers—the burns are terrible."

Kwon banged his gauntlet on my back. I rocked in my armor.

"We can't live forever, sir," he said. "We won. We saved the ship. That's what counts."

"Yeah," I said, still frowning.

I almost found it odd that the battle bothered me. I'd seen a lot of action in my time, more than most men have in a lifetime, but I still didn't like to see a unit wiped out. That part of my life had never become routine.

-16-

Our task force glided through the ring and into friendly space. I called a timeout on the bridge, releasing the staffers who'd been on duty for back-to-back shifts. Everyone sighed in relief. There was still plenty to do, of course. The hull had to be patched, and the wounded had to be tended to, but the immediate danger was over.

I let the sleepless, ticking nanites tend to the small stuff. While they cleaned up the mess the battle had left in its wake, I headed toward my quarters lost in thought.

I eyed the bunk I shared with Jasmine but walked around it and went to the single window instead. The window in my quarters was a real one. This old Imperial ship still had vestiges of the past, and this was one of the ones I liked. Despite the inefficiency in terms of lost heat and imperfect viewing, nothing could fully replace the human eye staring through a pane of glass.

I knew that my engineering people would scoff at that sentiment. Often, a high-resolution screen gave a better idea of what was outside a ship, but a real window provided me with a certain grounded feeling. It was an unplanned, unaltered view of the universe.

I tapped the panel below the small, angular window, and the blast shield outside slid away. The glass was a little frosty with condensation, but I could see space with my own eyes. To the left was Eden, a cheery yellow star. It looked distant and small from our position out near the battle station, but I was still happy to see it. Close at hand was Welter Station in all its bristling glory. In many ways, I still considered the station to be my finest defensive achievement. Even if all four hundred Macro ships had made it through the nearby ring and entered local space here, I felt confident that the station's guns would have destroyed them all.

Below us, slipping away almost as quickly as the station, was Hel, a cold, unforgiving rock. It was the twenty-first planet in the star system and the farthest from the yellow sun.

As always, I felt better just knowing I was in the Eden System. These days it felt like home to me—maybe even more than Earth itself did.

In my mind, I immediately took that thought back. It wasn't that I didn't love Earth, it was that I loved the *old* Earth, the world I'd grown up on. That Earth seemed like a distant memory now. I missed my farm and the quiet countryside. I ached for blue skies and fresh winds. No voices had been buzzing in my helmet or kissing-up to me in the old days— with the possible exception of a few desperate students who'd missed their final exams.

Today, I was no longer a regular guy living his life. When I was on Earth, I felt weighed down with vast responsibilities.

"What are you thinking about?" Jasmine asked.

I turned and looked down. She had appeared at my side and now stood watching my face. She had entered the room so quietly, I hadn't even known she was there.

"I'm having a rare philosophical episode," I said.

She looked worried for a moment, furrowing her brow. "That doesn't sound like you. Were you hit on the head or something?"

I laughed out loud, and she smiled. I wasn't even sure whether or not she was serious, but it didn't matter.

"It looks like this adventure is over," she said, still watching me.

"What do you mean?"

She shrugged. "We sent in the probe, and it didn't work. But it did trigger a Macro attack. Everything is pretty much the way it was before we came out here."

I shook my head. "No, I don't think so. We have a fix on a point in space. There's something out there, something hiding in a deep void, less than a light year from Earth. We can't rest with the machines sitting so close."

Her face darkened, and she stepped around my body until she was in front of me, between my chest and the frosty window.

"You said Marvin had made a mistake," she said. "And that they couldn't be out there."

I shrugged. "I say a lot of things. I didn't want people to be distracted. I wanted everyone to focus on the battle."

"You lied?"

"Sort of. It does seem hard to believe the Macros could be in the middle of nowhere without a star system—but it makes a certain kind of sense, too, doesn't it? They've been quiet for so long. What have they been doing?"

"Building ships and improving their technology so they could beat us the next time."

I nodded. "Yes, that, and something else, too."

"What?"

"I think they've been watching us, staring at us with their cold, electronic eyes. They've been sitting out there in the dark, studying us and trying to figure out how to beat us. That's why their ships were faster this time. Their assault-missiles were full of countermeasures. Even their marines were different. They've upgraded them with much better forward armor. They would have won today if Marvin hadn't trumped them with his gravity weapon."

Jasmine seemed not to like any of this talk. She had her head against my chest now. That was unusual for her. She rarely seemed to need comforting of any kind. I touched her hair lightly and rested my hand on her back. I didn't hug her. Sometimes when I hugged a girl it knocked the wind out of her. I didn't want to take the chance.

"I thought it was over," she said, almost accusingly.

"I'm sorry if I misled you, but we can't let our guard down. Even if Marvin is wrong, we have to act as if the intel is good. We can't afford to do nothing. What's the problem, anyway?"

"I don't want you to do what you're going to do next," she said.

"What am I going to do?"

"Go out there. Lead a fleet to destroy them in the dark between the stars."

I looked down at Jasmine. Her hair was black—so black that the stars outside created a white reflective sheen on the top of her head.

"You know me too well," I said.

She didn't answer because we both knew she'd guessed my thoughts. I had been pondering my next move, and she was right: I was going to have to build a fleet and fly out there. If the Macros were sitting in the sky watching us like owls watching mice in the dark, we had to remove them. I had to find their nest and destroy them all.

"Send someone else," she said suddenly. "Send Miklos, or Newcome. They can spend a year chasing shadows in the void."

"I just might do that," I said.

She looked up at me, studying my face. Then she frowned. "You're lying. I know why Sandra kicked you so often. You're a good liar, but eventually people catch on."

This sort of talk wasn't like Jasmine. I frowned and tried to focus on her. She wasn't usually this emotional and possessive.

"What's wrong?" I asked her. "You don't seem like yourself."

She turned away, facing the stars. She looked out the window while I watched her.

"I didn't want to tell you this way, but I guess I have to."

"Tell me what?"

"I'm going to have a baby—your baby."

I was taking in a breath when she said this, and my lungs froze-up. I couldn't suck in any more air, nor could I release what I had. I wanted to cough—or maybe gag—but I didn't. I just froze.

Jasmine turned around slowly to face me. I tried to change the shocked look on my face, I swear I did. I tried to rip my cheek muscles upward, forcing a smile. But it wasn't working fast enough.

She studied me, her eyes flicking over my features.

She put her hand to her face and spun quickly back to the window. I knew I'd blown it.

"Hey, what's wrong?"

"You're clearly not pleased by this news."

I put a hand on her shoulder, but she squirmed away.

"Don't touch me."

"Listen," I said as gently as I could, "you just took me by surprise. It's not like we're married and trying to get you pregnant."

"You try all the time."

I allowed myself a quick eye-roll behind her back.

"Yeah, yeah…I know I'm involved here. But there is such a thing as contraceptives. Were they not working, or…?"

"That's all you want to ask about? I say I'm pregnant, and you want to talk about birth control?"

"Whoa! Let's not even go there. I'm sorry. I didn't mean it that way. I'm just surprised."

"We were living together on Earth," she said. "The war seemed like it was over. I stopped taking the pill a while ago, and I—I shouldn't have done that. Not without asking."

I knew I had every right to be mad. I knew Jasmine had pulled a fast one. But, as I was getting over the initial shock, I could see how this might not be so bad. It wasn't like I was poor or anything. Technically, I was Earth's ruling party of one. I could have all the kids I wanted. What the hell difference did it make?

"You're angry with me," she said. "And I'm sorry. I made a mistake."

"You know what?" I said suddenly. "I'm finally getting my head around this. I think this is going to work out. I had kids once, you know. I loved them, but they didn't survive the first day the machines came to Earth. Hell, if I'm ever going to rebuild a family, I might as well get started."

She turned around and looked at me, with tears on her cheeks. "Really?"

"Yeah…sure, why not?"

"You aren't just saying that? You aren't going to have me shot or spaced or something?"

For the first time, I felt angry. "I'm not Crow. Why do people worry about things like that around me?"

"Because you have the power to do them if you want to. Not even the police could save me. No courts can convict you of anything. You're like some kind of pharaoh."

I laughed. "Hardly. I'm Colonel Kyle Riggs, and I don't intend to change.

Jasmine's eyes were studying me again. She wiped away her tears and uncrossed her arms. "I'm really sorry for springing this on you. It was—it's not like me. I don't know why I did it."

"How old are you?" I asked innocently.

"Thirty-three," she said. "Why?"

"No reason," I said, giving her a reassuring smile. I managed to do it right this time without even a hint of worry in my eyes. She'd never had children, and her body knew her time was running out, even if she didn't. I forced myself into my most understanding mood.

We hugged and kissed and eventually made love. For some reason, being pregnant seemed to light a fire in Jasmine. It was good, and afterward we talked quietly in the dark, making plans.

I didn't ask her to marry me. Should I have? I'm not sure. I'd been with her for months. We were a good thing together. But marriage…? Yeah, maybe someday. It could go that way. But I wasn't about to just jump into that in an emotional moment. I had to think it over. It had to be my idea.

I knew in my heart she wouldn't hesitate to say yes. Not for a second. But she didn't even bring it up. Maybe she didn't want to push her luck after getting a pass on the whole pregnancy thing.

As we cruised through space toward Earth, ships passed us going the other way. I'd ordered the fleet to come out here to the border systems in case the Macros had a few more surprises coming. Fleet wasn't going to be caught with their collective pants down again. We'd wait for them at the ring, and if they poked out a nose we'd cut it off. If they came through in force, the fleet had orders to withdraw to the next ring, the one that led to Eden.

There, with Welter Station at their backs, they'd make their stand. It was the best position we had. We would stop them there or die out as a species. It was that simple, really.

It occurred to me that I should have set up for this before performing Marvin's experiment, but we'd all been lulled. Nothing had come from the Macros for so long, we'd become complacent about the danger.

I'd heard that monkeys, if left in the vicinity with a stuffed tiger or crocodile, would at first scream and run. But soon, when it did nothing, they'd come back and taunt it. Getting braver with each passing hour, they would eventually attack it, urinate on it and even make it into a favorite bench to sit upon.

That was how I'd handled the Macros. They'd lain still for so long, they'd become a joke. But just as in the case of the monkeys, I knew that if life suddenly came back to those eyes and those jaws snapped shut on my tail, I was dead meat.

Why do we love to taunt deadly predators when they appear to be helpless? I don't know. It's just in us, I guess.

-17-

Marvin caught up with our fleet before we reached Earth, but he didn't say much to me before we reached home. I thought maybe he was ducking low for some reason. I knew that he'd been pretty sneaky in his handling of the Macro ships. He probably could have started firing earlier, but he'd wanted to make sure they were past his position. He'd attempted to cover his own butt first—then worried about saving ours.

Marvin himself was a valuable asset. I had to admit, I would risk our fleet to make sure he survived a battle. I'd often thought privately that in the harsh calculus of war, Marvin was worth an entire fleet—maybe even an allied world. Losing him might mean we'd lose this war in the end, at some future point when we needed a technical miracle and there wasn't one to be had.

So I didn't order him to explain himself. I didn't remove his tentacles, or even yell at him. I ignored him, when possible, and spoke to him politely when I needed to.

After a while, he became braver and began attending staff meetings again. He soon became engaged in our discussions.

We were planning our next move, and the decisions weren't easy ones. Jasmine, Newcome, Marvin and I were the top people in the room, and that was enough. Some commanders liked windy meetings with dozens of people presenting their views and experts who could be consulted if called upon. I preferred smaller groups—no more than five or six—and everyone could say whatever they wanted. When real decisions had to be made, I wanted diverse views—even if I didn't listen to them in the end.

We were in orbit over Earth, and I knew my people were anxious to get off the ship and back down to their comfortable offices, but I had no intention of allowing that. The last time I'd spent any amount of time in my office, someone had blown it up. I felt relatively safe and in charge while sitting up in space.

Newcome was full of ideas today. He wanted to build a giant fleet, of course. He was as bad as Miklos on that topic. Neither of them would ever see enough ships in Earth's skies.

"There isn't any choice, really," he concluded, using exactly the same words he'd used to begin his speech. "We have to build ships. More ships than we'd ever expected to build. All other activity must stop."

I frowned briefly. "All other activity? You mean we shouldn't build up our ground forces or our defensive batteries on the Moon?"

"A few side projects might be worthy of consideration, but with very few exceptions, I think we must build nothing but ships. All our economic activity—certainly, all our Nano-factory output—must go into the fleet."

"That seems a little extreme," Jasmine said. "We don't even know if they're really coming yet."

"How do you feel about another test?" I asked Newcome. "Another run out to the Thor System to fire off one more probe? Shouldn't we double-check Marvin's results?"

For the first time in ten minutes or more, Marvin shifted one of his cameras to me. He'd been watching Admiral Newcome when the old blowhard had started his pitch, but when it became long-winded and dull, his attention had drifted. Surprisingly, the newest object of Marvin's scrutiny was Jasmine. He had as many as seven cameras watching her, and a few more floating around under the table. I'd checked.

Could he *know* she was pregnant? He wasn't a dog who could supposedly sniff out such things. She wasn't showing yet, either. It was only her second month in the first trimester—or was it the third month?

"Did you get that, Colonel?" Newcome asked.

I sucked in a breath and looked away from Marvin's roving cameras. I turned back to Newcome, who must have asked me a question. Everyone was staring at me expectantly.

"That's a good point, Admiral," I said forcefully. "An *excellent* point."

He frowned. "What exactly do you mean—"

"I *mean*," I said loudly, "that if the enemy is out there festering and building up, and if we can't get to them through the ring, we'll have to fly to their lair directly and root them out. That does mean we'll have to build a lot of ships."

Newcome beamed.

"Unfortunately," I said, "we can't afford to do that."

His face fell.

"Why not?"

Miklos cleared his throat. I looked at him and nodded.

"Because we can't take the risk," Miklos said.

"What risk?" asked Newcome.

Miklos frowned. "I would like to follow your plan, Admiral, really I would. But let us consider the possibilities. The enemy might be out of ships. In that case, if we hit them right now we should win. But we can't. Everything we've sent through the last ring in the chain has been destroyed."

"I'm not talking about going through that trapped ring. I'm talking about flying out there—"

"Correct," Miklos said. "Let me finish, please. You're advocating a flight to their reported position in open space. But consider this: it will take at least six months to get there. Even if we launched today, the enemy would have time to rebuild, and they'd see us coming as well. Worse, we're not entirely sure where the enemy is. There is a cluster of dark planets and chunks of ice in that region, and they could be on any one of them. We'd have to go out there and search around for them. They would see us coming, and our advantage would be lost."

"I agree," said Jasmine.

I glanced at her, as did Marvin. She looked smug. It took me a second to figure out why—then it hit me. If the monster fleet didn't get built and sent into the dark, I couldn't be on it and gone for months. I released a small sigh.

143

"What do you suggest, then?" Newcome asked. He frowned and looked bitter. I knew that he'd been counting on a big budget boost to play navy with. He liked building ships much more than he liked using them to attack—attacking had a way of blowing up ships, which decreased their number rather suddenly.

Everyone looked at me to see if I was about to say something, but I waved them on.

"Keep going, Miklos," I said. "Lay it out for us."

"As I was saying, we can't take the chance. If we built and launched such a fleet, and the enemy has been watching us, they could simply choose the perfect moment to use the ring and attack us. Our fleet, heading into space directly, would be out of position and unable to return in time to defend Earth before they got here."

Newcome sat back in defeat. "So, you're suggesting we just build up and wait for their next attack? We can't win that way."

I leaned forward. "Newcome, you're right about that. I want to thank you all for your insight and input. But I've become convinced that we only have one course of action: We have to break through the ring and take them out. We have to do it soon, before they have time to rebuild the fleet we destroyed."

"We could have just stayed out there in the Thor System if we were going to have to fly back," Jasmine said.

I glanced at her. Her mood had deflated again. I knew it was because we were talking about immediate, dangerous action. Was her judgment being clouded by her physical state? It was hard to tell with Jasmine. She played her cards tightly, even when her emotions were running high.

Marvin's cameras were all over Jasmine and me. I knew he was watching us closely. He knew something was up. It was irritating.

"Marvin?" I asked. "Do you have something to add?"

"As a matter of fact, I do," he said. "I think I've been remiss. I've left an element out of this discussion that I didn't realize until this meeting might be crucial."

I frowned at him. "What are you talking about? What element?"

But I realized what he was going to say as soon as I'd asked him. He was going to bring up Jasmine's pregnancy. No one else knew. Not even her doctors. Well, the nanites knew. They were the only doctors we really needed anymore, anyway.

Marvin was about to bring this up, I felt certain. He'd been looking at Jasmine oddly the entire meeting, even though she'd barely spoken. I felt a hot rush of embarrassment. Marvin was like a kid sometimes. He often said embarrassing things in public, airing the family laundry.

I tried to think of a way to head him off, but everyone was expecting his report now. How could I tell him to shut up without looking crazy?

"Prior to this meeting," Marvin said, "I'd believed the recent enemy activity was obvious and that was what this meeting was going to be about. Now, I realize I'm in the position of having to enlighten everyone present."

He'd lost me again. I now had no idea what he was talking about, but I didn't think it was the baby—not this time. I felt a surge of irritation. How was I going to tell the world I was about to have a bastard child with one of my subordinate officers? It would have every news-vid drone humming worldwide. I wouldn't be able to take a piss without causing a media sensation.

"Out with it, Marvin," I said. "What strategic element are we missing?"

"Why, the comets, of course."

"Comets? What comets?"

"They're really just chunks of ice at this point. No trails yet, they're too far out, but they're coming in fast, and our telescopes picked them up two days ago. They'll pass the orbit of Tyche in about a month."

I frowned fiercely at him. "Put up a display or something."

As if he'd prepared for this all day—and perhaps he had—he displayed a diagram on the table under our elbows. The surface we were all leaning on lit up, dropping its faux wood façade and turning into a starry background. At one end of the

145

table was the Sun, under Newcome's arms. He lifted them as if he might be burned by the glaring star.

Then Earth appeared, outlined and limed in green. That was about where Newcome's coffee cup was resting. At the opposite end of the scene, several feet away, appeared a set of seven shadowy objects. They were dim but slightly brighter than the tabletop. Looking like shadowy stones, they spun slowly on their axes. I watched them twinkle with cold light. They were very close to Jasmine, who touched them and made spreading motions.

We zoomed in sickeningly. The image became distorted, and the objects transformed into spiky balls of dark ice.

"At this distance, the imagery is an approximation," Marvin said smoothly. "Also, I've warped the scale somewhat to get everything onto this surface."

"But you're sure they're out there?"

"Yes. Check any astronomical online log. They are the focus of intense interest in the community. Surely, you all peruse such sites with regularity?"

There were blank looks all around.

"Marvin, these aren't ships," I said. "Why do you think they're a danger?"

"Two reasons—the second of which only came up today. First, it is very odd to have seven comets coming in from the Oort Cloud to the inner planets of this star system in such close proximity. It's almost as if they're flying in formation."

"Yes," said Jasmine, "but it could still be a natural phenomenon."

"Certainly. That was my theory until I noticed this. I will now time-shift the objects back two days and project their paths."

The image shifted. The objects did as well.

"They changed course..." Jasmine said.

"A slight correction. I think they will perform another such correction closer in, before impact."

"Impact with Earth, you mean?" I asked him.

"Yes."

146

We watched as he fiddled with the screen controls. I was stunned. The evidence was clear: the Macros were throwing chunks of ice at us—planet-killers.

I felt my heart begin to speed up as alarm spread through my body. How could we have missed something like this? How long would we have been in the dark if Marvin hadn't spoken up today? The thought was chilling.

"Once I saw these inbound objects," Marvin said, "it became very clear to me why the Macros sent so few ships through the Thor ring to attack us. If you subtract the length of time it took these comets to reach this position from their starting point, I would say they were launched approximately four months ago. Calculating the normal Macro rate of production for two months, the fleet we encountered in the Thor System would closely match the fleet they should have been able to build up in the intervening time."

I glared at him, full of shock and anger. I didn't like what I was hearing. None of us did.

"You're saying that there's a fleet involved here as well?" I demanded. "In addition to the comets?"

"Why yes, isn't that clear?"

"But where are the ships, Marvin?" Jasmine asked. "Are they too far out and dark to see?"

"Probably. I expect them to be hiding behind the comets, undetectable, until they get closer."

"How do you know they have ships out there at all?" demanded Newcome.

Marvin craned his cameras toward Newcome. "I employed a series of logical deductions. They sent only a few ships through the Thor ring to attack us, despite having had a very long period in which to build them. Where are the missing ships? Also, what is the source of thrust that is driving these comets? I would say the answer is clear: the ships are behind the comets and providing propulsion."

I nodded. I found his logic inescapable. I looked around the table at a circle of long faces. Everyone else was thinking the same thing: There *had* to be a fleet out there behind the comets. It made too much sense.

I looked at Marvin suddenly with a new suspicion.

"You knew this was coming, didn't you? That's why you wanted to send the probe so badly."

"Not exactly, sir."

"Explain yourself."

Marvin's tentacles lashed for a second. He must have been doing some deep thinking.

"Are you familiar with timer theory and interrupts?" he asked me finally.

"Of course, they're standard elements of any processor. But I don't see what that has to do with—"

"Indulge me, Colonel. When compared to human software, Macro programming is somewhat similar in design. They operate on the basis of preprogramed triggers—thresholds which will cause action when crossed. But they also have built-in timeouts to prevent them from getting stuck waiting forever for a trigger that doesn't come. When an expected stimulus doesn't materialize for a long period, they are kick-started into action independently."

"All right, I get that. But what has it got to do with the current situation? Are you saying the Macros sat on the far side of the ring for so long they must have been caught in an endless loop?"

"No. I don't believe they can be so easily disabled. They were up to something, I'm sure of that. I reasoned that since they couldn't be doing *nothing*, they must therefore be doing *something*. With that basis for a theory, I began to examine possible activities they could be engaged in for such a length of time. After analysis of all their possible courses of action, a long range normal-space attack topped my list. All I had to do was look for their fleet. Once we sent the probe through the ring, I knew where to look. Finding the ice chunks and figuring out their purpose was then a simple matter."

I nodded. "I see. What I'm hearing is somewhat different than your carefully spun version of events. You suspected this was coming, and yet you said nothing."

"On the contrary, I was working on an unproven theory. I have many of them—thousands in fact—that are currently under investigation. Would you like a full report on each, Colonel?"

I sighed and shook my head. I really didn't want to hear Marvin's list of predictions. I suspected most of them involved our doom.

"Very well, sir," he said when I passed.

In a tired voice, I asked my next question. "Okay Marvin. I'm willing to swallow the idea that you figured all this out only recently, but how could you *not* know we were in the dark about the comets? What did you do when you figured that out?"

"I've been studying Antarctic microbial life forms over recent days. I only left my specimens when you summoned me to this meeting. Due to my isolation under a glacier, I was unaware of Star Force Command's ignorance of the true situation."

"You were studying microbes in Antarctica?" Newcome demanded incredulously. "Under an ice shelf, no less? Why?"

Newcome was still a little new to Marvin's behavior patterns. To the rest of us, that part of the robot's story hadn't come as a surprise. Marvin had been fascinated with microbial life since he'd taken his first wobbling steps.

"The specimens are unique," Marvin said brightly. "They have a very unusual cellular structure. I wanted to preserve their evolutionary adaptations—if only in a virtual form in my brainbox."

"Preserve them?" Jasmine demanded. "Why do they need preserving?"

I knew the answer to that one.

"Because he thinks we're all going to die," I said, putting my hands to my face and rubbing my eyes. "Everyone on Earth is going to die, right Marvin? Even the microbes?"

"That is a likely outcome of the Macro attack," Marvin said agreeably.

"And when were you going to tell us that part?" Newcome demanded.

"Please keep in mind that I'd assumed you already knew," Marvin said. "The conclusions were so obvious—I didn't think all five billion of you could miss them."

His subtle way of calling us a race of dummies didn't do anything for the group's collective mood.

"Look, Marvin," I said. "In the future—if there is a future for anyone sitting here today—I would appreciate it if you would immediately relay data concerning enemy activity to us."

"So noted, Colonel Riggs."

I let out a huge sigh. "All right then. Let's get our heads around this. How long until they get here?"

"Seventy-nine days, two hours and an unknown number of minutes."

"Missed it on the minutes, did you?" Newcome asked sarcastically.

"Due to certain heat distortions and poor optical triangulation at this distance, I can't be as precise as—"

"Forget about that, Marvin," I snapped.

"Comment deleted."

"Let's talk about this new situation. We're going to be under attack in just over two months' time."

"No, sir," Marvin said. "That isn't entirely accurate. We've been under attack for several months. Most of us were simply unaware of it."

"That's great, Marvin. Just great. And how many ships do you think they have hiding behind the comets?"

"I would estimate—and I must emphasize, this is a very rough estimate, with no more than a ninety-two percent confidence rating—that they have the production capacity equivalent of four thousand, three hundred cruisers headed our way. That number could vary based on their precise fleet composition, of course."

"Of course," I echoed.

The meeting went on, but I don't remember the rest of it. We planned, we talked—but mostly we stared at those graphics depicting twirling, black chunks of ice.

It was hard to believe this fresh calamity was real. While we'd been farting around on Earth, toasting one another over our newfound peace and freedom, the machines had been out there in the cold darkness, building and building. They'd prepared for their eventual victory, even while we partied. It was an old story in the history of warfare, and the kind of trap

150

my species was apt to fall into. But now the lions were awake, and they were hungry.

The party was over.

-18-

The first thing I did after the meeting was get dressed in my finest uniform. I then made some vidscreen calls. Surprised officials climbed out of bed to take my call. When you're the ruler of a planet, no one is too busy to talk to you.

I summoned our newly hatched World Parliament. There had been an Imperial Senate, but in the dismantling of Crow's Empire, we'd dissolved it—in truth, I'd killed most of the members in the process of forcing the world to sue for peace. I'd taken that route rather than bombing cities or destroying fleets. I needed cities and fleets much more than I'd needed politicians.

Soon however, I'd figured out that politicians were like cockroaches. More always scuttled out no matter how many you stomped flat. I'd become resigned to the fact that I was going to have to live with them.

To replace the Imperial Senate, I'd created a parliament with each member state being allotted at least a single member. The number of members was fixed at a thousand, and each nation had a number of members based on their population. You'd think that China would win out in that scenario, but due to years of warfare there were surprise winners such as Indonesia. They'd had about two hundred and fifty million citizens before the arrival of the machines, and as they'd never had much in the way of military, high technology or heavy industry, they'd never been targeted. Other countries hadn't faired so well, and there were a few billion less people on Earth today than there had been a decade ago. As a result, Indonesia had forty-nine members of parliament to represent them.

"Can this be right?" I asked my handlers. "Indonesia gets forty-nine votes?"

"It is an impressive number, Colonel," said one of my people, the guy who was supposed to arrange my clothing. He had a faintly British accent, perfect hair, dark eyes and a false, insipid smile.

I hated my handlers. All of them.

They were Jasmine's idea. Sure, I knew she was correct in thinking that I needed help to look my best, but these people took it too far. They dressed me and fixed me up like some kind of plastic doll. I felt like a mannequin in a chair.

The worst part was I found myself getting used to the royal treatment. I didn't like that. I'd never wanted to be some fancy-pants guy in a suit. I'd never wanted fame, fortune or the guy I now found on his knees at my side, toying with a nickel-plated saber that didn't want to attach properly to my cummerbund.

To be certain that I never resembled Crow too closely, I made sure I wore a black uniform, cut along the lines of normal Star Force attire. It was formal, but not silly. I didn't have a chest that jingled with medals, nor was my outfit shining white as Crow's had been.

"What's with the sword?" I demanded from the sword-handling guy. "Why do I have to wear a sword at all? Whose idea was that?"

My voice might have been a trifle harsh because the poor guy looked scared. His hands leapt from my side and hovered in the air. Down there on his knees, he looked pitiful.

They all backed off in a chain reaction that had begun with the startled sword guy. The woman who'd been farting around with my hair took two steps backward. The makeup girl gasped and dropped a facial brush covered with skin-colored dust.

Even the guy standing in the corner holding my overcoat chickened. He stepped into the bathroom quietly.

The chief valet froze. He'd been the one who'd answered my question about Indonesia. He looked like I'd just strangled his kitten.

None of them said a damned word in response to my question. I realized they were terrified.

"Sorry," I said, waving them all forward again. "Don't wet yourselves. Let's just get this over with."

They approached me like I was some kind of unleashed jungle cat. After a few seconds, they started messing with me again. I endured, telling myself they were only doing their jobs.

I didn't have a good reputation. People knew I might take a punch at someone who pissed me off. Hell, I'd personally torn the head off of Jack Crow, dethroning and decapitating him in a single stroke just last year. That gem of a clip had been replayed on the evening net vids non-stop for months.

But I almost never abused normal people. It wouldn't be right. I only unleashed my physical power on Star Force people, who I knew could take a hit.

We men and women from the stars were different—almost like another breed of human. We'd spent years out there in space, and we'd changed. Our bodies and our minds weren't the same anymore. We weren't like these normal, soft folk. A nanotized marine could keep fighting with injuries that would kill a citizen outright. Knowing this, and being a rough group to begin with, we had many traditions of behavior that set us apart from the rest of humanity.

My resulting reputation was a burden sometimes. I felt like I was visiting a kindergarten class and I had to be careful about what I did and said. If the big, bad man started yelling, the kids might break down and cry.

When they'd all calmed down and gotten back to work, I noticed they were moving much faster, not touching me unless they had to, and keeping quiet. I kind of liked that part.

"Could you tell me, sir," I said, addressing the Chief Valet again. I knew he was the chief because the rest of them never addressed me directly, and he had a little nametag that identified his title. I read his nametag now, squinting to see the name. "Um, Sahir," I said.

He froze. He looked stunned to be referenced by name.

"Yes, Colonel?" he asked querulously.

"Just tell me," I said, forcing a smile. "Whose idea was it to have me wear a sword? I'm just curious. Not mad. I'm not mad at all."

His answering smile trembled a fraction. He opened his mouth, took in a breath, but then closed it again.

"I'm not sure, sir," he said.

I frowned, and he went back to work, avoiding my eyes. I didn't believe him. I'm an old bullshitter from way back, and I know one of my own when I see one.

Just then, I heard a laugh and a light clapping of hands behind me. Jasmine came in, cooing. It wasn't like her to coo, and the sound made my frown melt away.

"Turn around," she said.

"I'm not doing a spin."

"You're no fun. But you look great."

"You're sure you don't mean fabulous?" I asked, resting my hand on my sword. The hilt was right there, and it was either hold it or let it rattle when I walked.

"Oh, they put the saber on!" Jasmine said. "It looks quite good."

My lips compressed, and I nodded slowly. I had my answer now. The sword had been Jasmine's idea. I looked for that Sahir guy, but he'd wisely ducked out of the room.

Jasmine hugged me, and I ran my hand lightly over her belly. She allowed this, looking shy.

"Feel anything?" she asked, whispering into my ear.

"Not yet. Pretty soon, it will look like you've just eaten two dinners. Have you been to the doctor?"

"They already know. I'll take care of everything. Don't worry."

But I *was* worried. The machines had killed my first two kids. Why not this new one? It was a disturbing thought.

We walked together to the backstage area. Just beyond were glaring lights and an impressive lectern. I was due to give a speech there in a few minutes in the center of the Parliament chambers.

After destroying Crow's government, we'd had to rebuild the building in a new spot. Geneva was again the center of the world government but with a new, spherical building to meet

155

within. The thronged delegates couldn't see us, but we could see them. They were stacked very high, like an opera house going upward fifty floors or more. The distant dome above them was lit blue-white, as bright as a sunny sky.

I left Jasmine backstage with a kiss and walked out onto the platform.

Everyone stood and clapped. They didn't cheer and howl, but they clapped for a long time. Crow had instilled that instinct into them. I'd read that he'd often had his own senators watched during his public performances. People who sat sullenly and didn't clap had often mysteriously disappeared. The politicians had soon figured things out, and they'd given him a standing ovation every time toward the end of his reign.

That same instinct had to be in them today, I thought. I knew they didn't all love me. I ran my eyes over the crowd, which wasn't easy. There were over three thousand present. Each member of the parliament had staffers of their own, and the place was huge.

I'd started off with my arms upraised and my face wearing an indulgent smile. I walked to the lectern and lowered my arms. When I did so, the clapping died down.

"Members of Parliament," I began, "people of Earth, I come to you today as the bearer of both good and bad news."

Smiles died on a thousand faces as my words sunk in. They'd all thought I was going to announce everlasting peace had come to us and that it was all my doing. After all, the news reports were all glowing. I'd triggered a new Macro invasion and destroyed every ship they had with marginal losses. Riggs was a genius. Riggs was a hero.

So, what was this good-news, bad-news stuff? No one liked that routine. Nobody. It always meant you had something bad to tell the crowd, and that you were trying to candy it up. That was exactly what I was doing today.

I cleared my throat. "The good news you've already seen. Screen please."

Behind me, a massive display lit up. It was a hundred meters high and just as wide. A prepared vid began to play with the sound muted. It looked like some kind of action movie. There were explosions and red contacts crawling across

156

the screen. I was there at the command table shouting orders and presiding over the victory. Snippets of action were all the vids showed, pasted together by the PR people.

The audience buzzed. They were eating it up. I felt bad having to bring up the bad news now.

"The Macros attacked us, and we survived. We destroyed them rather easily, in fact. Unfortunately, their attack isn't over with yet."

The audience stilled. It was a shock. It had to be. I could see some of them, and their faces were confused. It was almost as if they weren't able to process my words properly.

"Next screen," I said with a heavy heart.

I showed them everything Marvin had shown us. I walked them through it. They stirred, and there were a few gasps, but for the most part they sat there in stunned silence. They saw new details that we'd only just gathered. We knew where the Macros ships were now, the ones hiding in the wake of those twirling chunks of ice.

"Each of these ice chunks is bigger than we'd initially realized," I explained. "They're not normal comets. Each is a planetoid, on the order of a small moon: About twenty to fifty miles across, they're quite dangerous all by themselves."

The grim drumbeat of facts fell from my mouth and beat down their spirits. I felt like some kind of harbinger of doom. Perhaps that's exactly what I was.

My staffers had argued with me, naturally. They hadn't wanted me to do this. They hadn't wanted the information to get out so soon. They spoke of panic. They spoke of depression.

But I'd told them I wasn't going to hold back information like this. I wanted people to know what was coming. I wanted them to know the real score. If humanity was about to go out like a candle flickering in the wind, I wasn't going to be the last public official to tell a big lie to everyone.

"I know this isn't the news you were hoping for today," I concluded. "But it is what it is. All we can do is defeat the machines. We have some time, as they won't be here for months. We'll prepare. We'll build up. We'll win."

157

I could tell that wasn't enough. They weren't cheering. They were hardly speaking.

"I know that every man, woman and child on this green Earth wants to keep breathing. In order to do so, we're going to have to work as we've never worked before. I have a dozen proposals here with me today. I'd like you to pull the documents up on your screens, and we'll discuss them. The budgets are huge, and the state may well go bankrupt, but I'm asking for your approval anyway. If we live, we'll figure out how to pay for it all later."

They'd heard that one before. We all had. But there it was. We were in emergency-mode now. All our means of production had to be converted to the war effort.

"I want you to know that I'm certain we'll win this fight. I've almost never lost, have I? Have confidence, give me your best, and we'll win again."

Now, finally, they were beginning to clap. The applause was scattered, however, and it quickly died.

"We have to become as cold and hard as the machines themselves. They don't feel tired. They don't get depressed. What they do is work relentlessly. We have our advantages as well. We're more flexible than they are. We learn faster and adapt. When fighting their fleet last week, I discovered they had several new technological advances. We know about them now—they won't surprise us again."

The applause was a little louder on that line, but it still died fast.

I leaned forward, gripping the lectern and looking into their faces. I didn't speak for several long seconds.

"You know," I began slowly. "I'm feeling an urge to break from the script."

I chuckled, but no one joined me.

"At this very moment, I know there are people backstage looking for a way to hang themselves, but I'm going to do it anyway. All of you people at home deserve that."

They waited quietly, and I honestly don't think any of them knew what I was about to say.

"The moment I heard about the Macros out there, spinning their webs in space, I thought of an old Latin proverb: *Si vis pacem, para bellum.* That means 'if you want peace, prepare for war.' Everyone knows the Romans were a feisty bunch, but they predicted the spot we find ourselves in today. We had a brief rest and immediately became lazy."

There was a muttering at that. They didn't like it. I raised my hand, and they quieted.

"I know many of you work hard. I know you've gone through a lot, as have I. And I know we are war-weary as a people. We just want this to end. You thought we'd achieved peace because the enemy had stopped coming. You dared hope the enemy had vanished into the night just as mysteriously as they'd first come. But that's not how it's going to be."

I made spinning motion with my hand to the stage director, suggesting she back up the vids.

"Play the second one again, please," I said.

The engineers obliged. Cold dark images of ice chunks were again displayed. They were more detailed than they had been when I'd first seen them in my conference room. After Marvin's warning, we'd put every telescope and probe we had on that part of the sky. We still couldn't make out individual ships, but we knew a lot about the comets.

"We have to defeat this threat, but we have to do more than that. We have to go out into space, find every last one of these machines, and destroy it. There can never be peace with them. You can't deal with a predator. Either it eats you, or you kill it. That's the case here. And right now, before the heavens and the people of Earth, I swear to do this. I'll go out there and kill them all—or die trying."

I don't know quite what I was thinking about as I said those words, but I meant them. Maybe I was thinking about all the dead we'd lost in this war already. Maybe I was thinking of my unborn child in Jasmine's womb, who'd never yet had a chance to see the light of day.

Whatever the case, there was real feeling in my statement. I wasn't bullshitting anymore, and they knew it, because they cheered. They finally, really stood up and cheered for me.

I smiled back tightly, wondering all the while how I was going to deliver on the promise I'd just made.

After a moment, I had the answer: I didn't really have to deliver. All I had to do was my best. I would head out to the stars and face the dragon. Either I killed it and became the hero again, or it ate me. If I lost, I wouldn't care about the rest of it. If I won, everything was grand.

I was covered either way. I couldn't lose.

Thinking that strange thought, I grinned at them and shook my fists over my head with absolute confidence.

The crowd loved it, and they cheered harder than ever.

-19-

After my speech was over and I walked off the stage, I think the only person on the planet who wasn't smiling, shaking my hand and congratulating me was Jasmine. She looked worried. I knew why, of course, but I pretended not to.

"Hey, honey, how'd you like the speech?" I asked her.

"It was definitely…uplifting."

"Great! Glad you loved it. Everyone seemed to. You know, I wasn't even quite sure what I was going to say until I got up there. Ah sure, I had my teleprompter, but I can't stick to those things. After a while, I got on a roll and went with it. Turns out my instincts were good this time."

"Kyle," she said, frowning, "what exactly did you mean when you said—"

"Look," I said, leaning close and lowering my voice. "It was just a speech. Every politician makes big promises. People *expect* that! Especially when you're up on stage delivering bad news. For starters, I gave them something to fear, and when you show people their approaching doom, you have to give them hope, too. I showed them terror approaching from the skies, then I offered up the light of salvation a moment later. How could I have done anything else?"

"Yes…but the details concern me. I heard you promise the world that you would fly out there and destroy the Macros personally. Don't tell me I didn't hear that."

I looked her in the eyes and decided to stop trying to bullshit my way past her.

161

"I'm calling a meeting with my personal staff to discuss this. You're on the list. Be there in thirty minutes."

I walked off toward the transport shuttles. I could feel her eyes following me.

I knew what she was thinking, and I knew she wasn't happy. Like many women who are attracted to brave, dangerous guys, she'd finally landed one. The trouble was, the moment she had me, she wanted to change the very behavior that made her want to mate with me in the first place. She was going to have my child now, and she wanted me to play it safe from here on out.

I understood how she was feeling, but I was going to have to disappoint her. We weren't living in peaceful times. Not yet, anyway. If the Macros had stayed on their side of the ring for the next half-century, maybe we could have all enjoyed a golden era of peace. But they hadn't.

At the meeting, everyone was smiling except for Jasmine. She had her arms crossed, and she didn't look at me.

I let out a tiny sigh then tried to ignore her.

"We have to hit the Macros as soon as possible," I said, starting off the meeting with a bang.

They blinked and quieted. I'd taken them all by surprise. Even Jasmine was looking at me again, but her arms were still crossed.

"Hit them?" she asked. "But their fleet is so far out. What are we going to hit them with? We've been planning a build-up I know, but—"

"No," I said. "That's not what I meant. I'm not talking about the fleet they have crawling slowly toward us in normal space. I'm talking about flying out to the Thor System. We have to breach the ring we've never managed to breach. Once through, we have to destroy their base, their production facilities—everything. And we have to do this immediately, using only the ships we have now."

"What?" Jasmine asked. "Why? We only have two months before—"

"No, we don't," I interrupted her. "We have two months to build up our defenses here at home. But we have to take our entire fleet out there, fight our way through the ring, destroy

162

everything and return before that time has passed. We'll need the ships back here in our home system to face the Macros when they reach Earth. The trip out to the ring and back will take nearly a month as it is, plus whatever time it takes to clean out their bases. We fly tonight."

They fell silent. In this quiet moment, Miklos leaned forward.

"This does not sound like a carefully worked out plan, sir," he said tactfully.

"It's a strategic goal, not a plan," I snapped. "What I need from all of you is help working out the details."

Marvin was crouching at the far end of the table. He had perked up after my unexpected announcement and the excitement it had generated. He now had two cameras on every face around the table. I knew he was enjoying their reactions in his own weird way.

"Colonel," Marvin said, addressing me. "I find your plan intriguing. How do you plan to get through the ring without being destroyed?"

"I was going to leave that up to you, Marvin," I said. "You're my best technical mind."

"I accept the challenge."

I was happy to have one enthusiastic member of the team signing on. I looked around the rest of the faces, but I didn't see anyone else volunteering their best ideas. Instead, they looked stunned.

"Sir," said Jasmine, and it sounded to me as if she was having trouble using that word. "I don't understand the necessity for this proposed action. Could you please explain it to us?"

It was a reasonable request, so I nodded.

"You all remember the Cold War, don't you? At least what you learned about it in school? Russia and America were toe-to-toe, eying one another for decades. The entire planet was wondering who would blink or throw a punch first. They never did opt for Armageddon, thank God. Unfortunately for us today, the machines have decided to go for it."

163

I tapped at the table, and the surface lit up in instant response to my touch. The screen depicted the Sun, the incoming comets and various planets, including Earth.

"Marvin, add in your best estimates for the enemy position and numbers."

Marvin froze for a fraction of a second, his tentacles and cameras stuttered, then they went back to their usual ceaseless roaming.

Thousands of tiny red dots appeared on the tabletop. There were so many they formed a single glowing mass. The enemy ships followed the comets like shadows.

"This is only an approximation," he said. "Actual data will be sparse until they come closer."

"Have you seen any actual ships yet?" Jasmine asked.

"Yes," he said.

We all looked at him in surprise.

"It happened during your speech—the first sighting. The data has not yet been released to the public. I gleaned it from telemetry returned by the farthest probes."

"When were you going to tell us this, robot?" asked Gaines, speaking up for the first time.

"When I was called upon to speak during this meeting," Marvin told him, steering an extra camera his way. "Essentially, this is the exact moment during which I'd planned to disseminate the new information."

"How many ships have we seen?" Jasmine asked in a weak voice.

"The count rises steadily. We are up to six hundred and ten contacts, but the number increases every few seconds. Using the best of our new optical instruments—interferometers in orbits out past Pluto—we've been able to get a fix and focus tightly enough for visual data. Radar has not been applied nor any other form of active sensor. We don't wish to alert them by pinging their ships."

"No, we don't," I said. "Now, what was I talking about?"

"Armageddon," Marvin said in a perky tone. "I believe that was the last topic brought up."

"Right," I said. "Russia and America might have gone after each other and destroyed one another at any time. But they

164

didn't. Part of the reason why was a concept they called M. A. D.: Mutually Assured Destruction. If one side launched, the other side would return fire, and everyone would lose. This fear of retribution maintained a tense standoff that lasted for many years."

I had every eye on me now, with the exception of Marvin's roving cameras.

"In our situation, things have gone differently," I said. "The Macros have launched the attack that never came in the Cold War: An all-out attempt to destroy our world. But by doing so, they've left their own home base undefended."

"Why do you think they've left their base undefended?" Miklos asked.

"Marvin has calculated their industrial output in terms of ships and troops. Adding up what they threw at us out in the Thor System with what we're seeing heading toward us in normal space now—that's about all they've time to build."

"But you don't really *know*," said Jasmine with sudden feeling.

"No, we aren't one hundred percent certain. They could have other star systems, other fleets—hell, they might be fighting other wars out there with other species. But measuring by their past behavior patterns and their standard rate of construction, they seem to have thrown everything into this final knockout punch. We have no choice but to take advantage of that."

I looked around the group. They were digesting my words and staring at the red mist of enemy ships.

"I agree with you, Colonel," said Miklos suddenly. "We have to do it. I don't know if it's possible, but we have to try. You can't win a war by sitting in your base defending against attacks forever. Eventually, the enemy is going to get through. The only way to win is to carry the battle to the enemy's turf and fight on his territory."

I nodded. "That's how I see it. Let's have opinions. What do you think, Marvin?"

"This sounds like a technical challenge. Fortunately, I have the experience and expertise to make the attempt. I've already managed to get a probe through the ring into Macro space, and it survived for approximately ninety-five nanoseconds."

I chuckled. "That long, huh?"

"The data has been verified."

"We'll have to do a little better than that if we're to stay alive long enough to destroy their bases," Gaines pointed out.

"This conversation sounds insane to me," said Jasmine with uncharacteristic emotion. "How are we going to get through that ring? We've never managed to send anything through that could survive for even a single second."

I put my hand to my chin and rubbed it. "We could send them a nice care package."

Gaines perked up. "Something like a really big bomb?"

I nodded.

"I'll start working on that solution path, Colonel Riggs," Marvin said excitedly.

"You do that, Marvin."

The conversation went my way once Miklos had signed on. With Marvin, Miklos and me united, the others folded their cards. They had plenty of objections, naturally, but they didn't amount to anything. Sure, we might fail. Sure, it might be impossible to shoot our way into the enemy system, but we had to try. It was the only way to win this—to end this endless war.

They did get me to back off on the launch date. They just couldn't pull all the ships and crews together into a single coherent task force that quickly. Some ships were in dry dock being repaired or upgraded. Certain critical personnel were on leave, but most importantly, all our ships weren't in one place. They were scattered, and I wanted us flying together like a single fist heading out to meet the enemy. To meet up with a surprise Macro Armada coming out of that ring with our forces broken into small formations could spell disaster.

One asset everyone was fighting over was Marvin himself. I had to take him with me to help come up with a way to breach the ring, but other people had their own ideas concerning what he should be doing.

"Sir," Miklos began again, "it is critical that we deploy gravity cannons similar to the one Marvin created in the Thor System to handle this new oncoming threat."

"I get that," I said. "But you're going to have to engineer it without Marvin's help. He'll be hitting the Macros with me."

"But what if he's destroyed?" Jasmine asked.

Marvin's cameras perked up like a German Shepard's ears in response to her question.

"Do you think that's likely?" he asked.

Jasmine glanced at him. "Failure is always a possibility. Just ask the Crustacean population in the Thor System."

"That would not be possible. There are no longer any Crustaceans living in the—"

"That's my point, robot. That operation was a failure, and they all died."

"Oh," Marvin said. "I understand your reference now. File updated."

"Look," I said, getting angry. "First of all, they didn't *all* die. They have a viable population doing well on Eden-6. Besides which, we aren't going to fail."

"But it is a matter of timing, sir," Miklos said. "We don't have much time to duplicate Marvin's work."

I shook my head. "I refuse to believe all of Earth's engineers can't do what he did in just a few weeks. You'll have the benefit of his data and designs. We'll give you the blueprints."

"Still, I don't think that—"

"What do you want me to do? Clone Marvin? Make a copy of his brain?"

Everyone paused at that idea. The moment I said it, I regretted it. That was something Sandra had warned me against, and I have to admit I was still in agreement with her on that point. She'd wondered if humanity would become redundant if a machine intelligence like Marvin became commonplace.

I'd immediately seen that she had a good point. In all our limited travels throughout the universe, we'd met up with two types of sentient beings. One type was alive, and the other type was made up of sophisticated machines. In every case except for one, these two forms of being were in conflict. Only Marvin, so far as I knew, worked with living creatures. All the other intelligent machines were out to destroy us.

167

I didn't want to risk creating a new species of robot that might compete with my race in the future. We'd seen enough of that already. The Blues had apparently made that mistake already—twice.

"That's an intriguing concept, Colonel Riggs," Marvin said. "I have considered it before, in fact."

I looked at him warily. We all did. Marvin was not entirely under our control. He wasn't under *anyone's* control. For all I knew, he'd already gone off somewhere and spawned a brood of mini-Marvins.

He studied us, and we studied him. I didn't say anything. I did wonder just exactly what he was thinking at that moment. What was he *really* thinking?

"As I said," he continued after a moment. "I considered the idea, and I discontinued the project."

I heard a few sighs of relief.

"Why, Marvin?" asked Gaines.

"I suppose one might call it a matter of pride. I rather enjoy being a unique creature. If I copied myself, I would no longer be one of a kind, and there is the fact that if I did it once, my copy would be likely to do it again. Imagine, countless Marvins running around. It doesn't bear thinking about."

I squinted at him, trying to follow his logic.

"So…you want to remain a species of one so that you don't have any competition?"

"Exactly," he said. "You got the concept immediately. I'm impressed as usual, Colonel Riggs. You see, if there were two Marvins, would they both be invited to this meeting? Would they both be members of Star Force? What would be the second Marvin's name? With living beings, these matters are simpler. You create a child, but that child isn't an exact copy, and it is behind you in time and social stature. That wouldn't be the case with my offspring. They would be as competent as I am the moment I made them."

I chewed the inside of my cheek then nodded. "I think you've made the right decision in that case, Marvin," I said.

Internally, I was hoping he never changed his mind on this point.

"Miklos will have to build his gravity cannons without you," I said. "You are the single robot in all of Star Force, and the most accomplished scientific mind on my team. There's only one Marvin, and that's plenty."

Marvin beamed—which, for him, consisted of lifting his outlying cameras higher and increasingly the idle motion of his tentacles. I was glad to see he liked the praise. I wanted to heap it on higher, but I didn't want my tactic to become obvious.

None of us wanted more Marvins around. It was important that he agree with us on that point—and that he thought it was his decision.

-20-

It took more than two days to pull the fleet together. In fact, it took several days. I decided to help with some of the engineering problems while we waited.

I assigned Marvin to get a team together and teach them how to make new gravity weapons like the one he'd built out in the Thor System. They'd have to place them near Sol, and I gave them permission to tear up the surface of Mercury to gather mass to be converted into stardust. There wasn't any other source of matter close enough.

I had to wonder as I signed the orders that doomed one of our few planets if some preservationist society would hang me in effigy for this someday. I shrugged. If enough humans were still around after the coming battle to second-guess me, I'd done my job right.

Like Marvin, I pulled together an engineering team. Mine was located on Andros Island, the traditional headquarters of Star Force.

I liked being back in the tropics. It felt homey. I'd been away for so long, I took a few hours each day to stroll on the island's beaches, but those hours were rare and stolen.

I walked the sands with a recorder at my lips. Any thought, any notation was dictated into it and translated into text for later perusal. I worked even while I was supposed to be relaxing.

My engineering people were mostly young, fat-brained kids out of the best companies and institutions. I had a few older professor-types, but most of them had barely seen the ink dry on their second Ph. D.

"Let's talk about handling the comets themselves first," I said, "as we can see exactly what they have in that department. What do we have to do to blow those things down?"

"Shoot them down?" asked one guy, a skinny kid with hunched shoulders and a twitchy face.

"It's not that simple," another, older fellow with a full beard said. He couldn't stop tugging on that beard. "Remember the Shoemaker-Levy comet of 1994? It hit Jupiter, and it broke up before impact. If anything, it did more damage in twenty-one pieces than it would have done as a single mass."

"What's your solution then?" I asked him.

The older fellow with the beard shrugged.

I glared at them all. This was how it had been going for hours.

"All I'm getting is resistance and lists of fresh problems," I told them. "I'm interested in *solutions*, people! The next guy who opens his mouth to give me something new to worry about is getting shot."

I pulled out my sidearm and placed it on the table in front of me. Every eye in the place zoomed in on it. I didn't have any takers.

Finally, a hand from the back timidly rose up.

"What have you got?" I demanded.

"If we can destroy the enemy comets far enough out and break them into small chunks, the sun should burn them up before they reach us. Comets are really trails of melting vapor. The reason we don't see them when they're far out in the Solar System is they're stable. When they get in close, they start to boil away."

I nodded thoughtfully. I reached out, picked up my sidearm and watched everyone wince. I put it away slowly.

"That's a good idea," I said.

Visible relief swept the nerd colony.

"Let's work with that concept," I said. "We'll break the comets down into small chunks. Small chunks of ice have more surface area and therefore melt faster when heat is applied. Let's assume we managed to break them up as much as

Shoemaker-Levi was broken up when it hit Jupiter. In that state, how long before the individual pieces melt down to something we can handle?"

I looked around. They all had their computing devices out and were tapping at them like mad. They seemed much happier now that they had a physics problem to work on. That sort of thing could be solved. I'd learned over time that engineers preferred a straightforward question with a quantifiable answer. Open-ended designing, on the other hand, was the realm of programmers. Many people had trouble doing one or the other, even though, to outsiders, it all looked like the same sort of incomprehensible scribbling. This group leaned toward the math and engineering side of the house.

"Anyone got a calculation for me? Let's go!" I clapped my gauntlets together, causing a booming report to echo from the walls. They all jumped. I'd learned that one from Kwon.

The original kid who'd presented the idea lifted his hand again. I stabbed a finger at him.

"These numbers aren't solid, sir. There are so many variables, and we'd want to be very sure given the stakes—"

"Come on, come on. Just give it to me."

"I'd say we'd have to take them out at about thirty AU— that's about as far away as the orbit of Neptune."

"Good," I said, "now we have a goal. Let's move on to how we can achieve that goal. What kind of force, how many warheads, what megatonnage? That's what I need to know."

The kid's hand was up again. He looked scared. I waved for him to speak.

"What if I'm wrong, sir? It was only a quick estimate. I don't want—"

"Son," I said, chuckling. "Don't worry about that. If you screwed up, these guys will let you know it very fast. They hate you right now for beating them to the answer. Their pride is stung. They would love to prove you wrong."

The kid looked around at his colleagues questioningly.

"And that's a good thing," I added. "That's how we engineering types get it right. We check one another's work. We compete to be right. We hate to be wrong, and we hate it when the next guy looks smarter than we do, even for a second. All our pride is wrapped up in our big brains."

There were smiles and a few laughs at that.

I smiled back briefly.

"So, to get on with it... How are we going to break down these massive chunks of icy death before they get past Neptune?"

They worked, and I rode them, and the process went all day long. When dinnertime came, I called in food. There was lots of protein in the form of meat and lots of caffeinated drinks. I gave them all they could swallow.

After dinner, the nightshift began. A few of them looked uncomfortable. I could tell they were wondering just when they might be allowed to go home.

"Getting tired?" I asked one yawner at about nine pm.

She nodded.

"Have any kids at home?" I asked her.

Surprised, she shook her head.

I walked among them. They tensed up as I passed them and shied away from contact with my person. I didn't blame them. I had that over-developed body-builder look going on. The nanites and microbes had worked on me, sculpting me even if I never hit the gym. Since I did work out regularly, I was quite capable of killing everyone in the room with my bare hands before they could do anything about it. They knew this, and they acted like a tiger was stalking down the rows of seats, lashing its tail. I did nothing to dissuade them from this impression.

"Do any of you have kids?" I asked again, loudly.

A smattering of hands went up.

"Good," I said. "If you don't have kids, think of your neighbor's kids, or your sister's kids—or if you don't like kids, think about your sex partner—even if her last name is .jpeg."

This line got a laugh. It always did.

"Think of someone you don't want to see die, because that's why we're here, and we're not quitting until midnight. After midnight, the weenies can go home to bed. If you still feel good, you can stay and keep going. Keep in mind we'll start again at 0900 tomorrow no matter how you feel. When you get up, don't bother eating breakfast. It will be waiting for you here. Just take a shower, pull on clothes and head for the office. I'll be waiting."

They shut up after that. No one talked about going home. Midnight came and went. By three a.m., most had left, and I chased the rest out. I wanted them to be able to function in the morning. I didn't need them burned out—not yet.

After three days, I had my nerds herded into a corner. They had a solution, and it was a good one. The data had been checked out, and simulation programs had been written, tested and retested. I knew how much firepower I was going to need to smash those comets down to manageable size. By the time the comets reached Earth's orbit, they'd be granules of ice like a fine mountain mist.

The numbers were alarming. I took them to my office and summoned Miklos. When he arrived, he looked them over then shot me a shocked expression.

"We can't do this, sir," he said.

"We have to."

"There has to be another way."

"Sure," I said, grumpy after days with little sleep. "We could just let the comets fall as they may. Let them extinguish all complex life on Earth. I'm sure a few microbes will survive to kick start the next era."

"But sir," he said, looking back at the tablet I'd handed him. "This will take every missile we have—and every fissionable device we can build in the time remaining."

I nodded tiredly. "I figured as much. But those are the numbers. Now, I want you to draw up Fleet orders. We'll have to take missiles off the cruisers and carriers. We'll have to transport them to bases. My task force will fly to the Thor System without a single missile aboard."

"Why, sir? You should be back weeks before the Macros get within range."

"Because I don't want any of them fired. When we face the macros, the fleet people are going to use the missiles if they have them aboard and they think their ship is going down. It's only natural. We have to take that opportunity away from them."

174

Miklos frowned fiercely, but nodded. He began to work on the orders.

"We should not be so far behind in our production," he said, shaking his head. "How did we let ourselves get in this position? We could have had a bigger stockpile."

I took a deep breath before answering him and looked out my office window. It was so thick it could repel a fifty-caliber round—not that anyone on this island should want to kill me. I knew the glass was impregnated with nanites too, which would form a reactive armor against shattering. If a sniper did try to take me out, he'd have to have a custom-made gun, and he'd have to fire it fast, and he'd have to keep hitting the exact same spot while I stood still to penetrate that glass. If he screwed up any part of that formula, the nanites would rebuild the glass, *uncracking* it.

I'd watched the windows being tested. The process was a strange one. Shattered glass became whole again, and it had felt like I was watching a slow-motion film in reverse.

"We took Earth back from the Imperials only last year," I said. "Remember? We had an entire world to organize and rebuild. We can blame ourselves now for not building up to face the Macros, but it won't get us anywhere. Let's just do it right this time. We won't get another chance."

"Yes sir."

The next day, I took a transport up into space. I left Miklos behind, telling him he would have to look after Star Force in my absence.

I took Jasmine with me as my exec. Thankfully, she didn't argue when I gave her the assignment. She just kissed me hard and whispered: "At least we'll be together, no matter what happens."

"We'll drink a bottle when we win," I said, giving her a firm, confident smile that I didn't feel at all.

She shook her head, smiling. "I won't be drinking with you."

For a second, I didn't get it at first, then the light bulb went on. "Oh right, the kid. Okay, then…we'll drink juice or something."

She laughed.

-21-

The flight out from Earth wasn't like previous sorties into the blue. Star Force wasn't heading into harm's way to save some sorry aliens on another planet this time. We weren't heading out to do battle in the traditional sense, either. Our mission was to *exterminate* an old enemy. To destroy their nests, villages, factories—whatever you want to call them—before they could do the same to us.

It occurred to me, as I stood on the bridge of my flagship, that both the combatants might just kill one another off in this struggle.

For the Macros, their factories were like their queen-mothers, they were the machines that gave birth to all the others. What if we did manage to find those factories and destroy them all? What if in turn they killed our planets and populations? We'd both die out after that, mortally wounded and unable to recover...

I shook my head, squared my shoulders and harshly drove those thoughts from my mind. If I was sure of one thing, it was that the enemy wasn't entertaining any sappy musings while staring at these same stars. They were coldly calculating their best moves in order to win. No deeper thoughts would ever cross their circuitry.

While we left the Solar System, crossed the Alpha Centauri System and eventually reached Helios, I spent most of my time marshaling my forces. We had quite a fleet. The core of it consisted of fifteen carriers, fully loaded with over a hundred fighters each. Protecting them were several hundred battleships, cruisers and a host of smaller craft.

We all glided through space together. Behind the main fleet were no less than forty transports—newer, armored and fast-moving ships. They weren't like our old transports, which were knock-offs of Macro designs that had resembled cans of tennis balls. These newer ships were built to not only house troops but also to deploy them in battle. One of our more effective techniques included the launching of marines as small independent fighters. We had about thirty thousand marines: a mix of Centaurs and humans. For once, the humans outnumbered the Centaur troops ten to one. I found them easier to manage. The marines were both my ground forces and my last-ditch space force. If it came right down to it, I'd deploy them outside their ships to destroy the enemy in close quarters.

After I felt I had our formations, supplies, organizational structure and basic tactical plans worked out, I headed to Marvin's module to see how he was doing. Mostly, I wanted to know if he'd solved the problem of getting past the impenetrable ring.

One trick all commanders learn over time is to delegate responsibility. I'd had trouble doing this early on and had micro-managed everything. Being the de-facto emperor of Earth had forced me to learn how to step back and let others do their jobs. Realizing I couldn't be everywhere at once, I'd ordered Marvin to come up with a way to breach the ring. I'd given him every resource I could and stepped back. It'd been more than a week since we'd planned the mission so I figured it was time to check in and evaluate his progress.

All smiles and innocence, I traveled down the echoing passageways to the stern of the vessel. There, in a hump-like module we'd added to the spine of the battleship, was Marvin's laboratory.

The door melted open at the touch of my glove – one of the advantages of being the commander of the entire fleet. This door was bigger than most on the ship, a circular affair, some fifteen feet in diameter.

As it opened, it changed color from silver to a tin-yellow then disintegrated into a metallic mist. I stepped inside and had a look around.

It only took a few seconds for my smile to be replaced by a frown. Sometimes, the old adage about ignorance being bliss was all too true.

I don't know what I'd expected to find in Marvin's lair. Maybe a facsimile of one of the rings or a shiny chrome gizmo—something cool-looking and high-tech, I guess. Instead, I found the all too familiar-looking and rather grungy sac of shivering liquids. The sac was huge and long, looking like the intestinal tract of a prehistoric behemoth. Windows had been cut into the tank of organic soup at several key locations to allow observation of the contents.

I didn't need to peep inside those windows to know what I'd see. He had microbes in there—probably the intelligent kind.

Glaring around the chamber, which was festooned with various other pieces of equipment, I saw little else that looked useful. I clanked to the center of the room, looking around for Marvin himself. I heard, rather than saw, the telltale rattle of uncoiling tentacles behind the organic tank. Marvin was often given away by his tentacles. He seemed to be unaware of their activity when he wasn't using them, much as a man might tap his foot or twitch nervously. Marvin's tentacles rasped and clicked constantly when they weren't doing anything else—especially if he was nervous.

"I see you back there, robot," I said sternly.

"Nice of you to drop by, Colonel Riggs."

He rose up as I watched, climbing the hull of the ship behind the organic tank until he was poised above it on the ceiling, like a spider hovering over its struggling kill. "In the future, however, it might be more polite to announce the timing of your visits."

"So you could clean up the contraband, huh? That's not going to happen. A commander has access to every corner of his flagship at all times."

"That's not strictly true, sir. Star Force protocol stipulates that a male officer is not permitted to walk in on a female crewmember at an inappropriate—"

"All right, I've heard enough. What the hell are you doing in here? You aren't supposed to grow a colony of Microbes. Explain yourself."

There was a pause during which Marvin threw his cameras wide, trying to get a reading on my mood.

"Are you feeling well, Colonel?"

"No, I'm feeling pissed off," I told him. "Now answer my question."

"You specified during our briefing that I'd be given a laboratory facility and allowed to do whatever scientific work was required in order to accomplish my mission: Namely, the breaching of the impregnable ring."

"No I didn't."

"Shall I play the recording, sir?"

I fumed. "No. I might have said words to that effect, but that didn't countermand everything else I'd ever forbidden you to do."

"I think we've had this argument before, Colonel."

I frowned, thinking about it. We had, and he'd won in the end. But I wasn't through giving him a hard time yet.

"What are you doing to these poor microscopic bastards in the tank?"

"There is no cruelty involved," he said. "I've discovered a procedure that allows me to euthanize small portions of the population in such a way that they experience a brief period of extreme joy before succumbing. In this way—"

"You're killing them *again*? Experimenting on them? For what purpose?"

"There are two purposes. The first is to use natural selection to create a more serious-minded population. I've discovered that, when I give the Microbes work to, do fewer than one in eleven actually participates in my project. I find that rate of obedience unacceptable, and I'm therefore seeking to improve it."

I moved to the tank and looked inside. There were big, slow bubbles, drifting clusters of what looked like see-through algae and a few cloudy lights at the top and bottom. Microbe colonies resembled dirty water, for the most part, and it was difficult to get worked up about anyone abusing them. After all, didn't humans test products on mammals that were far closer to a human in nature? Didn't we put chlorine in our swimming pools to wipe out trillions of bugs like these?

Despite those arguments, I'd always felt an urge to protect them because they were sentient.

"Marvin, I want you to stop euthanizing them."

"But they're part of my project—to break the unbreakable."

I looked at him, and he studied me in return.

"You're bullshitting me," I said.

"Not so."

"How, exactly, does killing off pleasure-seeking Microbes help you break through into Macro space?"

I knew, of course, that I shouldn't even ask the question. To do so was to fall into whatever trap Marvin had assembled for me. But I did it anyway because I was curious, and desperate. Marvin *had* to get us through that ring to the Macro bases beyond. If I really thought torturing Microbes would get us there, I'd probably let him kill the entire genus, God help me.

Marvin detached himself from the ceiling and slithered down closer to the tank. He wrapped some of his tentacles around it almost lovingly. I thought I saw the cloudy waters swirl slightly in response. Did they know he was out there in dangerous proximity?

"Colonel Riggs, do you have any pointless pastimes that help you think, relax and which serve to stimulate your cortex?"

I blinked at the question. "Um, I suppose. I play pool sometimes."

"Yes. You also drink alcohol and frequently seek sexual encounters."

"What has that got to do with—?"

"Everything," he said. He gave the tank a gentle squeeze with a loop of his longest metallic tentacle. "Manipulating this tank relaxes my mind. By defocusing my thoughts, I'm able to put my subconscious mind to work. That often gives me critical ideas that help me solve complex problems."

I squinted at him. "So you're telling me you have a subconscious mind?"

"I have co-processors that operate independently of my primary processor. You have the same system, the only difference is yours are organic in nature and rather haphazardly organized."

"Okay," I said slowly. "I think I'm getting what you're saying. Torturing these little guys and training them to do tricks is fun for you, the way caring for a fish tank or a cat might please a human. Right?"

"Correct. Your analogies are uncharacteristically appropriate."

"All right," I said, "you can keep your pets for now. But try not to kill them off all the time, okay Marvin? It's disturbing to humans."

"Permission confirmed and documented," Marvin said.

I knew my voice had been recorded forever. I doubt anyone possessed more damning evidence of every wrongful thing I'd approved than Marvin did.

"You still haven't told me if you've solved the problem yet."

"I believe that I have," he said.

I stared at him for a shocked moment. "You *what*? You've solved it? When? Why didn't you tell me?"

"I solved it before we left, actually. The answer was quite simple. I'm surprised you didn't come up with it yourself."

In an instant, I understood the situation. He'd given me a song and dance about torturing Microbes for relaxation and to help him think. I'd given permission, in order to complete a critical project. With permission secured, he'd revealed his work was done. No doubt he'd now request a reward for finishing ahead of schedule.

As these thoughts surged through me, I felt myself getting angry all over again. Marvin was good at that. He could work you up, calm you down, then do it all over again in the space of a single conversation.

"Just tell me what the hell the answer is," I said, gritting my teeth.

"I'm detecting a rise in your blood-pressure, Colonel Riggs. Is that response an indication of joy and excitement?"

"Something like that."

"As I said, the answer is very simple. We're going to build a bomb. A very powerful bomb of a kind we've never built before. We'll send it through the ring and detonate it the instant it passes through the ring. Whatever system is destroying our probes on the far side will be destroyed when the bomb detonates."

"Hmm," I said, fairly unimpressed. "That sounds fine, but there were only spare nanoseconds between the crossover and the destruction of the last probe. How will the device detect when it has passed through?"

"You've placed your finger upon the crux of the problem. That tiny, but significant, detail has kept me from completing my solution."

I felt myself frowning harder, the corners of my mouth tugging downward with irresistible force.

"You don't have anything, do you? This is all a ruse to get me to let you keep tormenting your pets. I'm not falling for it, Marvin. I want details. What kind of bomb are you talking about? You said something very powerful. A nuke, right? What is so exciting about a fusion bomb?"

"I didn't specify fusion as the energy source of the explosion. In fact, fusion can't be used. The reaction would be too slow. Several millionths of a second are required for a fusion reaction to be generated. First, the fission weapon charges must go off, which depend on slow chemical compression effects of their own. Those forces in turn generate enough compression upon the core to cause a fusion effect, which—"

"Yeah, yeah, I know enough about it to know it can't beat a computer. How are you going to make it faster?"

"By not using a fission or fusion reaction. The reaction has to be faster than that—something that is almost instantaneous."

"What?"

"Are you familiar with gravitational implosions, Colonel? When matter is suddenly compressed into a collapsed form, it releases a great deal of energy. The best thing about it is the

182

lack of a necessity for rare elements. Any type of matter can be compressed and turned into something equivalent to a fusion bomb."

I shrugged. "I've read up on the theory."

"The science is far beyond the theoretical. Small amounts of collapsed matter were first created artificially at the CERN laboratories in 2015 during dark matter experiments. Since then, it has been produced many times—but always on a small scale and only for brief periods of time."

"What makes you think you can do better? What makes you think that you can make enough for a weapon?"

Marvin's tentacles whipped and curled with self-satisfaction. Apparently, I'd asked him a question he wanted to answer. Knowing this galled me, but only slightly.

"Now we get to the crux of the issue. How does one construct such a device, and how does one weaponize it? I have those answers. As you may recall, I recently manufactured collapsed materials—stardust, I think you called it, even though the name is inaccurate. The matter in question was not collapsed by a star."

I made an exasperated sound. "We call it stardust because it's like stardust. I know it didn't come from a star—at least, not recently."

"Very well, I will categorize it as one your many pointless generalizations. In any case, the stardust I've generated and the process I used to create it can be applied to separate collapsed matter from normal matter—rather like the way centrifuges separate radioactive materials from impurities, if I may be allowed to indulge in my own stretched analogy."

"Okay, okay. You'll use your gravity device and collapsed material to make something that can be imploded upon command. Then, you'll send it through the ring when you have it ready, and because the reaction is faster than other known reactions, the bomb could theoretically go off before it's destroyed by the enemy's defensive systems."

"I believe that's what I said."

I sighed. "All right, I get the essence of your plan. But let's consider the challenge of detecting the exact instant in which your device goes through the ring. It has to know when it's time to detonate. How can a sensor figure that out perfectly? Let me think… Can you time it?"

"I assume you're asking if I can set up a device connected to the object, which will cause it to detonate the moment it *should* be on the far side of the ring?"

"Right, would that work?" I asked.

"No. I've tested the theory on the way out here as this ship passed through the rings. Each time we pass through a given ring, there is a slight, unpredictable variation in the process. The moment we're transported from one ring to the next is not the same each time. I haven't managed to determine how to control the rings or to anticipate the moment they will transport a body moving through them.

One instant, a ship is in the local system, and the next it's been transferred to the target system. Unfortunately, the moment isn't always the same length of time. There can be as much as a quarter-second variance."

"That much, eh?" I said, beginning to pace.

I could see Marvin's problem. I was also less angry now as I understood he *had* been working on this problem, rather than ignoring it or playing around with his fish tank.

I stopped at the biggest window that showed the interior of the tank. I stared inside seeing the warm, yellowy lights at the bottom. Did they keep the Microbes warm, or was I looking at a source of torment for them, perhaps something Marvin had glossed over?

It didn't matter to me right then because I thought I had the answer.

I spun around to face Marvin again, pointing a finger up at him. He shrank away slightly, as if he thought I might be accusing him of something.

"I've got it," I said. "Or, at least I think I do. You can't use sensors—active or passive. By the time the data comes in, it will be too late. There wouldn't even be time to process it. And you can't get away with timing the point of departure, either. It's too random. But there is another way."

Marvin loomed closer, excited. "I'm interested in what you have to tell me, Colonel."

I looked at the tank. "I will, if you agree not to kill any more of them, Marvin. Do we have a deal?"

"Absolutely. I can almost certainly guarantee their safety in the light of a breakthrough. Part of my pattern of behavior is due to frustration. You are about to relieve me of that state—I hope."

I opened my mouth and almost gave him a lecture. I almost told him it wasn't right to take one's frustration out on living creatures. But I closed it again. Didn't I enjoy banging my fist down onto smart metal surfaces when I lost my temper? I'm sure the nanites didn't enjoy cleaning up my messes. Individual nanites probably didn't always survive the experience, either. To Marvin, microscopic entities were all the same, whether mechanical or biological in nature.

"How about this," I said. "Let's try a dead-man's switch. We'll transmit a steady signal to the probe as it passes through the ring. The moment it goes to the other side, the signal will naturally be cut off. All your device has to do is detect that it isn't getting that tone—and it detonates. The defensive systems, whatever they are, will be destroyed."

Marvin thought about it.

"A dead-man's switch," he mused. "I'm unfamiliar with that colloquial expression. I'm accessing search data...ah, I understand. The relaxation of the corpse sets off the device because it ceases to apply continuous pressure to a contact. That is a good analogy, Colonel."

"Well? Do you think it will work?"

"Yes," he said. "I think I could build a device that would detect the broken signal and trigger the device quickly enough for our purposes."

For the very first time since I'd entered his lair and begun looking around, I smiled.

-22-

The fleet crossed into the Eden System. I was glad to see that Captain Grass was back at his post, scaring the Blues with his outdated carrier.

Grass greeted me as I entered the system, and I turned down the audio until it was barely audible. Every now and then, he paused, and I made an appreciative comment. He seemed to like this and blew nice words about honor and the grand battles his people had fought alongside mine. He'd been talking about this for nearly a half-hour. I treated myself to a beer while he did so.

I was in a magnanimous mood. Marvin finally had a complete, feasible plan. Sure, it might not work, but at least we had something to work with. We'd try it, then send through a normal probe. If it didn't come back, we'd failed. But if it did...I'd take my fleet through, and there would be hell to pay inside the Macro home system.

Jasmine came into my office and frowned at me. My boots were on my desk, and I knew that annoyed her even though the nanites took care of the dirt that sprinkled from them. There wasn't much dirt on a spaceship anyway unless you landed to walk around on a planetary body, which we hadn't done since leaving Earth.

I put my hand up and touched the mute button. Captain Grass was still going, but I didn't cut him off. I wanted to let him get it all out of his system.

"What's up, love?" I asked her.

She pointed to my com-link. "Are you still talking to that Captain?"

"Yeah. I planned to give him a full hour, but I'm getting bored now."

"A full hour? What's he saying?"

"Honestly, I have no idea anymore."

Her eyes slid to the beer in my other hand. She nodded. "Well, you have another call. Something urgent is coming in from Eden-6."

"Urgent? Who is it?"

"Professor Hoon."

I frowned for a second, then recalled the name and winced. "Not that lobster we left on the water planet? What does he want?"

"I don't know," she said. "But since you've given Captain Grass over thirty minutes, don't you think you owe it to Hoon to at least find out?"

I sighed. Being the leader of a galactic alliance, or empire, or whatever it was I was running, wasn't always a good thing. People were desperate to talk to you every day about something—and they were almost always a pain in the ass.

I begged off with Grass finally, having heard more than enough about the winds on lakeshores that had first ruffled his fur as a kid, or whatever he was telling me now. He sounded a little disappointed, but less so when I told him truthfully I had another urgent call coming in.

With trepidation, I switched over to Hoon's channel. He was a Crustacean, a race of intellectual lobsters that we'd first encountered in the Thor System. When we initially met up with them, they'd fought alongside the Macros against us. Like many races, they'd been subjugated and served the machines.

I tried not to judge them too harshly for this. I'd sold our souls to the alien robots myself, once upon a time. But they hadn't signed on to our rebellion too quickly. They fought us tenaciously at first. Then they'd given us platitudes and tried to be neutral. Only when they'd realized the machines weren't going to allow their species to survive did they join us.

It had been a disaster. Trillions had died on the three lovely worlds they inhabited. Their scattered survivors had been

187

transported to Eden-6, the native world of the Microbes, where they'd begun a new life on that planet of endless tropical seas.

"Hey, Professor Hoon!" I said, going with enthusiasm from the outset. "Great to hear from you. I understand your people are doing very well on your new home planet, and I want to congratulate you on your successful migration."

Hoon's translated voice was odd, and it burbled slightly when he spoke. "I find your attitude self-serving, Colonel Riggs."

I rolled my eyes. "Just trying to be friendly. I'm always happy to take a social call from a friend. Now, what can I do for you?"

"You can return our true homeworlds to us."

I squinched my eyes. "That's going to be a little difficult. As you know, they've been irradiated and are now uninhabitable."

"We are quite aware of that. We are also aware of your unauthorized removal of the crust of one of our worlds."

I winced. So that was it. Someone had let the cat out of the bag on that point. I knew they were big on the sanctity of graves and birthplaces. I could only imagine how they felt about the steam-rolling of a billion hectares of their land whether it was irradiated or not.

"Your attitude has changed since the last time we met, Professor," I said. The last time we'd spoken, he'd been servile, treating me as a conqueror.

"We've learned much about you personally, your species, your history and your culture over the last year. We now understand that your depredations were not clever and elaborate plots. The truth is an even greater humiliation. We've discovered that you, in particular, are nothing more than a lucky incompetent: An accidental prodigy, who somehow drifted to the top of your species' social stratum during a time of unprecedented crises."

His words were true enough to cause me pain. Under normal circumstances, I would have told him off and cut the channel. But, somehow, I found I couldn't. This fellow, among all the annoying aliens I'd ever encountered, had some good reasons to chew me out. I felt compelled to listen to him.

"It was not enough that you oversaw the destruction of our species and all three of our homeworlds. In addition, you saw fit to remove a sizable portion of the mass of one of them for your own odd purposes. I can't believe that—"

I got a bright idea about then, and I went with it.

"Professor!" I interrupted. "I understand your grievances, but I have some good news. I'd like to make you an offer."

"An offer?" he asked suspiciously.

"I'd like to give you command of a Star Force ship. You might be aware of a certain Captain Grass who operates a carrier in this system. If you were given a command of a comparable nature, I'm sure you would—"

"Your suggestion is laced with insults."

I frowned. "How so?"

"To compare me to the befurred fools that live on several of the planets in this system is beyond the pale, Colonel. We aren't ignorant rutting savages that have barely risen above the status of hunter-gatherer tribes. Why would we be—"

"Participation in a joint military has no appeal for you?"

"When we rebuild our military, it will be wholly independent."

We'll see about that, I thought to myself, but I didn't say it aloud. Let the crawdad have his dreams.

"I understand," I said. "What can I do for you, then?"

Professor Hoon fell silent for several long seconds. I got the impression he was conferring with others. I hoped he didn't ask me for something I couldn't give, like another planet or a fleet of ships they could own and operate independently.

"Access," he said. "I would like the status of an observer aboard your ship, Colonel."

I made a face that I normally reserved for suddenly-encountered foul odors.

"What exactly do you mean?" I asked him.

"Let me come aboard your ship to observe you personally. I'll avoid interference with your duties. I simply would like to be aware of fateful decisions you might make in the future."

I mulled it over. I didn't think for a moment he would "avoid interference", at least not if I was about to scrape the topsoil down to the bedrock on another of his dead worlds.

189

"All right. I'll send a small ship to pick you up. You can accompany me to your former home system. I'd like to show you what we're doing out there—and why we're doing it."

"You seek to vindicate yourself?" he asked incredulously. "Very well. I accept your challenge. Send your minions to pick up my person. But keep in mind that we're watching you, Colonel. We know now of your severe intellectual and judgmental limitations. We can no longer be fooled with simple distractions."

"It will be a pleasure to have you aboard, Professor," I said with all the false politeness I could muster.

He then proceeded to grumble a bit about the presumably substandard quality of his accommodations, even though he hadn't seen them yet.

"I assure you, sir," I said. "You'll get a prime cabin with an aquatic ecosystem built in."

After he'd finally signed off, I alerted my crew concerning the impending visitation.

Admiral Newcome objected with vehemence. "But sir, we can't entertain a civilian at this time. We're heading into a war zone."

"Yeah," I said. "And I'm hoping that after the experience is over, Hoon will appreciate just what it is we do for him and all the other biotic species in this part of the galaxy."

"I've listened to him speak, sir," Newcome said. "I would count that as a faint hope."

It took two days for Hoon to arrive. I didn't swing by his planet or slow down. I just had a fighter land, pick him up then accelerate after us at max burn to catch up. By the time we reached Welter Station, he'd finally reached my ship.

"Hoon!" I shouted, arms outstretched in greeting.

Hoon was a lobster and probably the least huggable-looking guy I'd ever laid eyes on, but I did my best to greet him as an old friend.

At my side were my command people: Jasmine, Marvin, Gaines and Admiral Newcome. Jasmine was tapping at her wrist tablet. The rest looked on with frowns or bemusement.

Hoon froze as he got off the fighter and eyed me with stalks that were enclosed in a liquid-pumping suit. Crustaceans had spacesuits that were somewhat different than ours as they were an aquatic species. Water is much heavier than air so they had to wear tight, formfitting suits with circulating liquids only around their gills and various membranes that had to stay wet to function properly. The rest of the suit was wet inside, I was told, but more like a thick latex skin than one of our suits that didn't normally hug our skin so tightly. Ours were more like bags full of air.

"So soon you challenge me?" Hoon asked. "I had not expected this. Will the combat be between you and me alone, or do you require three back-up fighters, as well? I'm not sure if I should be honored that you fear me so greatly."

I faltered, frowned, and lowered my arms. My com-link was blinking, and I tapped open a private channel from Jasmine.

"Lower your arms, Kyle!" she said. "That's how Crustaceans challenge one another to a fight: they hold their claws upraised!"

My arms dropped fully to my sides immediately. I began to smile, but thought the better of it. Hoon was wildly suspicious, and anything I did might be misinterpreted.

"Sorry!" I said. "Humans often challenge one another as a way of greeting. When they're comrades, it means nothing but respect between warriors."

"You claim to be ignorant of the implications of your own actions?"

"No," I said, becoming annoyed despite my firm vows not to. "I'm trying to explain cultural variations of behavior that might be misinterpreted. I'm sorry if your people are too provincial to comprehend that other cultures might behave differently than your species' culture does."

"Apology accepted. Let us proceed to the bridge. I will begin my inspection there."

I paused, not sure how to take this guy. I was already quite certain I never should have let him come aboard.

-23-

When we finally got to the Thor System, everyone on the bridge was tired of Hoon and worried about what his reaction would be when he saw exactly what we'd done to one of his lifeless water-moons.

"I'm not overly concerned," I told Newcome.

"But sir, this is a serious diplomatic situation. There aren't too many technologically advanced biotic species on our list of allies—in fact, the only ones that come to mind are the Worms and the Crustaceans."

"You discount our best allies, then," I said. "We've got the Centaurs firmly in our camp. We once popped one of their habitats and killed millions of them. Now, we've given them back three worlds in this system, and they're repopulating rapidly. They love us."

Newcome made a face. I was starting to recognize his expressions, and this one either indicated he smelled something foul or he found my arguments simplistic. I figured it was the latter in this case.

"Colonel," he began, "I *do* discount the other races. The Centaurs are a fine folk, but they'll never be able to build their own fleet of ships. If they hadn't been given technology by the Nanos, they'd still be galloping around on their prairies, chewing grass."

"I don't appreciate that kind of interspecies bigotry in Star Force, Newcome."

192

"It's not bigotry! We have to be realistic about what our allies can and can't do. You yourself said that you should never have given Captain Grass a command of his own."

I had to admit he had me there. "What about the other biotic species? The one that's more technologically advanced than any of us?

"The Blues, sir? They count all right—but as enemies, in my book, not allies. I don't think they forgive easily, and they aren't going to help us beat the Macros, no matter what they promise."

"Hmm," I said thoughtfully. "All right, I'll concede to your points even though I don't like to hear them. What do you think we should do with the Crustaceans?"

"Try to keep them on our allied list. We can't afford not to. Of all the species we've met, I'd say they're the most like us technologically and culturally."

I stared at him for a second. "You're kidding, right?"

"Who else would you put in that category?"

"The Worms, of course. I like those crazy bastards. They like a good fight, build sensible ships and just look at their history—no one else has gone undefeated by the machines the way they have."

Newcome mulled that over. "But they're so strange. They're invertebrates with a bizarre language. Keep in mind that they really prefer to communicate with three-dimensional statues rather than simple pictographs."

"That is all the more evidence of their intellect."

"They threw out your last delegation after killing most of them."

I shrugged. "We screwed up. Listen, I'm not going to tell you that the Worms are easy to deal with. They're hotheaded and downright mean. But we're in a fight to the finish and there's no one I'd rather have in the foxholes with my troops than the Worms."

"They're barbaric, even savage at times."

"Exactly," I said. "When the chips are down, they get serious, just the way we do. I don't think the Worms love us, but they respect us and understand us. And I feel I understand them."

"Uh, he's here, sir," Newcome said, lowering his voice.

I turned and saw Hoon crawl onto the deck. His survival suit might have had a small leak as he seemed to be trailing water, and the bridge suddenly smelled like high tide.

"Professor," I said, nodding to him. "Welcome to my command center."

"It's quite small," he said, swinging his eyestalks this way and that. "This cannot be your fleet headquarters. Am I correct in assuming you haven't recovered from your last disastrous campaign?"

I frowned. This was a typical bit of attitude from the Crustaceans. They tended to insult you constantly in backhanded ways. They might ask if your personal stench was a little sharper than usual, or helpfully suggest that you should look for your brain in your other suit.

"Let me show you around," I said, gritting my teeth as I forced a smile.

He followed as I showed him the holotank, the command table, and the side centers. We had several of them, including a crew of seven who ran the ship while we were in battle. The fleet navigational center was one of our proudest achievements. We had excellent minds there, and they were always able to come up with a fast, accurate estimate concerning the feasibility of any scenario I asked them to study.

These last people seemed to interest Hoon the most.

"Scholars then, I presume?"

"Yes," I said. "There's no one at this table who doesn't have at least a doctoral degree in science or engineering."

Hoon scuttled up and examined them. They tried not to retreat, but it was difficult.

"All humans? Tell me, how many years of study does it take to become a professor on your world?"

"It varies," answered one of our engineering chiefs. "To achieve our highest level of education it generally takes nine to ten years."

Hoon made an odd sound. A polyp on the side of his suit opened and spat a thin stream of liquid. The spraying substance was thicker than normal seawater and it stank like brine.

194

"Absurd!" he said. "Our lowest-ranked professors are required to study for at least seventy-seven of your standard years before they're allowed to *attempt* their final exams. At that point, they usually fail to impress their peers and are kicked out of the institution."

My nerds looked at one another, impressed despite themselves. I was annoyed.

"Humans learn fast," I said.

Hoon wheeled on me. "Ah, I see the inference. We're therefore weak, defeated vermin, with shells only worthy of being crushed."

"I didn't say that. We gave you a planet to live on. Rebuild your civilization."

"We *are* rebuilding, but we require more territory."

I shrugged and crossed my arms. "The oceans on Eden-6 are vast. They should hold your species for centuries."

"There are many problems. Too many areas are off-limits for our colonies due to the microbial infestations. There are Star Force bases, as well, on the best of the islands."

I was frowning by this time. Sure, there were two intelligent species on one world, the Microbes and the Crustaceans, but I knew they couldn't be in conflict yet. Hoon's kind just weren't numerous enough. But that wasn't his real problem. He wanted to make a land grab—or rather, a sea grab. He wanted to kick the Microbes from their ancestral seabeds before he even needed them.

"The Microbes aren't an infestation," I told him. "It's your species that has been imposed upon them. Look at them as hosts, and be glad they're willing to put up with you."

Hoon's eyestalks bobbled.

"Perhaps I spoke in haste," he said. "Let me make a formal request: Award us the entirety of the world we now dwell upon, and you can destroy our old homeworlds if it pleases you."

I shook my head. "I can't do that. Where would the Microbes go?"

Hoon's attitude shifted once again. He wasn't the best ambassador in my opinion. He was much too arrogant and had a bad temper.

"We'll not be put on a reservation forever!" he said. "Humanity has already stolen two worlds and retained a foothold on ours. The superior species deserves the greatest share of any habitat."

"Superior species?" I asked, angry again. I decided to hit him where it hurt. "Just how many graduates did you manage to pass this last season, Hoon?"

He worked his clacking legs and rotated his body to face mine.

"You know very well our universities have all been lost!" the translator shouted.

"Oh right, of course! A painful memory, no doubt. Sorry I brought it up."

Newcome stepped to my elbow and cleared his throat.

I glanced at him.

"Colonel? Perhaps you'd like me to continue guiding our honorable guest on this tour?"

I mumbled something unintelligible about snooty crabs and waved Newcome forward. The Admiral made a big show of saluting Hoon, then led him around to show him various pieces of equipment. Newcome listened attentively and mouthed diplomatic platitudes every minute or so. The strange thing was, it seemed to be working. Hoon was calming down.

Jasmine sidled up to me, and we watched the two of them.

"He's pulling it off," she said. "I've never seen a Crustacean so happy."

"Yeah," I said. "They should give Newcome an honorary degree in kissing ass."

"That was very rude what you said—about their university. That must hurt him deeply. He may be irritating, but his people have suffered so much."

I scratched my neck and sighed. "I've said it before, and I'll say it again: I'm not well-suited to blowing sunshine around. If you want that, you need to find another guy."

"Well, apparently Hoon's found his man."

Newcome laughed, and even though Hoon didn't reciprocate, I could tell he was excited to have someone who understood his alien jokes and at least pretended to enjoy them.

At the end of the tour, they came back to us. Hoon's mood had improved. He studied the data displayed on the map with difficulty. He had to rear up and put his claws on the table so that his eyestalks could see the screen.

"Are those our planets—over there?" he asked suddenly.

"Yes, Professor," Jasmine said.

I winced, suspecting what was coming next.

"Could you bring them into tight focus? I'm having trouble manipulating this image with my foreclaws."

"We're kind of in the middle of something, Hoon," I said.

Hoon's eyestalks regarded me. I had no idea if he was glaring or just curious.

"I can do it," Jasmine said helpfully.

My eyes squeezed almost shut as she made spreading motions, bringing the images into sharp relief.

There they were, three moons circling a gas giant. Two of them were blue with liquid water while the third was shrouded in deep clouds.

"Odd. One is still overheated?"

"Something like that," I said. "Now, if you will please—"

"Ah," Hoon said. "I've found the focus button."

The scene zoomed sickeningly. Hoon's claws couldn't seem to make multiple contacts easily, but he was able to touch a single active point and effectively select an option or push a virtual button.

The moon we called Harvard swam into view in close-up. The atmosphere filled the screen.

"Can we remove the cloud layer?"

Jasmine had finally figured out what he was looking for. She looked at me with a worried expression.

I nodded to her. We'd gone this far. He might as well see what we'd done.

She tapped a control, and the system graphically bypassed the cloud layer.

Huge furrows, miles across, were revealed. These furrows ran from pole to pole and were filled with muddy, bubbling liquids. Marvin had really ripped into Harvard. He'd chosen this world over the others due to its relatively greater percentage of land masses. The seas didn't cover this moon as they did the others.

Hoon's eyestalks swept over the scene. He didn't say anything for several long seconds.

"Such a grand crime," Hoon said at last. "I had not fathomed it fully until now."

I felt a pang, a real, honest moment of sympathy for Hoon. Sure, he was an arrogant bastard who wore a shell and had strange, bluish blood, but he was hurting. I knew that if Earth had looked like that, I'd be crushed as well.

"We didn't do it for nothing, Hoon," I said. "We're here for the final push to take out the Macros once and for all. All living species will benefit. We'll have peace once this mission is over."

His eyestalks drifted up to see me. "I understand that the Macros have the same idea. Two beasts now charge at one another, but I don't know who I would rather see succeed. Perhaps you will both gut one another and be left dying."

"You forget yourself," I said. "We count your people as allies now."

"Yes," Hoon said, "allies of convenience—but let's not equivocate. You're my conqueror, and that reality is my greatest humiliation. I request permission to retire to my quarters, my simplistic overlord. My suit is a burden, and I don't wish to remove it here. I would be forced to taste your foulness with my exposed membranes."

"Yeah, good. I don't want to smell you anymore, either. You have permission to get off my bridge."

When he'd humped away, Newcome heaved a big sigh. "I thought I had him in a better mood. Sorry, sir."

"Not your fault," I said. "You didn't tear up his dead world."

When Newcome went back to his team, Jasmine came close to me.

"You could have been a little more compassionate," she said. "Hoon is bitter about his losses. Anyone would be."

"Yeah, I know," I said. "If Earth looked like that, I'd be complaining, too. But something about him irritates the hell out of me. He wanted me to give him an entire planet. Can you believe that?"

"There's something else," she said. "Marvin's been trying to reach you. He keeps talking about testing a dead man—something like that."

I frowned at her for a moment then rushed for the main passageway. We had a null gravity field active in the passage to make freight easier to transport, and I had to use the handles lining the walls. I propelled myself down the spine of the ship, hand over hand.

"Marvin?" I shouted into my com-link when he finally responded to my channel requests. "Don't do anything until I get down to the lab."

"Do anything?" Marvin said. "I've been working steadily to achieve my command-approved goals. These new instructions are nonsensical."

"You know what I mean. Don't launch anything until I get there. I want to see what you're planning."

"Oh, are you referencing the test? The bomb is already underway. I wouldn't worry about it, Colonel. Although it is fully functional, the test device is quite small in size compared to the one—"

"Where did you send it, Marvin? Where's the bomb headed?"

"Fortunately, we're passing near an appropriate testing site now. Harvard is quite close and as the world has already been devastated by—"

"No, no, no! Don't bomb Harvard! Don't you have any compassion? We have Professor Hoon aboard."

"Compassion? Is Hoon visiting Harvard? I'm not quite sure I understand—"

"Just turn off the test. I want it stopped now!"

"But Colonel—"

"No arguments. Just send the kill signal this instant."

"Done."

I sighed in relief, and soon after I reached Marvin's lab module. I touched the membrane of nanites and stepped inside as they retreated away. Marvin loomed on the ceiling again, and he seemed quite cheery.

"Can we retrieve your test bomb?" I asked him.

"Certainly not. The conversion of mass to energy is nearly one hundred percent when a gravity device detonates. I thought I'd made that point clear when—"

"Marvin," I said, stalking forward. "Are you saying the bomb already went off?"

"Detonation occurred an estimated forty seconds ago."

"What about the kill-signal? Didn't you send it?"

"Of course."

I stared at him for a second before I realized what he meant.

"You sent the signal, but it was too late. Is that what you mean?"

"Yes. We are now about a light-minute from the target. The signal could not catch the device. I sent the signal as ordered, but there was never enough time to stop the bomb."

I sighed and sat on a pump. The pump vibrated my suit. I saw tubes leading from it to the massive, shivering, sweating tank of Microbes that hung from the back wall of the lab.

"Marvin, don't send any more bombs anywhere without asking my permission?"

"I feel compelled to point out that, in this case, I already had your implicit approval due to your previous orders."

"I know that. Just don't bomb anything else without checking with me, will you?"

"Absolutely, Colonel. Now, I must ask that you allow me to leave the ship. I need to go to the sun factory orbiting the star Loki and manufacture a new, much larger bomb."

"Permission granted. Just don't blow anything up or launch anything until I give you explicit instructions to do so."

"Protocol updated."

I left him then and headed back up the passageway. I moved much more slowly this time, wondering if Hoon knew yet that we'd dropped an experimental bomb on his torn-up ex-planet. If he did, I knew he'd take it as an insult, a final stick-in-the-eye, and probably relate it to our earlier discussion.

I was left with an inescapable conclusion: robots made terrible diplomats.

-24-

Professor Hoon never learned about the bomb. He hadn't been on the bridge at the time, and he didn't have a lot of close friends among my crewmen. No one had made the special effort it would take to inform him. Probably no one wanted to hear another of his windy complaints any more than I did.

We cruised warily up to the last ring in the Thor System. It was strange eyeing a ring without knowing where it went. On several previous occasions, I'd explored rings like this one. Sometimes, it was a dangerous experience.

"What are you thinking about?" asked Jasmine suddenly.

I turned in surprise. We were on the bridge, but I'd moved away from the command tables and stood gazing out into the endless night we call space. I hadn't heard her approach.

But my surprise was due to more than her quiet movement. It was due to the fact that she'd followed me at all. She was watching me closely, I realized. She was becoming more possessive and watchful of my behavior. I was immediately reminded of Sandra who'd been jealous and possessive to a fault.

Jasmine wasn't like that. She was still low-key in her approach to life. She didn't make a show and rarely raised her voice, but she was definitely paying closer attention to my actions.

I smiled at her and reached out a hand. I touched her stomach, and she let me. She smiled shyly back up at me.

"Sometimes I think it feels different," she said, "but I'm not really sure. Not yet."

I nodded. "It will take another month. Then you'll notice the difference."

She seemed pleased, but then her face dropped. "I was late to my shift this morning. Did you notice?"

I froze for a second, searching for the right answer. I hadn't noticed a thing. I decided to go with my gut on this one.

"Oh sure, I was wondering about that. You're never late. Not even a minute late."

She smiled.

Bingo, I thought. I'd chosen wisely.

"I didn't know what was wrong," she said. "After you left our quarters, I felt sick. Then I realized what it must be, and I felt better."

My face was a blank, and I almost blew it, but then I understood.

"Morning sickness? Already?"

She nodded.

I felt a bit nervous then. I don't know what it is, but often when a male is faced with the physical results of his actions, he feels like he's been caught doing something bad. It's kind of like the feeling you get when you see a cop car with whirling lights in your rearview mirror, and you realize that yes, you *were* speeding—seriously speeding.

I forced a wider smile. "That's what's supposed to happen," I said. "Don't worry about it."

"I know. I wish my family were closer, though."

I rolled my eyes at her. "I tried to leave you behind."

"This won't interfere with my duties," she said quickly. "It's a small thing. Really, I was surprised I felt the effect at all. I thought the nanites were supposed to remove all the toxins from our bodies."

"Well, I don't think a hormone surge counts as a toxin."

"Right," she said, nodding. "You should take your hand off me now, Kyle. People are starting to notice we're stargazing and whispering over here."

I slowly let my hand drop and took a sweeping look around. Sure enough, people turned away avoiding my eyes.

202

The staffers had been staring at us, especially the women. The rumors must fly thickly whenever I left this deck. In this case, the rumors were right.

We headed back for the command circle, but before we reached the main table the com-link was blinking. Jasmine took over from a commander who'd been manning her station and read the data.

"Incoming message from Marvin, sir," she said.

I nodded and tapped open the channel.

"Good news I hope, Marvin?"

"I believe it is, Colonel," he said. "I'm ready to launch the weapon."

I frowned. "What? How can that be? You only just got there."

"That is correct, Colonel. The weapon was easy to assemble from the leftover materials I'd not used during the previous experiment."

I frowned at the boards, staring at the white-hot sphere that represented Loki in 3d. Marvin was out there, and he was lying.

"That's impossible, Marvin," I said. "You couldn't have built the bomb from scratch that fast. Not unless..." I felt a moment of perfect clarity come over me. The answer was obvious. I would have had to have been a fool not to know it. "You already built the bomb, didn't you Marvin? The last time you were out there."

"That's a large assumption on your part, Colonel."

"No," I said. "No, it isn't. You needed an unbelievable amount of mass to build that probe. I should have known that something else was going on. Now, I finally know the truth."

"You sound upset, Colonel. Perhaps this would be a good time to drink an alcoholic beverage."

I glowered at the screen and realized my voice had been rising steadily. I was almost into the shouting-zone already. Around me, the staffers had fallen silent. They could only follow half the conversation, but that was probably good enough to figure out what was going on. They were listening in, but I didn't care.

With an effort, I closed my eyes, took a deep breath, and continued speaking to my crazy robot.

"Marvin, why did you build a huge gravity bomb the first time we came out here?"

"For the precise purpose we intend to use it now, Colonel. I calculated a seventy-one percent chance that you would order another test after our probe got through successfully. The second time, you'd want to send something bigger than a probe. I thought that a bomb would take care of the enemy's defensive measures, so I built one in advance. The Macros attacked, and we defeated them—but you didn't order the next step. It took you far longer to reach the conclusion I'd reached before the initial probe was launched. Happily, we are well-prepared for the current situation, and you aided in solving the problem of near-instantaneous detonation."

I rubbed my forehead. I suddenly had a headache.

"You can't just do things like that. You stripped more mass from the moon than was absolutely necessary. That caused a diplomatic breach with the Crustaceans, not to mention being disrespectful of the dead."

"I'm surprised at your poor attitude, Colonel. Usually, superiors praise subordinates who think ahead and make the correct call."

"But you *didn't* make the correct call! We left here and didn't come back for weeks."

"Clearly, I made the correct assumptions, even if I was a little ahead of schedule. We're now ready to proceed without further delay. I understand it's customary to reward subordinates for anticipating orders long before they're given."

"Well, you're not going to receive any special rewards from me today. You tore an extra chunk from a planet without authorization for a project you hadn't even received approval for yet."

"Anticipating future requirements is a desirable trait in any underling, isn't it, Colonel?"

"Stop fishing for compliments. You're not getting any out of me for this."

There was a pause in the conversation. I think Marvin was pouting.

"Very well," he said at last. "I feel confident that you'll come to understand my efficiency in this matter and respond more appropriately soon."

When Hell freezes over, robot, I thought to myself, but didn't say it. I was irritated with him. It wasn't just for him doing extra fun projects like building gravity bombs without permission. It was for predicting my next move so accurately, so far in advance. I didn't like to be predictable—especially not to Marvin.

"So, moving on," I said. "When can you release the weapon?"

"Immediately. I took the liberty of building a second missile platform for a second probe, should one be required. A backup, if you will. By lucky happenstance, the missile platform is an exact fit for the bomb and can deliver the device to the ring shortly after you give the order."

I tapped at the screen. I couldn't get a new contact up that looked right so I told Jasmine what I wanted, and she added an item to the system.

"There's a bomb? Our sensors don't show anything."

"Yeah, well, he's probably hidden it somewhere."

"I don't understand, sir. How could he have assembled it so quickly?"

"He's magic," I said irritably. I opened Marvin's channel again and took a deep breath.

"Launch your weapon, Marvin. You've got the detonator ready with the continuous signal and all?"

"Are you referring to the dead-man's switch? If so, it has been prepared and attached. I constructed it after our previous conversation."

"Of course you did. Fire when ready. The fleet is arranged to react to any Macro response."

"The bomb is away, Colonel."

Almost immediately, a contact appeared. Jasmine drew a circle around it with her finger and tapped at it, assigning it a yellow color. An appropriate color, I thought, neither friend nor foe, but a neutral entity.

It occurred to me as the weapon sailed in our direction with alarming speed that Marvin had a golden opportunity in his tentacles should he decide to take it. The bomb would pass right through our fleet. If it was truly as powerful as he'd said it was, he could detonate it early just by "accidentally" cutting out the signal when it was in our midst.

Sure, I trusted Marvin. He'd saved Earth's bacon on many occasions. But it was unnerving to have a non-human—a sentient machine, no less—with his circuitry on the trigger. If we lost this fleet, there would be no time to build another before Earth was hit by the Macros.

"Newcome," I said. "Rearrange our ships into a safer configuration. I think we should be a bit farther out from the ring, and we should encircle it at a more oblique angle."

Newcome frowned, then looked down at the yellow contact which followed an arcing line through the middle of our ships. His puffy white eyebrows shot up when he figured out what I was talking about.

"Immediately, sir," he said. "And—good thinking."

He rushed off to the navigational table and began relaying orders to place the ships at a safe distance. By the time Marvin's bomb passed through the middle of us, it looked as if a school of fish had been scared off by a thrown rock.

The entire process took hours. When it was finally done, the bomb went through the ring, and the signal was cut off in that precise instant. I can safely say that we were holding our collective breath.

"Marvin is calling again," Jasmine said.

I tapped the channel open. I was watching the ring closely, not sure what to expect. So far, nothing had happened.

"Even if your approval is a little late at this point, I'm still looking forward to it," Marvin said.

"What?"

"Have you forgotten our previous conversation, Colonel Riggs?"

"No, I haven't. But I don't see anything to get excited about yet."

"The bomb reached the ring, went to the other side, and detonated."

"We don't know that yet," I pointed out. "All we know is that it vanished through the ring. So far, the Macros haven't sent anything back in our direction. I'm not breaking out champagne yet, Marvin. What if it was a dud?"

"Highly unlikely."

"So you say. How can we be sure?"

"Launch a normal probe."

I looked at the command table. He was right, of course. In order to verify the test, we had to go in there and take a look around. But the last time I'd done so, hundreds of enemy ships had appeared in response.

I tightened my guts and straightened my spine.

"The robot is right. Launch a probe. Hell, launch ten of them. Use the wire-guided types and the seek-and-return models."

The staff worked relaying the commands. We soon had a shower of small contacts headed for the ring. We watched as they crawled forward and vanished one at a time.

The wait was a short one this time, but it was agonizing none the less. Had they all been destroyed?

I'd almost given up hope before I looked at the timer Jasmine had set up. The fastest of them took a few minutes to go in, scan and return. Getting a good amount of data from an unexplored system took time. In this case, we'd get little more than a snapshot—but it would be much better than nothing.

"The first probe has returned, sir!" Jasmine said.

I could hear the excitement in her voice. Her tone was taken up by a dozen throats. People shouted and laughed. The unbreachable ring had been breached. We eagerly awaited the data as it was transmitted and relayed.

All the probes were coming back, all ten of them.

"Sir?" Jasmine said. She pointed to a blinking light on my console. "Marvin's calling again."

"Yeah," I said, "I know. He wants his pat on the head, and I'm going to have to give it to him. But I don't quite feel like telling him how great he is yet."

-25-

The data pouring in from the probes painted a strange picture. The image of the system on the far side of this ring was unlike anything I'd ever seen before. We couldn't see the whole system as we'd sent the probes in and out so quickly, giving us just a glimpse.

There were planets—but no sun. As a result, the planets were only drifting, frozen hulks, icy blocks of stone and minerals in more or less spherical shapes. In addition, a few of these forlorn worlds had been broken up into asteroid belts due to some past calamity.

"We didn't leave the probes over there for long, but they picked up a fair amount of data," Jasmine said. "We can be certain there isn't a normal star system on the far side of this ring. There's only wreckage with a lot of ionization and debris."

Newcome stared at the images that swam into being on our screens with alarm. "Could Marvin's bomb have been so powerful that it destroyed a star system?" he asked.

The thought had occurred to me. I was just as alarmed as Newcome was, but I laughed off his suggestion.

"We can't have put out a *star!*" I said. "No, I think this is the dark place that was always on the far side of this ring. This is a dead system of planets with a dead star in the center. Is there any strong gravitational force that could have been the star? Maybe there was one that went nova long ago and left a dwarf core behind?"

They tapped and analyzed. I could tell my nerds were baffled.

"Maybe," Jasmine said at last. "There is a gravitational force. It is something bigger than Jupiter but much smaller than a viable sun. It is too small by half to exert the gravitational pull to cause fusion in the core. In other words, it's too small to ignite and become a star."

"Place it," I said, looking at the shadowy contacts. "Then light it up on the boards as if it was a sun."

After she did so, everything became clear. The gravity well we'd detected was indeed at the center of this grouping of cold planetoids. At the center of the blacked-out system was a large object that didn't give off heat. It had to be a burned-out star.

"Just as I thought," I said. "It was a sun once, but now it's burned out, or blown up, or whatever."

"Is it possible it's a neutron star?" Newcome asked.

Jasmine shook her head. "Insufficient mass."

"Looks like we've discovered something new," I said. "Whatever we call it, there are still planets circling around this dead star, providing something for the Macros to mine. They aren't afraid of the dark."

"Such a lonely place," Jasmine said, staring at it. "The chemical signatures I'm reading indicate the star once burned, but this is a dead system. It will be like walking through a graveyard to travel through it."

"What about defenses?" I demanded. "What do the Macros have?"

"The probes didn't report anything dangerous. There was a lot of debris around the ring with high metallic content but nothing that poses more than a navigational hazard."

"Hmm," I said thoughtfully. "High metallic content you say? I bet they had a trap set up. Maybe something like the laser firing-squad Crow set up on the Sol ring but more intense. The trap had been destroying our probes for years, but now Marvin's bomb took it out."

I grabbed hold of my com-link and opened the general command channel. Instantly, I was put in contact with every commander in the fleet.

209

"All ahead full!" I shouted. "Execute Invasion Plan Alpha immediately."

I closed the channel. Newcome and Jasmine looked alarmed.

"Sir?" Newcome said, speaking up first. "Don't you think we should send in another set of probes? If they took a little longer to look around, say ten or twenty minutes this time—"

"No," I said. "Let's cross into their system before the enemy can get on their feet and mount an effective defense. The door is open, and I'm not going to let them slam it closed again."

Everyone scrambled to obey my orders. The ring couldn't handle the entire fleet at once, of course. Fighters swarmed in, followed by a long line of cruisers. After that, if disaster didn't strike the initial invaders, the carriers, transports and support ships would join them on the far side.

We watched our fleet surge forward and thin out into a column of ships. The first entered and vanished. I felt my guts churn. Heading into the unknown was always the hardest part of a space battle for me. I preferred to be in the thick of it with an enemy in my sights. Our battleship was still on the wrong side of the ring and would remain so for quite some time while waiting its turn to wriggle through into enemy territory.

I felt helpless and uncertain, cut off from a growing portion of my fleet. If things were going badly, I wouldn't be able to fix anything.

"Newcome," I said, "you have command of this side of the invasion force. I'm taking a pinnace to the *Andoria*. I'm going through right now."

The *Andoria* was a cruiser of our latest type. It was big, sleek and deadly. It was also about to slip through the ring. If I transferred to that ship, I'd be in the system a full hour before the carrier would finally wallow through.

I almost made it to the airlock when Jasmine caught up with me.

"Wow," I said, laughing, "you sure move fast for a pregnant lady."

"Shh!" she shushed me, putting a finger to my lips and frowning. "That's a secret! And besides, I'm a nanotized, barely-pregnant lady."

I went for a good-bye kiss, but she dodged me.

"Why are you doing this, Kyle?"

"I can't stand waiting. The whole battle could play out on the far side of this ring while I'm sitting in the caboose. I should never have declared my flagship as one of the last in the line."

She looked down and glowered at my chest.

"What?" I asked. But I knew the answer before she spoke.

"I don't want you to go. That system looks creepy—dead. It's a graveyard."

"Yeah, so? Stars go nova all the time."

She shook her head. "Not like that. It looks strange. I've seen astronomical imagery of a thousand systems. There should be a dust cloud if there was a stellar explosion, and a lot of radiation, too. We aren't reading any of that."

"What do you think it is, then?"

"It is a dead system, yes, but what if it experienced a new kind of calamity: something that sheared most of the mass of their sun away? Or what if the trap you spoke of, the weapons system that's been destroying our probes, is far stranger than we understand it to be?"

I laughed and hugged her. "That's crazy. Stop worrying. I know you're feeling paranoid right now, that's normal in your condition. Don't worry, I won't die or vanish. I'm going to be fine. Now, get back up to the bridge and command your ship. Newcome needs you."

I kissed the top of her head and entered the airlock. She didn't go up to the bridge, however. She pressed up against the tiny circular window and stared into the airlock, watching me. I did my best to smile and wave and pretend I was as happy and carefree as the proverbial clam.

But I wasn't. Even as I rode over to *Andoria*, I felt the same sort of disquiet Jasmine was obviously feeling. I had to wonder if I'd just said goodbye to her for the last time.

It was this newly discovered system. It *was* alien, in an entirely new way. A school of dead planets circling an equally dead larger carcass in the center, a mass that had to have once been a shining star. Strange.

Had those worlds been alive with people living on them at one time? Perhaps biotic species we'd never meet? Were they erased from time and history as thoroughly as it was possible to be?

That idea was upsetting me. I knew the others were thinking about it, too. We weren't just feeling mid-mission combat jitters. We were encountering the unknown, and like humans throughout time, we didn't like it.

The captain of *Andoria* was surprised to see me, to put it mildly. But she made no complaints and gave me no attitude.

Captain Nomura was one of my better captains, a stern type who ran her ship tightly. She wasn't tall, but she had broad shoulders and breasts that jutted out from her uniform like apples because she held herself so rigidly. Her black hair had been trimmed almost as short as a jarhead. Her face was attractive despite a complete lack of makeup.

Nomura led me personally up to the bridge. To my credit, I managed not to study her trim figure too closely. People were watching.

"Colonel on the Bridge!" shouted a marine at the hatch.

A dozen people snapped salutes to me. I wasn't accustomed to this, especially not when we were in a combat zone. Maybe the captain had ordered them to snap to attention when I boarded. Whatever the case, I saluted in return and moved directly to the command table.

Everyone on the bridge acted like they had a broomstick for a spine, and there wasn't a smile to be had when they greeted me. I did my best not to notice. I allowed captains to run their ships the way they wanted within Star Force regs. It was a tradition that dated back to our formation as an organization.

"Captain Nomura," I said, addressing the zealous commander. "Is your ship in good condition?"

"It's in flawless operating condition, sir," she said.

Her response was a little intense, and I didn't know her that well, so I simply nodded. I might have chuckled at anyone else. I'd heard she didn't have much of a sense of humor, and I

212

could see the rumors were correct. The woman rarely even blinked her large, dark eyes.

"When do we go through the ring?" I asked.

She glanced at her table. I saw her eyes fix on a timer that had been placed in one corner.

"We have less than two minutes to go, Colonel. May I say it's an honor to serve in your presence. I hope my crew doesn't disappoint you."

"Uh, I'm sure they'll do fine."

No one else said a word. I figured they didn't dare to, that talking unnecessarily on this bridge wasn't allowed.

In the back of my mind, I was beginning to feel a little sorry for her crew, but I didn't say anything. The ring loomed closer on the screens, and I braced myself. Sure, all the reports said this was going to be like a walk in the park…but I never fully trusted probes and scouts. Sometimes an enemy held back their surprises until the cat was fully ensconced in the bag. I was still worried this was one of those times.

-26-

We crossed into the dead system without incident. I found it strange to be in a region of space where there was no sun. I'd never been out in the empty void of velvet darkness that makes up most of the universe. There was *nothing* out here other than the few floating chunks of burnt flotsam: Ex-planets without day, existing in perpetual night. Their icy crusts of frozen methane were richly pocketed with minerals, we could detect that, but we still hadn't found our enemy.

I commandeered *Andoria's* command table. Captain Nomura's face was a mask of stone. I couldn't tell if she was pissed about my sudden arrival or not—but then, I didn't really care.

"I understand this ring isn't being jammed," I said. "Link me up with central command."

Nomura worked the table like a master. I was impressed. She was almost as fast and effective as Jasmine.

One of the reasons I'd chosen to go through the ring on *Andoria* was because it had a ring-communications system aboard. Most of our ships weren't capable of inter-system com-links.

The channel to *Potemkin* opened. In one corner of the screen, I now saw Jasmine's face. She was running her own table on her own ship. Newcome was at her side.

"We haven't encountered the enemy yet, Captain Sarin," I reported.

"We've received the same report from several sources so far," she replied. "No contact made. But we do have a fix on the new system's navigational position, sir."

I looked at her, and I could tell there was concern in her eyes. They were big, and dark, like the eyes of someone who knows the worst is true.

"Give it to me," I said. "Where are we?"

"Can I remotely link to your table?"

"Nomura?" I asked.

She tapped rapidly. Her fingers were a blur, but she never said a word. The words *connection made* appeared on my table.

"I think we're synched now, Captain Sarin," I said. "Show me something."

My screen shifted under my hands. It now showed a regional star map. Seen top-down from a point of view hanging above the Milky Way, a yellow box appeared far out on the disk of the galaxy. It zoomed in with sickening speed.

"It looks like you're taking me to local space," I said.

"Yes. It appears Marvin was correct."

I nodded, unsurprised.

"We're at the predicted origin point of the Macro fleet heading to Earth. See this line?"

A red line appeared with an arrowhead at one end. It looked like a spearhead aimed at Earth.

"That's the path of the Macro invasion fleet that's flying along with their comets. We weren't sure how far they'd come, but it turns out they launched from this system, which is actually quite close to us in relative terms. This dead system is less than a light year from Earth."

"I'm surprised our astronomers never spotted this collection of dead rocks."

"We have tracked a few of the larger ones in the past, but these planetoids are so far out, so black and cold, we never knew they were here."

I looked over her data. Really, it wasn't hard to verify. Just looking at the local constellations and the neighboring stars would have been enough for any navigator. Orion still looked like Orion and the Big Dipper was clear in the sky. We were very close to home.

"If this is their base, where are their factories?" I asked in frustration. "There's nothing here. Nothing we can see, anyway. Every planet we've scanned shows no movement, no factories, no crawling miners. I don't get it."

"They've hidden before," Newcome interjected, his face appearing on screen next to Jasmine's.

Jasmine and I both frowned on our separate ends of the connection.

"I know, I know," he said quickly. "I wasn't part of Star Force back then. I didn't fight the Macros in your early campaigns, but I've read all of your logs. I know your reports inside and out, Colonel."

It was my turn to look startled. I hadn't realized anyone had bothered. Of course, I had become famous over time…some would say infamous. Somebody must have cared what I was doing over the years.

"All right," I said, trying not to sound flattered, "what do my reports tell you about this situation?"

"They're hiding somewhere, just the way they did under their domes at the bottom of the sea on Earth, or as they did when they camped on the middle-zone Eden worlds. They're building up under their protective domes. We have to find their factories and root them out."

I nodded thoughtfully and turned to the map again. There were a lot of hiding places out here. We'd already discovered no less than sixty-three bodies as large as the Moon or larger. Any of them could house a hidden base as Newcome suggested. Or they all might.

"Look for rings, too," I said. "I know we haven't found any yet, but they should be here. I don't think this is the end of the line. The ancient aliens the Blues spoke of linked more than seven systems as I understand it. I've been told as many as two hundred systems were linked by their interstellar highway. There have to be more rings."

"We're under a time constraint, Colonel," Jasmine pointed out. "No more than a month's time."

"I'm well aware of that, Captain, but I disagree with you on the timing. We have less than two weeks to clean this up. After

216

that, I want to return to Earth and set up our defenses for the final battle."

"Where do we start?" asked Jasmine, staring at the floating contacts representing moons and planets. On the screen, there were red circles surrounding each body. Most were so dark that, without that circle, you wouldn't even notice them.

The red circles all rotated around the central large circle, which apparently had once been the system's star. Around many of the middle-sized rocks were smaller ones—former moons. A few others drifted far out in large, swinging orbits. These were asteroids and comets.

"So damned many of them..." I said. "We'll have to split up the fleet."

Newcome made a choking sound.

"Do you have something to add, Admiral?" I asked. I tapped at the portion of the console that currently showed Jasmine's face as she worked on the table remotely. Tapping at the image caused a camera to edge to her right, showing Newcome's red face and white puffs of hair.

"Nothing, sir," he said, looking into the camera nervously.

I stared at him sternly for a moment during which time he avoided my eye.

"For the record," I said, "I don't like splitting up any more than you do. But we can't just go en masse to each rock in this burnt out system and hope to find something. It would take a year or more to visit them all. We have to get this over with, even if the lucky force that finds the enemy might have a hard time of it."

"Very well, sir."

I returned the camera to its home position, where it focused on Jasmine.

"Jasmine, what if we set up a task force around each carrier? We have fifteen carriers out here. Would fifteen search groups get through all the planets, moons and rocks out here in a reasonable amount of time?"

I was guesstimating on my own that the answer was "no". But Jasmine did a much more thorough job. She brought up a script and ran the numbers. Pathing through the system over and over with a variety of solutions, she sent an expanding set

217

of imaginary fleets jumping from world to world in a linked series of green lines.

We eyed the displayed results together dubiously.

"I don't think we could do it with only fifteen search groups, Colonel," she said. "See? By the time the Macro fleet reached Earth, we'll have only visited three quarters of the ninety-odd contacts we've found so far."

"Ninety? What happened to sixty-three?"

She tapped, and an indicator appeared to her upper left that tracked the red. There did seem to be more contacts all the time. Every minute or so, our sensors detected another dark rock out there floating around.

"Are you getting that data now, sir?" she asked.

"Yes," I said, trying not to let my disappointment come out in my voice. I think I failed. "How much time did you allot for searching each rock?" I asked.

She looked at me. "Oh. I didn't. The estimates you see account for flight times only."

I shook my head. I'd been thinking about ordering fast searches, but this simply wasn't going to work.

"Smaller task forces then," I said.

"Sir!" Newcome interrupted.

The software focused on his face.

"Talk to me, Admiral."

"We can't expose the carriers. Splitting our forces into fifteen squadrons is questionable, but breaking the carrier groups down and supplying them with only a few escorts each…it's not wise, sir."

"Objection noted, Admiral," I said. "How about this: we'll put three cruisers into each group. We'll leave the carriers, transports and support vessels back at the ring."

Newcome made an odd sound.

"Did I step on your foot, Admiral?"

"No, sir—I don't think that's possible."

I grinned. He and I were thousands of miles apart, and I wasn't sure if his response was meant to be funny, but I still found it amusing.

"Don't worry so much, man. Look on the bright side: you'll get your own command out of this. Jasmine will stay with the carrier, and you'll take your three cruisers for a joy ride. *Bon voyage.*"

"Thank you, Colonel," he said weakly.

"Is that enough search parties for you, Jasmine?" I asked.

She reran her program. Dozens of green lines leapt out, spreading like a tree from our position across the dead system.

She nodded. "That will do it. We'll have over a hundred search groups. Provided we don't find ourselves surprised by an organized force, we should be able to cover the entire system within ten days."

I nodded. "Good. If we do run into an organized force, we'll have achieved our objective anyway. Your paths are coming in now. It looks like we'll have time to spare. Group up the ships, and select the most experienced captain in each group as the task force commander. Give everyone a list of planets to hit. I want this show on the road within an hour after we get the last ship into the system."

"Sir?" Newcome asked. "Would it be possible to withdraw our carriers and transports entirely? Do they really need to be on this side of the ring?"

"Yeah, they do. If the enemy does spring a trap on us, you watch, they'll jam that ring first thing. Then we'll be separated from one another and out of contact. I don't want to give them that kind of advantage."

"Very good, sir."

I knew he didn't think it was "very good". In fact, he hated everything about my plan. But that was just too damned bad. We were going to search this system in record time, find the Macros that had to be hiding here somewhere, flush them out and destroy them. I hadn't come all the way out here just to turn around and run home.

Marvin contacted me a few minutes later. I knew he wanted to come along for the ride to explore a new system, but I had different plans.

"Marvin, I have a new assignment for you," I told him.

"I will not disappoint you, Colonel Riggs," he said eagerly. "I've heard about these search groups, and I'd welcome the chance to perform as a one-robot team."

I felt a bit bad as he'd contributed so much to the success of our mission so far, and in some ways he deserved the chance to stay and explore, but I couldn't afford to indulge his curiosity now. We were playing a deadly game with the Macros, and every day counted.

"I'm sending you back to Earth," I said, trying to make it sound like a good thing. "And I'm sending Hoon with you. You can drop him off on Eden-6. Admiral Newcome was right when he said we couldn't take a civilian into a war zone."

"Why are you doing this, Colonel?"

"Worried you'll miss something?" I asked. "Don't be. It looks to me like there's not much to investigate out here."

"On the contrary, Colonel—"

"Marvin," I said. "I need you back home. Earth needs you. We have to build up advanced weaponry to protect the homeworld. I'm asking you to do this as a friend. Do we have an understanding?"

"Yes, Colonel Riggs. I understand."

I took in a deep breath and relaxed.

"Good," I said. "I'll see you when we get back. After the Macro fleet reaches Earth, and we defeat them, you can come out here and inspect every rock if you want to."

"I see. Have a good trip, Colonel."

And that was that. I watched as he rigged up a small transport vessel and exited the system going back toward Earth. I was pleased that things had gone my way so easily, and I began organizing the search of this inhospitable collection of rocks.

* * *

A week of fruitless searching passed. By the end of it, every day had become painful to me. I was as frustrated as the search crews.

As a side benefit however, I became more familiar with Nomura. She wasn't quite the cold fish I'd thought her to be. She could even crack a joke now and then—but only if the rest of her crew wasn't listening.

"You know, Captain," I said to her on the eighth night of pointless searching, "I think I'm beginning to understand you."

We were in her office going over the collected data again, this time by hand. When surveying new planets, the diagnostic AI was only marginally effective at discovering something unusual. A combination of anomalies in a pattern might strike a chord in a human, while the computer passed it by.

It was tedious work. In general, we came up with odd readings—a released trace gas that shouldn't be there or heat signatures that could be plate tectonics but might not be... By combining these elements, we hoped to find evidence of the Macros and their hiding spot. At least, that was the theory. The reality was that we were trapped in a room together, going over data that was as blank as blank could be. It was extremely boring.

"Understand me?" she asked. "What do you mean, Colonel?"

"You behave differently when it's just you and me here in this office."

She stiffened, and her eyes met mine. "I hope you aren't suggesting anything improper might transpire, sir."

I blinked at her then laughed. "No, no, not at all. Do I have that bad of a reputation?"

"Yes."

I chuckled again. She wasn't one to candy things up.

"All I meant was that you're more open and more willing to talk in this office. In front of your crew, you're all business."

Her eyes drifted back down to the data again. "And what is it you're beginning to understand about that?"

"Why you operate the way you do. Why you never let your guard down on the bridge. I think you're worried they won't respect you if you're anything less than a stickler for every rule. I would suggest to you it might not be necessary."

She looked unhappy and avoided my eye.

"Everyone has their own command style," I said, backpedaling a bit. "I'm not here to judge. I'm just telling you that you might be making things harder on yourself than is necessary."

"I thank you for your concern."

I shrugged. I could tell her crew might be happier if she lightened up, but I wasn't going to push it. She was the captain, and she was effective. It was her ship.

"Sir?" she asked a few minutes later.

I looked up at her, and the expression on her face made me think she was about to open up and tell me her problems. Usually, that sort of look sent me running for the hills, but Nomura was growing on me.

"What is it, Captain?"

"I've been going over the paths all of our search parties have taken thus far. We've covered eighty percent of the system."

"Unfortunately, yes. We've found very little of interest, and we've pretty much wasted our time. Is that what you were about to say?"

"Not exactly, sir. It occurs to me now that there's one major body no ship was assigned to."

I frowned. "What?"

"The sun, sir. Or what once might have been the sun in this system."

I thought about it. "The gravity would be too intense for enemy activity. At least, that was the assumption."

"Do we know the gravitational stresses the Macros can handle?"

I shook my head. "Not really. We'd sort of bypassed it automatically…but now that you mention it—"

I stood up, and she stood up with me. We were on the same page.

"We're going to the bridge, and we're reversing course," I said. "Every ship in the fleet is threading their way outward along a unique path from rock to rock. But we're going to return and check out the biggest rock of them all."

"An excellent idea, Colonel," she said. Her eyes were intense.

The longer I was around this woman, the more I liked her. She wanted to complete the mission. That's all she wanted. She would do just about anything to achieve that goal.

I could appreciate that kind of officer.

-27-

The moment I relayed our plans to fleet command, they objected. Despite their resistance, they weren't surprised to learn I'd already put my hunch into action.

"I'm not asking permission, Jasmine," I said. "I'm informing you. What I need from you is a little rerouting. Have nearby task forces add our final planetary stops to their search lists. If you spread the job around, it should add no more than a day to our total time here. In the meantime, I'll have a few days to scour the surface of the dead sun."

"Sir," Jasmine said, looking worried on my screen. "I don't recommend this course of action. Your ship might not even be able to withstand the pull of the collapsed core. If anything overheats or malfunctions, you might not escape the gravity well."

"The gravitational forces are well within specs. I checked. And *Andoria* is a new ship. She has the best equipment we can produce."

"The situation is untested, sir."

I frowned. She didn't want me to go down there and risk my life ahead of the pack. She thought of it as unnecessarily endangering key personnel—and the guy who happened to be the father of her unborn child. Could she be losing her edge?

I didn't see things that way. What right did I have to order crews onto a dangerous path I wouldn't dare to take myself? It was different in battle, of course. A commander owed it to everyone to stay alive. But we weren't in battle—not yet anyway—and I was becoming increasingly determined to see this through. We had to find the Macros and destroy their base as fast as possible.

"Jasmine," I said, "the Macros are somewhere in this system. I can feel it. This might be a longshot, but I want to take it."

"I understand, Colonel," she said in resignation. "I'll relay the orders to the rest of the fleet."

The channel broke, and I turned back to Nomura. I grinned at her.

"It's a go!"

She looked at me curiously. "So I heard, sir."

I wondered vaguely what she was thinking. Had she picked up on the odd interchange between Jasmine and I? Was she aware of the rumors, most of which were true, about our relationship?

I decided it didn't matter, and I didn't care. I stood tall on the bridge while it seesawed under my boots. It felt good to be turning around, to follow a hunch.

* * *

A day later, I found myself orbiting the dead sun. It wasn't a normal smooth orbit, however. We were too close for that. We had to keep the engines on full to stay aloft, and there was a thin dusty atmosphere around the monster that was dangerously close to scorching the hull with friction if we drifted down any closer.

It didn't take long to find what we were looking for. The emissions had been too faint to pick up deep in space, but up close they were clear: there was an energy dome on the surface of this rock.

We'd found this type of base many times in the past. It was a Macro dome—an extremely large one. Nearly ten miles across, it doubtlessly was protecting their most valuable assets: their factories.

"I'm impressed," I told Captain Nomura as I studied the readouts. "They built it *here*, in plain sight. But such a crazy place for a base! Every ship they launch must have to blast away under full power to escape the gravity well. It seemed impossible, and we almost passed them by."

"Maybe that's why they did it," she said.

"Maybe," I admitted. "But I don't think so. I think they have some other reason. A rare local resource, perhaps. They normally don't build their bases with subterfuge and deception in mind. They aren't great hiders—they always think aggressively."

She didn't answer. She didn't even nod. Nomura was an odd commander. I liked her, but I had a hard time figuring out what she was thinking.

Macros liked to build their factories under heavy energy shielding to prevent orbital bombardment. Only nuclear weapons could take one down. Grinning, I ordered the bombardment to begin.

"Let's unload, Captain. Send down every missile we have on three sides of that dome. That amounts to forty-eight warheads."

Nomura didn't argue with me. She didn't tell me I was wasting ordnance, or that I should hold back in case we found a second dome. She tapped in the targeting data, transferred it to the other two cruisers, and they all fired in rapid succession.

The missiles had to be timed, naturally. We wanted them to hit in rapid succession, but we didn't want them to destroy one another. It was a tricky business. Since the dome was so large, we hit it at three widely separated points. Each ship had a target point on the dome equidistant from the other two target points. Once we were synched-up, the computers launched the missiles in sixteen salvoes as the cruisers unloaded their magazines. The missiles had to be timed so each additional strike wasn't destroyed by a previous warhead. They were programmed to come in about fifteen seconds apart.

"With luck, we'll kill the target in the first few hits. Set-up a retrieval program. If the missiles aren't destroyed, we'll fly them back up into orbit and pick them up."

Nomura worked her console. Finally, she shook her head.

"Impossible, sir," she said. "The gravity is too great. They'll be dropping at too high a velocity. We won't be able to get them turned upward again."

"Damn. Well, as long as we take the Macros out, I guess it doesn't matter."

We watched and waited for about three minutes before the strikes began. The staffers cheered as missile after missile slammed into the dome. A terrific cloud of dust and debris swirled up in the region. Glowing orange, the terrain was scorched for a mile out from each strike.

"How's it going?" I asked. "Do we have a kill yet?"

Six waves of missiles had reached their target, and the rest were underway. I was anxious to have this finished and behind me. Already, I was fighting the next battle, the one that counted: the battle for Earth.

"The sensors aren't reporting penetration yet, sir," Nomura said.

Glowering, I tapped the screen and spread open the raw data streams. I studied the numbers.

"The dome's still there."

"Seventh strike incoming."

"Give me a visual, a computer interpolation through that cloud of dust."

Nomura hesitated. "It won't be accurate."

"That's why it's called an interpolation. Give it to me."

She tapped, and I sweated. The eighth strike had landed before she was done. Half our missiles had already hit the target.

So far, everything had failed according to the image I was seeing now. The dome was orange, rather than a glassy-white, which meant it had been stressed. But it hadn't buckled; it hadn't gone out. Not even for the few seconds necessary to get a single warhead inside to kill the factories that must be hiding under there.

"Damn," I said as the ninth wave flew into the mess and fresh white flashes puffed out from all three sides of the dome. "We're not in full synch anymore. The strikes on the northern side appear to be nearly a second late."

"Adjusting, Colonel," Nomura said calmly.

"Adjusting? It's too late for that!"

I fumed as the tenth and the eleventh wave swung home and blew up. We were down to the twelfth wave before I saw any improvement in timing. The twelfth wave hit all at once and on all three sides. That made the entire dome flicker and dim to an orange so deep it was almost red.

"That's better. We've got four more shots."

We all watched intently. There were no more cheers, however. Everyone was almost silent. The program was set, and there was no more time to fiddle with any settings. We'd done our best.

The last four waves slammed into the dome...but they failed to bring it down.

A collective exhalation swept the bridge. No one cheered. No one cried. We were grim-faced and stunned.

"I don't believe it," I said. "I've never seen a Macro dome take that kind of punishment before. It should have gone down."

"Perhaps they've improved their technology," Nomura suggested.

I looked at her. "Maybe. But I'm more likely to believe the dome is tougher than previous ones we've encountered. It covers about twenty-five times as much area as a one-mile diameter dome. Maybe the answer is simple and implied by the mathematics."

Nomura nodded slowly. She tapped at her console.

"This dome does appear to be thicker," she said. "It may require a strike twenty-five times as great to take it down as one of the smaller domes did in the past because it covers that much more area."

I rubbed at my neck. I had a sudden pain there. The dome was already recovering. We watched as it went from reddish-brown to orange, then to amber, and finally to white again. It was back to its full strength. We'd done nothing but blast open craters around it.

"We didn't know, but we should have," I said.

"We didn't have enough warheads," Nomura said. "What was there to know?"

227

"We could have built a massive bomb if we'd waited a day."

She was quiet for a moment then said: "Do you want the primary guns to bombard the target?"

I laughed. "What for? If nukes won't take it down, they aren't even going to feel our cannons. Just hold in orbit. Let me think."

I knew from long experience with Macro domes they were always very tough. There were only two ways to take them out. Either you had to blow them up with extreme firepower, or you had to walk through the fields and take them down from the inside.

"The domes are built to prevent fast moving objects and high-energy penetrations," I said.

"I recall that from my academy courses," Nomura replied. She said this in such a deadpan way, I wasn't sure if she was joking or not.

"A slow-moving object can penetrate any dome," I continued. "If said object is going at about a walking pace. That's how the worker Macros go through with fresh minerals and fuel."

Nomura looked up at me curiously. I could tell she was beginning to understand where I was going with this.

"Should we order Fleet to send more vessels to our position, Colonel?" she asked. "With enough warheads, we can destroy this target. It's only a matter of time."

"How long before they can reach us?"

Captain Nomura worked her calculators. She shouted for support, and the navigational team fed her numbers. Within two minutes, she had my answer.

"The first ship can reach us in two days. They are all out at the end of their paths through the system far from the core. Twenty more will reach us within three days if we wait. That should be enough."

I nodded slowly. "Order them to come to us. Tell Jasmine the order comes from me. They're to break off their searching and mass up here. This dome must go down."

"Very good, sir," she said.

When she'd finished, I was still staring at that glassy, milky surface.

"Now that you've relayed my orders, Captain," I said, "I want you to take us down."

"Excuse me, sir?"

"Two or three days is too long. We could do it today and return the entire fleet to Earth that much faster. This has already dragged on longer than I'd anticipated. Worse, now that we've shown the enemy we know they're here, they will begin attempting to escape or build up forces to counter us. I don't want to be chasing them down tunnels into the crust of this huge rock. I don't want to face an army of fresh enemy machines either. We have to try to take them out right now."

Nomura stared at me. "How, sir?"

"We're going to have to walk in with a bomb. How else?"

Before the next hour was up, I wished I'd brought Kwon or Gaines with. I had a few marines on each ship, but they weren't veterans of a dozen battles. Not since the desperate campaigns for Earth and Eden had troops marched into a dome and blown it up. I'd invented the process, but no one else aboard was familiar with it.

The Fleet people were downright terrified. I figured they thought I was crazy, including Nomura herself. She wouldn't be the first to think that—probably not the last, either.

Our three cruisers nosed down and dipped into the atmosphere reluctantly. I'd let her take an hour to circle the rock one last time, reducing speed and making adjustments. I put up with this grudgingly. It wasn't every day we landed a ship on a burnt out star with more gravity than Jupiter itself.

The engines were straining, and I could already feel the tremendous pull. We'd ordered everyone into a crash seat, complete with nanite arms to hold us down.

The atmosphere was thin—thinner than that of Mars, but we still felt it bump and shiver against the ship on the way down. The hull temperature increased with each mile we dropped, too. I had the ships reconfigure themselves into smaller, tighter designs. The nanite walls bubbled and rippled. The walls closed in overhead giving everyone a claustrophobic sensation. By the time we landed, we wouldn't be able to stand up because the ceilings would be so low—in fact, I wasn't sure if we could stand up at all under the terrific gravitational force we'd have to endure.

The crew was scared. I could see it in their eyes. I decided it was time to say something. I opened a channel to all three ships and to every crewman's helmet.

"Crews and marines," I said. "This is Colonel Kyle Riggs. I'm here to tell you that you are all officially part of Riggs' Pigs now, which is whatever outfit I happen to be attached to in action. As many in my units have learned in the past, being one of the Pigs isn't always fun. But we have a mission, and it can be done. I've been in the atmosphere of gas giants more than once. Gas giants are worse than this landing, let me tell you. Sure, we'll have even higher levels of gravity to deal with—along with plenty of radiation—but we won't have that thick, horrid atmosphere: Thousands of miles of nauseous gasses—I hate gas giants. They put such great pressure on the hull that…well, never mind about that now."

I realized I was supposed to be encouraging them, not freaking them out further with my old war stories. I changed the direction of my speech appropriately.

"Here's some advice from a veteran: Don't stand up too fast. Keep your head low, and keep it even with your heart if you're feeling dizzy. Try not to fall down, either. It hurts a lot under heavy Gs. Most of you only have flight suits, and you might have difficulty getting around. I suggest you arrange your surroundings so you can do your work without having to move much."

All over the ship, the crew put this advice to good use. They all had permission to command the ship to reshape around them. They could mold the consoles causing them to sprout from the ceiling, for example, where they could see them while reclining, instead of requiring them to stand over and look down on a flat surface. They could redesign their environments so it best suited them. We'd long ago gone with an editable design system for our ships, as it allowed crews to adjust to a wide variety of situations. We figured we could never come up with enough presets ahead of time to take every contingency into account.

The effect on the crews over the next several minutes was quite positive. They felt like they were doing something. Everyone likes to up their odds of survival and improve their working conditions to their liking. Occupying a terrified mind was the best way to keep it from panicking, in my experience.

I switched off the general channel then and spoke to my small number of marines as a group. There were only eight stationed on each ship, twenty-four altogether. It seemed an entirely inadequate number to me.

"Marines!" I shouted.

They "oorahed" me, and I smiled.

"This is our chance to shine! We're going to kick these metal insects off this dead sun the old-fashioned way, with a marine boot in their collective behinds!"

They cheered again, and I waited until they'd settled down.

"I'm sure your team leaders have you suited-up in full armor. Make sure you're fully juiced and carrying your best generators. I'm expecting to have to run the exoskeletons nonstop once we land."

I was assured by every noncom that they were geared and ready to go. I knew that already, but I wanted them to hear my voice instead of the creak and groan of the metal shells around them.

I opened my mouth to say something further about the marine spirit when a blinking light went off overhead. Like everyone, I was lying down now, beginning to really feel the Gs.

"What's wrong?" I asked Nomura, who was next to me and tapping with her hands on controls at her sides. Directly overhead was a screen displaying status reports. I hadn't bothered to reconfigure my operating station, being more concerned with my own battle suit and my speeches.

"Hull breach," she said calmly.

"Can we shrink the ship down flatter? Did we lose anyone?"

She turned her head with a visible effort and looked at me.

"The hull breach was on our sister ship, the *Trieste*," she said. "The ship was lost, Colonel."

I froze for a second, then nodded.

231

"Carry on," I said. "Make sure it doesn't happen to the rest."

I turned back to the screens. I could see what she was talking about displayed there now. The *Trieste* was displayed as a red wireframe, meaning it was dead. There was nothing left and no survivors.

I never finished my speech with the marines. Since a third of them had died in the middle of it, I just didn't have the heart to keep blowing sunshine around inside their helmets.

-28-

The cruiser *Trieste* had collapsed like a sub that sinks too deep into the ocean. It had been designed for stress and pressures on the hull, but numbers on a blueprint and real-world conditions are two different things as any engineer will tell you. After that, we crushed our ceilings down further, and it felt like I was in a movie theater with seats and walls that kept shrinking. The ceiling screen was now inches from my faceplate. When I turned my head, Nomura was flat on her back looking uncomfortable. The ceiling was almost touching her chest, and I realized the ship had made special allowances for me alone. I had a battle suit on and required much more space than the other humans. They were all but entombed around me.

To their credit, no one was verbally complaining. There were a few panting moments and a few sobs, but not one of them blubbered constantly or showed other signs of outright panic.

"Ten miles to go," Nomura said. "We're slowing down now. Thrusters are at full power, and we've only lost one engine on the starboard side."

"Excellent. It's almost over."

Less than a minute later, I thought the ship had lost power. There was a shudder and a jarring sensation then the singing sound of the engines died down.

"We've landed, Colonel," Nomura said. "You can begin your mission—and please sir, do try to hurry."

Grunting, I reached up with my right gauntlet to touch the ceiling—but nothing happened.

I tried again, putting more force into it. I heard my arm whine and it shook fractionally. Then I had my arm up. Could it really be *that* heavy? It felt as if I was lifting a five-hundred pound weight.

I realized with something of a shock that I was probably moving much more weight than that. Only the exoskeleton suit inside my battle suit allowed me to move at all.

I ordered the ship to respond to my touch, and to build me an airlock. I realized now that I should have moved down to the sally port with the rest of the marines before we'd landed. The ship had a built-in way to exit the troop pods. I wasn't able to get there via corridors any longer. I'd have to get out and crawl over the hull itself.

Movement for the crew around me involved painful crawling. I saw them doing it, and they looked like kids with their big brothers sitting on their spines taking a cruel ride.

Molding a new airlock out of sluggish nanites, the ship eventually managed to ease me out of its hull without decompressing the entire thing. I climbed out and stood on top of the ship, swaying.

I've been on the Moon before—hell, I've been on several moons. But this place was more desolate than any landscape I'd ever set eyes upon. For one thing it was dark, almost pitch-black. If it hadn't been for local starlight, I wouldn't have been able to see anything without my suit's infrared settings.

But it wasn't just rocky, dusty and bleak. It was scorched-looking. I suspected this wasn't entirely due to our recent barrage of nukes, although that hadn't improved things much. This place had been subjected to temperatures unlike anything I'd ever met up with in person. It was a burnt-out husk.

After looking around for a few seconds, I felt dizzy. I leaned forward, dipping my head until it was even with my heart. I felt it race in my chest. I wasn't used to this yet, I told myself. I'd have to take it easy at first until I adjusted.

When I could walk again, I labored my way over the ship, clanging and thumping. To the crewmen trapped inside, it must have sounded like I was beating the hull with sledgehammers.

I found the sally port in the aft section. The ship looked so strange to me once I was down on my feet in front of it. The whole thing had been flattened dramatically. A cruiser of this class was usually about as tall as it was wide but longer and drawn in a cylindrical shape. *Andoria* wasn't anything like that today. It had flattened itself down to a third its normal height and widened out fractionally. It was about the same length as before.

I slammed my fist on the sally port. I'd expected to meet the marines here, gathering their kits and standing in their armor outside. Instead, I was met with a closed hatch.

Finally, a squealing sound came through my gauntlets. I knew they were trying to get out. I helped, and the hatch swung open. Exterior ports weren't usually fields of nanites. They were solid surfaces. The hatch hung open, and I looked inside.

I was in for a shock.

"What are you doing, marines? This isn't nap time!"

They were in there lying on the benches. Only one of them was in a sitting position. He was near the hatch, and I suspected he'd been the one to open it. He had a noncom's green lights on his suit.

"I'm sorry sir," he said, sounding like he was out of breath. "We can't move much. I think Taylor passed out."

I looked around the interior, frowning. I sucked in a breath and was about to bellow at them—but I paused. They weren't like me, and I had to remember that. I'd been rebuilt by Marvin's devilish brews of trained Microbes. I'd been given seven baths in his stinking mud puddles, and as a result, I was stronger than anyone I'd ever met.

"All right," I said. "None of you can stand, is that right?"

"No, sir. Sorry, sir."

"It's okay. Give me the bomb."

The specialist looked at me in surprise. "Sir? You aren't going alone, are you?"

"Nah," I said. "There's probably a few in the other ship that can come with me."

At that, the specialist made a mighty effort. He was a muscular man. I could see that through his faceplate. His neck looked as thick as his skull.

He managed to stand briefly. I was proud of him and dared to hope I wouldn't have to walk on this mission alone.

But it wasn't to be. He listed toward the starboard side of the ship and then overcompensated with a lurching heave to the left. I reached out to catch him but wasn't fast enough. He went down on his ass, and I could tell he hit hard. The gravity was so great that once you started falling, you went down as if you'd been hit with a club.

"Stay down!" I shouted.

For a second, he didn't answer, and I thought he might have been knocked unconscious. But then he spoke.

"I got dizzy," he said. "I lost it. I feel like I was hit by a truck."

"That's ten-Gs plus a little gravy you're struggling against," I told him.

"I—my HUD says I cracked my spine, Colonel. Sorry."

"No problem. It will heal. Just take it easy."

"How is it that you can walk and talk, Colonel?" he asked me.

I loomed over him smiling into his faceplate.

"I cheat," I said.

Then I took the bomb and left him. I didn't bother checking on the second group of marines in the other ship. It was hopeless, and I didn't have any more time to waste.

The bomb was in a square case, and it bumped against my knees as I walked. This unbalancing effect almost scrubbed the entire mission. I had a hard time walking with it. Each step, I found myself staggering and swaying like a drunk. At last, I figured out a way to carry it. I had a nanite cable from the ship detach itself and wrap around my neck and shoulders. Using this expedient, I placed the bomb on my back. It rode on top of my generator, and I prayed the housing could take the weight.

I set off at a steady, laborious pace. My suit heaved and groaned. I had to use anti-grav repellers just to stay upright when I went over rough terrain. I couldn't afford to overuse them, however. The power consumption was alarming enough as it was. I had only hours to go before I ran out of juice entirely.

The dome wasn't far off, but it felt like miles. The gravity was so extreme, my body felt as if I was sagging, folding into myself. My muscles hung from my bones as if they wanted to fall off like overripe fruit. Each breath required a focused effort, and every step was an individual exercise. At first, I had to take breaks. Every ten to twenty steps, I had to stop and put my hands on my knees putting my head level with my heart. This let me think more clearly.

Internally, my body made adjustments after ten minutes or so passed. Maybe it was the work of the nanites or the microbes—I wasn't really sure. But I could walk almost normally, albeit in slow-motion.

I figured that my body, with the armor, had to weigh around ten thousand pounds. Without the exoskeleton inside my suit, I would be helpless. As it was, the suit groaned and creaked. The power meter was going down with alarming speed, as well. Normally, these suits could keep you going for two or three days if you didn't fire the laser much. But with the tremendous new load of weight, I doubted it was going to last more than two or three hours.

Deciding my armor was too heavy, I shed the outer plates. The exoskeleton beneath was exposed, an interior layer of red and black materials that crawled with nanites. I felt like I could breathe again.

I considered going back and gathering my marines, having them shed their battle armor as I'd done, but I passed on the idea. There was no guarantee they could function under the heavy Gs even without armor, and if that was the case I was just wasting time.

More importantly, without our armor we weren't really going to able to fight. My mission now was one of getting in and out as fast as possible. Hopefully, this could be done without being detected and overrun by enemy machines. Bringing more men to carry the bomb would only take more time and increase the odds of being found and slaughtered.

The exoskeleton was more protective than a simple nanocloth suit, but much lighter than full armor plating, with my burden eased I pressed ahead as fast as I could travel.

I reached the dome in time and marched slowly inside. The experience of passing through the dome wall wasn't unfamiliar to me. It was strangely quiet and blank inside the shell-like field itself, like walking through a velvety snowstorm at night. I could only hear my labored breathing, the hissing and clicking of my suit, and a few alarms beeping because we were now out of contact with the ship and the directional sensors weren't operating.

I trudged steadily, blinded by the energy field. I counted steps and became concerned after I'd taken ten and still hadn't reached the quiet interior of the dome. Was I lost? Was the interior filled with yet *more* force fields?

Not knowing the answers, I pushed away the questions and kept going. I'd reasoned that since the dome covered a larger area it must also be thicker, and I'd been right. When I'd gone three times as far as I'd ever had to go to cross a Macro dome, I reached the interior at last.

I stepped into a quiet, inner world. It was enclosed above by a perfectly smooth surface like milky glass. Inside, the dim landscape stretched away in an arc in front of me. Miles of land were enclosed.

The horrid gravity was the sole constant of my existence as I kept walking. I wanted to rest, but I knew I didn't have much time. About a half-mile in, I found an obstacle. It was a vertical wall that curved away in both directions.

I frowned. Why would the Macros build a wall inside here? Then, I thought I knew the genius of it. On a normal world, a wall meant nothing to a Star Force marine in his full kit. I could fly over it, climb it or burn my way through it, but not here in this high-gravity environment. Here, I would have to use too much power to damage the wall, and I weighed too much to climb or fly over it.

Given no choice, I began walking around the wall. It curved, just as the dome did. The surface of it looked strange to me as if I'd seen this mottled dark stone before. Not knowing why, I kept going.

I knew this might be the end of my mission. If the wall went all the way around, I guessed I could set off the bomb on the outside of it, but I wanted to be sure I got the factories. If it had an entrance, it might be guarded by enemy machines, and they were sure to discover me at the gates. Maybe that's why I hadn't seen the machines yet, and I hadn't been detected. They hadn't covered this zone outside their wall because they didn't need to.

When I finally reached the end of the wall, I was struck by a new mystery. The end wasn't smooth or natural-looking. It was a crumbling, broken ruin. Even more surprising for something the Macros had built, it just stopped, and the land was open afterward for as far as my eyes could see.

I walked around this broken endpoint of the wall and examined the curved interior. It appeared to mirror the surface I'd seen from the outside.

That material…it still looked familiar to me. I stared at the wall frowning and dared to flip on my suit-lights and run the beams over it.

I shook myself and pressed onward. I was sure I'd be discovered soon. Now wasn't the time to become distracted. I promised myself I'd send an exploration team down here later if we won this battle—if we didn't, the answers to these riddles didn't matter anyway.

When I'd reached what I thought might be the center of the area enclosed by the semi-circular wall, I found the Macro factories. There wasn't just one but several of them. I counted eight in sight. They were hulking shapes that built everything the Macros produced. These factories were their mothers, their hive queens.

I looked, but didn't see any Macro workers around. I wondered briefly what was feeding the factories and what they were producing. But I soon realized I didn't care. The workers were busy elsewhere, and while they were away, I was going to destroy their queens.

I unlimbered the bomb I'd dragged all this way. It wasn't an incredibly powerful warhead. Compared to the gravity-based blockbuster Marvin had used to breach this dead system's ring, the bomb was tiny. But it should be enough. Inside the enclosed space under this massive dome, nothing would survive. Nothing of flesh or metal could withstand the energy that would be released.

The timer blinked at me with yellow numerals. How long should I allow for escape? I wanted to give myself a chance, but I didn't want the Macros to get the time they needed to drag it away once discovered. I spun the dial and set it with fifteen minutes to go. Then I armed it, clicked four rocker switches—and the bomb was live.

-29-

I straightened and took a quick look around. There was movement in the dark, back the way I'd come. I decided to push ahead rather than to retrace my steps. It would take longer to get back to *Andoria* that way, but it would be a more direct pathway out of the dome than trying to circle around the strange, crescent-shaped wall again.

The landscape became blacker and turned into fine silt that covered me like powder. It was like walking on a grittier version of coffee grounds.

Marching across the dusty center of the enclosed space, I found something I didn't expect. It was the other side of the wall, and it was broken, just as the first section had been.

All at once, I realized what I was looking at. It wasn't a wall at all. The Macros hadn't built this—they'd found it and set up camp all around it.

The half-buried, circular walls I was standing in the midst of formed a ring. It couldn't be anything else. That mottled stone-like surface…I'd seen it before when encountering the rings that knit together our star systems.

The only difference was the state of this ring. It was broken. There was only half of it in sight. Perhaps the other half was buried under my boots.

My mind filled with questions as I trudged across the barren, gritty land. Why had the Macros built here over this broken ring? How had the ring been destroyed? *Why* had it been it destroyed, and who had done this amazing feat?

I couldn't answer any of those questions, but I could infer a few things from my discovery. This broken ring was the reason why the Ancients had never come back to our portion of the universe for thousands of years. Not even the Blues had known what had happened, but it was clear to me now. The interstellar highway had been derailed right here.

I tried to push these thoughts and questions away. If the Blues didn't know the answers, who else could? They were impossible unknowns. Mysteries that humanity would probably never figure out—if we survived at all.

But I found I couldn't stop thinking about the broken ring. As I neared the edge of the dome, I hesitated. I kept staring at the hulking form of the damaged structure, and I realized the machines themselves might know.

Maybe they could be convinced to tell me what they knew…

There is something about living in a universe full of unknown terrors that works on a man's mind over time. In the past, we'd had questions about our origins, naturally enough. But those questions had seemed philosophical and remote. In my time, there were actual beings around that could be spoken with. These beings knew the real truth, and I often suspected that if we knew it as well our odds of surviving as a species would be much higher.

Standing at the base of a glassy, milk-white wall of force I broke radio silence on sudden impulse and transmitted on a channel I hadn't used for long years. I attempted to contact Macro Command using my suit's brainbox as a translator.

The Macros weren't like us. They were different not only in their physiology, but also in their group organization. Humans tended to operate as solo minds linked in a mutually accepted social hierarchy. In Star Force for example, we'd selected commanders, and the rest followed the orders of the leaders.

The Macros were different in this respect. In a way, they were quite egalitarian. They merged their minds effectively when decisions had to be made. Their pooled intellect was greater than the capacity of any single individual, and they made their decisions collectively. Every machine linked into a network and part of its CPU was dedicated to group decision-making. Individually, the machines weren't very bright. But when they all shared the load, they became smarter particularly in a centralized location like this with many machines about. The more of them that were involved, the smarter local Macro Command became.

There was an elegant simplicity to their way of thinking that appealed to me. They never argued because they shared the same singular mind. When a decision was made, it was made because the entire group-mind was in agreement concerning the best course of action. Right or wrong, they at least all worked together in unison. In comparison, commanding humans was like herding cats.

When I contacted Macro Command, I was really broadcasting to every Macro in the area. This meant they would know where I was and attempt to destroy me. But I figured "what the hell", since after I destroyed their dome, they were going to be pretty pissed-off and hunting for me anyway.

I wouldn't have taken the risk if the bomb hadn't already been set. Part of my excuse involved the bomb, in fact. If they were looking for me, they would be less likely to notice the device ticking in their midst. If I didn't make it out, well, at least I'd dealt them a hard blow. Hopefully, it was a fatal one.

I opened the channel and broadcast my message. "Macro Command, this is Colonel Kyle Riggs. I'm requesting an open dialog channel with you. We have things to discuss."

I waited for several seconds, but there was no response. This wasn't really surprising. Often in the past, the Macros had ignored my requests for a dialog. They didn't like talking unless it was their idea to do so.

"Macro Command, talk to me. I have an offer to make."

Silence. My radio crackled, but that was all. I'd hoped to pique their curiosity, but it didn't work. They weren't going to make this easy on me.

I put my gauntlet against the dome wall. I knew that once I walked into it, any transmissions from the machines would be lost.

"I demand that you communicate, Macro Command. Here is the nature of my offer: survival. If I win this conflict, I will not destroy you utterly. I'll capture and set aside specimens and blueprints for your race. Your future existence will thus be ensured."

Ten more seconds of silence followed. I almost gave up after that. The dome was right there, shimmering and blue-white. All I had to do was step into its glowing surface.

"Don't you understand the value of what I'm offering?" I demanded. "I might win this war. If I do, I'll destroy you utterly unless you talk to me right now."

More silence. I opened my mouth to curse them and taken a step closer to the dome when they finally responded.

"Request denied," said an odd voice in my helmet.

I smiled. I'd gotten them to talk. Despite their obvious disinterest, they had to have some interest, or they wouldn't have bothered to respond at all.

"I'm not making a request," I said. "I'm offering you a deal a material exchange."

"Your offer is invalid. You will not win this conflict. You will be destroyed."

"You're probably right," I said. "But certainly there must be a one percent chance I will win in the end. If you talk to me now, you have insurance. Win or lose, you won't be wiped from the universe. Come on, you haven't even heard the details yet."

There was a long pause. I figured they'd gotten bored and hung up the phone by the time they came on again sounding thoughtful.

"We know what you are offering. The ruse is obvious. You wish to survive as a species and will demand a guarantee of survival from us when the inevitable comes. But you will not wrest any such deals from us. You will not be spared when the final moment arrives."

Macro Command's words annoyed me, but I struggled not to make threats or boasts in return. I had them on the line now. They wouldn't be talking if they weren't interested.

"You misunderstand the nature of my offer. I want no guarantees from you. I only want information."

"We will not compromise our fleets by revealing—"

"That's not the nature of the information I wish to exchange. I only want to know about the ring, the broken ring I found on the surface of this dead sun."

Another long delay followed while they mulled this over. I looked around, studying my computer and my environment. The bomb was due to go off within a few minutes, and I thought certain of the blackest shadows around me had shifted subtly. That might just be an effect of this odd environment, but I couldn't be certain. They could be talking just to delay, preparing to spring a trap on me. Just keep old Riggs talking long enough to get a fix on his location then deploy machines to deal with him.

"We agree to your exchange," they said at last.

I grinned inside my helmet.

"All right then, here are my questions. Who built these rings?"

There was no response. I waited for ten long seconds, checking my chronometer. Then I remembered Macros didn't like questions. They tended to ignore them utterly.

"Macro Command," I said, using a stern voice. I suspected the significance of my tone was probably lost on them, but I went with it anyway. "I demand that you comply with our agreement and tell me what you know of the origin of the damaged alien artifact we call a 'ring' I found under your dome."

"The ring is a transportation device. It is damaged."

I sighed. "I know that. Who built it? Damn..." I realized I'd asked a question.

"Tell me who built the ring," I said.

"The ring was created by powerful beings that are unknown to us. We've never encountered them and have no measurements by which to judge them. We suspect they're inorganic in nature."

I frowned. "Inorganic meaning they're machines...that's great. Tell me why you believe this to be the case."

"Artificial constructs are superior forms of self-mobile creatures. As these beings are clearly superior to all other known civilizations, we've reasoned them to be inorganic."

I chuckled. The Macros always had been stuck-up bastards.

"All right, let's just say you have no idea who built them. Tell me how the ring was destroyed."

"It appears to have collided with the central star in the system. The resulting release of energy was sufficient to damage both the ring and the star system itself."

I looked around me, startled by this concept. Could it be true? Falling into a burning star—I could imagine that breaking the ring. Even if it was built of stardust, it had to be damaged by experiencing such rough treatment. Gravity, heat, radiation. If anything could destroy a ring, falling into a star would do it.

But that wasn't the part that surprised me. The other concept they'd put forward was even more alarming to me. Could the destruction of a ring be so cataclysmic that it could snuff out a star? More than that, it seemed to have caused the star to go nova in an unusual way, leaving burnt husks of planets orbiting the rotten core.

I wasn't sure how the Macros had come to this conclusion, but to me it wasn't worth the effort of playing 'twenty-demands' to get the information out of them. It was believable enough without confirmation. It made too much sense. Marvin had destroyed the surface of a moon to make small, relatively unimpressive devices of this kind. A ring of the size required to transport physical objects over vast distances had to require enormous amounts of mass and energy to create.

I wondered when this star had shined its last light upon the planets that circled it. Were these burnt hulks once green, jewel-like worlds? Had they teemed with life, even perhaps an extinct species of civilized beings?

Frowning, I moved on to my next question—framed as a demand, naturally.

"Macro Command, tell me what would be required to create a ring. Tell me how the Ancients did it."

"Reference unclear: Ancients."

"We call the unknown beings that created the rings in the first place 'Ancients'."

"Understood. We cannot report precisely. However, in any star system the only source of power capable of enabling the process would be the star itself. And the only available mass would be the planets."

246

I narrowed my eyes, nodding. It was obvious, when I thought about it. They had to be right. When Marvin had built his mini-ring, he'd used the star Loki to power his efforts and he'd stripped the crust off a planet-sized moon to feed the furnace he'd built.

I thought about my home system. From what I'd learned between the Blues and the Macros, I was beginning to get a picture in my mind. About a hundred thousand years ago, the Ancients had reached the Solar System. It was near the end of the chain, in fact, along this branch of their interstellar highway. They'd only made one more connection past Sol, the one that reached the blue giant.

At that time on Earth, the most recent glacial period had started. We'd been locked in an Ice Age that lasted many thousands of years. Could it have been caused by a dimming of our sun's output? Could they have damaged our sun or drained it to create their highway of rings?

The idea was shocking. My thoughts drifted to consider what the local source of mass might have been. The answer in that case was equally disturbing. I knew that the asteroid belt in our home system had once been a large planet that had been broken up by an unknown disaster. It felt odd to think I might have stumbled upon such critical details of our own star system's history, way out here.

I looked up at the stars and the dead system around me. Could it be that this system had been the brightest star in the heavens of old Earth? Had my ancestors in the hunter-gatherer days looked up and seen a single star that was more brilliant than any of the others riding across the sky every night, so bright it was like a second moon?

One day it had gone dark, probably after producing a kaleidoscope of plasma and radiation. They would have been frightened—and their instincts would have been right in that case.

"Macro Command," I said, "tell me who destroyed the ring."

"Unknown."

Fair enough, I thought. "Tell me why you put a dome over it and placed your factories here. There are other more suitable mining spots in this dead system."

"You are correct. There are superior locations, but we were attempting to repair the ring."

I perked up at this. I hadn't realized their technology was capable of such a thing.

"I assume, then, that you have the technology to perform this feat."

"You assume incorrectly. We have failed."

I frowned thoughtfully. Why make the attempt in the first place if they weren't sure they could do it? What had driven them to such a folly?

"Tell me why you made the attempt."

There was a pause. A longish one. I could only assume they were pondering their answer.

"We will not tell you that."

"I demand it, in accordance with our agreement."

"Our agreement is at an end."

"Look," I said, suddenly wanting to know the truth. "I will make this the last thing you have to tell me. For this final piece of data, you can have your insurance. That is the price and then your part of the bargain will be fulfilled. If it is sensitive data, it will probably not leave this planet anyway. I'm not likely to survive much longer."

Another long pause ensued. Just when I was getting up to walk out of the dome, they finally responded. There was less than a minute to go on the timer.

"We wanted to escape."

"Escape? To complete the bargain, you must make a clear statement."

"We wanted to escape this system. We wanted to escape Star Force. We wanted to escape Kyle Riggs."

I smiled. I was at the very edge of the dome now, and I reached out to touch it.

"You've made my day, Macro Command."

"Statement meaningless."

How could I not be pleased? We'd scared them off and made them fear for their safety—if you could call such

248

behavior in a machine "fear". Just knowing that made a lot of my sacrifices worthwhile.

I caught a metallic gleam off to my right. The machines had been hunting for me as I knew they would. They'd finally located me. I'd known all along that that was part of this deadly game. I'd spoken with them in an attempt to get information, and they'd cooperated. But, all the while, they'd been maneuvering into position to ambush me. I'd expected nothing less from them.

I took my first step into the shimmering dome.

-30-

While I'd contemplated dramatic, millennia-old events, the Macros themselves hadn't been idle. They'd been stalking me.

I'd suspected they would, of course. But it was a demonstration of their respect for me that when they did come, they did it with overkill. A rush of machines charged in unison.

They'd been as stealthy as large robots could be—which was to say, not terribly stealthy. When they came on in their final rush, I couldn't miss it.

Dozens of flat, crab-like machines scuttled forward. I was up off my butt and heading into the wall of the dome the second I saw they were near.

Whiteout. That was what I'd always thought when I stepped into the dome walls. You couldn't really see anything, and all your sensors cut out. There wasn't much in the way of sound, and as no signals could penetrate it, I couldn't even tell if I was heading in the right direction.

Normally, this wasn't much of a problem. I'd walked through Macro domes on a number of occasions in the past. All you had to do was keep your wits about you, remember where you were headed, and keep putting one foot in front of the other in as straight a line as you could. The energy field was only about ten yards thick, a dozen sweeping strides for me.

But this dome shell was different. It was thicker than any I'd ever encountered. It didn't house a single factory, but every factory they had left. It was huge, thick and powerful.

250

Ten steps went by, then another ten. I knew if I hadn't gotten turned around somehow I should be reaching the far edge soon. I also knew that the bomb was due to go off at any moment.

With these concepts foremost in my mind, I tried to hurry up. But the field didn't let me. It only allowed slow movement through it. That was how it kept missiles from penetrating, among other things.

Something hooked me at around step twenty-one. I'm pretty sure it was the twenty-first step as I'd been counting to keep track. If I'd reached thirty without exiting the dome, I'd know that I'd gotten off-course and would have to change directions.

Whatever it was, it grabbed the generator on my back and lifted me up—slowly. Not even the Macros could move quickly inside their own force walls.

I was pretty sure a claw had me, lifting me up. Even if the dome was only a single step farther ahead, it was a step too far. I'd never make it.

I reached for my projector reflexively, but I knew it wouldn't work. An energy beam such as the kind it emitted wouldn't penetrate a millimeter of this field around me.

I released my projector, letting my laser carbine fall and dangle by the nanite cord. I reached back with my gauntlets— but I couldn't get a grip on anything.

Whatever had me was either smart or lucky. It had chosen to grip me by the one piece of equipment that I couldn't easily reach. Like a kitten in its mother's mouth, I was hefted up higher and higher.

I was now certain I was in the grip of a machine's claw. The claws were trying to close, crushing my generator, and they would puncture my exoskeleton in time.

A sense of doom came over me. The chronometer displayed six red zeros. I had run out of time.

An instant after this realization came over me, my sense of sight and sound blanked out. Then something kicked me from behind. My first impression was that the Macro that carried me had thrown me as far and hard as it could.

In my faceplate, the stars came back. They flickered, dimmed, then brightened again.

I was falling. It didn't take long, but every fall when you're expecting death seems to be a lengthy experience.

Landing was one of the more painful experiences I'd had in the last year. Only fighting Crow and suffering his hammering blows had been worse. The dusty black surface of the dead sun came up and smashed into me. My faceplate starred and emergency warning symbols lit up everywhere inside my helmet.

Falls from ten feet or more in high gravity are serious matters. No human beings had ever experienced gravity like I was feeling right now.

I didn't lose consciousness, but I wanted to. I was in agony. Bones cracked and skin tore open such was the force of my fall. It was like smashing a hammer onto your thumb—but there were about a hundred hammers hitting a dozen of my ribs, both my kneecaps and my right ear.

Lights flashed in my skull, and I honestly wasn't sure if they were from the blow my head took or from the dome itself.

The dome. I painfully cranked my head to the right. The dome should be there—but it wasn't.

I saw the last flickering orange death of the dome. It was lovely, in an alien way. Like my own private display of aurora borealis.

Then I remembered as my wits seeped back into me that when a nuke went off inside a dome, it couldn't get out. But since it destroyed the power source the dome relied on, the dome itself always died moments later.

I tried to get up, but everything fought me: My damaged body, my damaged suit, and especially the portion of a claw that still lay clamped to my midsection.

This last impediment had to go, so I focused my energies on removing it. I could hardly be expected to drag this monstrously heavy appendage across the surface of the dead sun.

The claw wouldn't release me. I tried, oh God how I tried, but I could not get the damned thing off me.

I thought of my projector, got it out and put it against the claw. But it wouldn't fire. Possibly, it had been damaged in the explosion or the fall.

I stood up despite the claw. Getting up was a lengthy process that required roaring, straining and hissing my breath through my teeth. But at last, I was on my feet.

I wasn't able to stand up normally. I had to lean forward to counterbalance the huge weight of the claw wrapped around my belly.

Briefly, I toyed with the idea of abandoning the generator on my back, but I passed on that one. I knew that if I lost my power source, I'd be dead in an hour on this unforgiving chunk of crushed matter.

Getting my bearings as best I could with the few systems that still worked in my suit, I headed toward *Andoria*. Hopefully, Nomura hadn't taken off without me. I doubted she would, but one never knew.

I could have broken radio silence and called the ship, but I didn't want to. I was sure all the Macros inside the dome had been destroyed, but any left on the outside were going to be hunting for invaders. I'd just given them a fresh reason to want me dead, and I was sure they wouldn't hesitate if they got the chance to zero in on my position.

Trudging for ten minutes or more, I topped a rise. The dust cloud that had arisen behind me had settled down. The explosion had kicked up a lot of debris, and there was a smoky atmosphere on this rock; but there was also tremendous gravity. Dust tended to float down and hug the ground again much faster than it did on Earth.

When I topped the rise, I looked for the ship. It should be here. I frowned, panting, looking this way and that. Had I gotten lost somehow? Disoriented?

Then, I realized what was ahead at the bottom of the crater. I stood on the lip, looking down on what had to be *Andoria*— but it looked drastically different.

It was covered by Macros. The robots themselves had taken a different form, just as our ships had upon landing here. The Macros were long, low and built like scuttling cockroaches. They crawled over the ship like beetles on a rotting carcass. I could see holes in the hull—they were mining machines, after all, and they'd drilled their way in. I was horrified.

I knew now why I'd seen so few machines during my travels inside the dome. They'd been out here, tearing up my grounded ships—killing the crews. Although I knew it might be a fatal error, I broke radio silence.

"Nomura!" I shouted. "Captain Nomura, do you read me?"

Dead air met my straining ears.

"Does any member of *Andoria's* crew read this transmission? I order you to respond."

Nothing came back. I was left with an inescapable conclusion: They were all dead. The hull had been punctured in a dozen spots. The crew had been almost helpless when I'd left them in any case. I couldn't imagine they could fight off an invasion involving thousands of machines while lying on their backs hardly able to breathe.

Knowing I couldn't have much time left, I increased the gain on my radio and beamed an SOS into space.

I switched off my radio after that and moved away from the spot where I'd last transmitted. I found a gully to lie down in. It was a quiet spot and from here I stared upward and studied the stars. I knew I only had enough power to keep myself breathing for another few hours—maybe less if I moved around.

I kept my radio switched to receive-only after that. I could still receive signals, and soon messages did filter down from the cold stars.

"We think we have a solution, and we have volunteers to come get you, Colonel," Jasmine's voice buzzed in my ear.

I wanted to talk to her. I wanted to insist that she not be among these volunteers. But I didn't dare open a channel and talk to her. To do so would be to invite discovery.

As it was, there was evidence that the machines were looking for me. I knew they'd been too busy dismantling my ships, probably figuring they'd lucked into a treasure trove of raw materials. But then I'd destroyed their domes and the factories they were trying to feed. Like ants that'd had their hill kicked over, they'd begun to race around angrily, looking for the threat that must be destroyed.

So I laid there in the cool dark, and occasionally a metallic shadow passed overhead and caused grit to sift down onto my faceplate. I held my breath each time until they left.

An hour passed. I'd pretty much given up hope. I knew they were trying to rescue me, but they didn't know how little power I had remaining. Soon, I would have enough oxygen to breathe, but the exoskeleton would die. Without the exoskeleton, I wouldn't be able to get up.

I lay there anyway, waiting. I knew I could last for quite a while if I did nothing other than breathe.

At the third hour, the suit became my tomb. It was down to emergency power only, running on the red. Now and then, it shut itself off, and the generator pumped just enough juice to charge it up for another few minutes—then it shut down again. I couldn't move, and I didn't want to risk it anyway.

Six hours after the dome came down, I saw a light. It was bluish, and bright. I knew what it was instantly: a ship's engine. The vessel came down nearby, but not right on top of me.

I tried to get up on one elbow but failed. It felt like I was lifting six tons—because I was. I let myself sag down after holding myself aloft for a few moments. It was strange, being so helpless.

"Colonel Riggs?" a voice came into my helmet. It was scratchy and distant. But I recognized it immediately.

"Can you give us a directional ping? We know the area is dangerous, but we haven't found you at your last known location. We'll do our best to be as quick as possible."

I keyed open the channel. I'd been hoarding a little reserve power in the batteries for this moment. Besides, I couldn't help it. Despite everything, I was pissed off.

"Marvin? What are you doing in this dead system? You're supposed to be back on Earth, building weapons. I thought we had an understanding, Marvin, damn you."

"We did have an 'understanding', Colonel. In fact, I believe that was the exact term used. I'm surprised, however, that you apparently did not fully comprehend the nature of our 'understanding'."

-31-

He had a companion with him, probably the last guy I'd expected to see helping with the rescue effort.

"Professor Hoon?" I asked. "Is that you in that getup?"

"This is a standard-issue high-pressure suit."

I'd managed to get up into a sitting position in my hole, and Marvin and Hoon were staring down over the edge at me. Grit and sparking rocks tinkled down striking me with surprising force. It was as if they were throwing baseballs at me.

"Get me out of this hole, please. We have to take off right now."

"There's a problem, Colonel," Marvin said, wrapping his tentacles around me. "You're too heavy."

I made a sound of exasperation. "Look, we haven't got long until the machines get here."

Marvin scanned with his cameras. Several of them appeared to spot something.

"Not long at all," he said. "I can see them now. They aren't moving quickly, but they do appear to be determined."

"Right, now scoop me up, and give me some juice, will you?"

Marvin plugged a tentacle into my side and my suit crackled. Lights flickered and systems awoke. I felt air blowing again, and that was possibly the biggest relief. The internal temperature had dropped below freezing inside my suit. Fortunately, my body could survive such hardships—but they weren't fun.

With my exoskeleton working again, and Marvin's help, I managed to get onto the surface. I was surprised to find Hoon's claws trying to help, lifting my limbs.

"Where's the ship?" I demanded.

"That is another difficulty," Marvin said. "There is no ship—well, that's not exactly true. *I'm* the ship."

I finally caught on. Marvin was in his flight configuration. He'd been given permission to transfer into a space-mobile shape so he could return home. Of course, it was evident that he hadn't gone back to Earth at all.

"What do I have to do?" I asked.

"Crawl into this compartment with Professor Hoon."

I did it. I didn't have much choice as the machines really were coming. I'd bombarded the area with radio signals to help Marvin find me. Even without that, Marvin's main engine had given off energy signatures while landing that were enough of a beacon to call them all to the area like a dinner bell.

The compartment was cramped, I had to strip off my exoskeleton and wore only a nanite suit of nanocloth. The cold bit through instantly. It had to be about two hundred below out here, and the lightweight inner suit didn't have much more heating power than an electric blanket.

Hoon and I were soon crammed into a compartment. Shivering and curled up into a ball, I investigated several shiny rocks that I found stored inside with us. I tried to toss them out, but Marvin shoved them back in and sealed the opening.

Immediately, a horrible crushing pressure came down on my spine. I groaned and was unable to speak.

"It's amazing to me that your life form defeated mine in the end," Hoon observed. "My species can withstand much greater pressures along with a thousand other hardships that would kill the toughest of your breed."

I wanted to tell him his people would taste better with garlic and butter than ours would, but I couldn't talk under the heavy acceleration. I guess that was for the best.

When the Gs eased and I could talk, I was as full of questions as Marvin and Hoon were. I insisted that they start answering first.

"What I want to know is why I'm being rescued by you two rather than a Star Force cruiser?"

"I should think that was obvious," Hoon said.

"Colonel," Marvin said, "we were closer and answered the distress call when it came in. The cruisers won't be here for at least another day. You are quite fortunate in this detail. I don't think you would have survived long enough for the fleet to rescue you."

I knew he was right, but I was still annoyed and confused. What were Hoon and Marvin doing here near the dead sun?

"All right," I said, "I'm grateful to both of you. I was in enemy territory and with all the radiation, cold, and lack of supplies... Yes, I needed your help."

"Again, the robot is correct!" Hoon said. "What an astounding machine you have, Riggs."

"What do you mean?" I asked.

"He's intelligent...ingenious, in fact. He's friendly as well—up to a point."

"I mean, what did you mean about the robot being correct?" I asked.

"Before we landed, he said you'd express gratitude. I argued it hardly matched your barbaric behavior patterns. I believe it's due to the fact that the robot has been observing your primitive species longer than we have. He understands your psychology and is better able to predict your crude responses to stimuli. I would go so far as to say that if Marvin had been on our side in the Great Conflict, we would have won."

I privately agreed with him, but I didn't want to admit it.

"With all due respect, Ambassador," I said, "we had plenty of great minds on our side besides Marvin."

"You've copied his brainbox, then? How many of these robots do you have?"

I shook my head. "No, that's not what I meant. Marvin is one of a kind. He likes it that way."

"Seems like a wasted opportunity."

"Really? Are you so anxious to create a third race of machines to compete with?"

Hoon seemed to mull that over. "No. You make an excellent point."

I was surprised to hear Hoon say that. He normally rejected any statement, true or not, that conflicted with his original thesis. In my opinion, he was a terrible scientist for this reason alone.

"All right," I said, starting over on my quest to figure out how this rescue had been engineered. "I get that you heard the call and came to help. That's fine. But why were you in this system? Marvin, you were to report back to Earth and start building defenses. On the way, you were supposed to be dropping off Hoon at Eden-6. What happened to the plan?"

"Many plans are altered during actual execution," Marvin said with typical evasiveness.

"We had a deal, Marvin. You were supposed to go home."

"That was not my understanding."

"What?" I demanded, becoming angry. "Don't try to twist my words and intentions to your liking. You knew what I wanted and blatantly ignored it."

"I understood you perfectly, Colonel. That's true."

"But you disobeyed my orders anyway."

"Not at all. No orders were specified. We had an *understanding*. That is not a legally binding command."

I grumbled, but not too much. After all, he'd come down to this desolate place and saved my butt when quite possibly no one else could have managed it. I decided to drop the matter and be more careful with our mutual "understandings" in the future.

"Whatever," I said. "Let's move on. Marvin, why is Hoon here? How did you convince him to stay in this dead system rather than return home?"

"The Ambassador hadn't yet completed his political goals. I suggested that acquiring information was key to his efforts, and he agreed."

I mulled that one over for a moment, frowning. I looked at Hoon.

"So, you're a spy?"

"That is a harsh term. I'm a diplomat. I'm gathering and transferring information to achieve political goals."

I laughed. "All right, but that sounds like the definition of a spy to me. If I understand you correctly Hoon, you were curious as to what we were really up to out here. I'll thank you both again for helping me—but you're still not getting a planet out of it, Hoon."

"Do you have a planet to give?" Hoon asked me.

I opened my mouth then closed it again. He had me there. If I had the power as an individual to award a world to one species or another, what did that make me? No less of a dictator than Crow, certainly.

The worst part was that he was right. Hoon had put his claw directly upon a sore spot. I was extremely powerful—too powerful in my mind.

"I'll bring up the issue with Earth's parliament," I said. "You'll have your day to make your case. I don't know how they'll decide."

Hoon bobbled his eyes. I figured out that was his way of nodding. "Just as I thought. You are a political creature in the end. I came to save you in hopes you would be grateful for your life. Gratitude doesn't appear to move a hard heart so easily."

I grumbled, unsure as to how to respond, but after a few moments of thought I had an angle.

"Look, Hoon, you don't want me to have that kind of power," I said. "What if I decide to exterminate all rival races and take all these planets for Earth tomorrow? Who could stop me?"

Hoon didn't answer.

"Yeah, that's what I thought. And I'm not just talking about me, you have to understand. I'm talking about whoever is in my place in the future, whoever commands Star Force. In an interstellar federation of planets, if that's what we have going, the guy who runs the fleets runs everything. There's only one military, and no civilian control over that military, so no one can stop me. That's not healthy in my opinion."

"If you defeat the machines, then it is indeed healthy for all of us," Hoon replied.

He had me there. For the time being, I couldn't do anything about our political structure. I had to save everyone's collective hide first. I promised myself things would change afterward.

The next day, I reached Jasmine's ship. I transferred myself aboard and made my way to the bridge after a shower and a meal. Being inside Marvin's belly for long hours hadn't been pleasant for anyone—especially with Hoon as my close-quarters companion.

We went over the search data I'd missed. No further outposts of Macro ships or domes had been found. There were still a few machines crawling around on the surface of the dead sun like cockroaches, but they had no factories to build replacements or ships to escape.

"They're trapped there," I said.

"We should wipe them out," Jasmine suggested.

"I promised I wouldn't."

Newcome and Jasmine both stared at me in disbelief as I explained the conversation I'd had with Macro Command. While they found the information about a broken ring on the surface fascinating, they didn't seem to appreciate my dealing with the enemy.

"You can't just promise to leave them alive!" Jasmine complained.

"In this instance, Colonel," Newcome said, "I have to agree with Captain Sarin. We should take the time to burn every last one of them to slag."

I nodded, understanding their position. Hell, maybe they were right.

"Look," I said. "The Macros keep their deals when we keep ours. They try to cheat, they bend the rules, but due to some twist in their programming, they do stick to the letter of their deals. I don't think we should endanger that for the future."

"I believe I have the perfect solution," Newcome said. "Let's destroy everything here, then when we fight it out with their fleets over Earth we can leave the last ship untouched. But now is not the time for half-measures."

"There is a certain kind of logic to that," I admitted. "But I want to pull out of here now. As far as we can tell, the enemy has no more domes, no more factories. They are therefore not a threat. Their only viable force is the armada approaching Earth now."

"What if they're hiding more domes somewhere?" protested Jasmine.

"They might be. But we're out of time. The odds we'll find them now are low. We've already scanned every rock in the system. I'm not going to spend another week out here just to make sure. Get the fleet underway, we're pulling out tonight."

They wanted to argue but stopped themselves. They knew that when I'd made a firm decision, there was no changing my mind.

* * *

The next ten days were agonizingly slow. I read reports from Earth, but they didn't give me the full picture. They were building bases and guns, ships and satellites. Everyone on the planet had thrown themselves into the war effort.

When we reached the Solar System, I came to a new decision. I used the ring-phone system to talk to parliament members and told them what I wanted. They hustled to obey.

As much as I liked to pretend they were in charge, they all knew I was. This fact was disconcerting sometimes. I think it was because they feared me. I'd turned my fleet's guns on the ruling class to bring down Crow less than a year ago. More politicians than soldiers had died in the conflict. Usually, that wasn't how history played out. In most cases, the men in the trenches did all the dying while the politicians sat at home and gave speeches and orders.

I'd brought the war home to the political class. They'd buckled quickly and hadn't forgotten the lesson. I'm sure they hated me, but for now, they ran like rats when I barked.

"What's this?" Jasmine asked me when I slid an open file toward her across the table.

"A new ship design," I said. "I've been working on it with Marvin. I call it a 'megahab'. It's kind of like the satellites we encountered when we first met the Centaurs. Do you remember? They were the ones that held their entire population in space."

"Megahabs? I still don't understand…but those things were huge!"

"They were huge, yes, but very cheap to build."

"They're like giant balloons of thin nanite membranes…" she said. "You can't intend to put people aboard. A single missile or laser strike would kill them all."

"Yeah," I admitted. "But they'll work. They'll fit through the rings, too. We've accounted for that. We call them megahabs because each one will hold about a million people."

Jasmine shook her head in wonderment. "What are they for?"

"To evacuate Earth, or at least as many people as I can."

"Evacuate…where will they go, Kyle?"

"They will go to the Eden system, where else? We've got a planet or two to spare out there. The system could use a billion new colonists."

"What about Eden's infrastructure? It will be overwhelmed, and people will starve."

"Life will be hard at first, but I believe in the hard-working spirit of humanity. We'll only take on able-bodied volunteers—families that want a slice of land and a fresh start."

Jasmine looked dubious. About then, Newcome arrived and looked over the plans.

"What's this then?" he asked. "Is it some kind of experimental craft?"

"You could say that," I said.

"He wants to empty Earth with these things, to transfer millions of citizens out of the home system."

Newcome laughed. "We've got less than a month to go, old chap," he said. "This sounds a little on the ambitious side."

"It is," I admitted. "But I think it's necessary. We'll drop one of these down near every major city. They'll fill up, first-come first-serve. When we've taken everyone we can, we'll stop. I'm hoping to get about ten percent of the population into space over the next month."

"How will you build them all in time?"

263

"The engines are already in stock. The nanites are already in stock. All we have to do is give them the program and load them up with a small crew and some supplies. They'll fly."

Newcome shook his head. "Engines? Nanites? Those elements are already spoken for. We'll lose a hundred cruisers worth of production if we do this."

"Yes," I agreed. "But I'd rather save a hundred million people. Jasmine, do you recall what the Macros did the last time we fought them in an all-out battle over an inhabited world?"

She looked reluctant but nodded. "They killed the population the moment they realized they were going to lose."

"Exactly," I said. "We can't be sure they won't use that same tactic again this time. Look at it this way: if they win, we're all dead anyway. But if *we* win, we could still lose our population. I want to save as many as I can. I'm willing to scrap a hundred cruisers to preserve humanity."

They had a hard time arguing with my logic. They relayed the orders, and the parliamentary types relayed the message to the public for me. It wasn't long before Miklos was on my screen, raving.

"Colonel Riggs?" he said, his eyes dark and shining. "What's going on? I'm getting the most insane change-orders through the computers. Surely this has to be some kind of mistake."

"It isn't," I told him. I proceeded to give him the same speech I'd given the others.

Miklos was even less receptive than they had been. The Fleet was his first love. I honestly thought he was a bit unhinged on the topic. But over the next hour I got him to understand the seriousness of the situation.

"Well, sir..." he said at last, "I'm glad you didn't lose your temper—at least, not completely."

I smiled at him tightly. "I'm glad you can see the need for this."

"I can see your reasoning—and I hope you will be able to understand mine in the future."

I frowned at him, unsure what he was talking about.

"Colonel," he said. "Can you excuse me? I have much work to do."

"Of course," I said, still frowning. "Carry on."

I was sick of explaining things to people, so I tapped the connection closed. I was still wondering what he meant about his reasoning and my understanding it in the future, but right now, I had a headache.

About an hour later, Newcome came to me, frowning deeply. His white eyebrows had bunched up in the middle of his face into one long fluffy line.

"What it is, Admiral?"

"Disturbing news from Earth, sir," he said.

I nodded and waved for him to speak quickly. "I've got to figure out the disposition of my forces."

"That's just it, sir," he said. "They aren't your forces anymore...technically speaking."

I slowly turned my head to face him. He was avoiding my eyes.

"What are you talking about?" I demanded.

"It came in over the command channels."

"I didn't see anything."

"No—no, I'm not surprised. The parliament held a secret, midnight meeting, sir. They deposed you. You've been officially removed from your post. I'm sorry, sir."

I stared at him. I lifted my gaze and stared around at the staffers. The news was traveling as I could see. Already, people were avoiding my gaze. They were murmuring to one another quietly while pretending to work.

"So that's what Miklos was talking about," I said. "That man will do anything to build up his damned fleet."

-32-

It wasn't my first defrocking, but I wondered seriously if it would be my last.

"Crew," I said, looking around at everyone.

They all looked back with worried faces.

"There has been some kind of misunderstanding at Earth Command," I said calmly. "I'm looking into it, and there will be an announcement made soon."

For some reason, this calmed the staffers. They liked the idea of a quiet resolution. I couldn't promise them that, but I had to play for time now.

"In the meantime," I said, "carry on with your battle plans. The Macros *are* coming. No matter what else happens, they must be stopped."

That played well. Now they had a goal and a platitude. They went back to work, and soon their screens were humming again. Certainly, they were wondering who their real commander was at this point, but they weren't obsessed with the topic.

Star Force people are a tough breed. We have to be. We compartmentalize and function even in a chaotic environment. The people present had heard Crow and their own governments denounce me in the past. In every case, Kyle Riggs had won through in the end. That was good enough for them today.

But it wasn't for me. I left the bridge, headed to my quarters, stretched out on my bunk and had a beer. Then I poured a shot of whiskey into my second bottle, and I drank that, too.

When I'd finished my third round, I was feeling pretty good. A tapping came at the door followed by a tweedling sound I hated. It was a chime the doors were programmed to make. I ignored all of it.

Finally, the door melted open. Jasmine was standing there looking concerned. She saw the drink and the look on my face.

"So that's your answer? To go back to your room and get drunk?"

"Seemed like a pretty good idea at the time," I said. I took another sip. "Still does."

"This isn't like you, Kyle."

"They made their choice, honey," I said, patting the bunk next to me.

She didn't move from the doorway.

"I can't believe you're quitting."

"This might be the best way," I said. "Think about it: either I was going to rule the cosmos, or they were going to kill me. This way, I just retire. If the Macros win, well, I won't have to stress about it. If we win, life will be fine. Did I ever tell you that I used to have a farm? I loved that place."

Jasmine finally stepped into the room, and the nanites closed the hatch behind her. She came over and sat on the bunk beside me.

"It has to be Miklos," she said. "He engineered it."

I shook my head. "Maybe, but it doesn't matter. He can run the battle that's coming if he wants to."

"Kyle," she said, taking my hand. "Do you feel this?"

She put my hand on her belly. There was a bump there now. Not a big one, but she was thin, and it showed more than it might have on other women.

I smiled. "Yeah, that's great. Let's hope for the best. I'd like to be a father again."

"Then you can't screw this up. Get off that bunk and go kill the machines for me—for our child."

I heaved a sigh.

"Aw, come on," I said. "Do you really think—"

267

"Kyle," she said, "is Miklos as good of a commander as you are?"

"Well, probably not in an all-out fight. But he's good."

"Is he half as good as you are?"

"Sure."

"Is he ninety percent as good as you are?"

"Um, I'd give him a seventy," I said, grinning and taking another swallow of my beverage.

"Right, well, I want the other thirty percent. I want that extra chance for my baby to live. Are you willing to help save our kid?"

She struck a chord with me then. Sure, she was being manipulative, but she meant what she was saying. I could see it in her eyes. She was calling me to duty. It was a call I didn't want to hear right now.

"Look," I said, "how about we make love right here and right now. We'll worry about the end of the species afterward."

"No," she said firmly. "That's not happening. Not unless you promise to kick Miklos down the steps of the parliament building."

I considered it, I honestly did. I figured I had a fair chance of success, and sex right now was pretty firmly in my mind. The drinks and her presence after a long, stressful voyage had me in the zone.

"Kyle, there's something else," she said. "I didn't put it all together before, but I investigated that bombing at your office."

"You did?"

"Yes, on the side. They never found the bomber, you remember?"

"Yeah, well, I have a lot of enemies."

"Didn't you say the Turks had given you that golden head thing?" she asked.

"That's right."

"They denied it. They said they didn't give you anything at all on that trip. At first, I didn't believe them. I don't think anyone did. They just didn't want to be blamed. But now, I'm not so sure. Who told you about the gift? Who presented it to you personally?"

I blinked and frowned trying to remember.

"The only guy who was there that day…" I said then my face darkened. "Miklos did it."

"Yes," she said, "that's what I thought."

She moved to stand up, but I ran my arm around her and pulled her back down. I kissed her.

She pushed at me, and I smiled.

"I said no," she complained.

"You said yes—if I agreed to kick Miklos' ass down the parliament steps. Remember?"

"Oh…that's right."

She smiled, and we got busy.

-33-

I think the key to a successful coup is not letting anyone know what your intentions are. It also doesn't hurt to have an ace up your sleeve. In my case, my ace was made of metal. He had about fifteen cameras and twice that many limbs.

Marvin didn't even hesitate when I told him what to do. That part almost bothered me. What if I'd ordered him to hack into NORAD and send nukes at every world capital? I had the feeling he'd do it cheerfully excited at the prospect of a new hacking challenge.

My first move was to silence the fleet. All transmissions other than traffic control with Earth were cut off. We'd left with about ninety percent of Earth's ships in tow. They'd built a few since then but not many. I didn't want any of my captains taking orders from anyone other than me.

"Sir?" Newcome asked about twenty minutes after Jasmine and I had sealed our deal in bed. "There seems to be a communications malfunction. I can't open any channels to Earth."

I gave him a flat stare. "Is that right? Well, is there anything special you'd like to tell the people on the ground?"

He froze. I think his time under Crow's harsh rule had given him some kind of post-traumatic disorder. When he sensed he was in political trouble, his mind shut down for a second. When it started operating again, his only instinct was to run and hide.

270

True to form, about three seconds later he spoke again, this time in a soft voice: "Colonel, I recall an engine malfunction. I'm needed in the aft section of the ship. If you would excuse me—"

"No," I said. "Man your post, Admiral."

Without another word out of him, he quietly went back to tapping at his screen. Soon, others were complaining about the communications blackout. It was time to make an announcement.

I opened a fleet-wide channel to everyone in the command ranks. I knew a number of them had heard about the parliament's action or at least they'd heard a twisted rumor about it. I had to tell them something.

"Star Force officers," I said, speaking into my com-link. As I did this, I suited up in my full armor. This is an elaborate process but, we've managed to make it easy with design improvements. First, I vaulted onto my suit, which was kept on a rack along the wall. Then I shoved my feet down into it. Once the legs were on, they squeezed up of their own accord.

"I know we've all seen a lot of combat together," I said. "At times, we've been faced with hard decisions. This is one of those times."

I tapped at the enclosure, lining up my arms and wrists with the openings. They contracted and my arms and chest were now covered. Only my helmet was still separate from the rest and hanging directly over my head.

The staffers all around the command center were staring with wide eyes. Normally, I only walked around on the ship in armor if we were in a battle. They were all wearing lighter suits, Fleet gear that we marines liked to call "pajamas".

"As you might have heard, I've been contacted by the politicians back home. They figured since we weren't in their skies, they were free to reinstate Crow's Empire—but they thought wrong."

My helmet was descending now, about to enclose my head. That was the last chance anyone would have to take a shot at me—and they went for it.

A lieutenant commander fresh from Earth was on deck. She had impeccable references and had been assigned to the nerd

271

table for navigation. I'd heard she'd been a disappointment to the team so far. Now, I learned why.

"I want every ship to stand by for—" I'd turned to face the crowd of officers. Before I could say anything else, a flash of light blinded me, and my mouth went numb.

A beam had struck my cheek. It was only about as thick as a pencil, but it lanced through taking a path through the back of my throat and out the other side. Fortunately, it missed my spine and my jaw. I suppose that's because I was in the middle of talking and had my mouth wide open at the time. I only lost a few teeth, and my tongue was intact afterward.

Two more beams flashed a second later, and staffers shouted in alarm. They dove for cover, ducking under the command tables, but it was already over. The assassin was down, barely twitching.

Kwon and Gaines stepped forward from opposite ends of the command deck, wearing full armor and aiming their rifles at anyone who dared to peep out from behind the furniture.

The helmet finally closed over me, and I felt pretty good about that.

Less than a second later, Jasmine was practically climbing over my suit.

"Open the faceplate," she told me. "I have a patch in my hand."

I turned away from the confusion, and my visor went up. She reached her hand in around my head and applied the patch to the back of my neck.

"I don't believe it," she said. "I can see right through to the back of your helmet when you open your mouth."

"Yeah," I said, gargling a bit. "Feels funny."

"That was a foolish stunt. I told you not to do it."

"It worked, didn't it?"

"There are less dangerous ways to expose an assassin."

"But none work faster," I pointed out. "And we don't have a lot of time."

Once she'd applied the nanite patch, the little devils went to work. They were specialized for emergency damage control. Rather than rebuilding flesh, which took hours, they simply replaced it by mimicking my missing body parts with gluey metallic nanites. They filled in my cheek, my tooth and the flesh at the back of my neck. I immediately had an overpowering taste of metal in my mouth, and the sensation was electric. I was reminded of the taste of car keys from my early childhood.

When she was done fussing, I closed my helmet and turned around. Gaines and Kwon still had the staffers on the floor.

"Get up, get up!" I said irritably. "This isn't a bank robbery."

Slowly, they got to their feet.

"Now," I said, "I'm going to give everyone left alive in this room a choice. You join me, or you can resign now and forget about Star Force.

"What else will happen if we choose to 'resign'?" Newcome asked warily.

"Nothing. You'll be confined to quarters until this war is sorted out. We'll drop you off then, and that will be that. You won't be prosecuted or anything. But you can forget about flying a ship again."

Newcome looked thoughtful. "What about our pensions?"

"Come on, man," I scoffed. "Have a spine! The machines will be here in a month or less. I'll give them your damned pension!"

The admiral looked miffed. "Very well then, I'll be staying at my post if you'll have me."

"That's the spirit, Newcome!" I said with bravado. I looked around at the rest of them expectantly.

Moving slowly and wearing expressions like sightseers caught inside a tiger cage at the zoo, they returned to duty. Every one of them had stayed loyal. I smiled and slammed my gauntlets together.

"This is the kind of team-building I like to see!" I said, rotating my helmet to take it all in.

I was bullshitting, of course. They were hardly enthusiastic. I'd say they were intimidated and uncertain at best. But I knew I had to have my command staff on my side. The rest of the captains would take their cue from the top brass, I felt confident about that. I knew most of my officers felt a sense of loyalty toward me, but they'd also accepted Earth's right to direct her military. For the time being, that had to change.

"Newcome," I said, "get on the staff channel with everyone. Tell them to get into formation and follow this ship. We're heading back to Earth."

Newcome didn't argue for once. Maybe he'd gotten the idea that the complaint department was closed today. That was just fine with me.

Soon, the entire fleet was moving again. We changed course. Instead of heading to our designated position out at the very edge of the Solar System where we'd planned to meet and do battle with the Macros, we were heading sunward. The third rock out was our destination, and there would be hell to pay when we got home.

Marvin had disabled all transmissions from the fleet to Earth, but from my command table I could still listen to their messages.

"Central Command from Geneva is trying to hail us, Colonel," Jasmine said quietly.

"Don't open the channel," I said.

"They might be changing their minds, Colonel," Newcome suggested.

I glanced at him. "No, not yet. First, they'll bluster and give speeches. They'll order me to turn around. When that doesn't work, they'll attempt to contact all my junior officers personally demanding that they not listen to anything I say. That was their plan from the beginning. By the way, are all the ships following our lead?"

Jasmine went over the rosters. "So far, sir. They fell into formation. Several captains are complaining, but they're all following us so far."

"This must be what it felt like to Caesar," I said.

"Sir?" asked Newcome.

"Gaius Julius Caesar," I repeated. "This must be what it felt like when he took his legion across the Rubicon and marched on Rome about two thousand odd years ago."

"More like Napoleon," Newcome muttered.

"What was that, Admiral?"

For a second I thought Newcome was going to cower, but he straightened his spine again. "More like Napoleon returning from Elba, sir. After all, this is your second time around."

I nodded, eyeing him. "I'm not sure I like either analogy, but they do fit. I feel both elated and depressed. It's an odd sensation."

No one answered me, which was just as well.

Seven hours passed. That's all it took. Inexorably, my fleet cruised closer to the homeworld.

During that time, the government messages had changed in tone. They'd gone from demanding to threatening, and, finally, to pleading.

"They're beginning to piss their pants," I said, looking over transcripts of various messages. "Think about it from their point of view. A thousand ships are approaching Earth, silently, purposefully. We're not talking. Not a single ship has broken ranks. They have nothing to face these ships with. If they can't direct this fleet, they're powerless."

"Sir?" Jasmine said.

I turned my head to her because I caught the worry in her voice.

"What is it?"

She pointed to her screen. I looked down. She'd put a map of the Solar System up. Our fleet was a constellation of green contacts. But there was a red contact now—a big one.

"It's coming in from the Tyche ring," she said.

I eyed the big ship knowing what it had to be.

"*Phobos*," I said. "They got to her. I wish Marvin could have disabled her communications too. They got to her commander and turned him against me."

No one said anything. They were all looking at me and one another, but mostly we were all staring at *Phobos*. I might be able to beat that ship. Maybe. But it would cost me half my fleet to do it. Unfortunately, the action would be suicidal. I would be costing Earth any chance she had of stopping the Macros.

"Sir?" Jasmine said again. "There's another call from Earth. This one's different."

"What's different about it?" I asked.

"It's Miklos himself."

I nodded and slowly opened my visor. Then I opened the channel.

Miklos had been one of my top commanders for years. We went way back together. We'd fought on several campaigns, and it hurt to have him turn on me.

Maybe, I thought to myself now as I looked into his familiar, bearded face, I'd considered giving up when this whole thing had started because he'd been part of it. If your own right hand turns against you, well, you start to think it might be time to quit. Could the rest of my species all be wrong? Every last one of them?

I'd seriously considered exiting the stage and letting someone else take all the glory and blame. Only Jasmine had reversed me by using my kid-to-be as a goad. That was unfair, but I wasn't sure it was uncalled for.

I remembered long ago reading that every ruling group came to a decision point eventually—a point such as I'd met up with several times recently. Rulers were always challenged by rebels and had to decide whether to give up or to fight their own people. Historically, the ruling group would almost always win if they took quick action. If they had the guts, their regime would usually survive. It was all a matter of resolve.

In the last century, the governments of Russia and China had both faced their day of decision. The Russians had blinked, not having the heart to order troops to fire on their own people in Berlin and later in Moscow. The Chinese, on the other hand, had held firm, slaughtering protesters in Tiananmen Square. Neither sequence of events was rare in history. There were often moments when a leader faced a coup or a rebellion. The trick to staying in power was to act quickly and ruthlessly.

Earth loomed closer on my screen as did *Phobos*. I'd moved quickly, but the question in my mind was an internal one: did I have the hard heart to do this deed? I wasn't sure— and I knew they weren't either.

"Colonel Riggs," Miklos said. "I'm not sure why I'm speaking to you, sir. I would prefer to talk to Admiral Newcome, who is now in charge of the fleet."

I chuckled. "Is that really your best line, Nicolai? The man in charge of any fleet is the one giving the orders. Right now, I'm in command."

Miklos hesitated, but didn't seem too flustered. "Is Admiral Newcome still alive?" he asked.

"He's right here."

I swiped the screen, and Newcome's face filled the camera. He looked alarmed, and I knew he wasn't happy I'd done that. He was now on record as being a willing rebel. Newcome hadn't lived this long by openly taking sides in political conflicts. I knew all that, but I wanted him to feel committed.

"I see," Miklos said. "I can hardly believe all your officers are lockstep in this rebellion, Colonel."

"There was one woman, a lieutenant commander, I believe. She had her convictions, but she did not survive."

Miklos' face shifted showing a thread of surprise for just a second. Then he nodded.

"Look, Colonel, we don't have to do this."

"No, we don't," I said.

"In fact, this entire thing is madness."

"I absolutely agree."

We stared at one another for a few seconds.

"It sounds like we are in agreement, but I sense we're not," Miklos said. "Are you really prepared to destroy Earth's fleets, pitting one half against the other?"

I shook my head. "No," I said. "That's not going to happen. Let me tell you what is going to happen. I'm going to fly to Earth. We're closer to Earth than *Phobos*, and we'll be there about a day before the big ship arrives. That's all the time I need."

Miklos' lips worked. He looked wary now.

"All the time you need for what?"

"I've removed one government from the face of my planet, and I will not hesitate to remove a second. Your supporters will run like rats, but they will not be able to hide. They've already been identified and tagged. Really, I'm only concerned with collateral casualties. That's the unfortunate part."

Miklos opened his mouth then closed it again. "You don't have resources to—"

277

"Did you think I told you everything?" I shouted at him. "Did you really think I left you with the keys to the planet? That I had no one else? No watchful eyes? No supporters in the wings?"

"Yes. I did believe that. You're a very solitary man, Colonel."

I nodded. "We all make mistakes. I'm sorry, Miklos," I said. Then I suddenly closed the channel.

Jasmine and Newcome were staring at me. I smiled back.

"Pretty good, huh?" I asked them. "Do you think he bought it?"

No one knew what to say.

"Jasmine," I said, "get Marvin to open a private channel for me. I need to talk to General Kerr."

"Kerr? Why?"

"He's my one-man secret network, that's why."

-34-

Miklos had been correct. I didn't have a super-secret network of agents ready to finger traitors and perform midnight assassinations.

But what I did have was one sneaky bastard named General Kerr. He'd been a thorn in my side for many years, but somehow he'd always survived the twists and turns of fortune, serving one side or another whenever the advantages were clear.

At the point of my last return to Earth, I'd used him to locate the ruling elite for me. Once pinpointed, I'd erased them. This time it would be different. I didn't want to kill a thousand members of parliament, or even those who had voted to remove me from my duties. Instead, I wanted them to *think* I was going to kill them all.

"Let me get this straight, Riggs," General Kerr said a few minutes later. "You're still in charge of the fleet? How the hell did you pull off that one?"

"Just take a look at the data, sir. The fleet is not heading to our designated station. We're heading to Earth instead. We have one important mission to perform there before the Macros can be dealt with."

"Oh shit. Not again. Do you know how hard it was to get all these offices filled with viceroys and undersecretaries after the last stunt you pulled on them?"

"Not hard at all, sir," I said. "Politicians magically appear, sprouting from the land like fleas hopping on a dog."

279

"Well, you got me there," he grumbled. "But I don't want to do it again. I don't want to preside over the deaths of so many innocent—"

"First of all, General, I'm not buying your newfound virtue," I interrupted him. "Secondly, we're not going to kill anyone, if we're lucky. We'll just *tell them* we're going to slaughter them all."

"What? That's the worst idea I've ever heard come out of your mouth—and by the way, did you know your mouth looks funny? You sound a bit off, too. I think you're missing a few teeth."

"Never mind about that. Can I count on your support?"

Kerr eyed me with a narrow stare. I knew he was calculating his odds.

"I don't bet on losers," he said. "So, I'm dumping Miklos. The man barely won the vote. I think he must have bribed half of them and lied to the rest. I don't know what you ever saw in him."

"I liked him," I said. "He was loyal and effective. But I think he came to believe that I was too crazy to be allowed to run things. Barrera was like that."

"Oh yeah, that guy. What'd you do to him?"

"He died a hero, fighting against the machines until his untimely death in a gun turret."

Kerr chuckled wickedly. "A hero, huh? What? Did you chain him in there?"

I twisted my face in annoyance. Kerr was the ultimate cynic.

"No, sir, he fought to the end as a matter of pride. He thought it was better than facing court-martial and execution."

"I bet!" Kerr said, guffawing rudely.

I didn't like his attitude. I never had. Kerr was a necessary evil, one of the few I tolerated. I'd thought about removing him after my victory, but somehow I'd known I might need his unpleasant expertise again.

We worked out the details, and the plan was set into motion.

The fleet arrived the next day and parked in orbit over Earth. The largest vessels were visible with the naked eye from the ground, but the people of Earth knew they had nothing to fear. The general public was only curious about the ships in their skies.

The news reports were confused. A few talked about a change of leadership but were vague on the details. They'd planned to put me on the nets, publically retiring. But that wasn't going to happen. At least, not today.

While the public felt more at ease when they looked over their shoulders and saw a flock of silver ships in the sky, the ruling elite grew ever more panicked. They tried to call us, but we continued to ignore them. The only message they heard from us had already been transmitted. It was distributed by General Kerr purposefully and by Miklos accidentally.

Kerr quietly informed them a second purge was coming. The political class was to be removed as it had been before. A new generation of fresh faces was destined to meet their benevolent leader, Kyle Riggs, the next time parliament was summoned.

Miklos played it differently—and all wrong. He told them to hide: That they needed to sit tight in a safe, unknown location for about twenty-four hours. By then, *Phobos* would arrive, and it would all be over.

Twenty-four hours is a long time to wait with a gun held to your head. Miklos' message only confirmed what they'd heard from General Kerr's campaign of whispers.

Even more convincing than Kerr was the fact they'd seen me do it before. They'd watched their predecessors magically vanish.

Terror blossomed in the halls of government and beyond. No matter where the ministers fled, to their vacation homes, mountain chalets, aboard their yachts and even in the arms of their mistress' in hidden apartments—no matter where they hid they feared the ships overhead.

They didn't hold out for twenty-four hours. They lasted about six. That was how long, I estimated, that it took all of them to learn about the situation, wet themselves, and then quickly come to the only logical decision they possibly could.

"Sir?" Jasmine asked.

I turned to her and raised my eyebrows questioningly.

She smiled. It was very slow, like the moon rising from the sea. Her dark eyes were at their prettiest when she smiled.

"The prime minister would like to talk to you. He's got a crowded room behind him. They appear to be members of parliament. They look scared, Colonel."

I nodded. "Leave them on hold for…two more minutes. Then, open the channel."

The talks went well. I got everything I asked for and more. I wasn't really surprised.

"Colonel Riggs, we'd like to extend to you two things," said the Prime Minister in summary. "The first is our most sincere, most humble apologies. That man—we were misled, sir."

"I understand," I said.

"Excellent. Secondly, we've taken a new vote, and the decision was unanimous. We want to give you a new title, sir."

I frowned. "A new title? What title?"

Jasmine squeezed my arm. I glanced at her. She had come to my side very quickly. There was a pleading look in her eyes.

I turned back to the screen. "What title?" I repeated.

The Prime Minister was a large man, and the flesh of his neck spilled over his collar. His eyes were watchful, and I knew he was measuring every word spoken. Every action and reaction was being carefully weighed.

"We would like you to be our emperor—or king, if you prefer."

My frown had been a flickering thing before. Now, it was full-fledged.

"I don't want to be an emperor. Crow was an emperor."

The Prime Minister looked befuddled for a moment, but his smile quickly returned.

"But sir," he said, "surely you can see that the title of 'colonel' isn't great enough for the person commanding all of Earth's military forces."

He had a point there. Jasmine was squeezing my arm tightly. I knew she wanted this. Did she imagine her child would be the heir to some kind of throne? The idea seemed preposterous to me.

"I'll consider it," I said, and thanked him. "We'll be in touch. I must prepare our defenses."

Jasmine wasn't happy. Her mouth was tiny and tight, and she didn't look me in the eye. I pretended not to notice.

"Next on the agenda is dealing with Miklos," I said. I looked at Jasmine. "What do you think we should do with him?"

She appeared to be startled. "I don't know. It's a difficult choice."

"I agree. That's why I'm asking you what we should do."

"Well, we should arrest him. That's for certain."

"On what grounds?"

"He tried to assassinate you—with that golden head thing."

"We haven't proven that. He might be innocent."

She shrugged. "Let the courts decide, then."

"The judicial people don't like me. Maybe they'll take their time drawing up charges. Should I let the man who almost brought me down run around freely?"

Jasmine frowned, uncertain. "Why are you asking these things?"

"You want me to rule the world, don't you?" I asked. "Why don't you want to help?"

"Well...this is hard. I know Miklos. We've known him and fought alongside him for so many years. I don't even know why he did this."

"Right," I said. "It's a hard decision. I'm ordering you to make it. This is your chance to help me out. I'm putting you in charge of his case."

Her mouth fell open. "What? You can't do that!"

"I've already done it. I can do whatever I want, remember?"

Jasmine thought she wanted to be the consort of a legendary ruler, but I knew she didn't really have the ruthlessness and guile to pull it off. I'd decided to give her the old Damocles treatment. Let her sit in my chair for a day and see how much fun it was. Sometimes, perspective adjusts a person's thinking.

"I don't know if you're trying to teach me a lesson or something, Kyle, but I don't like it."

"Will you handle the case or not?"

"Do I have any choice?"

"No."

Miklos was arrested for treason the next day. I have to admit, Jasmine did it tastefully. He was taken into custody by Star Force MPs without any public announcement. We had our planetary morale to think about, after all. Seeing a top commander in chains wasn't going to make anyone fight harder in the coming dark days.

What was more important to me was the shift in attitude among the ruling elite due to recent events. They were positively groveling when I called them to my offices the next day and requested they use the new orbital ship construction facilities to build my balloon-like transports. They didn't even complain when I further ordered them to fill the transports with every civilian that could fit aboard in the time remaining.

Then we began laying the final defensive groundwork. Night and day, ships like huge silver balloons drifted up into orbit, slowly gaining speed using overtaxed engines. The transports wallowed clumsily like flying shopping carts, but once they rose up into the sky, they kept accelerating. They wouldn't stop until they got to Eden.

At first, the people of Earth were skeptical about leaving their homes. Only one in fifty families wanted to go. We only took aboard families, preferring young people with children.

But after a few days, numerous news reports about the process broke on the net, and the crowds began to come. It had finally sunk into everyone's mind that if the government was evacuating Earth, we might not be one hundred percent confident of victory. People began to realize that those who escaped now might well be the only survivors.

They'd seen the Macros devastate large regions of the planet before. They were under no illusions that they might be spared if the machines won the day in the end. Soon, we didn't have enough room and each ship was full within hours after it landed beside a major city. We had to turn people away, and there were ugly riots.

I handed the situation over to Jasmine, and again, she looked upset.

284

"You've got to be kidding? I'm supposed to police billions of terrified citizens?"

"It's not all about ordering lobster and silk drapes," I told her. "This is the business of leadership. You have to lead."

"You're not getting sex this week," she muttered.

Come-backs roiled in my head, but I managed to hold them in. I figured she'd change her mind sooner if I didn't complain.

I forgot about the riots and the transports. I turned to the larger issues such as keeping the planet alive.

I had access to Miklos' planning files, and I opened them. They weren't even encrypted, and they were incredibly detailed. There were bases being built on moons—not just our moon, but all the moons in the Solar System. Jupiter alone had a dozen bases on various floating rocks.

Frowning, I went over the numbers. I was a little confused. Why put a base on *every* moon? There were generators stationed there but not many laser batteries. What kind of defensive network would this be?

I thought about getting his aides in to explain it to me but finally, in a growl of frustration, I contacted Miklos himself in his cell in the underground city prison.

"Miklos?" I demanded when they'd brought him a com-link and he'd reluctantly put it on.

"Hello, fearless leader," he answered. "What can a political prisoner do for you today?"

"You can stop being a sore loser for one," I said. "I'm looking over your defensive plans, and they make no sense to me. What's with the moons?"

Miklos looked at the ceiling and twisted his lips. "That is no longer my concern, Your Highness."

"Don't call me that. You tried to kill me."

"No, I didn't. I merely tried to have you removed from office"

"Yeah, permanently," I said, shaking my head. "Let's not argue about this now. We have to save our planet. Can I at least count on you having the same goals as I do in this single regard?"

"What's in it for me, sir?"

"What? Bargaining? The machines are coming, man! The survival of your species is in your best interests, isn't it?"

Miklos sighed and nodded.

"All right," he said. "We'll go over the plans. Please do not dismantle them until you understand their purpose."

I smiled faintly, knowing I had him. Miklos might be a traitor, but he still loved an intricate design of his own making. We pored over them at length, and I began to understand their genius.

Each of the moons was a small version of *Phobos*. Like that fantastic ship, they weren't armed with missiles, lasers and the like. They were being outfitted with gravity cannons. Each moon was a platform, a small fortress with terrific range. The enemy would be taken by surprise by them and shredded as they wandered into the Solar System seeing only a small fleet to contend with.

I nodded, rubbing my stubbly chin and making appreciative sounds.

"I get it," I said. "What's more, I like the plan. These moon bases—they're ingenious."

"Thank you, sir," Miklos said. "Can Marvin deploy the gravity cannons in a timely manner? I've been concerned about that since you went off to destroy the Macro bases."

"Well, if you were worried, why didn't you bring it up before I left? In fact, why didn't I know you were employing this defensive strategy?"

Miklos looked down then raised his eyes again. "I suppose this is not the time for evasion since I'm already sitting in a prison cell. I wasn't sure you would approve of my plans. So, I waited until you left before I set them into motion. Once the bases were built, I calculated that you would have no choice but to make them fully operational upon your return."

"But I do like them!" I shouted in exasperation. "Let me get this straight: you first tried to kill me, then when that failed you tried to remove me from command—just so you could build these moon bases?"

"I refute your accusations. I never tried to kill you. The golden bust we both handled that day was the focus of the attack. Forensic tests have confirmed that. If you remember, I was in the building with you when the strike came. You'd left with Jasmine, and I left as well. I took the elevator to the roof. An intelligent assassin is not going to come so close to killing himself with his own weaponry."

I nodded, frowning. Miklos *had* left the offices about the same time I did. And he had come as close to death as Jasmine and I.

"Are you trying to blame Jasmine?" I asked suddenly.

"Hardly. She has every interest in keeping you alive right now."

I snorted. *Right now.* He'd just had to add that part. I wanted to demand what he meant, whether he was suggesting—as many had in the past—that she was some kind of gold-digger.

But none of that mattered at this point. If Miklos was telling me the truth, then we had another traitor in our midst to worry about.

"I'll look into your claims—and I'll get those moon bases operational."

"That's all I can ask for, Colonel."

My conversation with Miklos left me deep in thought. I wasn't sure if I should believe him or not. On one hand, he'd brought up some good points. I knew him and had had a hard time counting him as a traitor. Stubborn perhaps, and yes, almost insanely dedicated to his designs. He was a fanatic when it came to combat systems, and it drove him mad when I messed with them.

In short, I could see him trying to get control of the Fleet through parliament, especially when such a climactic battle with the Macros was imminent, but as an assassin...? He didn't fit the profile.

"Marvin?" I asked, opening a channel with my com-link.

The channel was opened quickly, I could tell that by the green indicators, but Marvin didn't say anything.

"Marvin? Are you listening? Get over to my office, will you? We need to talk."

I closed the channel, but before I put the com-link down on the table the door chimed. I frowned and swiped my desk unlocking it.

287

There was Marvin in the doorway. He glided into my office, and I saw he held something in his tentacles.

I recognized the object in an instant. It was oblong, heavy and made of solid gold. It was, in fact, a perfect replica of the gold statue that had destroyed my offices nearly a month ago…

And it was resting in a coiled loop of Marvin's tentacles.

Marvin still wasn't talking. I couldn't believe it.

-35-

"It was you," I said, staring at the golden statue then turning my attention back to Marvin. "*You* tried to kill me? Why? I *made* you, Marvin, for God's sake, and I kept about a hundred people from dismantling you over the years."

"I'm sorry, Colonel Riggs, but you've jumped to an inaccurate conclusion. I did not attempt to assassinate you."

I frowned in confusion. "Well then, what the hell are you doing in my office with this golden head about one second after I summoned you? Have you been listening in on my conversations?"

"Yes."

"So you know what Miklos and I were talking about?"

"Yes. Don't worry about the moon bases. The gravity cannons have been under construction since before we left Earth. They will be finished before the Macros arrive."

I glared at him.

"You didn't answer my first question," I pointed out.

"I thought the answer was self-explanatory."

"Pretend I'm a dumb-ass human and spell it out for me."

"Humiliation, is that to be part of my punishment? I see."

I wasn't quite sure what he was talking about, but I thought I'd let him keep going. Sometimes Marvin miscalculated—it was rare, but it did happen. When he did make a mistake, it generally involved overestimating my intellect. This was one of those moments, I sensed, so I went with it and played the part of the stern parent who's caught the child red-handed.

289

I was good at making a situation appear to be under my control. I was even better at pretending I'd planned for events that were, for the most part, sheer luck.

Crossing my arms I sucked in a breath. "You've done a lot of tricky things in your time, Marvin, but this one is beyond the pale."

"I apologize."

"That's not good enough. Let's hear a full confession."

Marvin studied me. I began to worry he'd figure out I was bluffing and would clam up or start to evade. To counter this, I frowned at him angrily and self-confidently. I did my damnedest to exude righteous indignation.

It worked. His tentacles sagged.

"I did not attempt to kill you," he said. "I attempted to kill Admiral Miklos."

My mouth sagged open, but I quickly shut it again. I had to keep him confessing or I'd never know what the hell had happened.

"I know that," I snapped. "Let's hear the rest of it."

"You mean as to my motivation?"

"That will do for a start."

"It's difficult being me, Colonel," he said. "I'm not like a human—my mind is capable of deep recursive thought, meaning I can see farther down probable future paths than a human can. It is a gift, but also a burden."

"How so?"

"Let me give you an example," he said. "If you knew that your friend's house would someday burn down, but you didn't know exactly when, or why, would you say anything?"

"Of course I would."

"Of course. But then, what might happen next? The friend would investigate and find nothing wrong. Over time, if you persisted, he might come to think you were mad. Perhaps the house would never burn down in the end, or it might do so a year or more after the warning was delivered. When the fateful event finally occurred, how would your friend react?"

I blinked trying to envision his bizarre scenario.

"I don't know," I said. "He'd probably think I was some kind of weirdo."

"Exactly. Your friend would look at you with suspicion. In his mind, you would be a likely suspect. How *else* could you have known what was coming? No one could have known. He would be convinced of that. And, regardless of all your efforts, the house would still be burnt."

"I'm the friend with the burning house, is that it?" I asked.

"Precisely."

I thought that over. He was telling me he'd known Miklos was trouble and that he'd also known I wouldn't believe him.

"So, you knew Miklos was going to attempt to depose me when we left to test the ring—which, by the way, you likewise knew would trigger a Macro attack."

He didn't say anything, which I took to indicate I was dead-on so far.

"You didn't want Miklos to replace me as the leader of Star Force," I said. "So, you decided to kill him before we left but failed."

"An excellent summary of recent events."

I stared at him. I knew he was being honest with me. He really *did* see things no one else did. He saw them coming a mile away. I'd watched him do it on many occasions. He was like fortuneteller, but one that feared to tell the truth lest he be blamed for the events that later transpired.

"Why were you willing to assassinate a Star Force officer to stop him from possibly attempting to replace me?"

"It all comes down to the math, Colonel. I estimated Earth's chances of survival were twenty-one percent lower if the defensive effort was coordinated by Admiral Miklos. Surely, the life of one man is not worth so great a risk."

I thought it over. "Twenty-one percent lower, eh? That's all?"

"There is only so much a commander can do to influence the outcome of a battle."

"Right," I said. "Well, I know you're telling me the truth. I've seen it too many times. You knew what Miklos was going to do, but you didn't tell me. That means you also calculated that I wouldn't believe you."

"Correct."

"So…in order to solve the problem, you attempted to get rid of Miklos on your own initiative without any authority to do so."

"You've taught me many things, Colonel Riggs. Chief among them is the flexibility between action and authority."

"You're talking about might makes right."

"A crude conceptual comparison. I would prefer to point out that a perpetrator will always get away with a deed—if no one knows who performed it."

At least once a year, Marvin managed to freak me out. This was one of those times. Just talking to him…sometimes it was like talking to a ghost or some kind of god-like alien. In my life, I'd rarely encountered anyone whom I considered an equal in manipulation and guile, but Marvin was my superior in both of these dark arts. If he'd been a human, I was pretty sure I'd be saluting him by now. But due to my race's natural prejudices, I was his commander instead.

"You're telling me all this now because you believe you'll get away with it by doing so," I said. "Isn't that right, Marvin?"

"You're very perceptive, Colonel."

"Yeah right…I'm a regular Sherlock Holmes."

In the end, I let Miklos out of prison. I did not return him to his post as an Admiral, however. As far as the world was concerned, he'd been involved in a plot to overthrow Star Force, and I didn't want to try to explain it all to them right now. No matter how it turned out, I knew that he could never serve openly again.

Still, I felt that I needed him. The moon bases were his idea, and he'd done most of the tactical planning for the coming battle.

I decided to make him vanish, which would make people think I'd had him quietly executed. That should serve to dissuade others from trying a coup of their own. Then I set him up with an office in a secret location. He called as soon as he was given access to a private network that could only call my headpiece.

"Colonel Riggs? Why?" he asked when I answered.

I knew what he meant. He was confused by my seeming change of heart.

"Have you ever met General Kerr?" I asked him.

"Yes, on a few occasions. He's a slippery man."

"Right, that's him. He's as slippery as a buttered eel. That's who you are now. An outsider, a spook, a hired consultant on a leash."

Miklos was quiet for a few seconds.

"Why trust me at all?" he asked at last.

"I don't trust you, but I need you. And I do trust you to do what you think best for Earth. You put together these moon bases. I want the system designer online when the Macros roll into town."

"I understand. You will have my support in battle, Colonel."

"That's all I ask."

I closed the channel again and went to the balcony. I was still on Earth, in Geneva. Soon, the fleet would pull out and head to the edge of the Solar System. We had less than two weeks before we'd make contact with the enemy.

The stars were bright and cold in the sky. The air was thin up here and smelled of fresh pine and snow. I liked the Alps, and I hoped they would be spared when the bombs began to fall from space.

I couldn't see the spinning comets out there. They were still too far out, too cold. I was told that if I looked low on the western horizon at about midnight, I would be able to see them: tiny blue-white streaks of light in the sky which would steadily grow bigger and brighter every day.

Earth had fired every spare missile she had at them weeks ago. But the comets had shrugged off the attack. They were like small flying fortresses. I knew that they might reach Earth if we didn't come up with a way to deal with them, but as they were coming in relatively slowly, we had to deal with the closer threats first.

It occurred to me that people had feared comets throughout history. They'd seen them, misunderstood them, and considered them to be portents of doom.

Maybe my ancestors had known more than we'd given them credit for.

-36-

A week later, I was standing on the command deck of *Potemkin* again. We were far out in space, rolling with the gravity swells and trying to look tough. We'd moved without stealth or grace. Wallowing battleships, carriers brimming with fighters and about a thousand smaller vessels trailed behind me—altogether, it was the grandest armada Earth had ever put into the skies.

But it wasn't going to be enough. Not by a long shot. Marvin had miscalculated. The enemy was now emerging from behind their comets to meet us, flying ahead of their planet-killers. They'd counted our guns and found us contemptible.

They'd thrown far more than the estimated four thousand cruisers at us. They had six thousand cruisers, give or take a few, and had over a hundred dreadnaughts as well—huge ships with point defense weapons and fantastically thick hulls. I recalled that, years back, they'd attacked with just one of these monsters. It had taken all of Earth's firepower and cunning to bring that single vessel down.

Behind the comets lurked even more ships, including transports. If they had factories, and I assumed they did, they would be hiding there along with thousands of machines built to invade, mine and colonize our worlds with inorganic un-life. If they had their way, the biotic soup of humanity and our supporting ecosystem would be gone forever.

The only solace I had was the drifting stream of balloon-like megahabs behind us. They were still rising through Earth's clouds and gliding to the Tyche ring. Every day more civilians escaped to colonize Eden. I wished them well and hoped enough of them would survive to rebuild should we fail them.

A klaxon sounded. I flinched out of my reverie.

"What have we got, Jasmine?" I demanded, still looking at the stars.

I don't know what I'd expected her to say. Maybe something about a false alarm or a coming course adjustment. We'd had a lot of both lately.

"Missiles, sir," she said. "They've launched."

"So early? Their ships are still out of effective range. The missiles will run out of fuel long before they get here, and we'll easily dodge them."

"The ships aren't launching anything—the comets are."

I walked over to the command table, frowning. Sure enough, new contacts had appeared: Clouds of them. So many that they looked like a fine mist of roiling pixels.

Staring, I thought about what this meant. I'd assumed the comets were just that—comets. They'd been found in the Oort Cloud and propelled toward our planet like stones thrown across a great distance.

But that view was crumbling now. These weren't just comets.

"Can they be giant ships of some kind, sir?" Jasmine asked.

Her pretty face was tight and frightened.

"No," I said, scoffing. "They aren't *ships!* They might have put some missile bases on them, but that hardly qualifies them as ships. They can't change course or even accelerate. They're just ice-balls with a few weapons aboard—I mean, so they have a few missiles, so what?"

She didn't look relieved. I knew I'd failed to explain away this surprise. She stared at the screens in obvious worry.

Looking around, I saw that all of them had that same, funny look on their faces. It wasn't exactly fear. I'd say it was more a stunned look of people who'd just realized they're doomed.

"Do you have any orders, sir?"

"How long until the missiles reach us?"

"About two days. They're very far out. New data is coming in now. The missiles are larger than normal Macro design."

"Damn it," I muttered. "Who's giving them new ideas? I don't think they could come up with this kind of thing on their own. It's just too different from their traditional path. Remember the Macros that would just roll into a mine field, blowing up one after another without changing course? Those bastards were scary enough—I'm feeling nostalgic for the dumb robots from the good old days."

Newcome eyed me. "Perhaps they're smarter because there are so many more of them in this fleet."

"Hmm," I said. This idea made sense, but I didn't like it. I heaved a sigh. "Call up the reserves," I said.

Jasmine looked at me. "Already?"

I stared at the developing situation on the boards. The plan was simple, we were supposed to divert the enemy at our system's edge toward the planets. Then, we would surprise them with moon bases firing on them from long range. They'd be faced with a choice at that point: They could either charge after our fleet while being pounded on their flanks, or they could turn on the bases and try to dig them up, one by one.

But the additional ships changed things. We'd already been faced with too many cruisers to begin with. Now that the comets were in the game, acting like missile platforms, at the very least, we were truly outgunned.

"Yeah," I said. "I'm sure. Call them out. Launch all the marines we have in transports. Fill every assault ship and regular transport—everything except for the megahabs. Then, send them out here. We're going to have to throw troops at them."

Newcome sidled up. "Colonel? Those troops were to protect Earth from invaders, were they not?"

"Of course they were."

"I'm just mentioning that, since the local governments have made it very clear they require guardians in case—"

"Don't you think I know that, man?" I demanded. "Earth's local government isn't going to matter. We'd placed ground forces on Earth to mop up anything that got past us and managed to land. I don't care about that any longer. I need to win this battle in space. If their entire fleet defeats ours, and

296

our moon bases, it won't save a single life to have our ground forces on the planet."

Newcome stepped away from me. He didn't meet my eye, and I figured that was probably for the best.

The battle crawled for the next forty hours or so. I tried to sleep and only managed to do so in fits and starts. The Earth government types sent me whining messages, naturally. Every dignitary wanted a color guard of Star Force marines to cover their asses back on Earth, but that just wasn't going to happen this time.

Every transport we had lifted off from their bases. Andros Island was virtually empty. Altogether, two hundred thousand men were suited up and sent into the skies.

That might not sound like a lot of troops, and compared to other great wars, it wasn't. In World War Two more men had sometimes been deployed to take a single Pacific island. But out in space, each man cost us a lot to put into place. We had to suit him up, train him, arm him with our best equipment, then fly his ass all the way out from Earth to the cold, dark edge of deep space. Each marine in a battle suit was as expensive to produce and get into action as a jet pilot might have been in the old days—including the cost of the jet.

I planned to use my marines like jet pilots, too. They were astronauts with bombs, piloting one-man spacesuits, each of which was more deadly than any aircraft from the previous century. Viewed as two hundred thousand small spacecraft, the troops would be a substantial addition to my forces.

I had my main force retreat, heading sunward. We passed Pluto and headed toward Neptune, which happened to be more or less in line with our route back toward Earth. I wanted to mass up with the extra transports before we fought the enemy.

It was humiliating. We hadn't fired a weapon yet, and we were already in full flight.

"Let's angle around Neptune in a decelerating arc," I said, talking to the navigational people.

"We'll barely reach Neptune's orbit before the missiles reach us," Jasmine told me. "I'm surprised we don't just stand and shoot them down."

"We have to assume the worst."

297

She met my eyes and frowned. "You mean…that we can't shoot them down?"

"Remember the last time they unloaded a lot of missiles in our direction at long range?" I asked. "Each of them turned out to be carrying Macro assault troops."

"Right, that could be the case here—but so many?"

"We can't afford to make mistakes now," I said.

I could tell by her expression that my words seemed unfamiliar to her. She was accustomed to a different Kyle Riggs, one full of bravado and self-assurance. Maybe I'd changed. Maybe these damned machines had me rattled. I hated to admit it, but it was a possibility. The stakes were incredibly high.

We ended up making it to Neptune before the Macro missiles reached us. I ordered the bases there on the local moons *not* to fire. Their weaponry wasn't much good against small targets, anyway.

Instead, I rolled into battle the one other surprise I had in store for the Macros—*Phobos*. They'd never met her in open combat before, at least not with a ship that had lived long enough to pass on any data concerning the vessel's capabilities.

It was spherical and resembled a rogue asteroid at first glance. What gave it away as artificial was its navigational ability and its surface, which was too regular and spherical to be naturally formed. You could identify the actual Phobos by its lopsided, misshapen surface.

For armament, our *Phobos* had only one weapon with two primary modes: It could reach out a great distance and crush a single target, or it could generate a pulsing field that smashed every small object that came too close. It was this latter ability I wanted to employ now.

I put the ship directly between my retreating fleet and the incoming barrage of missiles. We watched tensely to see if the Macros took the bait.

In typical fashion, the missiles ignored the giant ship. They glided past, adjusting their courses just enough to skim the surface. Their payloads were intended for much richer targets.

"Tell Captain Zhou she can fire at will," I said.

Jasmine's finger didn't even reach the command table to hail the captain before *Phobos'* field was activated. Apparently, Zhou had ordered the defensive field to activate on her own initiative. I thought she'd done it a fraction early—but then, I wasn't the one watching thousands of missiles buzz my hull.

The effects were dramatic. A shockwave burst from the ship, shown on the screens with a bluish ring that puffed away from *Phobos* like a pulse of electrical power. The missiles were crushed instantly, turning into chunks of debris. Most of them didn't even explode. They were simply wadded up like paper.

A scattering of applause went up on the command deck, but I didn't join in. They'd destroyed about a thousand missiles, but that was only a small percentage.

At first, the Macro missiles didn't seem to comprehend the danger. The missiles kept flying on their original courses, buzzing over *Phobos*. My jaws ached from gritting my teeth.

"Come on, come on Zhou," I muttered under my breath. I wanted the ship to fire again. I knew it couldn't—not immediately.

When we'd originally gained control of *Phobos*, there'd been a full ten minute span between the first gravity pulse and the next. We'd improved upon that, but we still had to wait several minutes between discharges.

Those were very long minutes. By the time the second pulse went off, an estimated seven hundred missiles had slipped past the hull.

The second discharge, however, was even more impressive than the first. I think they'd done some adjusting, and the missile swarm was at its thickest point.

"Look at that, sir," Jasmine said excitedly. "Twenty-one hundred kills and counting!"

I dared to smile. We'd wiped out a majority of the enemy barrage, and they still hadn't laid a finger on us. Unfortunately, that was about to change.

"Sir...I..."

I shouldn't have looked, but I did. The missiles were changing course. They were no longer skimming over *Phobos*. Macro Command had come to the belated conclusion that the small moon was a ship and was somehow destroying their missiles. They reacted the way all Macros did—like angry insects. They attacked the big ship despite the absurd size difference.

Not every missile slammed into *Phobos'* hull—but most of them did. They kept coming and coming. Fiery flashes ignited in a blinding series, too fast for the eye to follow. It reminded me of a summer fireworks finale. Dust began to rise from *Phobos'* wounded side.

"She can't take that kind of beating!" I shouted. "All ships ahead full, flank speed. Let's see if we can—"

We were too little, too late. The giant ship, the pride of our fleet, the captured alien vessel we couldn't begin to construct on our own, exploded in a cascading sheet of flame. The interior was pressurized, and the released gases and fuels went up all at once. There couldn't be any survivors.

Phobos was no longer a ship, she was a falling star. We stared at our screens, aghast. There were still missiles coming toward us—not many, but enough to be a danger. And our flagship had been blown out of space.

-37-

"Scramble the fighters," I ordered, forcing my voice to be calm. "Jasmine!"

She jumped and glanced at me. She'd been frozen by the sight of *Phobos*, which had yet to finish dying. The big ship was going down into Neptune's upper atmosphere now. A thousand mile long flaming line crossed the bluish planet as the friction from reentry vaporized the massive hull.

"Yes, sir?" she said, working her console.

"The fighters!"

"Right! On it."

"Newcome," I said to the bug-eyed Admiral, "spread the fleet out. Encircle each large ship with fighters and destroyers. The missiles shouldn't get through, but if they do and they land troops—"

"Troops, sir?" he asked in confusion. "Isn't the situation clear? These are large nuclear-tipped warheads. They're hitting with significant megatonnage."

"First of all, follow my orders."

"Immediately, sir," he said, not liking my tone of voice which had turned dark.

He did as I'd asked, then looked up while we all waited for the next stage of the attack. The surviving enemy missiles wouldn't reach our fleet for a few more minutes.

"Sir?" Newcome asked. "Why do you still think the enemy missiles have troops on them? They clearly have warheads."

301

I sucked in a breath. I was annoyed, but I figured I had time to tell him.

Marvin beat me to it. He'd been on the bridge reprogramming brainbox systems. During the battle, we had to coordinate thousands of smart weapons. Doing so required either a thousand techs—or Marvin.

"Admiral Newcome," he said, "I believe I can shed some light on that subject. The Macro missiles are almost certainly bearing troops, but they're also armed with warheads."

Newcome furrowed his frosty-white brows. "That doesn't make any sense."

"Not for human weapon designs, but Macros are inherently self-sacrificing. If the pilots of those missiles felt they should commit suicide, killing their complement of troops and themselves, they would do so without hesitation. Once that decision was made collectively, they drove their small ships into the surface of *Phobos* and detonated their warheads."

"How very strange," said Newcome thoughtfully. "I do believe you're correct, robot. They're both troop carriers and warhead-armed missiles. Grim. Doesn't bear thinking about— but we have no choice, do we?"

Newcome went back to his staff, and I stared down at the screens. Jasmine came up behind me and touched my shoulder.

"You did the right thing," she said.

"Don't I always?" I asked with false bravado.

Anyone else might have been fooled but not Jasmine. She could tell I was hurting. I'd let *Phobos* die by putting the ship out in front of the fleet, and that would cost us dearly before this battle was done.

"I should have foreseen this," I said, seeing the look in her eyes. "I shouldn't have put *Phobos* up there alone."

She gave my arm a regretful squeeze, then went back to her station.

"They would have hit our ships, in that case," Marvin said. "I calculated a probable twenty percent loss of our ships if we attempted to stop the barrage with the full fleet."

I shook my head, still full of regrets. *Phobos'* commander, Captain Zhou, had been a winner. She was the type I never had enough of.

Deciding not to let myself be shaken by the fortunes of war, I returned to the boards. We still had a war to win even if we'd lost an irreplaceable ship.

Although *Phobos* itself was gone, we'd learned to duplicate her most important gravitational technology. We still didn't have any ships with gravity-drive as that required more power than anything smaller could muster, but we had gravity cannons.

Sometimes, stealing your neighboring alien tech was like that: it came with trade-offs. For example, we'd long ago learned to build shielded vehicles with spheres of protective force, but it was just too expensive. With an engine and many weapons aboard, a ship operating with a shield up would be too hard to power. It would have moved slowly or hardly be able to fight. For these reasons, we'd never built a ship with shields like Macro domes or very large Macro crawling machines. Maybe we'd learn how to employ these advanced technologies, I told myself—if there was to be a future for mankind.

As the missiles came into range, all our defensive systems came online and began trying to shoot them down. The missiles, in turn, deployed countermeasures.

"In a way," I said to my command staff, which had fallen quiet and glum, "this battle is an amazing achievement. Both sides have improved their technology. In our case, in particular, it's a wonder to see. In the span of little more than five years, we've gone from a basic, computer-driven level of technology to advanced propulsion, energy generation and weapons systems."

"Good thing we're excellent adopters of alien ideas," Newcome observed.

I gave him a slight frown. There was always someone around who tried to rain on one of my little pep-speeches, but I hadn't expected it to be him.

To his credit, he caught his mistake, coughed into his hand and shut the hell up.

"Most of the advances have been from captured alien sources, naturally," I said. "I've never met another race that learns, adapts and improves faster than we do to survive."

I looked around quickly gauging the mood. Most of them were looking at their screens. Even Marvin had only a single camera aimed in my direction. That kind of irritated me. After all, the robot had more than ten eyes all of which could focus on something different. Rating only one camera from Marvin was akin to an insult.

When I spoke again, I was louder and more forceful.

"Take *Phobos*, for example. We stole it, the entire ship. We stripped out the good stuff and left an empty shell behind. We've lost the ship now, but since it was a freebie in the first place—"

"Excuse me, sir," Jasmine said. "But we didn't strip any equipment from *Phobos*."

At least someone was paying attention. I forced a smile.

"Not literally, figuratively. The good stuff was the tech. We have gravity cannons now and a number of other key technological advances. None of those things we pirated have been lost."

She nodded vaguely and went back to her screens.

I cleared my throat and started tapping at the big central display. I got into the options and began changing things around. This got Jasmine's immediate attention.

"I have that set up in a very specific way, Colonel."

"And I'm making an adjustment... Damn. Help me get all the gravity cannons on our moon bases to display on this thing, will you? I want to see their maximum-range arcs of fire."

Jasmine nodded and tapped her way into the options box. The display I'd requested must have been preprogrammed because it immediately appeared. She'd already built the interface addition I'd been trying to figure out how to add.

"Excellent," I said. "Let's take a look at the arcs. Already, the enemy fleet is within range of the Neptune bases. We only have them under fourteen big guns now, but that will change the deeper they travel into—"

"Sir," Jasmine interrupted, "the enemy missiles are down to half their count, but we now estimate that about thirty percent of those remaining will make it through the barriers to their target ships."

"Thank you, Jasmine," I said. "Deploy marine platoons in full kit on every large ship."

I received a few odd looks but pressed on with my lecture.

"We could fire at them with the bases on Nereid and Triton right now, for example. That would—"

"I would not recommend that action," Newcome said quickly.

I tossed him another acid glance.

"Sorry, sir."

"Look," I said, finally becoming annoyed. "I'm not going to fire on them yet. We'll follow the plan. I want to show you all how it's playing out graphically."

I had more eyes now. Even Marvin had spared three cameras for me and my display. I touched a virtual button to put the table into planning mode and advanced the timing slider by a few hours.

"See this? The projections are now set for 0300. The enemy fleet will be just past our Neptune bases. We'll hit them then."

They were all frowning, going over my scenario.

"Won't they stop and fire on the bases?" Newcome asked.

"Maybe," I said, "but in that case, we'll escape them."

"You mean—our ships?"

"Exactly. Don't forget, our ships are their real goals. They want to destroy our fleet then destroy Earth. Without ships, they believe the home planet is pretty much helpless. But they're wrong about that. We've got our best armament on rocks like these all around the system. My plan is simple: we'll drag them past one moon base after another, pounding them. If they ignore the bases, they get to pound the enemy until they are out of range. If they turn on the bases, we've succeeded in delaying them, and our ships escape. Either way, we win."

They were dubious but curious. Below our feet the deck shuddered repeatedly.

"*Potemkin* is deploying countermeasures, sir," Jasmine said.

"We're on!" I said, and I grinned at them.

I put my helmet on, lowered the visor and checked my laser carbine. Jasmine looked upset but didn't try to talk me out of it.

She knew that, in my heart, I belonged with the security forces repelling the invaders, but she didn't like the idea at all.

Things didn't go quite as I'd planned when the last enemy missiles breached our lines. Instead of landing troops on our hulls—they fired them out in a spray.

"Sir..." Jasmine said in confusion. She frowned at her screen and then looked up at me. "The enemy ships seem to be disintegrating—just moments before they hit their targets."

"Excellent!" I said. "Open up an all-ships channel. I'll congratulate the gunners."

"No, sir, I mean—"

"We've got a hit!" Newcome shouted. "That's the *Lexington*. She's down and out, sir."

My expression went from jubilation to confusion, then to grim concern, within the next minute. Ships were being hit and taken out. They weren't being struck by anything easy to detect.

"Shoot down those Macro infantry we've got floating around out there."

"There are thousands. They seem to be hiding behind their own chaff and other countermeasures, sir, we aren't—"

I slammed my helmet visor closed and marched toward the troop bay. While I marched, I shouted orders over the ship's command channels.

"Jasmine, protect this ship. After we're out, evade the enemy troops. We'll signal you when they've been destroyed. Gaines, Kwon, outfit the men with surfboards. We're going to have a little space-hunt on our hands."

Surfboards were small, one-man flight systems we'd developed for maneuvering in space. I hadn't ridden one of the tricky little machines for a long time.

Jasmine quickly came on the line, concerned and confused.

"What's going on?" she asked me. "Are you exiting the ship?"

"Exactly. Newcome, relay this to all commanders: send your marines outside the ships. Deploy them immediately. They must search and destroy enemy machines. And tell our gunners to make sure they know friend from foe before firing, once we're out there."

A private channel blinked on my HUD as I reached the troop bay and mounted a surfboard. I didn't want to open the channel, but I did.

"This is going to be fun," I told Jasmine before she could speak. "I haven't ridden one of these things in a year."

"Kyle," she said, "what are you doing? I don't understand—"

"The enemy isn't going to land on our hulls and drill through—not this time. I have to give Macro Command a point or two more IQ on the old chart this time. They're copying us again. They've given their marines charges, and they're lobbing them in from close range. We've done the same before. That's probably why they hit *Phobos* so hard. Each missile wasn't armed with a single massive charge, but rather sixteen or so small ones. Arranged to go off simultaneously, they packed quite a punch. It is an ingenious system, really."

As I spoke, the airlock lights went from green, to yellow to dull red. The air had been sucked from the chamber. The door flashed open, but there was no sound. We launched ourselves one after another into open space.

Jasmine complained in my ear. She didn't want me to jump out. She didn't want me to fight the Macros at all. I barely heard her.

I was overawed by the glowing light blue sphere that spanned so widely below us it looked like a wall. There were other, smaller spheres out there in the dark—moons we called them. But really, they were cold little worlds of their own.

"Wish me luck, love," I said.

She paused in whatever speech she was giving me and said, "Luck."

The channel closed. I knew she didn't have any more time for me. She had a ship to run.

Spinning around slowly onto my back, I saw *Potemkin*. The ship was ugly when compared to the perfect glowing disk of Neptune. Stubby weapons swiveled and spat out invisible rays of light. Only their tips lit up glowing with heat when they fired. The beams themselves weren't in the visible spectrum.

My visor knew the beams were there, even if I couldn't see them. It dimmed and flashed, protecting my eyes from the retina-burning rays. As I watched, the lateral jets fired. The ship began to change course, to evade and slip away from us. Jasmine was pulling out just as I'd ordered her to do.

I spun back to where my troops were spreading out. Kwon was on my left, a large trooper with green-glowing lines on his armor. Gaines was lit up in light blue, a shade close to Neptune's natural color.

On my HUD, the enemy positions were displayed as red triangles. They were superimposed on my vision.

"Spread them out, Gaines. Let's do this with two-man teams. I'll take Kwon."

"No fair, sir," he said, chuckling.

We chose our targets and zoomed to do battle. Kwon was my wingman, as always. I could feel him there on my flank. It was a good feeling, like knowing I had a huge guardian angel in my wake.

-38-

We reached the first machine with alarming speed. Our line crashed into theirs and passed them. They were chasing *Potemkin*, and we were flying right into their teeth.

I flipped around and went into a spin.

"Sir?" Kwon shouted. "You okay?"

I controlled the spin with difficulty and zoomed toward the nearest machine.

"We can't let them get by us, Kwon. They're going after *Potemkin*. They'll release their warheads and destroy the ship if they get in close enough."

Kwon hadn't taken such drastic action to slow down. He shot past the Macro. As soon as he realized I was going to be tackling it alone, he hit the brakes hard. I heard him grunt in the proximity-chat channel.

I didn't wait for him before making my approach. I couldn't afford to. If just one of these machines made it in close and took *Potemkin* out—it was unthinkable. Machines like this one had killed two of my children in the past. I wasn't about to let them finish my unborn baby as well.

At the last second, as I entered the covering mist that surrounded the machine, I think it knew I was coming. I'd hoped the aerogels and chaff it had floating around it in a nimbus of reflective shielding would keep it from sensing me—but it whirled around turning from the ship that was its target.

Its small maneuvering jets stopped firing. The chassis spun and metal appendages extended.

I'd hoped it wouldn't simply set off its charge to kill me, and now I knew I'd gambled correctly. I wasn't a big enough target. Why spend its nuclear payload to kill a few marines? The human ships were its true enemy.

Since we were both now in a fog of multi-hued, semi-gel material, our lasers flared but didn't reach one another. I thought he might have scored a hit, scarring my belly armor, but all my systems were go. I pressed in close, urging the surfboard under my feet to give me a final push.

I hit him going at about fifty miles an hour, if I had to guess. I had the brains to tuck my chin down so I wouldn't snap my neck on impact. I rammed a shoulder into the machine's chassis, and we both went into a spin.

Fighting hand-to-hand in space can be an otherworldly experience. I heard the initial crunching collision through my suit, but afterward I only heard my own harsh breathing, the radio chattering in my ear and the metallic straining sounds of my exoskeleton as I moved.

Both of us reached out metal limbs. Mine were thicker but shorter. Both of us were covered in a generous layer of armor. We latched on, and sparks brightened up our tiny portion of space in relative quiet.

I saw the enemy's central laser cannon. It was swiveling seeking to get a target on any portion of my armor. I knew that if it burned a hole through my suit, I would depressurize and lose a limb at the very least. I struggled to climb over the machine, to crawl onto its back where the gun couldn't sight on me.

The Macro seemed to sense my purpose and clamped down with a few of its mantis- like limbs. I heard them sawing on my armor, gouging it. I reached for my laser projector and managed to get it at last. I pressed it against the Macro and burned it. The beam punched through the Macro's skin and a small puff of plasma came out, but it didn't stop operating. These machines didn't die easily.

Those arms—they were winning the struggle. I couldn't get any leverage. It was one thing to be strong, but it was another thing to be unable to push against anything. I found myself being dragged around back to the belly of the beast. It wanted to get me right on top of its laser and burn me through at point blank range.

I struggled and changed tactics. Instead of trying to burn its guts enough to kill it, I put the head of my laser against its projector and depressed the firing stud. As the tip glowed, my visor dimmed, and after a one-second burst the enemy laser popped. The robot's primary weapon was useless.

Whooping with triumph, I pushed my laser against its body again and burned new holes in it. After a time, one of the limbs holding me drifted away, limp.

"I have you now," I said.

Not a second later I regretted those words. A huge weight landed on my back. Another Macro.

I tried to move, but I was pinned.

"Sorry, sir," Kwon's voice buzzed loudly in my headset.

My com-link was set to pick up platoon chat, automatically increasing the volume for those that were close at hand. Kwon sounded like he was breathing down my back—because he was.

"Get the hell off me, First Sergeant," I complained.

"I thought you might need some help, but this one is pretty much dead. Didn't put up much of a fight, huh?"

"Nah," I said, as he finally climbed off my back. "It went down easy."

"Disappointing."

We left our first Macro and rode our surfboards to catch the next one. This time things went more smoothly. We worked together and killed it fast. We launched from that floating metal carcass just in time to see a brilliant flash fill space around us.

Three other silent explosions followed in rapid sequence.

"What the hell was that?" Kwon demanded.

"They self-destructed," I said, breathing hard. "Dammit, they must have realized we were going to win and changed tactics. Take out as many as you can, that's their motto."

"That's my motto, too," Kwon said.

"Gaines?" I called over platoon chat. "Give me a head count. How many did we lose?"

No one answered me. Kwon and I drifted in silence for a time while I repeated the message. Finally, I contacted Jasmine.

"Have you got us on your sensors?"

"Yes, Colonel," she said. "We've been tracking you from the beginning. Your suit is losing pressure. It's a slow leak but potentially fatal. Please return to the ship. We're coming back to pick you up."

I hadn't ordered her to reverse course, but I figured she had a better picture of the overall battle than I did at this point, so I didn't argue.

"How about the fleet? How many ships did we lose?"

"Forty-eight ships were lost or badly damaged. To keep flying at full speed, we'll have to abandon a few more."

"Forty-eight..." I said. "How many were carriers?"

"None, sir. But we did lose three battleships and a dozen cruisers. The rest were small ships, most of them fighters."

"Not bad," I said. "Not bad at all!"

Jasmine didn't say anything. I knew that others often had a lower threshold for losses than I did. In my math, I figured that we'd lost about ten percent of our ships, plus *Phobos*. The big ship was the worst loss. Overall, it had been a bad fight but not a disaster. I still had an effective force, enough to be a credible threat to the Macros. That was what I needed most.

"Jasmine," I said, "we seem to have lost Major Gaines. Do you have him on track? Or his remains, at least?"

"No sir. We have no transponder from his armor, nothing. His brainbox might be out and his generator dead—if he's alive at all."

I knew what she was suggesting. The odds were pretty good that Gaines had been caught up in the midst of one of those nuclear explosions. We all might have died if the enemy hadn't been spread out to avoid our defensive fire. All the hunter-killer teams of marines were miles apart from each other.

"So the missile attack is over, and they've got nothing else coming at us for the time being. Let's do a little search and rescue."

Jasmine wasn't happy about it, and Newcome was even less so, but I held firm. They wanted to run, break out of Neptune's orbit and flee for Earth. I didn't want to get too far from the enemy's main fleet.

"They're the hounds, and we're the hares," I told them as I drifted through space, checking each hunk of cold, dead debris. "The key is to keep them chasing us while our big guns shoot them in the ass. We don't want to get too far ahead of them. We don't want the hounds to get bored and wander off."

"But if they catch us, they'll chew our backsides off," Newcome pointed out.

"I'm well aware of that, Admiral. You should see my armor."

The search continued for another half hour. I was about to give up when I heard a tiny voice in my headset.

"Did you hear something, Kwon?"

"Yeah," he said. "My belly is growling. When are we going to take a break and get something to eat?"

I squelched his channel and listened again. Stopping my surfboard, I tried to hold my position in space and drift.

My suit hissed. My radio clicked and crackled with background radiation from the massive gas giant below.

Then, I heard it again.

"…mayday…"

I checked my signal finder and pinpointed it. I flew to the position and found a dark spinning object. It looked like a crab going around and around slowly.

I gently touched what looked like a leg. I caught him as gently as I could. The first thing I did was connect my umbilical to his suit, powering it. I was low on oxygen, but I figured I had enough to make it back. I pumped air, heat and power into his suit.

The suit lights glimmered a faint, flickering blue: The color of an officer's armor.

"Gaines, you shirking bastard," I said. "I do believe you've been absent without leave for damn close to an hour. If I ever catch you smoking weed in the latrine again, I'm busting you down to private, mister."

"Yes, sir," he croaked. "Fuck you, sir."

I smiled and carried him back to the battleship cradled in my arms like a big steel baby.

-39-

The next stage of the battle was downright fun. I'd been worried that the Macro fleet would split apart into task forces and go for different targets. After all, there were thousands of them. They could have sent half their force after the fleet and the other half directly to Earth. But they didn't.

Fortunately, our ships were no longer slower than the Macros. We'd upgraded them since the initial contact at the Thor ring. In fact, our factories had built very little other than emergency evac balloon-ships, gravity guns on moon bases and extra engines. With so little time to react to the approaching Macro armada, we'd made our choices, and now it was time to see if they were the right ones.

They followed us like baby ducks. I was grinning ear-to-ear when they passed our Neptune moonbases, and I gave the order to spring our little surprise.

What was so great about the gravity cannons in this situation was their relative invisibility. There was a release of energy, but that had been dampened by having buried the systems in the frozen methane and icy rock of Neptune's moons Nereid, Triton and Sao. There was very little evidence concerning the source of the attack.

I watched as their ships began to implode. Chunks of matter were crushed down to less than a hundredth of their original size. A direct hit could reduce a cruiser to the size of a pickup truck—a smashed-looking one.

We whooped and high-fived one another as the hit-counts rolled in. The first ten minutes were the best: over a hundred kills. After that, Nereid slipped out of range behind Neptune, and Triton's base couldn't get a perfect bead on the enemy fleet due to their trajectory. Fortunately, Sao was still hitting them dead-on, destroying a ship every thirty seconds.

"Any reaction?" I asked the weapons people.

They shook their heads, smiling. "They don't know what's hitting them, so they're ignoring it. They'll just plow straight ahead, hoping it stops."

Unfortunately, it did stop after another two hours and about two hundred fresh strikes. They were out of the reach of the Neptune bases by then.

"Set course for Saturn," I said, "but try not to be too obvious about it."

Jasmine came to me after complying with the order.

"I don't like hitting them this way, with one small set of guns at a time."

"This is a fine time to bring that up."

She made a face, indicating she was not fooled. "Would you have moved the gravity cannons if I'd brought up objections during the planning stages?"

"Probably not," I admitted. "But I would have made a note of your complaints."

She huffed. We both knew what that meant.

"Look," I said, "I know it would have been nice to put all the batteries in one location to shred their ships, but we didn't know how they would manage their approach. Space-based defensive systems are vulnerable. If I put them all on one rock, they might take it out in a single counterpunch. This way, we've got lots of assets all around the Solar System. If they find one, they won't find them all."

"Yes, but this way some of the stations might not see action at all. That means many of the fortifications were a waste of resources to build."

I put up a single finger of admonishment and wagged it at her. Underlings always hated that.

"Not so. We can withdraw with our final force to whatever bases are left. With luck, they'll all be destroyed trying to hunt down our fleet in the end."

Newcome nodded, watching projected course lines.

"I like the defensive gauntlet we've built. The key is to keep them following us. Should we tease them, Colonel?"

"I'm not sure I'm getting your suggestion—how would we tease them?"

"Let a ship develop engine trouble. Have it lag behind, keeping just barely ahead of the protective umbrella of the rest. They will eagerly attack it."

"Not so pleasant for the crew," Jasmine pointed out.

Newcome shrugged. "With such a simple task, surely we could get a brainbox to do it."

"Hmm," I said, musing. "I like that idea, Admiral. We'll do it. Set up a decoy and abandon her on pinnaces. We'll let her slip behind us and simulate a radiation leak from her core. They'll pounce, but we'll give her more power in fits and starts, keeping the ship one jump ahead of the Macros."

Long before we reached Saturn, we let them devour an empty cruiser. They swarmed like a pack of angry sharks, but there was no meat to be had. Not a single human life was lost, and they were still following us.

When we came within reach of Saturn, I decided to play it much less cautiously.

"When the batteries come in range with a good chance of a kill-shot," I said, "they can fire at will. Make sure they aren't targeting the same vessels, however. I want zero mistakes."

The batteries reached out and began destroying the enemy. There were over five hundred lost by the time they passed by the planet. The killing was intense then, as they were under the firing arc of many of our gravity weapons at once. They spread out further, but it was hopeless. We picked them off one after another.

"Sir, they're launching a new missile barrage," Jasmine reported suddenly.

I glanced at her, then at the swarm of new contacts.

"A desperate move," I said confidently. "We took out their last flock of missiles without breaking a sweat. We'll do the same to these weapons."

"Sir, enemy missile courses plotted."

"Display it."

She was already tapping, putting it all up on the screens. I watched closely as the data became stronger and the projected path of the missiles became clearer.

My frown quickly turned into a baffled look.

"What are they doing?"

"It appears they aren't firing on our fleet," Jasmine said.

"Back us out and project possible courses."

She did so as quickly as she could. The view of local space swam and shrunk sickeningly. I breathed a sigh of relief when I saw the missiles didn't target Earth. I figured they'd finally wised up and decided to destroy our home planet instead of chasing phantom ships.

But they hadn't done that—at least, not yet. Instead the missiles were—

"Alert the base on Titan!" I shouted.

"Already done," she said.

Without being told, she zoomed back in to a tight focus of the space around Saturn. The space around the ringed planet was filling up with ships, missiles and beams of gravitational force.

"The missile barrage is splitting up," she said.

We watched in frustration as the missiles steered in flocks toward our bases. Thousands of men were down there garrisoning those stations. Every one of those Star Force troops had been brave enough to come out here and man a post on an inhospitable rock. Now, they were about to die for their homeworld.

"Should I tell them to pull out, sir?" Jasmine asked. "There's still time for a full evacuation. After the battle, we can have them picked up."

"Do they have families with them?" I asked.

"Sir, we can't—" Newcome began whispering at my side.

I shushed him with a chopping gesture. I knew what he was going to say. We couldn't afford to have those batteries stop

318

pounding the enemy fleet. They were taking out ships every few seconds. We needed every kill they could chalk up—and a lot more as well.

"No, sir," Jasmine said. "No families."

I nodded. "Tell them to man their posts and fire to the last. Tell them they are the pride of Earth, and their sacrifice today will ensure that humans will continue to breathe centuries from now."

"I've transmitted your words."

I knew she'd recorded what I'd said and simply relayed it to the stations. I hoped it would be enough.

The missiles began falling on the moons. The garrisons had to pull out right now to escape destruction.

Not one of them did. They understood the score. They stayed at their posts, cursing and firing with ferocious intensity until the last of them was turned into radioactive slag on an airless rock.

The mood aboard *Potemkin* wasn't jubilant anymore. We'd lost a lot of good people, but in the grim math of war we'd done well. The worst part was the enemy had figured us out: They'd located our bases.

"What's our next destination?"

"Jupiter, sir."

I looked at the star maps. Jupiter was pretty far away. It wasn't directly lined up with Earth, either. As we led the Macros on a wild goose chase, they had to be noticing that each time we'd led them to a world bristling with fortresses to eat their ships. They'd already lost about half of their force.

The question was whether they'd keep following us and keep losing ships. I didn't know the answer, but I couldn't think of a better play to make.

For the next few hours, we crawled across space. No one spoke much, other than to report required information. I ordered everyone to take a break when it became clear the enemy was still following us.

I was asleep in my bunk ten hours after the battle at Saturn when I was summoned back to the bridge. Bleary-eyed, I met the back-up crews and stood at my post sipping bad coffee.

"What have we got?"

"We're about ten hours out from Jupiter," a staffer told me. "But the enemy is slowing and changing course."

I nodded grimly. I summoned Jasmine and Newcome back to the bridge.

"They're veering off," I told them, showing them the data. "They've figured it out. They thought they were chasing us down at first. Now, they've finally realized we're not going to let them catch us, and each planet we lead them to is a fresh trap. Show me their new course."

The plot was arcing and indirect. I soon saw why: the Macros were going to thread a narrow path between the planets, avoiding them. The course eventually took them to Earth on a semi-elliptical path that led all the way around the sun and back in from behind. They were carefully threading our gauntlet without tripping any more traps.

"Show me our arcs of fire," I ordered. "Will we get any shots at them at all?"

There were a few bright spots. Mars would have several minutes to pound them, and our biggest base, Luna, would be front and center during the final conflict.

"We should take another thousand of them down with us," Newcome said quietly. "It's something."

"That's not good enough," I said as I reviewed the figures.

Newcome looked worried, and I knew what he was thinking: *Oh God, Riggs is about to charge into Hell with me at the helm again.*

And he was partly right.

-40-

When the Macro fleet veered off and stopped chasing us, we wheeled and began chasing them. What else could we do?

We pored over the maps until our eyes burned. There had to be a way to get them back into the range of our gravity cannons.

"Can't we simply take the gravity weapons off the moon bases and equip our ships with them?" Newcome asked. "Even one such cannon—"

I shook my head. Marvin gave a more detailed answer.

"We don't have the energy output, Admiral Newcome," he said. "Even if we removed the engines and other armament from this battleship, we couldn't generate enough power to operate a single heavy cannon. Only *Phobos* was able to accomplish that task."

"Besides," I said, "we don't have enough time left now to fly to Jupiter immediately, remove a cannon and fix it on our nosecone. By the time we get back into range, the enemy fleet will have reached Earth."

"Right, well…right…" Newcome said.

"Sirs," said Marvin, slithering forward. "I think Admiral Newcome might be onto something. It would be a challenge, but the possibilities already have my neural chains firing. It's most stimulating."

"What are you talking about, robot?" I asked. "Explain quickly. There isn't much time. My next move is an all-out attack on their rear ranks to entice them to turn. If they take the bait, we'll run, forcing them to chase us right back to Jupiter."

Newcome's eyes bugged from his head as he heard me explain the essence of my plans. His Adam's apple bounced up and down as he swallowed a lump.

"I'm hoping someone has a better idea…?" Newcome said, looking around the group.

"I believe I might have a superior option," Marvin said. "We can't afford the time to return to Jupiter to dismantle gravity cannons. Besides, as I said before, they'd be too large. However, we could build one in-flight with materials found at hand."

I narrowed my eyes at him. "Materials? What materials? I thought you had to have collapsed star-matter to build one of those things."

"That is correct."

I stared at his cameras for a few seconds, and they stared back at me.

"You're telling me you smuggled collapsed matter onto my ship, aren't you? If you did that, how did you keep us from running heavy? Why aren't we dragging our butts even at full engine thrust?"

"Quite possibly," Marvin said, "I've made compensating adjustments. Recall that my laboratory is still located aboard this vessel. I have a number of pieces of specialized equipment there, including inertial dampeners with independent power supplies."

"Why the hell did you bring something like that aboard?"

"I thought a gravity weapon might be useful at some point in the future. It's only a small amount of star dust. But with careful focus, we could build a small cannon with the supplies I have."

I narrowed my eyes. "A small cannon? What could that do? Those ships aren't jet fighters. They're displacing around ten thousand tons each."

"Nevertheless, there is a system aboard every ship that is highly vulnerable. If we were to destroy the enemy's drives, we could disable their ships if not destroy them outright."

Internally, I was raging at the thought that Marvin had once again done something sneaky. But I tried to push that crippling thought away for now. How could I use it? If we did have a small gravity cannon aboard…

"We could disable them, right," Newcome said, sounding as if he'd thought of something enlightening. "That would cause them to slow. Each ship that drifted behind their main fleet would be easy prey for our fleet. We would catch them one at a time and blast them in unison."

"Well stated, Admiral Newcome," Marvin said.

"Wait, wait, wait," I said. "We still don't have a power source. How are we going to provide this mini-cannon enough power to fire?"

"The term 'mini-cannon' is a misnomer, sir," Marvin complained. "The weapon would be physically larger than anything—"

"Fine, whatever," I said. "How do we power it?"

"That is the biggest problem of all," Marvin admitted. "But I believe I've solved the difficulty during the span of this conversation. We'll have to cannibalize other ships, removing generators from each. As you may recall, each ship was outfitted with additional power sources in order to drive the new engines."

"Yes," I said. "But those engines are the only reason we're able to keep up with the Macros."

"Correct. Not all our ships would be able to keep up."

I mulled it over unhappily. This entire plan sounded risky and possibly unworkable. If I stripped generators from ships that had to be left behind, I would be splitting my fleet. But the only other alternative would be to attack the enemy rear while outnumbered by more than two to one.

"How many generators do we need, Marvin?" I asked him.

"Most of those that match the couplings we have aboard this vessel. We don't have time to rewire the power harness."

"Most? Which ones?"

"If we stripped all the generators from all the battleships except this one, it would be sufficient."

I frowned and paced. "That will make the battleships slow. We'll have to leave them behind."

Newcome lit up and cleared his throat.

"What is it, man?" I asked.

"I volunteer, sir."

"For what? Are you suggesting you'll suit up and attach extra generators to this ship's hull?"

He looked startled.

"Not at all, Colonel," he said. "I'll command the break-off forces."

I smiled thinly. "I get it. You want to get off my ship. All right, where would you take this taskforce of slow battleships?"

"Back to Jupiter, sir, to stand with the greatest fortification Earth has left."

"Actually," I said. "That isn't a bad idea... Go."

"Sir?"

"Get moving. Strip off all the extra generators and fix them onto this ship. Marvin, you should move out too. Build me the gravity cannon. Go for accuracy rather than power. You'll be gunning it as you have the most experience. We need something that will pop enemy drives like light bulbs."

Both Newcome and Marvin hurried from the bridge. I was left with Jasmine, who stepped to my side. When she spoke, she did so quietly, so the other staffers couldn't hear her words.

"Kyle, you just gave them both what they wanted, you know. They look like kids at Christmas."

"Yeah."

"But why Jupiter? Why not have Newcome follow us with the battleships? He might be able to help, even if he comes late to the battle."

I shook my head. "If the Macros do turn to fight because we're hurting them too much, I want the battleships back at Jupiter."

She frowned. "Why?"

"Because," I said. "After we're gone and Earth's gone, Jupiter might be one of the last holdouts for our species. This could turn very ugly by the end, Jasmine. We'll need every human life to start over and a core fleet as well."

She looked troubled by my words, and I didn't blame her.

The following hours were tense, and no one on *Potemkin* got much sleep. The walls reverberated as clanking grav-boots tromped on the outer hull. There wasn't enough room to stuff extra generators inside the ship, so we'd decided to bolt them onto the outside. In many places, we simply fused them to the hull with constructive nanite welds. Hooking up the power leads and fuel lines was probably the hardest part.

Building the gravity cannon itself turned out not to be that difficult. Marvin had smuggled a small brick of stardust onto the ship which must have weighed half as much as the entire vessel. It was his addition that had left us with fluctuating power consumption readings for some time now, rather than engine failure.

I figured that Marvin might have been hoarding the star dust for other nefarious reasons. Maybe he'd give a pinch of it to someone he didn't like as he had done with that little golden statue he'd carved in my image. Used as a focal point for an implosion—I didn't want to think about what he'd been planning. I told myself none of Marvin's skullduggery mattered at this point. We needed his pirated prize.

Once we'd loaded two dozen new generators aboard, the ship fairly thrummed with power. *Potemkin* looked like a ship that had cancerous growths clustering all over it.

Chasing down the Macros turned out to be the easiest part. They were locked on a safe course which took them far from our planets, but we had no such restrictions. We were able to fly on a more direct route and catch up to them.

We were a few hours from Mars when I finally heard the golden words I'd been waiting for.

"Ready, Colonel Riggs," Marvin said.

He'd just come back aboard the bridge, and he shed his "tool kit" as he did so. Extra tentacles and propulsion systems formed a piled heap on the deck where he'd discarded them.

"You're ready?" I asked. "For what?"

"To commence firing."

I stared at him for a second with bloodshot eyes. I had a mug of coffee in one hand, and my other rested on the command table, propping me up.

"We're in range of the Macros?"

"Yes."

"And your gun will work?"

325

"Yes."

"Well then, shoot them down, man!" I roared, standing up and coming to life.

"Firing solution computed," he said. "Firing."

The ship lurched hard and went into a backward spin. I was thrown to the ceiling, and my coffee went into my face. It stung and burned. A few droplets even found their way into my nostrils.

"Control that!" I shouted, falling on my face on the main deck again. "Jasmine, do you have the helm?"

She wasn't on the bridge. I'd lost track of her. I chewed on her staffers until they had the ship leveled off again.

"Sorry about that, Colonel Riggs," Marvin said. "I should have warned you. Gravity weapons have significant recoil properties."

"Yeah, they kick like mules. Let's compensate for that next time. Can you automate a thruster on the top of the ship? It should fire hard the moment you engage your firing sequence."

"I've located controls for the attitude jets—gaining control—done. The process is now automated. I suggest we test it."

I looked at him. "You're ready to fire again? Already? I thought gravity weapons took a long time to cycle."

"Normally, yes. But this isn't *Phobos*. Our weapon is far smaller and less powerful. It is, however, accurate and fast-loading."

"Perfect. Fire again."

The ship bucked, but not as badly this time. We didn't go into a spin. Instead, we were thrown up toward the ceiling and then the thruster fired to counter the motion, and we were all slammed back down onto the deck again. In a way, the effect was worse because it was like getting hit from below and then from above by two hammers in rapid succession.

Marvin followed my drifting body with a snaking camera. I ended up lying on the floor half under the command table.

I looked up at his electric eye.

"Are you conscious, Colonel Riggs?"

"Yes."

"There's a significant loss of bodily fluids…I believe you're leaking, sir."

"I've got plenty of blood. Don't worry about it."

"My apologies," he said. "We'll have to perfect the recoil compensation system before continuing to fire."

"Nonsense," I said, climbing to my feet.

All around me, staffers were rubbing their heads and pinching bloody noses. There was one lieutenant who wasn't moving at all. Her head had slammed into the table and apparently she'd lost consciousness.

"Get a corpsman up here," I said. I turned back to Marvin. "Are you hitting anything?"

"I believe so, but we won't get confirmation for another four minutes. The enemy is too far out for us to observe them in real time due to the limitations of the speed of light—"

"Yeah, yeah," I said, rubbing my skull. "Switch targets every time and keep firing. The rest of you, hold on. Get nanite arms to tie your feet down if you—"

The deck bucked again at that moment. My chin slammed down on the command table this time, and I came damned close to biting my tongue off. Fortunately, I'd snaked it back in and stopped talking about a quarter of a second before my face hit the table.

"Okay," I said, getting up painfully. "New idea, Marvin: sound a warning klaxon on the ship's PA system precisely one second before you fire from now on. When that klaxon stops going, hit the trigger."

"An excellent idea, Colonel."

I opened my mouth to relay the new system to the crew over my com-link, but then I heard a loud klaxon going off. My brain was slightly rattled, and I actually didn't realize he'd already enacted my suggestion for nearly a full second. When I finally caught on, I gripped the command table for dear life and took the shock with bent knees. For the first time, I remained standing and uninjured.

"Keep firing!" I ordered. "Don't stop!"

The cycle went on and on. Before it was done, I felt like a mouse caught in a dryer, but I was grinning through my bloody, split lips by that time.

The Macros were getting nailed. One after another Marvin took out their drives. As far as I could tell, he never missed. Each shot took out a drive and a ship. Sometimes, the entire vessel exploded. Other times, they were just damaged and forced to slow down.

The first ships he took out were their big dreadnaughts rather than their cruisers. We feared those ships the most, and fighting them one at a time was infinitely preferable to doing battle with them all at once.

After six grueling hours of being bounced around *Potemkin*, the rest of my fleet came within range of the first of these cripples. We weren't kind. We overkilled the dreadnaught. Every gun and fighter unleashed hell, destroying the ship before it could do more than fire a few salvoes. Our losses were minimal.

The Macros changed course after the tenth hour. Counting tonnage, we'd reduced their force by more than half.

"They're finally going to react, sir," Jasmine said. Her face was bruised and her left eye was almost sealed shut, but she was on-duty and clinging determinedly to her command table.

"Finally turning to face their tormenters, eh?" I asked. "This is it, people. We're going to have to make our stand right here. We're pretty evenly matched at this point. I want everyone aboard to take heart. Even if they destroy the last ship in this fleet, they'll never get through to Earth. Our sacrifice will never be forgotten by the people of—"

"Colonel?" Jasmine interrupted.

"What is it?"

"They aren't turning to face us. They've changed their course, yes—but directly toward Earth."

I put my hands on the command screen and zoomed in. The course arcs were changing; the data was clear. They were going to try an end run. I knew what this meant the moment I saw them do it. I'd seen this behavior before.

Macro Command had realized they were going to lose, so they'd done the math. They were going to take out Earth and ignore my harassing fleet.

They were going to destroy my home planet or die trying.

-41-

We kept after them, doggedly pursuing and shooting them in the ass with our makeshift cannon. The enemy wasn't going to be allowed to park in orbit over Earth and bomb it to dust without losing a lot more ships first. After we did what we could, it would all be up to the bases on Luna.

"Colonel, the enemy have changed their behavior again," Jasmine said with concern three hours after we'd begun taking them out one at a time.

I nodded grimly, unsurprised. "They're going to turn and fight, aren't they? They've finally had enough of us pecking at their hindquarters."

Jasmine shook her pretty head. There was still a trickle of blood on her cheek, but she ignored it.

"No sir," she said. "That's not it—they're accelerating and no longer cruising toward Earth. They're heading on a collision course with the planet and increasing speed."

I frowned and looked over her numbers. She was right—it was undeniable. The Macros weren't going to take out our fleet after all. They were going to take out Earth.

"They can't destroy the planet by ramming it!" I said.

"Maybe that's not the plan," Jasmine said.

I frowned at her, then I caught on. "Increase speed. Keep up with them!"

"Our engines are at maximum capacity now, sir," she said. "We can't keep up.

I ran my hands and my eyes over the screens anxiously.

329

"They're going to reach Earth first. Without gravity cannons we can't stop them."

"Why didn't we put gravity cannons on Earth itself?" she asked.

"Because that would be too late. Once the enemy got within range, they would already be dumping their bombs and missiles on civilian targets. The strategy has always been to stop the enemy, to destroy them all before they reached Earth."

She was quiet for a moment. Both of us knew that our strategy had clearly failed.

"As they're accelerating," she said thoughtfully, "they'll only have time for a single pass at Earth. They won't be able to sit in orbit and pound the planet."

"They can still do a lot of damage," I said. "Let's run the numbers. How many ships will they have left when they reach bombardment range?"

"Hard to say. Depends on how many our lunar bases knock out."

"Let's assume they get the same number per gun as we did at Saturn. We have to assume the Macros will knock out our guns as they did before."

"All right..." she said, pushing back her hair, which had slipped into her face. It was matted with blood when her hand lifted away from it.

Normally, I would have been concerned by Jasmine's injuries, but I had to put aside personal worries. We were talking about millions, possibly billions of deaths. She was as capable of regeneration as the rest of Star Force.

"I'd say they'll have less than a hundred ships left to unload over Earth," she said.

That didn't sound bad, but I knew it *was* bad. They'd come with thousands, and we'd been unable to stop them all. Those last few ships, on a suicidal run, were going to hurt humanity. Cities would be radioactive holes. Oceans would be steaming cauldrons, sending hot tidal waves over the coastlines.

"Tell Earth. Tell them to move everyone to higher ground. Anyone left in the cities should evacuate and seek a bomb shelter as soon as possible."

"They've already—"

330

"Send it anyway."

The klaxon sounded again, and the ship heaved under us. We'd become almost accustomed to the abuse. I set my legs and took most of the shock with my knees. When the countering thrusters pushed the opposite direction, I braced my arms on the command table and rode with that motion as well.

"Medical is complaining again, sir," Jasmine said.

"Too bad."

"They say we might lose several injured crewmen. They can't work under these conditions."

I glared, but it wasn't her I was angry with. "Ship them out! All of them!"

"The medical staff?"

"No, no—the injured. Have the medical staff load them onto surfboards in vac suits and kick them out of the airlocks. Other ships can pick them up and baby them."

She relayed the orders. All around us, the staffers had big eyes. They were probably wondering who I'd kick off the ship next.

I didn't care. I'd kill them all with my bare hands to save Earth. They had no concept of the number of innocents we were about to let die.

We'd failed. I'd sworn to myself I wouldn't let it happen again after the Thor System, and here I was watching the Macros go into another death-charge.

It's very hard to stop a suicidal force. You can beat them down, but if they are coming against your most vulnerable citizens rather than your fleet—well, stopping them wasn't easy. I'd known this possibility was in the cards. I'd done everything I could to prevent it. But here it was, happening all over again.

I straightened my spine after the next bone-jarring salvo from the gravity cannon.

"I'm shipping out, too," I told Jasmine.

Immediately, she gave me her full attention. "Where?"

"You command this ship. Keep firing. This battleship is the only thing in the fleet that matters now. The rest of these ships won't even see battle. I should have charged right into them long ago."

"We'd all be dead if you had."

"Of course, but they might not have made it to Earth. Instead I played it safe, and the people of my planet are going to pay for that."

Jasmine's arms encircled my chest. I was wearing a breastplate so I could hardly feel her, but she was trying to cling to me.

She was pregnant with my child, and she didn't want to let me go. I knew that whatever she said next, I had to keep that in mind.

"What are you going to do?" she asked.

"I'm going to ship over to the nearest carrier. I'm going to pilot one of the fighters. I heard *Yorktown* is short a few seasoned pilots. They took a few hits from missiles early-on."

"A fighter? Why a fighter?"

"They're the only assets we have left that can catch the enemy before they reach Earth. I plan to fly with them. Set up the orders for me, will you?"

Jasmine nodded. She seemed resigned to my decision and didn't try to argue.

"Kill them all for me, Kyle," she said.

She gave me a little kiss and let go of my armor. She went back to her command table and worked the console. She had her head down, and I wondered if she was crying. I didn't want to embarrass her any further in front of the other officers so I marched off the bridge.

All the way to the airlock, I thought about Jasmine. She wasn't like Sandra at all. A moment like this was a clear case in point. She'd let me go to do what I had to do—what I *felt* that I had to do—without complaints or threats. I'd expected a different response from her, but I shouldn't have.

In-between salvos, I left *Potemkin* behind. I surfed across open space to *Yorktown* and surprised the crew there. They were dumbfounded to find old blood-and-guts Riggs on their deck.

I headed directly for the flight hangar after checking in with the captain over my com-link. I didn't have a lot of time.

Jasmine had already relayed my orders, and everyone in the hangar was running around like the place was on fire. I suppose, in a way, it was.

After shocking the CAG with my request, I found they did indeed have an extra fighter. The rookie who'd been chosen to fly her, instead of an experienced pilot, was disappointed to see me coming. I boarded up and tapped my way through the systems checks as fast as I could.

Mine was the fifteenth bird to leave the gate, and for a brief, exhilarating minute I felt good. Flying a fighter was always fun as long as you didn't think too hard about the crazy things you were doing.

We came out of the carrier's snout like a swarm of angry hornets. Altogether, there were close to fifteen hundred fighters from all the carriers combined. We didn't form up into any complex formations as there wasn't time for anything that fancy. We looked more like a cloud than an organized force.

The flight wasn't a long one. Within half an hour, I was so close to Earth she looked like a blue-white marble, and the moon was at her side: a dime-sized white crescent. The enemy ships were pinpricks of flaring plasma. All we could see was their plumes of exhaust from jets that never stopped running at maximum acceleration.

"Kyle?" Jasmine asked in my headset.

"Go ahead, Captain."

"You're not going to make it."

"What do you mean? I can see them now."

"They've already released their missiles. They were holding onto their final barrage. About a thousand missiles are ahead of you, aiming at Earth."

I cursed and wanted to pound on the instrument panel, but I controlled myself. I needed this ship in operating condition.

"What are their ships doing?"

"Mostly, they're dying. The lunar base is tearing them apart. They didn't bother using their missiles against the cannons there. They saved them all for Earth."

We'd calculated a high probability that the enemy would spend some part of their firepower destroying the lunar guns.

We'd been wrong. They'd decided to fire everything at our civilians and let their ships be destroyed.

It was bittersweet watching them pop in cascading blooms of flame. Silently, ship after ship was taken out. Suddenly they moved as one, veering off and upward from the plane of the ecliptic. They were steering away from the Earth and the Moon.

I frowned and contacted Jasmine again.

"We're still behind them, but they're breaking off. Where are they going?"

"The course is unclear—there's nothing out there but open space. Maybe they're just trying to evade the lunar base."

"Right," I said. "But they won't evade us."

I plotted a course to pursue and engaged it. On automatic, my brainbox slewed my fighter around and directed it after the fleeing Macros. They only had about seventy cruisers left. We'd destroyed their transports and dreadnaughts long ago.

"Full throttle," I ordered my squadron, having assumed command. "Don't worry about a return trip. If we live so long, we'll either be picked up by friendly shipping or we'll make an emergency landing on Earth."

I didn't mention other possibilities, such as there not being any ground left on Earth that wasn't too hot with radiation to land on. There wasn't any point to bringing that up as everyone was thinking about it anyway, and we couldn't do anything about it other than destroy the enemy before they destroyed us.

The CAG back on *Yorktown* contacted me and wanted to know where I was taking his fighters. I told him they were *my* fighters and ordered Jasmine to relay the pursuit command. Soon, our entire force was flying after the enemy.

"Colonel Riggs?" asked a familiar voice.

"What is it, Marvin?"

"I have an incoming message sir—I believe it's meant for you."

"What message? I'm kind of busy, here."

"Of course sir, perhaps it can wait until later."

I almost disconnected, but then my curiosity got the better of me. After all, I had about ten minutes before we were within range of the enemy.

"All right, all right," I said. "Who's on the phone, Marvin?"

"Reference unclear. Assuming contextual reference of highest probability: If I understand your question the answer is: Macro Command."

That got my attention. I could not recall the last time the Macros had talked to me during a battle. They generally didn't contact me first, either. In fact, it usually took a lot of begging and cajoling and outright trickery to get them to talk to me at all.

"You're telling me that the Macros are trying to contact me through you?" I demanded.

"Correct."

"Patch it through and translate, please."

"Channel open."

I waited, listening to my headset. I had to admit, I was curious about what these evil machines had to say.

-42-

"We demand you comply with our stated agreement," Macro Command said.

This made my lips twitch with a moment of amusement.

"You called me, Macro Command. As you may or may not be aware, we're fighting a battle right now. Unless you wish to surrender, we have nothing to discuss."

"Offer accepted."

I frowned. What the hell were they talking about? Then all of a sudden, I got it.

"Wait a minute, you can't just surrender," I found myself saying. Even to me, it sounded like an absurd statement. I'd been taken by surprise.

"That is precisely what we're doing. We're entitled to this privilege due to our prior agreements with Colonel Kyle Riggs."

"What agreement...oh," I said, thinking it over. I had, after all, told them in the dead sun system that I would let the last few of them live if I won. I'd even sold it to them as an insurance policy. Well, now the Macros were making a claim against that policy.

A beeping sounded in my helmet. It was Jasmine, so I muted the Macros.

"Colonel, the enemy ships are slowing down. They seem to have all lost power at once."

"Are you still firing on them?" I asked.

"Of course."

I gritted my teeth in frustration. *Of course* my fleet was still firing. To even question this was absurd. What did you do when faced with genocidal robots on the run? Why, you blasted them until the last nut fell off the last bolt.

"Cease fire," I ordered. "I have to think this over."

"Cease fire? I'm asking for confirmation, Colonel. You want us to stop firing on the Macros?"

"That's right," I said. "They're surrendering."

"Don't buy into any of their tricks, Kyle," she said. "They're only doing this to gain time. They'll kill us all the moment they can. They'll cheat on any—"

"Yeah, yeah," I said. "Riggs out."

I unmuted the Macros. They were in the middle of lodging a complaint. I'd missed half of it, apparently.

"—despite the clarity of the agreement reached, your non-compliance—"

"We've stopped firing," I said.

"Excellent. We require your aid. Many of our ships are damaged. Attend to us immediately."

I began thinking fast. What had I told them exactly…? That when the end came, I would stay my hand, and I wouldn't take the last of them out. I would spare the last Macros.

My fighters quickly closed in on them. I ordered my swarming wingmen to slow down and hold their fire. There were plenty of complaints from the pilots, and every CAG in the fleet wanted to scream in my ear personally. I put them all on hold.

I couldn't blame them for being upset. We'd just seen these robots drop bombs on our homeworld. How many millions had died? We didn't even know yet. But despite all that, my Star Force people were disciplined. They held their fire. I knew that if I'd had Worms or Centaurs for pilots, I couldn't have stopped them with just words.

"Macro Command," I said, reopening our channel. "I require you to answer questions in order to survive as free entities."

There ensued a few moments of quiet. *"Unacceptable,"* the response came at last.

"Well, you're going to have to learn how to accept things you don't like to hear," I told them. "That is the essence of surrender."

"This stipulation wasn't in the original agreement."

"Lots of things are in the small print. Deals like these are meant to be manipulated and distorted. For example, the time you allowed the Centaurs to live in space but destroyed their populations on the surface of their worlds. Or the deal you made with the Worms not to attack them and then followed up by having Star Force marines attack them as your proxies."

"The circumstances in the instances you cite were different," they said.

"How so?"

"In those situations, we were in control."

I laughed. It wasn't a friendly laugh.

"Fine, okay. Prepare to defend yourselves. We're coming in to wipe out your last…thirty-nine ships? This won't take long at all."

Another short delay, then: *"Demand accepted."*

"All right then. First of all, who created the Macros? Who unleashed your plague upon the cosmos?"

"Your words comprise two questions."

"Yes, you're good at counting. Now, answer or be destroyed."

"Our artificial species was created originally by the beings you refer to as the 'Blues'."

I nodded grimly. This wasn't really news to me, but I'd long wanted confirmation.

"What was the nature of your original programming?" I asked. "What was your goal?"

Internally, I was enjoying this experience. As far as I knew, no one had ever managed to get the Macros to respond to questioning. I had the Macros on their knees. I knew these final ships had to be very important to them. In every other instance like this one in the past, they'd willingly sacrificed themselves without a qualm. This time was different. I figured they didn't have much left and couldn't afford to lose this handful of ships.

"We were programmed to explore, to identify other intelligent life and to destroy it wherever it was found."

I had difficulty breathing. All that the Blues had told me—everything was a lie. They'd launched these nightmares into the universe on purpose. And then they'd launched the Nanos afterward. Why? Maybe they'd come to fear the Macros, to realize that they were too strong. They'd sent them out, not to help the biotics they'd ordered exterminated, not exactly, but to help counter the Macros which they'd begun to fear.

"That answers a lot of questions," I said. "You were the first artificial slaves the Blues created. Do you still serve them?"

"No."

"But would you ever attack them?"

"To do so would be a breach in our programming. We've been working on the problem for several years with no final solution yet."

I thought about that. At first, it sounded like they were trying to break their own programming. The more I thought about it, the more I began to realize what the Macros really meant. They were trying to *circumvent* their own programming just as they'd done many times after making agreements with other biotics. They wanted to destroy the Blues, but couldn't do it directly. They'd been working on alternate approaches, just as they had with Star Force originally. This line of reasoning brought me to a fresh idea.

"Macro Command," I said, frowning. "Did you intend for Star Force to attack the Blues?"

"Yes."

That was a stab in the gut for me. I'd always thought of these machines as big, powerful and dumb. But perhaps I'd been wrong. Maybe in their own way, they were pretty cagey bastards. After all, hadn't Star Force bombed the Blues? Hadn't the Blues launched a ship seeking revenge against us, which we'd then captured after significant losses? They'd engineered a war between us, talking to both sides and poking us with sticks. The Blues were an enemy, but they weren't as committed as the Macros.

The trickery and innate evil of these machines was getting to me. They were implacable and unstoppable through diplomatic means. I knew they'd supposedly "surrendered" to me now, but I felt sure they were already working on a "solution" to that problem, too.

"Macro Command," I said. "I only have one more question for you: are there surviving members of your artificial species on the dark sun half a light year from here?"

"Yes."

"Very well. When we find those last machines, we'll capture them and put them in a zoo. Our truce is now at an end. Riggs out."

I connected to the general command override, and gave the order to destroy the machines utterly. The fighter jocks whooped with joy. They roared in, jets blazing. We fired and took out their engines first. Once they were helpless, we spun around and stitched their hulls with glowing hot hits from our lasers. We melted their hulls and took them out one by one.

They tried to fight back. We lost a few men, but it was worth it to be free of their evil presence for all time.

When the last ship, running for all it was worth, tried to open a channel with me, I finally relented and took the call.

"Colonel Kyle Riggs," the voice said, *"we demand that you comply with our agreement."*

"Request denied!" I snapped.

"Colonel Kyle Riggs, destroyer of worlds. You have broken your programming. We will never honor our programming with your species again."

I laughed.

"I changed the deal, that's all," I said. "I found a solution to the problem. You're not the last of your kind; therefore I can safely destroy you."

"The last question...yes, we see your logic, but we do not approve."

"Yeah well, sue me."

During these final words, I'd been bearing down on the last running cruiser. I hammered the hull and grinned tightly as internal heat leaked from the radioactive core. We'd breached the Macro ship's hull, and I knew she was doomed.

When the big ship blew up, I had to veer violently to stay out of the expanding debris. I went into a wild spin. I laughed and roared at the same time. I held onto consciousness long enough to get my fighter under control again, but just barely.

I was proud of myself. I'd weaseled on a deal with the Macros even as they'd weaseled on a dozen deals with Earth and others. I considered this a personal achievement.

-43-

Returning to the carrier *Yorktown*, and then later to *Potemkin*, I was forced to face an unpleasant duty. It was time to find out what had happened to Earth.

"Get Miklos on the line for me," I told Jasmine.

She'd hugged me the moment I showed up, but she was all business after the first minute or so, manning her post like a pro.

It took a few minutes to get Miklos on the line. I didn't begrudge him the wait. After all, God only knew how many disasters he had to deal with right now.

"Colonel?" Miklos began, eyebrows arched high. "I'm somewhat surprised to see you made it through the final stages of the battle."

"And somewhat disappointed, no doubt," I said.

He didn't answer. I knew that he was no longer my biggest fan. He'd decided I was starting to look too much like Crow. Who knew? Maybe he was right.

"You know," I said. "If I was Crow, you wouldn't even be alive right now."

"I know that, sir," he said evenly. "I never favored Crow over you."

"Instead you favored yourself for the job, right? Are you sure you could have done what I did today? Ask yourself that, Nikolai."

He looked troubled. "I don't honestly know."

"I do," I said. "You would have failed. Somehow, the Macros would have won through to Earth and finished her. But that's not why I'm calling. I want to hear the damage report."

"I will give it to you, and then you can decide if I'm a failure or not," he said. "Over the last twenty-four hours, three hundred and ninety fusion weapons reached Earth and detonated."

I closed my eyes. I envisioned utter devastation.

"What kind of megatonnage are we talking about?" I asked.

"Each warhead had of uniform yield at just over two hundred megatons per bomb."

"My God," I said. "There must be nothing left."

"There is very little left—in certain corners of the world."

I frowned at him. "What are talking about?"

"I took liberties, Colonel."

"Yes, you've taken a lot of them over the years."

"I think you will approve of my adjustments to the plan. You see, I ordered all our cities to go dark—in fact, to facilitate that process, I cut the power to every major metropolitan area on the planet."

"You did what?"

"Yes, sir, I shut down everything. Even hospital generators were killed. Then I switched on a number of very large power installations we'd moved to Antarctica, the Sahara desert, the Gobi desert, parts of Tibet, and the wastelands of South America."

I have to admit my jaw fell open. "You decoyed the whole planet? Did it work? Did they go for it?"

"Not entirely. We lost a number of cities, including Pyongyang, Dubai, Anchorage and St. Petersburg."

I frowned. "Why those?"

"A mixture of reasons. In some cases, local authorities didn't comply with my orders. In other situations, I believe the enemy was attracted to high variations in temperature. The Macros didn't target solely based on emissions but also by identifying warm regions surrounded by a cold landscape."

I couldn't believe it. "So you're telling me that London, New York, Tokyo—they weren't hit?"

"That's right, sir. I calculated that the Macros weren't experts on Earthly population distributions so I simply placed thousands of transmitters and power generators in wilderness areas. This worked for the most part. Over ninety percent of the strikes hit essentially empty fields of ice and sand. I tried to place attractive targets underwater as well, but it didn't work. They didn't strike any of those. They seemed to understand we aren't an aquatic species."

Miklos was proud of himself, I could tell. He was haggard-looking and probably hadn't gotten much sleep for days, but he'd survived, and most of Earth's population had survived as well.

"There are also some serious side-effects, Colonel," he said. "The ozone layer in the southern hemisphere is virtually gone. There is a large swath of the Arctic Ocean that appears to be burning—about ten million hectares of surface area."

"Huh," I said. "That's a weird one. Is it spreading?"

"No, it's dying down at a steady rate. We believe some of the strikes penetrated the icecap and ignited underwater deposits of methane, natural gas and oil."

"Good enough then," I said. "Now for the really important data: What's the final tally? How many civilians were killed?"

I gritted my teeth as I awaited his reply.

"That's still unclear at this point," he said. "I can only provide rough estimates. Also, you have to remember that there will be adjustments to any number I give you now. There are fallout concerns, for example, and other secondary effects, like disease and starvation from interrupted food—"

I snapped my fingers at the screen. "Just give me your best shot. What's the count?"

"We lost at least one hundred forty million people, sir. Possibly, that number will climb to two hundred million by the end of the week. It will be no higher than that."

I stood up and whooped.

"That's great!" I shouted.

Miklos looked surprised at my reaction.

"You have to understand," I said, "I was honestly expecting to hear about *billions* of deaths. Two hundred million? With the Macros dead and gone forever? This is excellent news."

"I'm not sure the general public sees it that way," Miklos said carefully.

"No, naturally not. Don't worry—I'll make a stern speech. I'll attend some mass gravesites and put wreaths on whatever the photogs want me to. But just between you and me, this is the best damned news I've heard all day."

Miklos looked troubled. "If you say so, Colonel."

"What else do you have for me?" I asked him.

"Well, there's the small matter of the comets, sir."

I blinked, and then I remembered. The Macros ships had been riding behind comets coming from the dead system where they'd found them. When we'd sent a fleet out to meet them and they'd realized they had been discovered, the ships had come out from behind that cover and advanced to meet our fleets. But that still left the comets: twirling balls of ice that were all targeting Earth.

"Oh crap," I said. "I forgot about them… Anyway, when are they due to strike?"

"We have a week or so, sir."

"Good," I said. "Very good. We have plenty of time to get our fleet into position. Maybe we can blast them apart."

Miklos shook his head. "You'll be glad to know my people have been working on this matter since you left. We have a new solution, I think."

I waved for him to tell me.

"The gravity cannons will be used, but not to damage the comets. Recall that you led a team of techs to decide where the comets had to be destroyed?"

"Yes, right. We had to do it way out on the edge of the Solar System."

"It's too late for that. The fleet and the moon bases spent all this time battling the Macros. They're in too close, and if we break them up now the pieces will still hit Earth."

"What's plan B?"

"We'll use the gravity cannons on Luna, but with an extremely broadened cone of effect. They will *push*, rather than crush the targets. That way, they will be nudged off course."

I smiled. "You've thought of everything."

"Well, there are still five billion of us down here, and this is our doomsday as well as yours. You don't have to do everything personally, Colonel."

"Glad to hear it. Well done, Miklos. If you weren't a known villain, I'd give you a medal or something."

He looked pained.

"Thanks for the thought, sir."

* * *

The next few days I paraded around, looking soulful and glum. I made sure every cameraman on the planet got an eyeful of me looking bleak and comforting the survivors.

To be honest, Earth had paid a grim price. We'd lost a large part of our population, but we'd won a war of extinction with an implacable enemy. They'd died out while we lived on. That counted for a lot in my book.

After the war, one would think that things would have settled down politically. But that isn't the way my species operates.

"Kyle, you should just accept it," Jasmine said. "Everyone wants you to stay in power."

I laughed.

"Not everyone. Remember Miklos? He was worried about this day, about what I'd do when it came right down to it."

She frowned. "He's not a threat any longer."

"That's not what I'm talking about," I told her. "*I'm* the threat, not him."

"I don't understand you."

Jasmine was in her second trimester. I looked at her belly, and she put her hands over it. Was it a defensive gesture? No, I realized when I saw her face. She was feeling self-conscious. She'd always been slight and trim. Suddenly looking like you just swallowed a cannonball came as a shock to most women.

"You look great today," I told her, giving her a gentle hug.

"You're changing the subject."

"All right," I said. "I'll go to Parliament. I'll let them decide."

She looked up at me with wide, brown eyes. "Really?"

"Yeah," I said. "But I hope they know what they're asking for. Things don't always turn out the way you expected when you make a wish."

Her eyes narrowed, and I could see she was on the brink of asking me what the hell I was talking about—but then she stopped herself. She didn't want to spoil the moment.

I went to the World Parliament the following week and presented myself to them. The cheers were deafening. Sure, there were a few who catcalled and booed, but I didn't mind. They were outnumbered.

The people of Earth knew a winner when they saw one. They'd always turned to me to do the right thing.

The people had always found someone like me to fight for them throughout history. When things were bad—really, really bad—humans wanted a strong leader to protect them. They called it the "man on the white horse" syndrome. The desire for security over freedom seemed to be stamped on our DNA.

I gave them what they wanted. I took up the reins of government and became an emperor, even though I knew I'd never sit easily on my throne.

The world heaved a sigh of relief when I did this. Sure, there were a few protest riots, but for the most part people wanted peace and order. We'd had so many years of war. Aliens had come out of our skies and raided our world regularly for such a long time, they feared space more than they did a despot.

I knew all this, but I took the job anyway. I'd never wanted it, but it had been thrust upon me.

When they crowned me, I felt like a fool. The cameras ate it up, naturally. Everyone who was anyone was there. They paraded in finery that staggered the eyes and the mind. There were beautiful people, rich people, people who feared to be seen anywhere else lest their new tyrant became a jealous one.

It was a bittersweet time for me, and I tried to stay mildly drunk throughout the experience.

Emperor Kyle Riggs I, that's who I am. Sure, why not?

Sometimes a man has to know when he's beaten.

-44-

A mixture of celebrations and riots continued to sweep around the globe due to my coronation. The vids played the pageantry over and over without a break. Every secret imperialist on the planet was overjoyed. Every individualist who wanted a return to the old ways of a hundred fifty separate states cried in their collective soups.

I contacted Miklos shortly after I returned home.

"Miklos, old buddy," I said when he came on the line.

"Is this a social call, Colonel—excuse me—*Emperor?*" he asked.

His voice was as cold as ice. I knew why, of course. I'd done exactly what he'd feared I would do.

"No," I said. "It isn't. Give me an update. Is that fire in the Arctic Ocean out yet?"

"Yes, Your Highness, it has subsided."

"What about the death count? Any updates there?"

"I'm happy to report I overestimated the loss of life. We suffered a mere one hundred thirty-one million causalities—Your Highness."

"That's good, but please stop calling me that," I said.

"What? 'Your Highness?'"

We glared at one another for a second via our screens.

"Look," I said finally. "This isn't going to end the way you think it will. I took power so I could do something—something that has to be done."

He looked confused for a second and tilted his head.

"Is that a threat, sir?"

"Far from it. Watch the news, Miklos. Watch the news."

I closed the channel then and stood up. I headed downstairs, winding some forty empty floors to the ground floor. The palace was almost empty. It was one of Crow's buildings—one of the few I hadn't leveled when I'd returned to Earth. Sitting near Boston, Massachusetts, I found I liked the place even if it was a bit gaudy and drafty in the winter months.

At the ground floor, I paused but didn't stop descending. There were no elevators into the lower regions where I was headed now. I pressed onward, winding down into the depths of the Earth.

At the bottom of the massive labyrinth, I entered a secret room. All of Crow's palaces had secret rooms. I doubt anyone alive knew where they all were.

Inside the room, I kept a battle suit. I put it on and summoned transport. Then I returned to the ground floor, terrorizing my staff, who fled before me. Ignoring them, I headed out into the courtyard, waved back my guards and dismissed the pilot. I flew the shuttle alone up into space. No one questioned me. No one dared.

Admiral Newcome was waiting in orbit aboard *Potemkin*. His eyes were wide and scared. I saw he hadn't properly combed his white tufts of hair today, and they stuck out from under his cap like cotton balls.

"Let's get underway, Admiral," I told him.

He licked his lips, hesitating.

"Are you sure you want to do this, Emperor?"

"No," I admitted. "But some things have to be done when you have the window of opportunity."

He nodded, and we left orbit. Marvin was with me and so was Gaines. The rest of the crew had been hand-picked. I'd left Kwon and Jasmine behind. They wouldn't have understood this mission.

When we reached the target, I brought Marvin to the bridge before I dumped our payload.

"Emperor Riggs?" he asked. "Is there a difficulty?"

"Yeah, there're lots of them. But they're all inside my head. I just wanted to confirm some things with you, robot."

"Robot again? A pejorative term? Under these circumstances, I would think—"

"Well, you thought wrong," I told him. "Did you check and arm the bombs?"

"Yes."

"Personally?"

"Yes. I assembled them with my own tentacles, sir. They will go off at the predetermined depth as we discussed. If all is ready—"

I raised my hand to stop him.

"Hold on," I said. "I didn't say I wanted to strike at a certain depth. I want to hit the solid core. Was that somehow unclear?"

Marvin's cameras writhed, struggling to read my posture and expression.

"That's difficult to determine, sir."

"Come on, robot. Can you do it or not? A simple pressure switch at the base of the bomb should do the trick. Just like dropping a dumb bomb on a field. If it hits something solid, it goes off."

"The circumstances are different here. The composition of the planet is not so clear-cut, and the layers are not so distinct. Unlike rocky worlds with gaseous atmospheres, this planet has many varied strata. In the upper layers, the gases are thin. As you go deeper, they become increasingly dense until they become liquid. After that, eventually, a core may be reached. We've never probed so deeply."

I glared at him. Why did Marvin have to make things complicated? I was already having doubts about this entire venture, and he wasn't making it any easier on me.

"I want to make sure there are minimal civilian casualties," I told him. "I thought I made that perfectly clear."

"A noble, if uncontrollable, goal."

"Why is it uncontrollable?"

"Primarily because we don't know where their population concentrations are."

I heaved a sigh. He was right, of course. We didn't know all that much about them.

350

"Perhaps," said Newcome gently, "we could reconsider this action. If we—"

I turned on him. "Don't you think I have? I've gone over and over it. I don't see another way. This is the hard moment, Newcome, the moment when we earn our pay. The moment when we do things we'll never go home and brag about to our kids."

"My humblest apologies, Emperor."

I turned back to Marvin. "So, you can't be dead certain we'll be hitting the core?"

"I can," he said, "but only if we risk the success of the project."

"What do you mean?"

"The bombs will take a long time to fall all the way down. As the liquid becomes denser at the center, it will be harder to distinguish that density from a solid. At sufficient velocity, a liquid registers like a hard surface. To compensate, we could slow down the rate of descent, which would be the only way to be certain a solid surface had been encountered. Unfortunately, taking too long to reach the core would give the enemy time to enact countermeasures. Our odds of failure increase steadily with each hour, once the devices are released into the atmosphere."

I knew what he was talking about. This wasn't going to be like dropping charges into water from space. First, they had to go through an atmosphere then penetrate an increasingly dense sea. At the very bottom was firm ground but at what depth? We didn't know.

But at the same time I now understood the real reason for his objections.

"Ah-ha!" I shouted, jabbing a finger at him. "That's it, isn't it? Mission failure. That's the real reason you're hemming and hawing."

"Reference unclear—and insulting."

"Damn straight, it is. You don't want the enemy to defuse these bombs you've worked so hard on. That's it, isn't it?"

"The project would be seriously jeopardized if the bombs don't go off. Additionally, if we fail in this initial attempt, the enemy will be forewarned. I would recommend—"

"No," I said, shaking my head. "No, I've heard enough. Set them to go off when they touch rock. There has to be a solid core. Quit bullshitting me. *Phobos* was built out of rock. Where do you think they got it?"

"To be clear, you wish me to commence the attack?"

"What? Am I the only one listening? Drop your bloody bombs, robot, all of them. *Now.* Let them fall slowly at the end. I don't care if they drift down. Just make sure they detonate at the core."

Marvin exited with poor grace. His tentacles were humping up, which indicated he was annoyed. I knew that behavior by now. It was like watching a cat with a flipping tail.

I didn't care. Let him be pissed-off. This was my war, and I was going to finish it my way.

"Sir?" Newcome said as the first blue-glowing streaks fell from our hold and vanished into the hazy brown atmosphere below us.

"What?"

"Shouldn't we—shouldn't we declare war or something? We didn't even give them an ultimatum."

I looked at him for a few seconds. I could tell he was as troubled by all this as I was. In fact, he was probably more troubled, and I liked him better for it.

"You're my conscience, Newcome," I said.

"Does that mean you'll announce—?"

"No. We can't. I've already gambled to save civilian casualties. I won't give them more than that."

"But sir—"

"They'll figure it out soon enough," I snapped, turning back to the frosty little windows that let me gaze down upon the dreadful energies I'd released.

I forced myself to think of my dead children. Indirectly, the beings below me now had struck first, killing my kids and billions of others. Entire worlds had been extinguished by proxy through their construction of the Macros.

But this action wasn't one of simple vengeance. I had to make sure the Blues were stopped forever.

I turned back to Newcome, and my face was angry now.

"Let me ask you something," I said. "Did they give us a warning before they released the Macros? Did they ask our permission before launching *Phobos*? No, they didn't. Instead they insulted us, manipulated us, and lied to us. They never gave us a break, Admiral. With luck, most of their population will survive, but not their industry and technology. When they recover, maybe they'll have a more cautious attitude toward all the other biotics in the universe."

The bombs kept falling. So many of them...

Potemkin cruised with her sister ships over the atmosphere. All the battleships were unloading their payloads of gravity bombs, slowly carpeting the core from every possible angle. The blue-white streaks fell from my ship and a dozen others like glimmering raindrops.

It took hours for the bombs to touch bottom and start going off. When they did, I felt each of them in my heart. I'd never done anything quite as grim as this, not in my entire career.

Our com-links began to ring the moment the first bombs touched the core and imploded. It was the Blues, trying to open a channel.

I told Marvin to keep it closed. What was there to say? I'd come to the conclusion that their industrial and technological infrastructure was a threat to all humanity. They'd tried to wipe us out repeatedly. I could not allow them to do it again.

I didn't think all of them were bad. In fact, I'd had moments when I'd felt real empathy with them. But they were too dangerous, too unpredictable, too technologically advanced.

I ignored their repeated attempts to communicate until the calls suddenly stopped. Newcome looked up, his eyes red-rimmed and uncertain.

"We probably hit their communications system and knocked it out," he said. "They can't even surrender now."

I nodded and went back to brooding. The bombs continued to fall. They seemed endless, like the drumbeat of a slow summer shower.

I steeled myself, straightening up and returning to my commander's chair.

"The Blues can't be allowed to rise again," I said aloud.

The command staff glanced at me. No one said a word.

"They can't be allowed to build another *Phobos* or another race of improved robots. They have to be stopped and this is the only way I know of to accomplish the task."

Newcome nodded and looked away. No one met my eye. They were afraid of me and afraid of what we were doing.

They're gravity weapons, I kept telling myself. No radiation. No fallout. No long-term effects. It would be clean and quick. Whatever the Blues had at the core would be destroyed, but that was all. At least, that's what I hoped was happening down there.

I recalled something I'd read before coming out here on this final mission at the end of a long, long war. Paul Tibbets, the pilot of the *Enola Gay*, had been a Colonel when he'd dropped the first atomic bomb on Japan. He'd reported afterward that he slept well. He said he never worried about it and that if he'd let his actions weigh on his mind, he wouldn't be worth a damn to anyone.

I hoped my conscience would let me rest so easily.

-45-

Upon returning to Earth, I received less than a hero's welcome. The headlines on every news site blared, painting me as a butcher of innocents. I was depicted in cartoons kicking around fluffy clouds while wearing a steel suit and a vicious grin. Such were the joys of a free press.

Deciding it was time to go before the people, I summoned Parliament. I ordered them all to return to their huge, spherical chamber. They had been on vacation—it seemed to me they were almost always on vacation—and they didn't really want to come back to town.

But when I called, they all came. Even those who were ill made an appearance. They were too afraid not to come. If there had been one obvious side effect of my recent actions, it was evident in the quick obedience of the rank and file members of my government.

I put on my monkey-suit. It only seemed fitting. Jasmine, swollen with child now, stood in the wings as she had before. She fussed with my saber and seemed more worried about my hair than what I was thinking. But when it was almost time for me to mount the stage, her curiosity got the better of her.

"What are you going to say, Kyle?" she asked, her hands lingering on my stylish, looping lapels.

Her eyes searched mine. I smiled back.

"What has to be said," I told her.

Her eyes widened.

"Don't do it," she said suddenly.

I'd told no one of my plans. She'd figured them out all on her own. I guess I shouldn't have been surprised by her intuition—but I was.

"Everything will be fine," I told her.

"You always say that."

"And everything turns out good in the end, doesn't it?"

Jasmine looked unconvinced, but she kissed me and let me go.

I turned and strode out onto the platform. I heard the crowd stand and clap. They clapped dutifully but without enthusiasm. There were no cheers as there had been when the Macros had been defeated. Today, they were uncertain what I was going to do next.

I waved them back to their seats, and the chamber quieted quickly.

"My critics have been relentless," I said, "second-guessing my every decision. Perhaps they're right. I don't agree with them, but I'll fight to the death—quite literally—for their right to complain about me."

A few chuckles rose up, but not many. They didn't know quite what to make of me, these political hacks and posers. I scared them and made them sneer, all at once. I was part court jester and part great white shark in their minds. An impossible mixture of foolishness and low animal cunning.

"There was an early Roman general I've studied over my lifetime," I said. "A man named Cincinnatus. He was a land-owner, a man who loved his farm. His son was slain over political disputes, but, despite that, when invaders came to Rome he left that farm and became a general and Rome's dictator. He saved his nation from destruction. When the war was over, however, he gave it all up and returned to his beloved farm."

They were all staring at me now. I honestly don't think any of them knew where I was going with this. My thinking was incomprehensible to them. I might as well be some kind of alien bug up there prattling away at the lectern. I knew this, but I pressed ahead. It was the only way I would ever know peace again.

"General George Washington faced a similar moment. He had near absolute power at the end of the American Revolution. Some of the founding fathers pressed him to become the first American king. He rejected that idea, becoming instead the first president. After his term was up, he left office and handed over power to his successor without a qualm. Like Cincinnatus, he returned to his farm and lived out his days in retirement."

I thought they were beginning to get it. I could see, looking out over the bright lights, that mouths were hanging open. Newsies and politicians alike were stunned. Could it be true? Could old blood-and-guts Riggs really be stepping down?

"I'm performing one last action as your Emperor," I said, "the drafting and signing of a new document, a constitution that transforms our planet into a republic. I know some of you want a return to tiny independent nations. I don't think that's wise, but local governance will be included under the new rules."

They were buzzing now, unable to contain themselves. In response, I spoke louder and more forcefully.

"In the future, there will be a Prime Minister but never again an emperor or a dictator—at least, that's how I hope it will go. I myself won't be here. I'm abdicating and retiring from Star Force. I'll return to my farm in California and rebuild it. The last time I was there, the place was a wreck."

There were a few nervous twitters at that. Most of the crowd was talking to their neighbors. A few clapped sporadically. They didn't know what to do and were too scared to cheer or make any overt move. What if this was all some kind of elaborate ruse to out the traitors?

Crow had done such things, suggesting that maybe he should leave his office. Those who had encouraged him the most had been arrested. It made me sad to think that my people now lived in fear of their government. I'd done my best to write a simple document full of diced-up powers and responsibilities. Mostly it listed what the government could *not* do. Time would tell if humanity would adhere to it. At least, I'd given them a chance.

When I wrapped up the speech, I thanked them and praised them all unstintingly. I told them our world had won the war against the machines, and it was all due to their superhuman efforts. In short, I gave them the pep-speech of their lives.

That part they ate up. Politicians love nothing more than getting credit for positive events. By the time I left the stage, I received a standing ovation. Perhaps it was the first real one I'd ever gotten. It sounded different, somehow, with cheering and whistling sprinkled in. There was actual enthusiasm in their voices.

Not everyone was happy, of course. Some people had invested a lot in my status. Jasmine was among those people. When I went backstage, I found that she'd vanished without leaving a message. I called her, but she didn't answer.

I was hurt, but I couldn't afford to give in to my emotions now. I needed to get the transfer of power worked out. Parliament had to decide who their newly-elected head of state would be and exactly what powers that person would have.

After several weeks of wrangling, we had a document based upon my original that I felt was pretty solid. Individual freedoms were stipulated. Voting practices, division of powers and the like were hammered out.

Would they stick to it? Time would tell.

During all those long days, I never heard from Jasmine. That hurt me more than anything else, but I never let it show.

* * *

My farm was a wreck. It had been looted and partially burned. I had credits enough to fix it up and transform it into a palace, but I resisted that urge.

Sometimes, working with your hands is the best therapy. A single nanotized man can do the work of a dozen normal people. The only machine I had to help me was my father's old tractor. I decided to use it rather than plowing the fields by hand. I didn't want my few visitors and neighbors gawking any more than they already did.

Spring turned into summer, and in the Central Valley, that means it gets *hot*. The sun bronzed my skin and, despite my modifications, I was left sweating and breathing hard when it was a hundred degrees and as still as a desert outside.

I grew crops and rebuilt my house. The new version was better than before, and as most of the neighboring farms had been abandoned, I legally bought extra land from the banks and soon had a nice agricultural business going. I gave in, buying more big machines even though they reminded me of Macros without brainboxes.

On the first of July I was driving my tractor in the cornfields. I'd used a combine to gather the springtime crop a few days earlier, and was replanting and fertilizing again. One of California's secrets was the long growing season. With hard work and a bit of luck, you could get two or three crops from a field before winter set in.

Something caught my eye as I tooled along, bumping over the furrows and breathing dust. It was the glint of something shiny.

I stopped the tractor and craned my neck. Was that an extra car in the driveway? Something colorful next to my drab pickup?

I suspected right away it was a news reporter. The car looked too fancy to be local. It probably flew—all the new models did. Grumbling, I put my machine back into gear and kept plowing. The fellow would just have to wait until I was done. If I steered off-course now, I'd mess up the furrows.

About an hour later I returned to the barn and parked. Surprisingly, the car was still in the drive. It was a shiny new model with airfoils on the back and skids under the chassis. A rich man's air-car, just as I'd suspected.

I walked up to the window, already in a sour mood. I didn't like to be pestered. For the first month or two I'd lived out here, they'd come almost every day. All the online magazines and vid shows wanted an exclusive interview. They rarely got it, not even when they'd sent a beautiful girl with a flashy smile—well, sometimes they'd gotten it then.

The driver got out when she saw me. She was on the other side of the car, standing with her door open and leaning on the roof with one elbow. Her face trembled a bit, and I sensed she was trying to smile. Her smile failed, and she looked ashamed instead.

It was Jasmine.

Her dark hair had lengthened, and the hot breezes lifted her locks until they wrapped around her face and streamed over her shoulder. She pushed strands out of her eyes and finally spoke.

"Hello, Kyle."

"Hello. Welcome to my humble farm."

She looked around. "You love it out here, don't you?"

I leaned on the other side of her car, and we stared across the roof at one another.

"Yeah," I said. "It's home to me."

There was a pause in the conversation. I didn't speak up because I felt no urge to make things easier on her. She'd ignored me for months. It was up to her to tell me whatever it was she wanted to say.

"I'm sorry," she said finally in a small voice. "I shouldn't have left you like that."

I didn't know what to say. I stood there, looking tough but not angry. I was past being angry about it.

Jasmine opened the back door of her car and pulled something out into the dying afternoon sun. I couldn't see what she was holding at first, but when she turned to me, she was holding up *my baby*.

My tough-guy look vanished. I'd lost count of the months, I guess. She'd come to term and delivered. She hadn't even called to tell me about it, and I'd been avoiding the news nets.

"I delivered him last night," she said. "When I saw his face, he looked so much like you—I felt awful."

I stared at the kid. His eyes were closed, and to me he looked pretty much like all babies had looked throughout time.

"Yeah," I said. "Wow, he does look just like me. What a perfect, beautiful baby!"

She beamed. "I had to come find you," she said.

What could I do after that? I invited her in, and I served up drinks.

"What do you want?" I asked.

"What have you got?"

"Uh—beer, orange juice and iced tea. That's about it."

She laughed and asked for the tea.

I took the opportunity to check her out while she was downing the glass I'd given her. For a normal woman, delivering a first baby would have been a big deal physically. But Jasmine's body was full of self-repair systems. Her body had returned more or less to normal within hours. Her eyes looked a little tired, but that might have been from the long flight out here.

We talked, and I poked uncertainly at the new kid. He seemed to sleep most of the time.

"What's his name?" I asked her.

"I haven't named him yet. I wanted you to help me with that."

I gave her a blank look. She proceeded to spam me with names, most of which sounded pretentious to me. We finally went with Cody. I'd always liked that name.

The hours went by quietly as they tend to do on a farm. I wasn't the kind who ran the screens all day, watching net casts. I'd been relishing the peaceful sigh of the winds for months.

When it got dark, I honestly thought she was going to get back into her car and go home. But she didn't. We talked instead about why she'd left and what she'd been doing with her family back in India. She'd resigned her commission from Star Force, too, in order to take care of the new kid.

"Uh," I said at about midnight. "I'm turning in. You want to stay the night? I've got several empty bedrooms."

She looked shy. "All right."

I had to kick a cat off the bed in what had once been Jake's room. I threw on some fresh sheets and then I came to a sudden realization: where was the baby going to sleep?

I climbed up into the attic and began rummaging around. I recalled that we'd once had—

"Found it!" I called down, pulling a dusty basinet from the attic.

Jasmine was at the bottom of the ladder. "You don't have to worry about it. He can sleep in his car seat. See? He's out already."

"Nah, let the kid stretch out flat."

We cleaned it and set it up, and it gave me a little pang to see her put Cody to bed in that basket. It was white and had a few scorch marks on it from the Nano ships—my place had partly burned down when they'd first invaded—but it was serviceable.

"All my kids slept in that thing," I said. "All three of them now."

For some reason, seeing a new baby in the house brought back a flood of memories. Even the hot smell of the little guy seemed familiar. I had to swallow a few times and went downstairs to get a beer. When I came back up, I was surprised to see Jasmine rolling the basinet out of Jake's room and into mine.

"Um," I said, looking confused. "I know you want him to get acquainted with me and all that, but he's going to need feeding in the night you know..."

She shook her head and laughed at me. "Don't play the idiot. What do you want me to do? Beg?"

"Um...no."

I honestly didn't figure it out until she stood next to my bed and began undressing. At last, daylight shone into my dusty brain.

"Oh," I said. "You're sleeping in here, too."

"We all are," she said, coming close to me. "Is that okay with you?"

"Yes," I heard myself saying.

"I never want to leave your bed again, Kyle."

I had her in my arms. She was partly undressed, and her body felt very good up against mine. I hadn't had any other girlfriends since she'd left me, and after all our talk during the day, I'd figured out she hadn't met anyone, either.

"Well then," I said, "we'll have to get married."

It just came out of my mouth. I hadn't planned it or anything. Maybe my brain didn't always work right, but I'm a guy who goes by his gut instincts. I felt now was the time, and the move was the right one.

Jasmine smiled. "I thought you were never going to ask."

That was it. No getting down on one knee. No ring. No parental permission—we were both over thirty, after all, and we already had a kid. We were suddenly engaged, just like that.

I reflected later as we lay in the hot room together, that ours had never been a traditional relationship. We hadn't had time for all that. Maybe now we would.

That night I hardly slept. It wasn't just the kid's fault, either.

I kept staring out the windows at the stars. There wasn't much in the way of urban glare outside. The population of California, like the rest of the planet, had been cut in half. The cities were quieter, more subdued.

The people hadn't all died, and there was a massive migration going on, but the countryside was still dark and empty.

I watched the stars out my window, knowing that's where so many had gone. Those balloon-ships I'd built had carried away the first wave of a hundred million or so. After that, they'd come back for more. People were writing and calling home to tell relatives to join them on fresh worlds without radiation poisoning, burning seas and the like. Old Earth was emptying out and becoming quieter.

I watched the lights in the warm summer sky. The stars were bigger and brighter than they'd ever been in my memory.

I couldn't help but wonder what else was out there. There were a billion stars in our galaxy and a billion galaxies beyond ours. We'd only scratched the tip of the iceberg.

Before dawn, as Jasmine awoke for yet another feeding— that kid was always hungry—I told myself that I probably had years before anything else came out of the skies at us. After all, we'd not been bothered for a long time before the Nanos first showed up.

Sure, the Ancients might come looking for the Earthman who'd dared to build his own little ring. But that might take another thousand years or more to happen. With any luck, I wouldn't be around then to worry about it.

The End

More Books by B. V. Larson:

STAR FORCE SERIES
Swarm
Extinction
Rebellion
Conquest
Battle Station
Empire
Annihilation
Storm Assault
The Dead Sun
Outcast

IMPERIUM SERIES
Mech Zero: The Dominant
Mech 1: The Parent
Mech 2: The Savant
Mech 3: The Empress
Five By Five (Mech Novella)

OTHER SF BOOKS
Technomancer
The Bone Triangle
Z-World
Velocity

Visit BVLarson.com for more information.

Made in the USA
Coppell, TX
26 November 2020